MUTED COLORS

gerald myers

Pittsburgh, PA

ISBN 1-56315-231-2

Paperback Fiction
©Copyright 2001 Gerald Myers
All rights reserved
First Printing—2001
Library of Congress #00-107592

Request for information should be addressed to:

Sterlinghouse Publisher, Inc.
The Sterling Building
440 Friday Road
Pittsburgh, PA 15209
www.sterlinghousepublisher.com

Cover design: A.J. Rodgers—Sterlinghouse Publisher, Inc.
Page Design: Bernadette Kazmarski

All rights reserved. No part of this publication may be reproduced, stored in a retrieval system, or transmitted in any form or by any means—electronic, mechanical, photocopy, recording or any other, except for brief quotations in printed reviews—without prior permission of the publisher.

This is a work of fiction. Names, characters, places and incidents either are the product of the author's imagination or are used fictitiously. Any resemblance to actual events or persons, living or dead, is entirely coincidental.

Printed in Canada

dedication

To Reneé, for her support, her patience, and most of all her unconditional love.

The Sick Rose

O Rose, thou art sick.
The invisible worm
That flies in the night
In the howling storm:

Has found out thy bed
Of crimson joy:
And his dark secret love
does thy life destroy.

—William Blake

chapter one

ride 'em cowboy

Moving away from Manhattan proved more complicated than Marshall Friedman had anticipated. Uplifted by the prospect of starting a new life back in his hometown of Pittsburgh, Pennsylvania, he handled the arrangements and unexpected snags with characteristic good humor.

A forty-year-old staff psychiatrist with a teaching position at Bellevue, the gangly six-foot tall physician tackled the daunting task of severing his professional and personal ties in a systematic manner. After tendering his resignation with the psychiatry department, he began the delicate task of reassigning his private patients to other physicians and clinics. The magnitude of this endeavor, however, had been greatly reduced by a recent shift in the focus of his professional activities.

A few months earlier his first self-help book, *When Good Men Feel Bad,* had hit the shelves. So preoccupied had he been with the research and writing of this work he hadn't accepted any new patients for nearly a year. Add to that a few strategic therapeutic successes in his private practice and his census had been shaved even further.

The remaining individuals still on his active list were informed of his departure by phone or during their routine office visits. Most patients took the announcement in stride, wishing him luck, while inquiring as to why he was leaving, while a few who were weaker and less independent, tended to abandon their deferential façade and assumed a defensive, almost hostile, posture.

Dealing with emotional reactions, Marshall knew, was the crux of his job. And patients' reactions seemed to take on greater magnitude simply because of the kind of bond he encouraged in the therapeutic setting. It was a connection both difficult and painful to break. Marshall genuinely liked the people he treated. This allowed him to forge a special kind of relationship with them. They were respected as individuals with interesting lives and real problems. He felt responsible for their welfare. And in return, he sensed they liked him too.

At home, the process of physical and emotional disengagement proved less distinct. As Marshall went through the process of finalizing his move from his wife Bernice who he'd shared a bed with for over eleven years, he sensed an eerie, pervasive, sense of unreality lingering in their Park Avenue condominium. With the declaration of his intention weeks earlier, Marshall had expected a litany of desperate pleas ensconced in highly emotional scenes. But instead of heated conflict, there seemed to exist a temperate, almost respectful coolness between them. As he drove the U-haul trailer back from the rental site on the morning before he left New York City, he thought about the evening when he'd expressed his intention to leave.

Marshall and Bernice sat in the dining room of their spacious Park Avenue condominium having a light meal. As had become evident over the past few months, the couple had less and less to talk about over dinner. This particular evening Bernice seemed engrossed by a pile of fashion catalogues and Marshall leafed through the *Times*. Despite his outward calm his insides were in turmoil.

Why hadn't she asked about his visit to her father's office earlier that day? She had certainly heard about the blow-up. She talked to him every afternoon. As for Marshall, he almost never raised his voice to his father-in-law. He knew better. Henry Tannenbaum was a multi-millionaire commercial real estate magnate, the owner of a chain of malls and shopping centers up and down the eastern seaboard, and a big reason why he and Bernice lived so well. But this time it was different. It had to do with his book, his pride and joy, and what he thought was an achievement that wasn't influenced by the old man's money. But, as Marshall had discovered, this hadn't been the case.

Months ago, without informing his son-in-law, the old man had ensured the success of Marshall's book by recruiting a cadre of investors to bankroll the purchase of enough of the first edition copies to propel the work onto the bestseller list. After that the larger retail outlets optioned the work and displayed it prominently.

One sunny morning in early May, while consulting with his father-in-law in his downtown Manhattan office on an unrelated matter, Marshall had inadvertently learned of this covert strategy to make him appear successful. Truly believing that the book had achieved notoriety on its own merit, Marshall felt betrayed and deceived. It was all a sham. And Bernice, privy to the ruse, had neglected to include him in on the ruse. But once he knew the truth—and she knew that he knew—he wondered why she *still* hadn't confessed her complicity? Perhaps, by avoiding the issue, she hoped it would simply go away. *Not a chance!* he thought vehemently.

After their maid, Maria, had removed the dinner dishes and set down coffee and desert, Marshall said matter-of-factly, "I called Bertram Hunter today."

"Who's he?" Bernice asked absently, still mulling over the Victoria's Secret catalogue.

"He's runs the Hunter-Neuman Clinic in Pittsburgh. Don't you remember? I met with him when we visited my sister for Passover last month."

"You mean the one that offered you that department head position?" She was looking up at him now. "Why did *you* call him?"

"I'm thinking of taking the job."

Her eyes widened and her dark eyebrows arched. "You're not serious, are you?"

"I believe I am," he replied meeting her incredulous stare.

"But why? I thought you were happy doing what you're doing here. In fact, didn't you tell me you rejected his offer right after you spoke to him?"

"That's right. I wrote back to him about a month ago and told him I wasn't interested in the position."

"But now you are?"

"Yes."

"Why?" He heard the hint of desperation in her tone. This announcement was disconcerting, probably frightening. She seemed anxious to hear what he was about to say.

"Because I'm tired of having my life run for me, Bernice. I'm tired of being a kept man, dependent on my wife's endowment fund. I'm ready to assume responsibility for my own life."

"What in the world are you talking about, Marshall?" she asked, rattling her coffee cup down on the saucer. "I thought you liked the things my money provides, the kind of lifestyle we enjoy *because* of it. I thought you didn't mind using my trust fund to pay for the extras."

"'Extras'! That's putting it mildly, Bernice. Admit it, if it weren't for what your father chips into our monthly expenses, we'd be holed up in a two-bedroom condo in Paramus, for god sakes. Hell, for what I contribute to our upkeep, I might as well be working for free."

"Well, whose fault is that?" Bernice countered, defiance now evident in her voice. "If I remember correctly, you chose the kind of psychiatry practice that suited you."

"Yes," he replied honestly. "I guess it was my choice. But that was because you wanted me close to home with plenty of time on my hands. And even *that's* part of the problem. Even my position at Bellevue is due to your father's influence peddling and name-dropping."

"Don't you think you should be grateful for that, Marshall, not resentful? If it wasn't for my father, you might be working in one those mental health clinics in Brooklyn or the Bronx."

"Which, come to think of it, wouldn't be so bad. Even though it wouldn't impress your snooty high society friends, *I* know I really made a difference at Menninger when I helped out there a few months ago. But that's all beside the point, Bernice. What I'm telling you now is I'm through. After what I found out this afternoon, I realize I've had enough. It's time for a major change in my life. I'm ready to move on."

"Is that so?" she retorted, her hard brown eyes ablaze. "You mean to *Pittsburgh?* Just like that. You're gonna pick up stakes and run."

"That's right. It happens in everyone's life. Not often, but it happens."

"And what about me, Marshall? What am I supposed to do while you're running off to find your new life? Where do I fit in this grand plan of yours?"

He had anticipated this question. He had his offer ready.

"You can come, of course," he said nonchalantly. "In fact, I want you to come. I think we could make a real life for ourselves out there, if you approach it with the right attitude."

"Are you're insinuating that there's something wrong with the attitude I have here and now?"

"Yes," he answered frankly, "to some extent."

"And what do you regard as the problem my dear husband, the all knowing, all-seeing psychiatrist?"

"The problem, as I see it," he began, enunciating slowly, framing his words carefully, "is that you think it's just fine and dandy that we, as a middle-aged couple, continue to live under your father's wing, dependent on his money and subject to the restrictions and conditions he places on our lives."

"That's ridiculous, Marshall! Father hardly ever mixes in our lives. And the money I receive each month comes from a trust fund set up long before you came along."

"A fund of which your father is the sole executor, I might point out." Marshall paused, then added, "But all that's beside the point. I know that you're satisfied with the status quo. It's all you've ever known. It allows you to have the life-style you covet. And I have to admit, from a purely materialistic standpoint, it hasn't exactly been burden and struggle for me either.

"But at the same time, you think it comes without strings. Speaking for myself, I've paid a dear price to stay here. I feel like I've sold my soul to the devil. But now I see that the cost is too high. Seeing how your father used his money and influence to manipulate my book behind my back made it all crystal clear."

"But we just did what we thought was best, Marshall!" Bernice cried. "We thought it would make you happy to see your book make the charts."

"What would have made me happy was to have had the book stand on its own merit. You knew that. You knew how important it was to get this thing published on my own. It's been years since I've felt this good about myself. The book was my resurrection. Now you've taken that away from me."

"So, just because of this one incident, you're ready to throw away everything we've created as a couple? You'd abandon eleven years of marriage just because of a little indiscretion on my part? Don't you think you're overreacting? Underwriting your book with outside investors wasn't such a big deal. According to Sandi, it's done all the time."

"Of course my literary agent would tell you that. She'd do anything to see my work hit the charts. But for me, succeeding *on my own* was the big deal. And you took that away from me, without telling me, knowing full well how important it was."

"But if I'd told you, you would have accused me of meddling."

"Which is exactly what you ended up doing."

With her face crestfallen, she conceded, "I suppose so."

Checkmate, thought Marshall.

They were silent for a while. Bernice absently toyed with a lock of her thick black hair and regarded him. Then she looked down at the table and he noticed the tiny creases around her mouth and cheeks deepen. She was making no effort to hide her distress. Tears were forming around her eyes.

"So what do we do now?" she asked almost rhetorically. "You talk like you're ready to pitch it all. Throw the baby out with the bath water, so to speak, and walk away from our marriage just because your precious feelings are hurt. Don't you think you're overreacting a bit?"

"I can't believe this," he replied, feeling a bit exasperated. "You're totally missing the point, Bernice. This isn't just a small incident that you can smooth over with a glib apology followed by a nice trip or an expensive gift. This is the last in a long string of insults to my integrity.

And that includes all the compromises I've made during our eleven years of marriage just so things would run smoothly. But I've finally had enough. Let me repeat; this is the last straw. It's the final offense. It's...my...wake-up...call!" he declared accentuating each word with a pound of his fist on the table.

"And what about me?" she asked again, her anguish more evident than ever. "What happens to me when you run off to Pittsburgh to start this great new life of yours? What happens to me, Marshall?"

"You come with me," he repeated calmly, noting how his composure contrasted starkly with her uninhibited emotionalism. "It'll give you a chance to sever that umbilical cord that's linked you to your family for all these years. You can finally reject the support your father gives us and join me on our own. It may not be easy at first, but I know we won't starve. Dr. Hunter has offered me a generous starting salary. The cost of living in Pittsburgh is a fraction of what it costs to live New York. I'm sure we'd do quite well."

"But will I be happy, Marshall? I mean, come on, Pittsburgh? How can I even consider moving to Pittsburgh after what I'm used to? I'd languish there. I'd whither like some rose on the vine. What would I do? Who would I spend time with? What kind of life would I have there?"

"A life of your own making," Marshall replied, his tone remarkably free of condescension. "The kind of life I plan on fashioning for myself, one with integrity and purpose. And one not contaminated by the unwanted influence of some less-than-impartial benefactor. It may not be glamorous, Bernice, but for me it's authentic and quite appealing."

His wife didn't reply right away. In fact, she sat there without saying a word for what, to Marshall, seemed like an eternity. Finally, he became so impatient with her silence that he was compelled to ask, "Well, what do you want to do? Will you come with me or not?"

With agonizing deliberateness she lifted her head slightly, raised her eyes so they were level with his, and simply said, "No."

During the subsequent weeks, although obviously upset about his decision to leave, Bernice had only made a few half-hearted pleas to urge him to remain in New York.

Perhaps, Marshall rationalized, *she really understands how committed I am to making this move. She probably realizes that nothing she could say could dissuade me.*

Which, he affirmed, was fundamentally correct.

And why was he so ready and willing to go? Was their marriage really over? What was wrong with it in the first place? His analytical mind frequently groped for answers to these elusive questions.

First he blamed himself, contending that there was a basic defect in his own personality that compromised his ability to stay committed and in love. Or perhaps it was some fundamental deficiency in their marital relationship, some fatal flaw that blunted his emotional reaction and tempered his sense of loss? Despite his extensive training in psychology, he couldn't tell.

Deep down inside he suspected it was the latter. Years earlier, when he'd first noted a mounting dissatisfaction with his situation, he'd came to the painful conclusion that Bernice was, rather than being the one true love he'd hoped for in a life partner, no more than a dear friend and trusted companion. And now, as he prepared to leave New York City, he sensed that his emotions were consistent with someone bidding farewell to a good friend, not a soul mate. It lacked the fervent charge associated with abandoning a person with whom he had a deep spiritual attachment. Perhaps that's why, despite the emotional scene that marked the start of the their separation, he had remained so detached during the process.

The day of departure, Friday, June 19, arrived under an overcast sky. He parked his Mercedes with its U-Haul trailer in tow in the loading dock bay behind the Park Avenue high-rise. As he stepped out of his car he glanced up at the brick building. All was in readiness. With the help of a psychologist friend from the Menninger Clinic and the delivery boy from a nearby delicatessen he loaded the vehicles.

Marshall had made it easy for them, only taking a portion of his clothing, his computer and its accessories, his stereo system with VCR and TV, and several boxes of books and papers. The rest, like furniture, kitchenware, and a bed, he planned to rent or buy in Pittsburgh. When he thought about claiming some mementos and knickknacks, he realized that there was little to which he had emotional ties. He left all the artwork, sculpture, ceramics, souvenirs, and photos behind. These had been purchased or accumulated almost exclusively under Bernice's auspices and he had little interest in them. He would travel light, unencumbered. After all, he was starting over, wasn't he?

All that morning Bernice had seemed uncomfortable, wandering around aimlessly like a stranger in her own home. Eventually she withdrew, isolating herself in her room and didn't emerge until he started to carry his last load to the elevator. Calling his name, she stopped him by the door. Walking over, she reached down and took both his hands in hers. Then she looked up into his eyes.

"I guess this is it, Marshall," she said, the sadness evident in her voice. He nodded. A lump formed in his throat. "At least I know you're not leaving me for another woman."

"Far from it," he agreed with a wry smile.

"You can still come, you know," he offered.

"I know," she conceded. "Not now. Maybe later."

"Okay," he agreed. "Let's see how things go at a distance for a while. Maybe we'll miss each other so much we'll change our minds."

"Maybe," she agreed, but seemingly without conviction. "We'll see."

They kissed tenderly then hugged for a long time. Before they separated Marshall could feel the moisture from her tears seep through his shirt onto his chest. Suddenly he was crying too.

"C'mon," he said, trying to be cheerful while holding back a sniffle. "Walk me down to the car. This is my last load."

"I know," she said, and they walked out of the apartment, he possibly for the last time.

Marshall took the Lincoln Tunnel to the New Jersey Turnpike then picked up interstate 78 east of Newark. The afternoon was warm and humid, somewhat unusual for this time of June. But he didn't mind. With a big smile on his face he powered down the windows and cranked up the radio. Behind him the small U-Haul rolled along, like a miniature horse trailer in a western movie. Marshall imagined himself a cowboy, dressed in Wranglers and a Stetson, towing his quarter horse out to the ranch.

Deep down inside he felt free. So free, that when he acknowledged the feeling, it was tinged with guilt—but not enough guilt to hunker down and reconsider his action.

The miles raced under his spinning wheels. He crossed the Delaware south of Easton and continued on through the steel towns of Bethlehem and Allentown, the latter made famous by Billy Joel in his hit song of the same name.

But not as famous as my hometown Pittsburgh, he thought proudly. *That was once the steel capital of the world. And that's where I'm heading today.*

He knew he wouldn't feel lost when he arrived, just unencumbered. He had some ideas about where he wanted to live but would wait and see what the woman from Howard Hanna Realty had chosen for him to inspect. Until he decided on a place, he'd store his stuff and get a room at the Hilton which was across the river, five minutes from the clinic. The last time they had spoken, Dr. Hunter assured Marshall he was welcomed to start his new job anytime he wanted.

"The sooner the better, Dr. Friedman," had been Dr. Hunter's cheerful greeting. "We're all excited about having you on board. We can't wait to have you working here."

Marshall was excited too. It was as if a whole new vista had appeared before his eyes and he was itching to explore it. He would shed the baggage of his past and embark on the journey of a lifetime. He couldn't imagine anything so wonderful.

He stopped for dinner at a truckstop near Exit 16 of the Pennsylvania Turnpike just west of Harrisburg. After savoring a favorite from his childhood, an open-faced turkey sandwich with mashed potatoes and gravy, he resumed his journey. At just before eight he pulled in adjacent to Point State Park in front of the Hilton.

chapter two

new beginnings

Marshall could already tell he was going to like this place. The coffee in the medical staff lounge was hot and the pastries fresh. It was a far cry from what the attending physicians were offered at Bellevue. As he bit into a soft, warm maple-cinnamon roll he tried to recall the last time he'd tasted anything this good.

Relaxing in one of the recliners, Marshall awaited his personal tour of the Hunter-Neuman Clinic. Earlier that morning he'd met with Bertram Hunter. Marshall sensed that his interaction with the current CEO had gone well. Hunter assured him that everyone who would be working with him was excited about his arrival. After that, some contractual benefits and perks had been discussed. Hunter, one of the co-founders of the clinic, also mentioned the Independence Day picnic he hosted at his estate in Sewickley Heights. He invited Marshall to attend. And now, as ten o'clock rolled around, his tour was about to commence.

"Dr. Friedman?" a female with a pleasant lyrical voice called from the doorway.

Marshall turned, expecting to see one of the secretaries he'd met earlier. Instead, standing there holding a thin manila folder was a pretty, middle-aged woman. She wore a long black skirt, a flowered silk blouse, and a white clinic coat over her slender frame. She had ashen-blonde hair and sparkling blue eyes. For some reason she looked vaguely familiar to Marshall. He stood up as she approached.

"In case you haven't recognized me yet," the woman said, her thin pink lips breaking into a warm smile, "it's me, Marshall. Sally Swenson, now Sally Steiner."

"Oh my God!" Marshall exclaimed, tapping the heel of his hand against his forehead. "Of course it's you, Sally. How are you? And what the heck are you doing here?"

"I'm fine," she replied, amusement twinkling in her eyes. "And I've been asked to escort you on your tour this morning."

"To be honest I was expecting a secretary or somebody like that," he admitted candidly. "Not the...," he hesitated while glancing at her I.D. badge. "Wow, Sal, Chief of Nursing at the Hunter-Neuman Clinic. That's some position."

"I suppose it is," she replied modestly. "Mostly it's a lot of work. But I'm proud of it. And today I get to give the psychiatry department's new chief his tour of the clinic."

"I suppose you do," he agreed.

"Ready?"

"Sure thing."

They exited the lounge and strolled down the long carpeted corridor that spanned the west wing of the old building. They passed the spacious George McGowen Auditorium, the stately wood-paneled boardroom, a host of administrative offices, and a few smaller meeting rooms. Finally, they turned left near the main entrance to the hospital.

"This place has really expanded since I left for Penn in 1980. I don't think they'd broken ground for the new tower back then."

"Probably not," Sally agreed, matching his long stride with her own graceful steps. "That was completed in 1982, a year after I finished my BSN at Presby."

Marshall recalled the University's teaching hospital set atop 'cardiac hill' in the Oakland section the city. But before he could unearth any more details about Sally's past, she directed him toward a small well-lit room off the main hallway.

Inside the audio-visual department, the hospital's photographer greeted Marshall then took a series of photos of him. There was a mug shot for his hospital badge and credit-card-sized I.D. A portrait pose would be published in the 'New Faces' section of the hospital weekly, *The Neuman News* then filed in the Department of Medicine office pending requests from newspapers and other local media.

"The Hunt's famous," the photographer commented proudly. "Members of our medical staff are often newsworthy."

After finishing in photography Sally led him toward to their main destination, the psychiatry department. They passed through a glass-enclosed pedestrian walkway that crossed over a large ground-level parking lot.

"You'll need your picture I.D. to pass in and out of that gate," she said pointing below. "But you'll probably use the indoor parking lot during the winter. The North Side gets pretty cold in January and February."

"Don't remind me," he commented. "I used to sell hotdogs at the Steelers games when I was a teen-ager." An automatic door slid open on the far side of the walkway. As they walked through it Marshall inquired casually, "So it's Steiner now? That your married name?"

"It sure is," Sally replied.

"And your husband? What's he do?"

"Howard was a neurosurgeon, Marshall. But he's dead now. In fact I've been a widow for almost seven years."

Marshall regarded this bit of sad news. "I'm so sorry," he told her. "What happened?"

"His Hodgkin's disease relapsed and he failed a bone marrow transplant. An overwhelming pulmonary infection killed him."

"How tragic. Do you have any children?"

"Two, both teenagers. Jared's fifteen and my daughter Stephanie's only eighteen months younger." But before she could elaborate any further Sally pointed to a door labeled Department of Psychiatry. "Well, here we are."

She preceded Marshall into the office complex and introduced him to three secretaries who occupied identical desks in the large outer-room. From there they headed down a short hallway where, on the door of the first office, Marshall read, DR. MARSHALL I. FRIEDMAN, CHIEF OF PSYCHIATRY printed in neat bold letters on the opaque glass. His chest swelled with pride. Wasn't this proof he'd finally arrived?

"Well, how do you like it?" she asked, her eyes searching his imploringly.

"It's great."

"Would you like to go inside?"

"Of course, I would."

The room seemed ample but not spacious, a little smaller than his old office in Upper East Side of Manhattan. There was a large dark red mahogany desk. The chair behind it was upholstered in soft cordovan leather. Bookshelves and filing cabinets lined the walls. A Gateway 2000 computer had been set up at right angles to his desk along with a laser printer and a scanner. To Marshall it seemed so enticing that he was ready to get to work immediately.

"This office is great," he commented to Sally. "Can I bring my stuff down tomorrow?"

"Anytime you want," she replied, her smile warm.

After leaving the Psychiatry Department they visited the clinical units on the seventh floor of the Tower Building. There, he met some of the nurses and aides then reviewed the facility's layout. The head nurse took a moment to brief him on the unit routines. One of the staff psychologists showed him some of the treatment algorithms and briefly discussed the psychological testing they had available. Finally he spent some time leafing through one of the prodigious procedural manuals.

"Let me show you where the physicians' dining room is," Sally mentioned after he finished. "I've got a luncheon meeting with my ICU head nurses, so I won't be able to join you. But I'm sure you'll get along."

"That's a shame. I was looking forward to sitting down and catching up on old times."

"I'd like that too. In fact, if you haven't made any plans for dinner tonight yet, why don't you and your wife join me?"

"Oh," he said with a brief stutter, "my wife's back in New York, Sally." After a brief hesitation he added, "I know this will sound a little strange, but I think we're separated."

"Hmmm," Sally replied. Marshall expected to have to elaborate. Instead she asked, "Then how about you? Any plans?"

"Not a one," he said. "In fact, where do you live? If you're interested in a casual meal, there's this place called Max and Erma's around the corner from my new apartment in Shadyside. Or we can go for something fancier if you like."

"When I mentioned dinner, Marshall, I meant at my house. I just thought a home-cooked meal might be nice for a change. After just moving back here, you probably haven't had one of those in a while."

"No," he agreed, "I haven't. Dinner at your house would be great. Should I bring anything?"

"Other than yourself? No, I believe I'm fully stocked."

An elevator took them down to the second floor. On the way Sally gave him a piece of paper with her address written on it and some directions to her house. It turned out to be just a few blocks from his old high school. As the door opened she pressed the hold button and added, "When the door opens just walk about thirty feet down that hallway and you'll see the cafeteria on your left. The physicians' dining room is to the left."

"Sure," he said, as the door started to close. "No problem. See you tonight. About seven?"

"Seven's fine, Marshall. See you tonight."

After lunch Marshall found the library and then located the audiovisual department on the same floor. Finally, around three o'clock, after signing some tax forms and setting up a credit union account in the Personnel Department, Marshall departed the Hunt.

While driving home in his Mercedes S 420, a fortieth birthday present from Bernice, he reflected upon what a fortunate coincidence it was that Sally Swenson, now Sally Steiner, was an administrator at the clinic. He tried to recall when he'd first seen her. It was during the first semester of his sophomore year at Pitt. Sunny Sally, as she came to be known, was sitting three rows in front of him in his Introduction to Poetry class, her wispy blonde hair hanging well below her shoulders, her expression intelligent as ever.

She looked like a typical shiksa, he remembered thinking the first time he saw her.

On passing in and out of the classroom they exchanged smiles. But he couldn't seem to muster the nerve to introduce himself. In fact, it wasn't until his fraternity brother, Michael Rosen, took her to the Greek Week Formal that he finally got to meet the girl.

After that their poetry class became the context for their friendship. Soon they were discussing assignments over the phone at night and sharing personal creations before turning them in. Toward the end of that fall semester they even collaborated on a term project, comparing and contrasting the lyrics of Paul Simon with those of Bob Dylan.

Through his final year at Pitt, Marshall had kept his link with Sally cordial, talking to her at fraternity functions or athletic events, running into her at the Student Union, or just strolling around campus. Occasionally he'd phone her for advice regarding someone he was dating. Twice she'd even fixed him up with sorority sisters. Neither match worked out well.

Pulling the Mercedes into the parking lot of a three-story apartment building on Kentucky Street, Marshall remembered where he'd seen her last. It was the day of the graduation reception in May of 1980 while he was sitting at a table behind the frat house with his roommate Michael, and a girl named, Karen Marcus. Sally, he remembered, was still involved with Michael at the time. They had even hinted about getting married.

We were so starry-eyed about our plans back then, Marshall reminisced. *Everyone had lofty aspirations, marvelous hopes and dreams. But amid the excitement we were a little sad, too. I was leaving for Philly in the fall. It was the first time I'd be living that far away from my friends and family. The rest of them were also leaving places they'd grown attached to.*

In earnest they'd exchanged addresses and phone numbers. Determined to delay their inevitable parting, he and Karen had escorted

Sally to Mike's white Mustang convertible. About to slip into the passenger seat Sally hugged her friends and wished them well. She then vowed to stay in touch by writing and calling each of them frequently.

However, except for two brief letters during his freshman year at Penn, Marshall had never heard from Sally again.

chapter three

a dramatic entrance

Marshall's first full week at the Hunter-Neuman Clinic was spent in a whirlwind of activity. After using the weekend to organize his office he dived headlong into departmental meetings, clinical rounds, ward conferences and patient interviews. On Tuesday afternoon he met with his outpatient staff to create a set of guidelines for his private practice. By Wednesday, July first, the new crop of psychiatry residents arrived.

Some initial trepidation notwithstanding, he found the scope of his new position exhilarating. Most everyone he came in contact with seemed good-natured, friendly, and accommodating. The majority of individuals who worked at the Hunt, from housekeeping through the medical staff, seemed to like their jobs and the institution that provided them. This universal attitude, Marshall conceded, was a credit to the hospital administration in general and to Bertram Hunter in particular.

Then, on Thursday, while doing a consult down in the recovery room, Marshall ran into Steve Heller, a former classmate from Penn. Later, over lunch in the hospital cafeteria, he and Steve, the interim chairman of the anesthesia department, caught up on old times. Then, on Friday evening they went to a Pirates game at Three Rivers Stadium. Three hours later, while driving home after the baseball game, Marshall decided that his reinvigorated life seemed particularly satisfying and multidimensional. He thought about Bernice living back in Manhattan and wondered whether he would have trouble fitting her into this new framework.

■   ■   ■

Independence Day morning dawned clear and warm. By ten A.M. the temperature hit eighty-five. The Hunters' picnic/dinner party was called for five. Marshall spent a lazy day reading and hanging around the neighborhood. At four-fifteen he left to pick up Sally.

Marshall had yet to visit his boss' suburban estate, but Sally assured him she knew the way. The traffic seemed particularly light as they cruised down the Parkway East toward The Point. Bypassing the downtown area they crossed the Duquesne Bridge, passed Three Rivers Stadium, and continued out along Ohio River Boulevard toward Sewickley Heights.

As he drove beside the wide river Marshall furtively glanced over at Sally. With her soft blonde hair gathered in a cinch, her cheeks and forehead lightly tanned, and her light blue eyes sparkling, he thought she looked fetching. He was charmed by the intense expression of concentration she wore as she scrutinized the directions Bertram had given her.

He shifted his gaze to the panorama before him, noting how much he loved the domesticity of the scene, driving along a four lane suburban highway, the Ohio River lazily lapping nearby, a blue cloudless sky above him, and an attractive woman by his side. He contrasted this setting with being back in New York, an over-crowded, concrete and steel jungle where, with Bernice, he'd been forced to rely on cabs and limousines for transportation while choking on the congestion of urban life. Being back in Western Pennsylvania seemed so much more pleasant.

"Oh!" Sally said excitedly, "Here's Beaver Grade. Marshall. Bear right."

He eased the Mercedes up the narrow tree-lined thoroughfare and soon entered the sleepy little township of Sewickley. Despite Marshall being here for the first time, it looked vaguely familiar to him, resembling dozens of small Pennsylvania towns he'd visited over the years. With narrow streets, boutiquey specialty shops, and stately homes it appeared both quaint and prosperous. Red, white, and blue bunting hung limply from the gas streetlights and storefront windows. A large banner sagged above the roadway advertising the Independence Day parade that had taken place earlier that afternoon. Piles of streamers, confetti, and other papers littered the deserted sidewalks and recessed gutters, like a lingering testimony to the celebration.

On Blackburn Road, a serpentine, tree-lined grade, they passed Sewickley Valley Hospital and War Memorial Park before entered the Heights. There, a host of fabulous mansions dotted the hills. Many, Marshall noticed, seemed almost plantation-like, boasting large white columns, rectangular casement windows, elaborate porticos, and massive wooden portals. Interspersed among these were more contemporary multileveled structures with oddly shaped floorplans, semidetached garages, and elaborate wrap-around decks. As impressive as the older structures seemed, Marshall decided that he favored the modern architecture more.

"It's coming up on your left, Marshall," Sally warned, "right after the orange belt sign. There it is!" She pointed through the windshield at a small driveway marked by two square stone pillars. "There's the sign, Fairview Acres."

Indeed, Marshall noticed the estate's grand title embossed on a pewter-colored plaque bolted to the far pillar. A separate sign announcing, PRIVATE PROPERTY, NO TRESPASSING was tacked up beneath it. Marshall pulled in and drove for about a half mile down a densely wooded, asphalt covered access lane. Suddenly the trees thinned, the road widened, and an impressive vista greeted them.

Marshall had heard that Bertram Hunter's home was impressive. Nestled in the rolling hills of four acres of prime Sewickley Heights real estate, it ranked up there with the largest residential structures in the area. But he was totally unprepared for its true magnificence. Broad, stately, and totally constructed of white brick and wood, it reminded Marshall of one of the Loire Valley chateaus he and Bernice had toured when they vacationed in France during the summer of 1992.

The access road split to accommodate an elliptically shaped front lawn. Marshall eased around it to the front door and parked behind a Lexus GS 400. A young man with sandy colored hair and a pleasant smile gave him a valet ticket and told him to leave the car running. Marshall admired his hunter green polo shirt with the Clinic's name and a caricature of the Tower stitched where the breast pocket should be. A second valet opened the passenger door for Sally.

They proceeded to the large door that opened after he knocked. A short, slim, gray-haired woman in an apron-covered summer dress greeted them. "Sally!" she said pleasantly. "I'm so glad you could make it. And who's this handsome young man you've brought with you?"

"Hello, Mrs. Hunter. This is Marshall Friedman. He's Hunter's new chairman of the psychiatry department."

"Well, welcome to our holiday celebration, Dr. Friedman. I believe Bertram has mentioned you to me. It's nice to have you join us for dinner today."

"The pleasure is all mine," Marshall replied, shaking the small, bony hand. "This place is truly magnificent. I'd love to see more of it."

"Remind me later," she offered with a wink. "I'll take you on a little tour. But right now I'm helping the cook stuff mushrooms with crabmeat. It's one of Bertram's favorites. Why don't you two get yourselves some liquid refreshment and join the other guests in the back of the house. The Mister is out there grilling the main course." She pointed to a corridor that seemed to bisect the huge mansion. "Brenda," she called to a liveried young woman holding an empty tray in her hand. "Could you please provide Dr. Friedman and Mrs. Steiner with beverages?"

A few moments later Marshall and Sally were standing on the back porch by a long table laden with an interesting variety of hors d'oeuvres. Surrounding them were clusters of guests sampling the food and conversing animatedly. Marshall turned toward and the rail and tried to absorb the majestic scope of the place. He was in awe of the handsome swimming pool in the immediate foreground, the twin tennis courts off to the right, an elevated deck on the far side of the pool, and what seemed like acres of rolling hills that reached a wooded boundary in the distance.

"Isn't Mrs. Hunter a sweety?" Sally asked, interrupting his muse.

"She seems charming," Marshall replied. "What's her story?"

"From what Hunter's told me, she's a real southern belle, born and bred in Charleston, South Carolina. He met her in the 1960s while he was at the Naval Academy. She was living with her aunt and uncle in Annapolis. They had this idyllic summer romance then continued it long distance until she finished college. They got married in 1965 and celebrated their thirty-fifth anniversary last fall."

"I thought I detected a bit of Southern hospitality in her manner. You know, sweet and very proper." Sally nodded and smiled.

Suddenly Marshall felt very hungry. After scanning the food table he selected two phylo dough pastries, a handful of cut vegetables, and two jumbo shrimp. Sally garnered her own sampling of the delicacies and they headed over to an arrangement of small tables that had been set up around the pool. They passed a tall, lanky man in khaki pants and a blue denim shirt standing alone near the diving board.

"He looks familiar," Marshall commented pointing with his plastic fork. "Who is he?"

"That's Chris Jeffries, chief of cardiothoracic surgery. He's supposedly one of the best vascular surgeons in the country. Toby Cosgrove from the Cleveland Clinic trained him. He's doing all our miniCABs and keyhole procedures."

Marshall had read about this new wave in heart surgery. "He looks pretty young to be that accomplished," he commented

"They say he's brilliant—and a wizard in the OR."

"He'd have to be to do that kind of work," Marshall agreed.

Sally nodded then took his arm. "Why don't we go over and say hello to Bertram?"

"Where is he?"

"Up there on the deck, standing by the grill."

They strolled around the kidney-shaped pool to where an elaborate multilevel deck had been constructed. Marshall suspected that the platform was normally used for sun bathing. But today it was replete with table and chair ensembles designed to comfortably accommodate forty or fifty guests. Off to the left stood a large outdoor stainless steel grill. Before the grill, partially hidden by a group of guests, stood a middle-aged man in a tan apron and white chef's hat.

Marshall and Sally ascended the trio of wooden steps. A warm breeze sent a row of colorful Chinese lanterns swaying. Just as they approached their host turned toward them. "Marshall, Sally," he hailed them and bowed briefly. "Welcome to my humble abode."

"Some humble abode," Marshall retorted. "This place is magnificent. It reminds me of one of the castles I toured with my wife in France a few years ago."

"You must mean Cheverny," Hunter commented. "That's what the realtor suggested back in seventy-five when she first showed us the place. And Marshall, if you're familiar with that particular chateau, make sure you check out our north wing library. It's an exact replica of the Early Empire style the count included in the original."

"Fascinating," Marshall said and made a mental note to ask to see that particular room when Mrs. Hunter gave him his tour.

"Has Sally been introducing you around, Marshall? Several of your contemporaries are here."

"She's pointed out some people," Marshall replied. "I'm sure I'll meet everyone before the night is through."

"Splendid," Bertram said. "Now tell me what I can fix you two for dinner. Most of my guests have requested steak. There's a choice collection of two-inch-thick filets already on the grill. But if you're not partial to meat, I can rustle up some pretty tasty barbecued chicken instead."

"Whatever you're having, Mr. Hunter," Marshall said, trying to be tactful.

"Oh, I'm having grilled halibut," he replied, gesturing with his spatula at two slabs tucked away on an elevated rack behind the twin burners. "They're marinated in tamari sauce."

"Fish?" Marshall asked. "You're not opting for one of those juicy steaks?"

"I'm afraid not Marshall," Hunter explained. "My cardiologist doesn't allow me to eat red meat, even if it's trimmed lean like those prime cuts over here."

"Oh," Marshall said, curious about the restriction. "I guess I'll go with the fish too," he indicated without probing further.

"Great. And how about you, Sally?"

"I'll have chicken, Bertram. I remember how tasty it was last year."

"All right. Now you two find yourselves a nice table up here on the deck and I'll bring them over."

Sally claimed the corner table near the front part of the platform. One of the young servers came around and took their beverage order. Sitting back Marshall absently watched the other guests as the murmur of their dozens of conversations melded into a low-pitched hum. Finally his glance returned to their host standing in front of the grill. Almost instinctively he felt compelled to ask Sally, "What's with the cardiologist? Does Hunter have a bad heart?"

"Yes," she replied simply.

"How bad is bad?"

"Pretty bad. Or so I've been led to believe. They think he had an attack of viral myocarditis a few years ago. It left him with a nasty case of cardiomyopathy. His last echo shows there's only about forty percent of his left ventricle left."

Marshall thought of the heart's main pumping chamber and how critical it was to the life-sustaining action of the heart. "Does that make him a transplant candidate?" he asked.

"He's on the list," she acknowledged.

To Marshall this was a sobering thought. The man appeared healthy and robust. Despite this he couldn't have more than a year or two to live. The man's sentence wouldn't seem so harsh, Marshall decided, if Hunter had been one of those hollow-cheeked, cachectic cardiacs he'd seen in the Coronary Care Unit back at Bellevue. But Hunter looked like the picture of health.

I guess he's pretty well compensated, he reflected. Out loud he commented, "I suspect that healthy diet's designed to preserve what's left."

"There's more to it than that," Sally offered. "He's got advanced coronary disease, too. The diet and whatever exercise he can do tends to slow its progression."

"I guess that accounts for him being so close to Jeffries," Marshall commented. "If anyone's going to help him squeeze out a few more years, it's going to be a thoracic surgeon."

"One would think so," agreed Sally. After that they fell silent, concentrating on the dusky sky, and waiting for their food to come.

"Why so glum?" inquired a cheerful voice from just beside them. Marshall glanced up and saw Steve Heller standing there.

"Steve," Marshall greeted him. "When did you arrive, old man?"

"About half an hour ago. But my wife's had me sequestered in the house talking to a couple of her friends. I finally told her I needed some fresh air and wandered out back."

"Have a seat," Marshall said, pulling out one of the plastic chair. "We'll save the other one for Maura."

Accepting the invitation Steve plopped down. "Beautiful night," he commented. "You two drive out together?"

"We live so close it was silly to bring two cars."

"Makes sense to me," Steve remarked. To Sally he added, "You're living in Squirrel Hill, aren't you?"

"Ever since I moved back to Pittsburgh in ninety-two. Why?"

"Just wondering. I thought you grew up in Mount Lebanon? No desire to go back there?"

"I wanted the kids to live in a Jewish neighborhood. It's something Howard felt very strongly about. We've raised them Jewish. In fact, Jared was Bar Mitzvahed two years ago. And Stephanie spent six weeks in Israel last summer."

"But you're not Jewish, Sally," Steve persisted. "Unless you've converted."

"I'm pretty much an agnostic, Steve," Sally explained. "So there was never a question of converting. And Howard agreed that it wasn't necessary. But I love the Jewish traditions and believe strongly in their moralistic teachings so I have no trouble following them. There's a lot of universality there that everyone could benefit from."

"That's for sure," Steve agreed. "But you're preaching to the faithful. I was just curious, that's all."

"Curious about a lot tonight, aren't you, Steve-a-reno?" Marshall asked lightly.

His question was designed to curtail the interrogation and it succeeded. Steve gave him a wry smile then asked Sally something about a committee on which they both served. Marshall started to track their conversation, but his mind wandered back to the precious little evening he'd spent at Sally's cozy home in Squirrel Hill, soon after his return to Pittsburgh.

It must've been hard, he reflected, a widow with two young children, picking up the pieces and going on after her husband had died. The rush of sympathy he felt turned into an earnest hope that somehow someone would come along and fill the apparent void in her life.

Bertram walked over carrying a plate laden with chicken and fish. He set it down on their table, inquired as to Steve's preference, then directed them to a table near the back of the deck stocked with an wide a array of, vegetables, salads, and fruit. Marshall and Sally added to their plates. When they returned Steve was still sitting there looking pensive.

"You're from Pittsburgh too, aren't you, Marsh?" Steve asked as he reached over and pilfered a celery stick from Marshall's plate.

"Born and bred," Marshall replied, starting on his salad.

"Parents still live here?"

"Yeah. After we sent my mom into The Heritage two years ago, Dad couldn't manage the house on Denniston Avenue in Squirrel Hill. So he moved to the Webster Hall last fall."

"That's too bad. What's with your mom?"

"It's mostly Alzheimer's," Marshall replied a little wistfully. "She can't remember anything past the age of twenty. I visited her last week. At first she thought I was her father."

"No? Really? That's so sad," Steve said. "I'm sure glad my pop's still firin' on all eight cylinders. He's pushin' seventy-five, you know. But he still gets up at six A.M. and walks five miles every day. And six months after my mother died he started dating a woman fifteen years younger than him."

"Well good for him," Sally offered.

Marshall was about to comment about how he wished his father had more of a social life when a flash of motion caught his eye. There was a swath of bold colors briefly illuminated by the row of ground level lighting near the pool. A woman appeared, clad in the loud dress. She stood about five feet six inches tall with broad shoulders and a buxom chest. His mother would have labeled her 'big-boned.' She paused at the top of the steps long enough to allow Marshall to get a good look at her. Her shoulder length auburn hair was combed to one side. Her expression seemed intense, her attitude deliberate. The loose-fitting dress she wore almost reached the ground.

She started walking—almost strutting—again, toward the far side of the deck. Marshall sensed that it wasn't so much her appearance that intrigued him, but rather the array of reactions she seemed to generate in the other guests. It was as if, with her unheralded arrival, everyone on the platform felt compelled to suspend his or her conversation in mid-sentence so as to track her progress across the deck. Their faces, Marshall noted, registered a variety of emotions ranging from breathless surprise, through amused pleasure, all the way to total disgust.

Everyone on that deck seemed to be familiar with this strange woman. And Marshall suspected that most had some strong opinion about her.

The woman walked straight up to Hunter. She greeted him with a kiss on the cheek and a big hug. He, on the other hand, appeared to shrink back a bit, almost embarrassed by this gesture. Then the woman began speaking in a voice that was loud enough for everyone to hear. First she thanked Hunter for the kind invitation then apologized to him for being late. She asked about dinner and told him she wanted a big juicy steak.

Marshall captivated by the scene, soon realized that he wasn't the only one eavesdropping. No one else on the deck was speaking. Then, as the bold woman in the multi-colored dress moved away from Hunter, the other guests seemed to collectively sense they'd been intruding. Like a spring of water bubbling out of a parched field, a smattering of conversation rose up again. Soon the low-pitched hum of dialogue filled the deck area.

Turning his head slightly toward Sally, but still not able to take his eye off the retreating woman, Marshall asked, "Who the heck was that?"

Sally, her voice curiously flat and dispassionate replied, "That was Rose Shaw."

"Rose Shaw?" He persisted. "Who's she?"

"Oh, you'll find out, Marshall," Sally replied mysteriously. "You'll find out."

And no matter how much more he probed, that was all she was going to say on the matter.

chapter four

rose

After Mrs. Hunter gave him a perfunctory tour of the grand mansion, Marshall browsed around the formal library inspecting Hunter's impressive collection of first editions.

Marshall found the room charming, rich with intricate molding, a pale inlaid ceiling, sectional bookcases whose complicated design matched the walls, and a beautiful Oriental rug covering most of the teak floor. As he ran his hand along the back of one of the exquisitely delicate chairs he imagined how it might have come directly from the court of Louis the Fourteenth.

While perusing the neat collections, Marshall had a thought. He located the psychology section and paused at the shelf containing works by Anna Freud through Carl Jung. There, next to *The Sane Society* by Erich Fromm, he saw what he dared to hope would be there.

"You dog, Hunter," Marshall said aloud. "You went out and bought it for your private collection. Now whaddya think about that?"

He reached over and pulled out a copy of *When Good Men Feel Bad* by Marshall I. Friedman, M.D. It was a first edition hardback in excellent condition. Marshall wondered if it had been read it yet. Then he noticed the Barnes and Noble bookmarker sticking up from about halfway into the body of the text and opened the book to the designated page. A small stain discolored the lower right corner.

The Hunters must like to eat while they read, too, he decided.

Satisfied that he had at least one subscriber in the Pittsburgh area, Marshall moved on to the fiction section. While browsing through a section devoted to a work of Hermann Hesse, a soft, husky voice from nearby inquired, "Good book?"

Marshall started. He turned to see to whom the voice belonged. It was the woman who'd been on the deck, the one who had stirred up such a commotion among Hunter's guests. Sally had called her Rose Shaw.

"It's one of my favorites. I read it while I was in college."

"What's it called?"

He told her.

"Never heard of it."

She eased over and stood beside him. As she peered over his shoulder at the novel he could smell her perfume. He was familiar with the scent, Opium, a fragrance Bernice had experimented with while they were dating. He breathed a little deeper, relishing the deep, rich aroma. It was a scent that reminded him of sensuality.

"I'm Dr. Marshall Friedman," he said extending his thin bony hand.

"Yes, I know," the unusual woman replied without taking it.

Marshall glanced at his palm, felt a little flustered and dropped it to his side. "How did you know?" he asked.

"Hunter told me."

Marshall nodded. While doing so he took a moment to apprise the mysterious woman that was standing uncomfortably close to him. She appeared to be about five feet, five inches tall, full-figured with a shock of wavy auburn hair combed to one side and reaching her shoulder.

She's certainly not unattractive, he decided.

But, on the other hand, she was no knockout. Her oval face seemed a tad asymmetric and she had red full lips, a feature to which he'd never been attracted. A tiny gap marred the continuity of her front two teeth. But her eyes were beautiful, hazel green and arresting.

"Did Dr. Hunter also tell you what I did?" he probed.

"You're a shrink," the woman replied. "A psychiatrist. You're the new head of the department."

"That's correct," Marshall acknowledged, intrigued that she'd gone to some trouble finding out about him. "And who are you?"

"My name's Rose. Rose Shaw." He waited for her to share more about herself. When she remained silent he felt compelled to inquire further.

"Do you work at the clinic?"

"I'm a geneticist. Dr. Hunter recruited me back in 1994. I head a major research project in molecular biology."

"Genetics?" Marshall replied, trying to look impressed. "That's real cutting edge stuff. On the verge of any breakthroughs?"

"My work is progressing nicely," was all that the woman offered.

Marshall nodded, again waiting for some elaboration. Instead, a silent interlude followed, one that set Marshall a little off balance.

What was it with this woman? he wondered. Why did she seem so intriguing?

Marshall glanced at his watch and noticed that in was almost eight o'clock. Mrs. Hunter had scheduled a music recital for her guests at eight o'clock.

"Are you planning to attend Mrs. Hunter's recital?" he asked Rose.

"No," she replied. There was no hint of embarrassment or apology in her tone.

"May I ask why?"

"I don't like classical music."

"Oh."

"And I don't particularly like Mrs. Hunter either," she added.

Once again caught off guard, Marshall tried to hide his uneasiness. He glanced down at his hands, noticed the open book and closed it softly. As he returned it to the shelf, Rose remained by his side. He could feel her eyes studying him.

"That's a beautiful shirt you're wearing," she commented.

"Well thank you," Marshall replied with pride. This was his finest silk top. All evening he'd been hoping someone would notice it.

"You know, I've seen a psychiatrist or two in my time," she offered without prompting.

"Is that so?" he said. "Why was that?"

"Childhood problems. My mother was killed in an automobile accident when I was twelve. My father was forced to raise me. I guess he couldn't hack it."

"That sounds tragic," Marshall said, fascinated by her unsolicited revelation. "Why did he have so much trouble?"

"I was a wild kid. He called me a bad seed. He needed my aunt to move in with us to help out."

"Oh," Marshall replied with a slow nod.

"Do you interpret dreams?" Rose asked him

Starting to anticipate these sudden curves in the road, Marshall rolled with this one. "Sometimes," he replied. "Why?"

"I've been having nightmares. They wake me up. Maybe you could help figure them out for me."

"I may be able to," Marshall agreed. But before he could elaborate Steve Heller strolled into the room.

"Marshall, my man, I've been looking all over for you. Sally's wondering if you're coming in for the concert. She says Maggie's a real master at that dumb little dulcimer. Then glancing at Rose he added, "Oh, excuse me. I hope I haven't interrupted anything."

"Dr. Shaw and I were just talking," Marshall explained. "Tell Sally I'll be right in."

With a nod the anesthesiologist backed out of the doorway. "Sure, thing Marsh," he said.

"It looks like I was missed," Marshall commented to Rose. "I suppose I'd better be going. I hope we can continue our little conversation sometime soon."

"We will."

Marshall slid into the folding chair next to Sally then sat up straight.

"Where were you?" she asked, her harsh whisper sounding more like a hiss. "Maggie's already into her second number."

"I was checking out the library—like Hunter suggested before dinner. He was right. It's fabulous. I couldn't believe his collection of first editions."

Sally, who kept her eyes fixed on the performer, turned partway toward him and put an index finger to her lips. A couple other guests cleared their throats. Twenty feet away Magdeline Hunter sat on a miniature bench before a trapezoid-shaped wooden instrument. It had two bridges with clusters of thin metal strings stretched over them. Using two curved-tip mallets, Mrs. Hunter struck the strings and produced a somewhat tinny sound. The melody, however, seemed bright and cheerful. Marshall joined the rest of the company as they listened intently.

But eventually a certain repetitiveness crept into the composition and its uniformity lead to a lapse of attention. His mind began to wander. His thoughts drifted back to his brief encounter with Rose Shaw.

So she's a geneticist, he reflected. *How intriguing. And she'd doing 'topical' research. Maybe it's one of those molecular biology projects where they try to eliminate a congenital disease with some elaborate gene transfer or gene manipulation. I'll have to ask her about it the next time I see her. But that assumes there'll be a next time. Which is how likely? After all, what pretense could I use to speak with her again? Maybe we'll run into each other in the cafeteria or at a staff meeting. I can use those dreams she's been having as an icebreaker. But that clinic is such a big place. We could go months before running into each other.*

An outburst of applause jolted Marshall out of his reverie. Maggie, a proud smile on her pretty face, turned partway on her bench and faced the audience. A guest seated far back in the room called for more.

"You flatter me," she said, blushing. "Since some of you wonderful people would like to hear another composition, I'd be delighted to oblige." The crowd responded with more clapping.

Despite Marshall's intention to pay attention, his thoughts soon returned to earlier that evening when he'd discovered Hunter's copy of his book on the library shelf.

It's amazing how little I've thought about that book since I came back to Pittsburgh in June, he noted. *I guess it got lost in all the commotion of getting settled in. And if it wasn't for Sandi's call a couple of days ago it would still be on the back burner.*

His literary agent had indeed phoned on Thursday evening to say hello, or so she said, and to reassure him that, despite his blow-up with Bernice's father, all was not lost.

"In fact, Marshall," she had reported, "standing up to Mr. Tannenbaum in the conference room like you did last month must've radically altered his opinion of you. The last time we met he said you showed him some character he never thought you had. And that observation alone has given him the impetus to renew his support of your book."

"Really," Marshall had replied, resisting the urge to get too excited. After all, wasn't his father-in-law's comment just a thinly veiled insult?

"But he doesn't want to throw good money after bad," she continued, "which buying up a few thousand more copies of your book would represent. Instead he's going to trust his business instincts this time and attack this project from a new direction. At least that's what he said."

"What's all that mean?" Marshall asked.

"He wants us to organize an all-out marketing campaign. He says he'll be willing to bankroll it. Actually, that's what I thought we were doing with all those book-signings and interviews you gave while still living in Manhattan. But this time he wants us to target a narrower public sector. Call it the 'enlightened minority.' We'll be using thirty-second radio spots and creative ads on the more culturally savvy televisions stations like A&E and The Discovery Channel to stir up some interest."

"That sounds promising," Marshall agreed, becoming more engaged.

"And he's anxious to take advantage of your new location and position. Being tapped to head the psyche department at Hunter-Neuman gives you the respect and credibility you lacked in private practice." While she paused to catch her breath, Marshall considered the ramifications of this statement and was pleased. "He also wants to target the professional community. We'll be working on the assumption that if we can sell the psychiatrists and psychologists on your stuff, they'll mention it to their patients who'll go out and buy it. And with those sales the book might gain enough commercial momentum to sustain itself."

"But how do we get at the professionals?" Marshall inquired. "Through journal ads and personal mailers?"

"Some of that," Sandi agreed. "But we also think it would be extremely effective if you could address your colleagues directly—in some professional forum or other?"

"A conference?"

"Or a seminar. In fact, that's another reason why I called. I've been in touch with the woman who runs the Allegheny County Medical Society's Continuing Medical Department. When I told her what I had in mind she was very supportive. She mentioned a talk on 'Depression in the Nineties' the Society has scheduled for July fourteenth downtown at the Westin William Penn. But her speaker unexpectedly cancelled on her. So, being the proactive person you know and love, I seized the moment and offered you up in his place. She sounded thrilled with the prospect. Before we hung up I told them I'd check with you about it." She paused again, her inquiry implicit. "What do you say?"

Marshall fended off a sense of excitement tinged with overwhelm. It had been months since he'd given a formal presentation and years since he'd done so to a group of his peers. He had to be rusty. But the notion of jump-starting his book back onto the charts was irresistible. Without hesitation he agreed.

"Great," Sandi had said. "I'll phone her tomorrow and confirm. Someone from the Society should be in touch with you by Monday. I've also got a list of pharmaceutical reps in the Pittsburgh area who detail psychiatrists. If I can get them to personally invite their clients to the talk, we should have a pretty decent turnout. We're thinking of billing you as the Alan Watts of the new millennia."

"Those are pretty big shoes to fill," Marshall cautioned. "But maybe I can get some mileage out of the association. We'll talk more once we finalize the plans."

After Sandi signed off Marshall had been left wondering what he'd talk about.

It was after ten when Hunter and Maggie started escorting their guests to the door. The valet was sent to drive Marshall's Mercedes around. Hunter shook Marshall's hand then draped an affectionate arm across his shoulders.

"It's so good to have you in Pittsburgh, Marshall," he said warmly. "I'm looking forward to spending many productive years with you here."

"So am I, Dr. Hunter."

"Call me Bertram—or Hunter. Everybody else does." Then he turned toward Sally and gave her a fatherly hug. "Well, thanks for coming, you two. I hope you enjoyed yourself."

"It been great, Bertram," Sally offered. "As always."

While Sally and Hunter said their good-byes, Marshall happened to glance past Maggie Hunter's tiny left shoulder back inside the house. There, off to the corner of the entranceway, standing by the foot of the large staircase, was Rose Shaw. Leaning casually against the wall, her arms crossed on her chest, she watched the pleasantries taking place by the door. For an instant her eyes met Marshall's, locked on them, and then looked away. The encounter, however brief, left him breathless.

Hunter must have noticed the direction of Marshall's gaze. As Sally started out toward the car, he grabbed Marshall's arm and held him back. In a low-pitched, even-tempered voice he cautioned, "Stay away from that one."

Startled that his thoughts seemed so transparent, he asked defensively, "Why do you say that?"

"Because she's trouble, Marshall—the kind of trouble you don't want to get mixed up in."

Marshall was intrigued by this reply. He nodded as if he understood. But he knew he really didn't. Sally was already in the car and he thought it better not to explore the matter further at this time.

While walking around the rear of his car he felt in a little off balance. And despite Hunter's solemn warning, Marshall couldn't help longing for an opportunity to stare into Rose Shaw's hazel green eyes once again.

chapter five

an unexpected attendee

The following week turned out to be more hectic than Marshall expected. But despite his ten-hour workdays at the Hunt, he did manage to squeeze in two comprehensive workouts at the Rivers Club in downtown Pittsburgh.

Another casualty to his busy work schedule was Marshall's social life. Except for a light dinner on Friday night and brunch on Sunday with Sally, most of the subsequent weekend was spent putting the finishing touches on his presentation for the Medical Society. On Sunday evening, Bernice called.

This was only the second time he'd spoken to his wife since his arrival in Pittsburgh. The first had been late in June, while he was still staying at the Hilton when she called to see how he was making out. She missed him and hoped something mutually acceptable could be worked out between them. She regarded their current situation as a "trial separation" forced by the assumption of his new position, and that perhaps, "if they felt it was appropriate," a compromise could be worked out so they could be reunited. As he had listened to her make these quasi-optimistic assertions, he detected neither enthusiasm nor conviction in her tone.

Bernice's second call also sounded more informative than expressive. She began by telling him that she would be spending the summer at her parents' home in the Hamptons and reminded him of the number in case he needed to contact her. Regarding the marketing of his book, she apologized once again for having deceived him and reiterated that she had meant him no harm.

"Truly, Marshall," she had said, her tone earnestly honest, "you have to believe me on this one. I only had your happiness in mind." After conferring with her father several times since late June, she thought he might be interested to know that the entire family was behind the new marketing strategy for his work. "As for me," she confessed, "I've decided to avoid any active role in putting this project into action. That's not to say I don't fully support your literary pursuits, Marshall. But given my track record I don't want to do anything to jeopardize any future relationship we might have. And of course, it goes without saying, I wish you all the success in the world."

After he hung up, Marshall spent some moments reflecting on the awkwardness of the conversation. Somehow he got the impression that Bernice was going through the motions of remaining in contact. Or perhaps, embracing this cool objective demeanor was her way of insulating herself from any hurt that may have surfaced in the wake of his departure. Either way, he was hard put to predict an optimistic future for their failing marriage.

The evening of his presentation arrived. Toting a briefcase full of outlines in one hand and a carousel loaded with slides in the other, Marshall checked with the clerk at the front desk who directed him to the Monongahela Room on the seventeenth floor. A small group of people mulled near a narrow registration area. Past them was the spacious conference room. Once inside Marshall took a moment to get oriented. He regarded the rows of folding chairs facing a slightly raised platform. A collapsible screen and a wooden podium also awaited him. He set down his briefcase and brushed his sweaty palms on his suit pants.

A dark-haired middle-aged woman in a gray suit walked up to him and introduced herself as Gladys Frazier. She offered him assistance in setting up, which he declined, content to load the carousel onto the projector himself before inspecting the podium. Lastly he tested the microphone and laser pointer. Everything seemed to be in working order.

During dinner Marshall sat with Mrs. Frazier and Dr. Morton Kastlebach one of the staff psychiatrists at West Psychiatric Institute. During his mother's many admissions for incapacitating clinical depression over the years, Marshall had become well acquainted with Pitt's famous mental health facility. Dr. Kastlebach, Marshall learned, was a highly respected, experimentally oriented clinician, who believed that most mental disorders were due to chemical imbalances in the brain. He tended to treat his patients with many of the wide array of drugs on the market. Thus, the title of Marshall's presentation, *Depression, A Crisis of Spirituality,* appeared to intrigue him. Such a topic, he informed Marshall seemed more suited to a minister's sermon than a board-certified psychoanalyst's presentation to a room full of physicians. Marshall, in turn, assured him that he fully intended to integrate both the mystical and the medical aspects of this vexing disorder. Kastlebach voiced skepticism but promised to keep an open mind.

At seven-thirty the lights dimmed. Mrs. Frazier took the stage, formally welcomed the attendees, then introduced Marshall. As he listened to her cite his numerous titles and accomplishments, he felt a rush of pride. He hoped that this review of his credentials would accord him the credibility he needed to get started.

About to begin his presentation Marshall stood behind the podium and peered out into the muted darkness. He hadn't been this nervous in a long time. Perspiration coated his armpits, his shirt felt chilly under his jacket. He introduced himself, shared a little about his background as a hometown boy then told a slightly off-color joke that met with a favorable response. Gradually his anxiety abated.

The slides started rolling and so did Marshall. He paced his talk with the pictures, diagrams, charts and tables. He began with a review of some of the traditional psychological theories of depression, moved through some well-described environmental and nutritional causes of the disorder, and finally segued into the crux of his presentation, a discussion of the etiology and treatment of depression based on a mystical, spiritual model.

Borrowing heavily from the work of Carolyn Myss and Deepak Chopra, he lectured on how unexperienced fantasies and unfulfilled expectations could lead to disappointment and distress. And if this disappointment festers it ultimately evolves into full-blown depression. He tossed out catchy phrases like assuming 'an attitude of gratitude' as one solution, then delved into the more mystical concept of 'the dark night of the soul,' to help illustrate a dynamic of his New Age theory. He talked about how the merger of Eastern and Western philosophies had created an opening for a new era of enlightenment. But before the average person could experience this rebirth of spirit, they had to go through both a mystical and a psychological cleansing. And while one was immersed in this soul-wrenching process, they passed through an emotional wasteland that manifested as a deep, dark depression.

He concluded, however, on an optimistic note, reassuring his audience that since the population as a whole was heading toward a more enlightened, less fragmented future, this age of depression was temporary and certain to pass. He knew that all this probably sounded ethereal to some of his conservative, less open-minded therapists, but it was the stance he'd assumed in his writing and one he was committed to endorsing in person.

Needless to say the question and answer period proved lively and thought provoking. Marshall found it amusing listening to his colleagues try to frame questions about his unorthodox ideas in their own more conventional terminology. But after reworking their inquiries into more of an 'enlightened' vernacular, Marshall responded to their concerns. When the dust settled he imagined a bit of common ground had been achieved. If nothing else he hoped to send them home with some food for thought.

Marshall remained on the platform busy collecting his materials. Suddenly he sensed someone by his side. Rose Shaw was standing there clad in a beige jacket that covered the top of a form-fitting black dress. He couldn't help but admire her shapely figure. She grinned and her eyes seemed to sparkle. Although he was certain the lighting in the room hadn't changed, it seemed as if it had intensified slightly.

"Brilliant presentation, Dr. Friedman," she complemented him, her voice more lyrical than at the Hunters, her words less clipped. Was that sincerity he sensed in her tone? "I loved the reference to 'the dark night of the soul.'"

"Is that material you're familiar with?" Marshall inquired, intrigued by her comment.

"You're very perceptive. The fact is I'm a strong believer in the metaphysical. I have been for a long time."

"Really," he replied. Rose tilted her head slightly. Marshall noticed how she had her hair pulled back tonight, which gave her a more casual look.

"I was just wondering if you had considered my proposal?"

"Proposal?" Marshall asked. "What proposal was that?"

"Your offer to help me work through my nightmares. They haven't stopped. In fact they're getting worse. To the point that my sleep is impaired and my work is suffering."

Marshall recalled the conversation they had at the Hunters'. He had initially regarded it as strictly casual and without any implied commitment. Now this woman was asking him to work with her in a professional capacity.

"I didn't realize you were soliciting me," Marshall said frankly. "However, now that I understand that you are, I'd be glad to be of whatever assistance I can."

"Marvelous," she replied. "When can we start?"

Marshall wasn't prepared for her bluntness. He considered his crammed schedule, acknowledged how over-extended he was, but for some reason still responded, "As soon as you wish."

"Wonderful. How do you want to structure our meetings? I appreciate that we are colleagues working in the same institution. You might find it awkward taking me on formally as a private patient."

Marshall considered this for a moment. It *would* be a little awkward seeing one of his fellow physicians in his office at the Clinic. No matter how discreet he was, and how sternly he cautioned his staff to honor the physician-patient relationship, word would surely leak out. A casual, less formal, arrangement might be more appropriate here. He indicated this to her.

She nodded and asked, "Could we start this weekend?"

Was that desperation he detected in her tone? Did she have a longing to unburden herself? This wasn't the first time he'd detected this attitude in the early phase of a new patient interaction. It seemed natural. He took a moment to consider the logistics of their meeting.

Recalling the pleasant afternoon he'd spent in the park near his apartment he asked, "Are you familiar with the Pittsburgh Center for the Arts? We could meet in the park behind it? It's peaceful and it will give us an open, informal environment in which to interact—especially if the weather cooperates."

"I know the place, Dr. Friedman," Rose informed him. "Meeting in a park is a wonderful idea. It excites me to see how imaginative you are." Her gap-toothed smile appeared, shining forth like a beacon.

"How's noon sound?" Marshall asked.

"Noon is fine," she replied, offering her hand as if to seal the deal. Without hesitation he shook it, finding her grip firm, her skin soft and warm. "And once again," she added, her expression reflecting earnestness. "Your presentation tonight was wonderful. Now I can understand why Hunter has picked you to head our psychiatry department."

"You flatter me Dr. Shaw," Marshall admitted and he knew he was blushing.

"I know," Rose agreed then let go of his hand and strolled away.

chapter six

informal therapy

Marshall awoke on that Saturday morning in mid-July to a misty overcast sky. His upcoming session with Dr. Rose Shaw came to mind. If the capricious Pittsburgh weather turned ugly he would have to move this initial therapy session indoors. He considered his apartment, but decided that this would seem highly irregular by setting too intimate a tone for a first interview. A restaurant or a coffee shop, he decided, would be more appropriate.

But a contingency plan proved unnecessary. By nine the rain had stopped and two hours later the heavy layer of clouds began to thin. Just before noon, as Marshall headed up Fifth Avenue toward the Pittsburgh Center for the Arts, the summer sun peeked through.

Once on Shady Avenue, Marshall turned left into the lot behind the Center. He walked beyond a row of parked cars through a narrow doorway in a gray stone wall that led to a large rectangular courtyard. The bulk of the park was located on the far side of the grassy enclosure. As he headed down a red brick path, he paused to inspect some stone sculptures on his way. The courtyard expanded into an oval field. Beyond that a group of cascading hills trailed off in three different directions.

He scanned the area for Dr. Shaw, expecting to see her sitting on one of the park benches or perhaps on a blanket in the grass. What he discovered was quite unanticipated.

"Hi," she called from beside a plastic-covered table nestled under a huge maple tree. On the table was an elaborate picnic lunch.

"What's all this?" he asked, trying to hide his amazement.

"You picked lunchtime for our meeting," she reminded him, "so I decided to bring lunch." He nodded appreciatively while stealing a wolfish glance at her appearance. She had tied her auburn hair in a ponytail and was wearing a white blouse opened past the second button. The rest of the outfit consisted of skimpy black shorts and black sandals with inch-high heels.

"How thoughtful," he remarked still resisting the temptation to stare at her cleavage. "But you've made me feel bad for not bringing anything."

"Your help with my problem will do, Dr. Friedman," she informed him. Her radiant smile seemed to bath him in light. "Consider it a down payment toward your fee."

This notion caused Marshall some embarrassment. He hadn't even thought about whether he was even going to charge her for his services. Was it happening again? Did she have him at a disadvantage already?

"Well, I've gotta admit, Dr. Shaw, I'm hungry as a bear."

"Then let's get down to it."

Slipping onto the bench across from her, he set a red and white napkin across his lap. Without asking what he wanted, she took a paper plate and began loading it with portions of the offerings. There was fried chicken, mashed potatoes, corn on the cob, and biscuits. When she had finished, she leaned over and set his meal down, standing close enough for him to get a whiff of her perfume.

Umm. He almost swooned. *Opium, again.*

He reached for the corn and began gnawing off the kernels, juice soon dripping from his chin. A gentle breeze stirred the humid air.

"So, Dr. Shaw," he began his tone light and friendly, "why don't we start by you sharing a little bit about yourself?"

"Sure, Doc. And let's drop the formalities. Call me Rose."

"Okay, Rose."

"I guess you want to know where I'm from?" she said as a way of starting. "It's a place called Millcreek, which is considered a section of Erie." Instead of saying 'Pennsylvania', she stressed the two-letter abbreviation. "It was a middle-class neighborhood just a few blocks from Presque Isle. The Isle was where I used to hang out a lot."

Marshall had driven past Erie on his way to Niagara Falls, but wasn't familiar with Presque Isle.

"Dad," she offered, "was your typical nice guy with little or no ambition. He finished high school in the mid-fifties, but couldn't hack college and dropped out of Kent State after his freshman year. After that he joined the Merchant Marines, but was out of the service before the Vietnam War. Then he worked as a laborer of sorts, holding down all sorts of odd jobs. The last was as a kiln master at the ceramics plant by the railroad tracks just a few blocks from our house. Mom was an RN and worked in the critical care unit at Hammet. That's the big medical center in downtown Erie."

Marshall interrupted her. He wanted to know a little more about her father.

"Like I said, he was the typical nice guy," Rose related. "Quiet and easy-going. He never yelled or beat me. In fact he left all that discipline stuff to my mom. 'Course he wasn't around much either. There was a stretch while I was young that he worked two jobs. That's when mom was still in nursing school. Then she got the job at the medical center and he cut down to just one."

"So he was home more?" Marshall probed.

"Not really. It just means that he had more time to get drunk with his buddies at the local pub. Until Mom died, that is. That's when I guess he felt guilty enough to start coming home right after work. Which, come to think of it, didn't make much difference, since all he'd do was sit around and watch the tube or tinker with his silly little projects."

Although Marshall was genuinely interested in her father, he had trouble getting past Rose's reference to her mother's death.

"Your mother died?" Marshall asked when Rose paused to catch her breath.

"Yep," she replied, almost matter-of-factly. "Killed in an car crash when I was twelve. And I was sitting in the back seat at the time."

"Really? That sounds horrible. What happened? Were you hurt too?"

"Knocked out," she replied her tone oddly upbeat, as if she was proud of the fact. "But in the end I was okay." Then, almost as if she realized the strangeness of her demeanor, she added solemnly, "But if it's okay with you, I'd rather not say anything more about it right now."

"We'll come back to it later," he told her, not wanting to jeopardize whatever rapport was forming between them. "Whenever it feels safe, you can share more about it."

"Good," she said.

He paused, waiting for the tension to dissipate. In the background a cacophony of sounds created a hum, an unusual amalgam of traffic, birds chirping and the chatter from the group of children playing tag nearby. Rose, meanwhile, seemed to be regarding him intently, her hands folded on the table leaning slightly forward.

She's really pretty in an unconventional way, he thought distractedly. *Her face looks almost cherubic in its fullness. And that splash of freckles on her cheeks gives her a certain childish innocence. Whatever strength of character she exudes is probably tempered by some underlying frailty.*

"We'll have plenty of time to explore the implications of your mother's death," he reassured her. "Share a little more about what happened after she died."

"All right," she agreed with a sigh. "After the accident Dad seemed lost. He could barely take care of himself, let alone me. That's when he asked his sister, my Aunt Agatha, to help out. She wasn't married and seemed to have plenty of time on her hands so she started coming over in the afternoon to clean and fix us dinner. Finally, after a few months of this routine they decided that it was silly for her to keep her apartment so she moved in. That's when we added the day room on to the back of the house."

Aunt Agatha, Marshall learned, had remained with the Shaws through Rose's sophomore year at Gannon College. Then, in 1983, when Rose transferred from the state-related school located in downtown Erie to Penn State's main campus in State College, she moved out. By then Rose was on her own, working two part-time jobs in order to pay room and board with her tuition covered by a higher education loan.

"I was working toward a B.S. in biology," Rose related. "The schoolwork was pretty tough. That and the two jobs didn't leave much time for a life. So I kept pretty much to myself."

"Sounds pretty austere," Marshall commented.

"Whatever that means, Dr. Friedman. All I know is, I did what I had to survive," she confided. "I had my goal. I wanted to get into medical school. I needed to get into medical school. It was something I had to do for my mother. It was something I felt she would have wanted for me."

Rose paused, lifted her cup, and took a sip of tea. Marshall noticed that her orange lacquered nails were clubbed. He wondered if she smoked.

"I remember how much Mom bragged about the doctors she worked with," Rose continued, "how smart they were, how caring. She was always telling us involved stories at dinner about the important work they were doing—the exciting research, the interesting experiments. She loved to brag about the difference they were making in lives of their patients—her patients. And, Dr. Friedman, I can't count the number of times she said how she wished she could have gone to medical school herself and become a doctor. So, after she died, I knew I had to become one myself. It was the least I could do for her."

Marshall nodded, impressed with the insight Rose displayed into her occupational motivations. With this kind of personal intuition, deciphering the dynamics of her psyche would be a cinch.

Rose's diligence at Penn State, Marshall then learned, had served her well. Early in her senior year she was accepted 'early decision' to Atlanta's prestigious Emory Medical School. While she excelled there, she financed the expensive tuition with two more state loans and a modest grant from Mary Hanson, the executor of the Hanson Endowment Fund and the widow of the founder of the Hanson Shoe Company.

Following dessert, Rose cleaned up, then stowed the picnic paraphernalia in her car. Back at the clearing she suggested they take a walk. Marshall agreed and they headed down the windy asphalt path which led to the next street over, Beechwood Boulevard. After turning right they ascended a gentle grade under the shade of tall oaks and broad maples. Large mansion-like homes, all with exquisite landscaping, occupied both sides of the street. Without Marshall's prompting, Rose resumed her story.

She'd remained in Atlanta for four years, savoring the challenge of medical school and sorting out her aspirations within its broad confines. During the first two years she found the core science curriculum exciting and sometimes daunting. She loved being in the lab, learning to use the scientific method, working out vexing experimental problems. Her junior year core clinical clerkships, however, and the half-dozen electives she took during her senior, proved tedious and less satisfying.

Marshall asked her to elaborate and she related how one afternoon during her internship her preceptor stood in the hallway reviewing a chart. While there he eavesdropped on her telling a patient, just diagnosed with lung cancer, that his chance of a surgical cure was only five percent. Furthermore, he would probably be dead in less than two years. From this interaction the second year resident concluded that Rose had, what he termed, 'poor people skills.'

"Dr. Friedman, I was just being straight with the guy. It was his right to know what was in store for him. But that self-righteous asshole had the audacity to call me cruel and insensitive."

It was this confrontation, she told Marshall, that did more than anything else to steer her away from clinical medicine and into research. "I wasn't heartless, Dr Friedman," Rose insisted. "I just felt this emotional sensitivity to their suffering. They all had horrible diseases with dismal prognoses and I felt obligated to be honest with them about their fate." He nodded in understanding, briefly recalling some of the unfortunate patients he'd cared for doing his medical internship at Penn. "But by doing that," she contended, "I exposed myself to their pain and suffering. And each time I got close to someone, they inevitably became sicker and died. This made me feel helpless and exposed. And ultimately it made me less effective as their doctor, which turned what my senior resident said into a self-fulfilling prophecy.

"I shared this with my instructor during a senior elective in neurology," Rose went on to say. "That's when he turned to me and said, 'Rose, let me give you some advice. If you're going to be successful at this game, you'll find that it's okay for you to treat your patients. But don't ever start to like them as people. Because when they die, a little bit of you dies too.'

"But, Dr. Friedman, I just couldn't see myself maintaining that level of detachment. So instead of torturing myself in clinical medicine, I opted for a career in research."

Marshall considered this for a moment. "That's very interesting Rose," he commented. "As for me, I've learned to walk a tightrope when dealing with my more disturbed patients. In the interests of cultivating rapport, I feel compelled to invest a certain emotional energy into their situations. In not doing so, I'd compromise the interpersonal integrity in our interactions. But ultimately I find that a certain sense of detachment is also required in order to function effectively as their therapist." She nodded, but didn't comment. This prompted him to add, "I suppose we all make compromises in this business. I do mine by withdrawing emotionally. The price, of course, is intimacy. But then again, it's my choice. To do otherwise would probably be terribly draining."

They started strolling up a particularly steep portion of the boulevard. As they reached Hastings Street, about halfway to Wilkins Avenue, Marshall glanced over and noticed how much Rose was struggling to keep up. Her breathing appeared labored and she was grimacing with every step. Alarmed, he forced her to stop.

"What's the matter? You can hardly breathe."

"I've got a touch of emphysema," she answered between gasps. Bending over, she rested her palms on her thighs and sucked in some deep breaths. "I used to smoke pretty heavily as a teenager."

"Are you on medication?"

"I use a puffer once in a while—if it gets really bad."

"Is it with you?"

She nodded

"Would you like to give it a try?"

He waited while she administered a dose. A couple deep breaths later she seemed better.

"You didn't warn me we were about to climb Mount Everest," she commented lightly, a meek smile returning to her face."

"I had no idea it would affect you like that. I bet I've walked this hill a thousand times. When I was a kid my best friend lived down at the bottom in Point Breeze. I'd go over to his place after school, then come home for dinner."

She nodded. "We can go on now."

He fell into step beside her.

"You know, the house I grew up in is just a couple blocks away," he mentioned. "Would you like to see it?"

"Sure," Rose said, her smile regaining its radiance. "I'd love to."

With a rush of boyish pride he led the way. They passed the Darlington Nursery on the corner of Wilkins and Beechwood where he spent one summer during high school delivering plants and shrubbery. At Northumberland Street they made a right. Halfway up the block he pointed across the street and said, "There it is, Rose, catty-corner to the Rehabilitation Center."

He indicated his boyhood bedroom on the second floor with the large casement window looking out onto a narrow back yard. Without prompting he shared about his parents, describing them as good people who worked hard and had precious little to show for it. Everything they did, it seemed, they did for their children.

"They were totally committed to us, my sister and me," he declared proudly. "They fully supported whatever we decided to do."

This last statement seemed to cast a shadow over Rose's countenance. The corners of her mouth drooped slightly and her bright sparkling eyes dulled. Such was not the case in her childhood home, he concluded.

They strolled along Northumberland for another block. At Shady Avenue they turned right. After a half-mile descent they were back at the Center for the Arts.

Rose's crimson Pontiac Firebird was parked facing the brick wall. They stood by the driver's side door for a moment.

"I can give you a lift home if you'd like," she offered.

"That's all right. My apartment's only a few blocks away."

"Okay then," she agreed with a nod. Reaching up she squeezed his shoulder beaming a warm appreciative smile. Her fingers through his polo shirt felt strong. "Thank you for being such a good listener, Dr. Friedman. I hope we can do this again."

"We can," he said. "And for god sakes, please call me Marshall. After all, we are colleagues aren't we?" She nodded and flashed him one of her radiant smiles. "Should we set up another meeting?"

"Why don't you call me? I'm in the book."

"All right," he agreed, accepting this new twist to their unorthodox doctor-patient relationship. "You'll be hearing from me then."

Rose slipped into the driver's seat, revved the engine, waved to him through the window, and then eased out of the parking space. As she did he found himself wondering about the true nature of their relationship.

I suppose time will tell, he told himself as he watched her drive off.

chapter seven

getting to know you

After their Saturday afternoon in the park behind the Center for the Arts, Marshall and Rose starting meeting once or twice a week for the next few weeks. Since neither had weekend hospital responsibilities, they spent a portion of the next two Saturday afternoons together. Two briefer sessions took place at a New Orleans-style bistro located just two blocks from the hospital.

After their first meeting in the park, Marshall had Rose focus more on her symptoms. She described the cluster of throbbing headaches she'd been suffering from. Also of concern were the nightmares, a series of dark, murky fantasies littered with grotesque monsters and sinister fiends engaged in gory acts of mayhem. One particular dream had recurred several times. It featured a pale young woman cloaked in a white robe trudging through a dark wooded area clutching a butcher knife in her outstretched hand. Sometimes the ghostly woman would approach a gnarled old oak tree that had a bloody red valentine pinned to its trunk. With maniacal determination she would raise the knife high above her head and stab viciously at the heart, sending inky black blood spewing forth onto the stabber and ground.

This sort of graphic violence intrigued Marshall. He wondered if the dream had to do with a former love interest and graphically catalogued the emotional scars left behind. Or perhaps a more maleficent force was at work here, some painful, albeit repressed, experience that continued to gnaw at his patient's subconscious. He encouraged her to share more of the gory details. She remained obscure. It was at this point in the dream that she'd always awoken.

At other times during their sessions he had her share more about her present life. Her work in the genetics lab was approaching the conclusion of a three-year research project, one for which Bertram Hunter had specifically brought her to the Hunt. It involved a very practical application of genetic engineering that was considered on the cutting edge of her field. Marshall probed for details but Rose resisted, commenting that prior to any formal publication the work was considered top secret. Once she submitted her preliminary findings she would allow him to review the manuscript.

During subsequent sessions Marshall delved more into Rose's childhood. He wanted to know more about her parents—what they were like, how they reacted in certain situations, how they related to their daughter. He hoped that this information would help explain some of the traumas and demons that haunted her. Sitting in their corner booth in the corner of the James Street Cafe, he would watch his patient struggle with her memories, perched anxiously on the edge or her seat, her hands tightly clasped on the table, her thick lips pursed. Her sentences were short and terse. The spindly tension lines around her eyes and mouth would deepen.

Frank, her father, was weak, thin in stature, taciturn, and mostly absent from her life. Karen Shaw, her mother, was a cold, domineering woman, a fanatic about order and a stickler about cleanliness who had kept Rose on a short leash while running their regimented household like boot camp.

At home Rose had been embroiled in an endless series of domestic conflicts. Her mother, the patient claimed, made an issue out of everything she did. There were rules about what Rose could wear, where she could go, what she could do, and with whom. And from mid spring through late autumn, when the days in the lakeside community were long and unstructured and the streets were teeming with visitors and vacationers, their battles escalated. That's when Rose would conspire to get away from her mother.

"What did you do?" Marshall wanted to know.

"Basically," she related, "I avoided being home."

As soon as Rose was old enough to be out alone, she spent her afternoons roaming the strip malls on Route Five. On weekends she'd pedal her bicycle onto Presque Isle and spend the daylight hours hanging out on the periphery of the lagoon where she became friendly with the fishermen angling by their boathouses. Soon most of the park rangers knew her by name.

This conflict between mother and daughter made Marshall more curious about Karen Shaw. But his effort to probe deeper into Rose's relationship with her mother was met with resistance. He sensed some deep-seated mixed emotions here. Marshall had suggested she tell him more about the accident that resulted in her mother's death.

They were in the car together, Rose related, a seventy-five Chevy Citation. Her mother was driving. Rose sat in the back seat, hurrying to finish an overdue homework assignment. Karen Shaw lost control of the car. The police never figured out how. Had Rose been up front, she would have most likely died too. As it was, Rose had been rendered unconscious by the impact and apparently suffered partial retrograde amnesia regarding the event. This traumatic shock was obviously why she remained so vague about the details. But recalling whatever happened in that car seemed crucial to Rose's mental health.

The more time they spent together, the more Marshall craved her company. At first Rose existed as a pleasant distraction. Then, gradually, like a faintly familiar aroma, she seeped into his everyday life. At odd times some whimsical expression on her face or a casual movement of her body would pop into his head. At other times someone would pass him with a pigeon-toed gait and he would think of Rose. Or he would notice the soft hiss of someone talking through the space between a pair of front teeth or glimpse a woman with auburn hair or detect the scent of Opium perfume and reflexively he would think of Rose. Yes, he admitted, his new patient was haunting him.

He found himself distracted by comments she'd made during their sessions together, a preoccupation that seemed annoyingly prevalent while he listened to other patients share their tales of woes. As their convoluted stories unfolded, an unexpected reflection about Rose would affect his concentration. And as he nodded or 'hmmmed' at random points during these office sessions, he would, in reality, be analyzing or sometimes fantasizing about Rose.

But it was during the nighttime hours that this distraction became most intense. Stripped of his professional posture, unwinding in his easy chair watching television, or propped up in bed reading a novel, an image of Rose would visit him. Rather than appear in conventional attire, she would float into his consciousness clad in some silky negligee or skimpy bathing suit. Elaborate fantasies ensued from there, she posing for him in a leopard-skin bathing suit trying to seduce him or strut across the pile carpet like a runway model flaunting her long muscular legs and buxom body. In his mind's eye he would rise up and reach for her, longing for the fullness of those breasts against his bare chest, the softness of her lips against his hungry mouth.

At first these daydreams possessed a vague, almost surreal quality, shadows moving in the twilight, hints of sensation, the promise but not the realization of fulfillment. But the more his mind inhabited this dream-like expanse, the more vivid became his musings. Assuming tangible shape and substance, they eventually reached a point where he could almost feel the warmth and satiny softness of her chest against his, smell the musky earthy odor of her skin, taste the intoxicating sweetness of her lips.

It was a hot afternoon in late July. Marshall made his way back to his car. The humidity was so thick he felt like he had to walk sideways to slice through it. Once inside his Benz he ran the air conditioner for several minutes before touching the steering wheel. Finally he headed off into rush hour traffic.

While crossing the Seventh Street Bridge, Marshall estimated that he still had enough time to work out before his seven o'clock dinner meeting with Chris Jeffries. The chief of thoracic surgery had called him earlier that day and commented how, now that Marshall was a member of the executive committee, he might find, "a little pep talk on hospital politics helpful."

Since it had been four days since his last workout and he was determined to get in a circuit training session that evening he suggested they meet at the Rivers Club. As he systematically progressed through his workout, Marshall kept wondering what Jeffries was planning to share with him. Perhaps it had something to do with the powerful alliances that inevitably existed between unit heads and the administration. Would he brief him on the backroom power politics that promoted their public and private agendas? Maybe the medical staff president was interested in assessing whether he could function in a responsible fashion in this milieu.

After all, he reasoned, *of all people, shouldn't I be uniquely qualified to review any series of facts and from it reach an objective conclusion? Aren't I the seasoned professional trained to deal with convoluted stories and well-concealed motivations?*

Suffused with this buoyant sense of generosity and open-mindedness, he dressed for dinner then rode the elevator from the third to fourth floor of the Oxford Tower Building. After the metal doors parted, Karen Sheptak, the club's social director greeted him. Hungry for dinner he strolled through the reception area and paused in the lounge.

"Has Dr. Jeffries arrived yet?" he asked Mona, a tall, attractive Eurasian woman who was serving the dining room hostess tonight.

Gazing back at him with a pair of bottomless brown eyes, she smiled politely and said, "No, Dr. Friedman, I'm afraid Dr. Jeffries phoned a few minutes ago and regretfully canceled. He mentioned something about a late case in the operating room tonight." Marshall felt his face sag. Mona then hastened to add, "but there is a young woman in the bar area who asked me to inform you that she was here."

"A young woman? Did she mention her name?"

"No, Dr. Friedman, I'm afraid not. But she did say she was sure you would recognize her."

Swept up in a wave of excited confusion Marshall nodded, and thanked Mona for her help. As far as he knew, Sally, and now Jeffries, were the only people who knew he belonged to the Rivers Club. And it wasn't Sally's style to just show up somewhere without making arrangements first.

As bright and homey as the lounge was, with its beige ceiling, maroon table lamps, rich mint green carpeting, and deep comfortable couches, that's how dark and foreboding the bar area seemed. Peeking through the narrow entranceway he could just make out the heavy burgundy walls, the dark wood tables and chairs, and the large rear-projection television near the back corner. A neon Miller High Life sign cast a cool harsh pale on part of the shadow-shrouded room.

It took a moment for Marshall's eyes to become adjusted to the muted light. Soon he discerned a young couple seated at a small round table near the far wall, their heads inclined toward each other, their beer glasses half empty between them. A group of older men boisterous and loud sat around a larger table by the TV playing cards. A professional looking threesome—a woman on a barstool flanked by two men in suits—congregated at the far of the bar. Marshall studied the woman's profile, her long almost platinum-colored hair, her prominent nose, the way she perched on the stool, one elbow set crooked on the polished wood surface, a taper-like cigarette held to her pursed lips by two slender fingers. He decided that she didn't look familiar.

There was another woman at the bar nearer to him, facing forward, her shapely legs crossed in front of her. She chatted with the bartender, a cocktail glass poised provocatively between the counter and her lips. Suddenly, for Marshall, recognition dawned.

"Rose!" he exclaimed, a bit too loud for the setting. Modulating his tone he added, "What are you doing here?"

"Marshall," she greeted him casually. He tried but couldn't remember when she started addressing him by his first name. "I was in the neighborhood so I decided to stop by."

He thought about this and the idea struck a dissonant chord. As far as he knew she wasn't a member of the club. She couldn't just 'stop by.' Before he could clarify the matter she added, "Actually, that's not at all true, Marshall. I ran into Jeffries at the hospital around four-thirty this afternoon. He was rushing to take an emergency valve repair into the OR. He mentioned standing you up for dinner tonight. I thought you might still want company, so I came over in his place. Disappointed to see me?"

"Disappointed? Of course not. I'm delighted. It's just so, uh, unexpected, that's all."

"And you like to have everything all nicely planned out, don't you, Dr. Friedman?" she said, gently patting his hand which was resting on the edge of the bar. "You like to be in control."

He considered this and knew she was right on, but retorted defensively, "Hey, who's the psychiatrist here?"

"Certainly not me, Marshall," Rose replied coquettishly, appearing to enjoy addressing him so familiarly. She raised her face toward his. The proximity allowed him to sample her vodka-scented breath.

How many of those has she consumed, he wondered? *Do I really care? Maybe it's better to just enjoy being together like this, in a nonclinical setting, acting like a couple, not like doctor and patient.*

He paused and appraised her. Even in the muted barlight he could see how her black dress hugged her curvaceous body, accentuating her chest and hips, her crossed legs pulling the hem several inches above her knee and exposing a fair amount of thigh. His pulse quickened with wanton desire.

"Let's eat," she proposed. "Or would you like something else first?" He blushed, wondering if she'd read his mind. "I mean a drink," she clarified with a playful grin.

Marshall, struggling to regain his composure, announced, "I'll have wine with dinner."

Then, with his entire body energized, he escorted Rose out of the sensual suggestiveness of the bar's murky light. As they left she caught the bartender's attention with a tap on her glass, "Scotty, put this on Dr. Friedman's tab. I'll settle up with him later." Then she took Marshall's arm and they strolled out of the dimly lit bar.

The dining room was finely appointed, continuing the same theme as the lounge with tasteful maroon and green wallpaper, dark brown beams and molding, fine wood furniture and deep pile carpeting. The tables were adorned with white linen, shiny silverware, sparkling crystal, and white bone China. Mona guided them to a small table along the large picture window that made up much of the far side of the room.

A tuxedoed waiter hurried over, lit their centerpiece candle, offered Marshall the wine list, and took their beverage order. As he handed them menus he described the evening's specials. After he left them to ponder their choices, Rose leaned across the table and commented, "This place is wonderful, Marshall. Do you eat here often?"

"This is my second time."

"Well, it's my first and I think it's great," she admitted. "And they have Cornish hens tonight, which is one of my all-time favorites. Aunt Agatha used to make them instead of turkey for Thanksgiving. She'd stuff them with wild rice and whip up a gravy that was scrumptious." With a dramatic flourish she raised her curled fingertips to her mouth and gave them a loud kiss.

Marshall smiled, nodded his approval, and then returned to the menu. He found it impressive and was tempted to try the rack of lamb, which he'd heard was excellent. He then recalled the few pounds he'd added since arriving in Pittsburgh and chose the trout instead. The waiter returned and recorded their choices. Marshall ordered wine, a Chateau St. Michelle Chardonnay. He told Rose that from what little he recalled, it was a quality vintage from a small vineyard in the southern portion of Washington State.

"My, my, Marshall," Rose commented after the waiter had left. "You sound like you know a lot about wine,"

"Not really. Right after Bernice and I got married she enrolled us in a wine tasting course. She thought it would help me seem more urbane when we ate out with friends. I've managed to retain bits and pieces from it."

"Bernice is your wife?" Rose commented. He nodded. "You never talk about her much. Which is because whenever we're together the attention is always on me, I guess. What's she like—you're wife, I mean?"

Marshall considered the question for a moment. "I guess you could say she's a very nice person," he offered. "Bright. Articulate. And very cultured."

"Is she pretty?"

"I suppose so. In a middle-aged, Jewish way."

"And she's from New York?"

"Yes, Long Island. The Hamptons, to be more specific. In fact that's where she's staying now, at her parents' home." He mused about Bernice being back there with her parents, their servants, cooks, chauffeurs, and landscapers, in that huge mansion near the Sound. "Bernice is heiress to the great Tannenbaum empire."

"Heiress?" Rose asked, looking confused. "Empire?" Then as if comprehending she said, "You mean commercial empire?" He nodded. "What do they build?"

"Shopping malls."

"Oh," Rose said. "And how come she's not in Pittsburgh with you?"

"Because she's more attached to her creature comforts than to me."
"But you're her husband."
"That's correct."

At first Rose frowned. Then a sympathetic expression washed over her complexion. With certain deliberateness she reached over and placed her hand upon his. Marshall found her touch gentle, her skin soft and warm. He was tempted to rotate his palm upward and take her fingers in his. But he wasn't prepared to deal with what she might infer from this gesture. So instead he kept his long slender fingers curled slightly facing down.

"Don't get me wrong, Rose," he declared, almost feeling obliged to defend his wife's decision. "Bernice is a good person. We've had a special relationship. It's sustained us for eleven years. But I always got the sense there was something missing for me. And then this job showed up. Accepting it turned out to be an opportunity to test the strength of that relationship. Suddenly I think we've discovered that what was missing was larger than I ever imagined."

"And what was missing?" Rose asked, as if on cue.

"Maybe you could call it 'true love'," Marshall reported without malice or regret.

Rose did not reply immediately. Instead she simply gazed at him; her beautiful green eyes studying his face; her expression a blend of sympathy and compassion. She smiled, a slight smile, not the broad cheerful grin he was used to, but a soft, mellow look, which, despite its subtlety, still projected the same radiance he'd come to expect from her. Somehow he felt satisfied that everything would be all right. Appreciating this his chest began to swell. A suffocating tightness took hold of his throat. Suddenly, without warning, tears welled in his eyes. For a moment he struggled to suppress them. Then he surrendered and let them flow.

She waited while he composed himself. He tried to figure out why he'd reacted this way. Was it the pain and sorrow from his lost marriage with its paucity of deep abiding love? Or was it gratitude for Rose, sitting across from him, extending support without his requesting it? Hers seemed like such a selfless, unconditional gesture. He couldn't help but be moved.

Marshall looked around self-consciously at the smattering of couples scattered about the large room. Then he turned and peered out the picture window beside them. Rose meanwhile reached in her purse and took out a scented handkerchief. She offered it to him.

"Whew," he said with a sigh. "That was quite a reaction! I've never done anything like that before."

"Which is sad, Marshall," Rose said soothingly. "I bet there's all kinds of emotions like that one stored up inside you. And you'd probably feel a whole lot better if you'd let them out once in a while."

"You know, Rose, you're probably right," he said with one final sniffle. "You're probably right."

The waiter came over and set their entrees on the table. They ate in silence. Marshall felt concerned that his outburst might have put a damper on the evening. But Rose seemed oblivious to his concerns and was busy sampling her dish. After a few bites she commented how good it tasted.

After that he began eating in earnest. Eventually their conversation resumed, a little more casual, a little less introspective. Rose shared about work and how her project was rapidly approaching a successful conclusion. With its completion she expected to finally garner the recognition such groundbreaking research deserved. It was this kind of accomplishment that might very well propel her into the soon to be vacated position of Director of Research Sciences. And with the proposed expansion of her laboratory into a new wing dedicated exclusively to genetic research she would be set at the Hunt for years to come.

All this was news to Marshall. It impressed him that Rose held such a formidable position in the hospital's research division. What he had inferred was important work now appeared to be almost monumental. He made a mental footnote to inquire further about it, perhaps with Sally, or Hunter himself.

The waiter set down coffee and a pair of peach gellatos. As Rose sensuously licked the creamy dessert with her outstretched tongue, she encouraged Marshall to share more about himself. Although he was thoroughly distracted by her lingual gyrations, he did manage to tell her about some of his accomplishments since assuming his new position at the clinic. There was an innovative series of outpatient therapy groups he'd helped get up and running. He was also making headway in shifting the basis of in-hospital patient care toward a more psychoanalytic bent. And his private practice was steadily growing. Rose lauded his accomplishments, commenting how proud she was of him.

"Related to your private practice," Rose segued, "I thought I should let you know that I had that nightmare three more times last week."

"That one with the woman and the butcher knife?" Rose nodded. "And it woke you?"

"Yes."

"Any insights?"

"No."

Suddenly Marshall had a thought. But before he could comment on it Rose added, "But there's more. Last night I had a different dream. It was still pretty gloomy, but a little more optimistic."

"Why don't you tell me about it."

Rose took a deep breath. "All right. From what I can remember, I'm dressed in my nightgown walking barefoot on a path in the woods. Then suddenly I come to a broad, rocky wall. In the center of the wall is a cave. The next thing I know I'm inside the cave in the dark. At first it's too dark to see. I get down on all fours and crawl along the floor. In the distance I hear wild animals wailing. Tiny pairs of eyes stare at me from all directions."

Marshall listened intently, feeling compelled to write all this down. But he didn't have his notepad.

"Marshall, I'm scared. But I feel driven to keep going. Far in the distance I see this shadowy white light. Which turns out to be a hazy figure standing on a pedestal, like an angel with a pair of wings. I stare up toward its face. Guess who it is."

Marshall couldn't imagine. "Who?" he asked.

"You!"

"Me!"

"Yes, you. And while I'm staring up at the angel, it scoops me up in its arms and we start flying up toward this opening in the ceiling. A moment later we emerge into the light. When I opened my eyes for real the sun was shining on my face through a break in the curtains."

Marshall considered the significance of the dream. "Perhaps your subconscious was trying to tell you there's cause for hope."

"I thought the same thing. And it looks like you're the one who's going to show me the way."

"Maybe so, Rose," Marshall agreed. "Maybe so."

Their waiter stopped back and asked if there would be anything else. Marshall signed for the meal and then rose to leave. While they walked to the elevator Marshall commented, "These dreams of yours are certainly intriguing, Rose. They may hold the key to your mental torment. There must be something repressed from your past which needs to surface. Something that's been haunting you but refuses to allow your conscious mind to know it."

"I wondered about that too. But what could it be? And how can we get at it?"

"There might be a way," Marshall offered. "A sort of shortcut that I use sometimes that usually avoids months of tedious analysis."

"What's that?"

"What do you think about hypnosis?"

She paused to consider her answer. "It fascinates me," she admitted. "But, the truth is, I really don't know that much about it. Why?"

"Have you ever been hypnotized?"

"By my boyfriend in seventh grade. But he just wanted to see me naked. I don't think it worked."

"Why do you say that?"

"When he woke me up I still had my clothes on. And I remembered everything that happened when he thought I was under."

"Well I'm not proposing anything like that."

"Of course you're not." The elevator doors to the parking lot level opened. They stepped out into the narrow corridor. Standing side by side in this confined space Rose peered up at him with a serious look on her face. "Do you really think it could help?" she asked.

"I do, Rose," he replied earnestly. "I really do."

"Then let's give it a try."

"All right," he said, feeling oddly relieved. "Meet me at my office after work on Friday. With the weekend coming the girls usually try to get out early. Having them gone will mean we'll have much less explaining to do."

"Wow, Marshall. That sounds like a date. I guess I'll see you then." She pulled open the parking lot door. He was on the level below. "And thanks for dinner," she said softly. Leaning over she placed a gentle kiss on his cheek. A moment later she left him standing there his fingertips gently touching the spot on his face where her lips had brushed.

chapter eight

member-at-large

While Bertram spoke on the phone Marshall leaned over to get a better look at the photograph of Magdeline Hunter and decided that she must've been a knockout when she was young.

And judging from the way they acted at the party, he concluded, *she really loves and supports him.*

Hunter set the phone down, leaned back in his padded leather chair, and formed a steeple with his fingertips. He smiled warmly at his newest staff member, the corona of fine lines around his gray eyes bunching, his bushy eyebrows arching expressively. Marshall returning his boss' gaze, decided he was indeed a singularly attractive man, vibrant and healthy, appearing younger than his age. It was hard to believe what Sally had said about his heart.

"It's good of you to stop by, Marshall," Hunter said affably. "Now that it's been over a month since you've dropped anchor here at the Hunt, how do you like it so far?"

"A lot," Marshall admitted. "More than I expected, actually."

"Doing the administrator bit different from being in private practice?"

"Much different," Marshall confirmed, "although I did get some experience working with the training program at Bellevue."

"Which I'm sure helps with the transition. How are things going in the department?"

"Okay," Marshall replied, starting to feel at ease chatting with this man. "Having primary responsibility for a bunch of young psychiatry residents is a real challenge, especially with my emphasis on psychoanalysis and spirituality."

"I think I know what you're talking about," Hunter commented. "So much of their training is in experimental psychiatry."

"That's right. Which utilizes things like drugs and electric shock to treat the major disorders," Marshall confirmed. "Not much Freud or Jung."

"Which you're attempting to rectify?"

"As best I can."

Somewhat abruptly changing the subject Hunter inquired, "And your wife? Sally mentioned she's still back in New York. What do you hear from her?"

"We've spoken on the phone a couple times. She's spending the summer in the Hamptons with her parents. Next month she's planning to go on a two-week cruise to the Greek Isles with one of her divorced girlfriends. It's possible that we'll get in a weekend together before she leaves."

"That sounds encouraging. Any chance she'll abandon the Big Apple for Pittsburgh?"

"Too early to tell," Marshall replied, knowing that he was being evasive. "All she's admitted to so far is our need to make sacrifices. You know, those famous compromises."

"Yes," Hunter agreed. "I've been told that's what marriage is all about."

The reality was that Marshall held out little hope for reconciliation with Bernice. Each day apart left him more comfortable with the separation.

"So I can assume you're pretty well settled in here then?" Hunter asked, as if reading his mind.

"For the time being," Marshall replied.

"Well, if my opinion counts for anything, Marshall, as far as I'm concerned you're on board for the long run."

"Which feels very reassuring," Marshall admitted candidly. "I appreciate your confidence in me, Mr. Hunter."

"Call me Bertram, Marshall, or Hunter. Everyone else does."

"Sure, Bertram."

The CEO stood up and walked over to a wall unit catty-corner to a large picture window that overlooked East Avenue. Behind a hinged door was a well-stocked bar.

"Can I interest you in some liquid refreshment? I know it's only two in the afternoon, but some of us like to get an early start."

"A soft drink would be fine."

"Admirable, Marshall. As for me, I'll have my first Scotch today. Jeffries tells me that two to four ounces a day does wonders for one's HDL cholesterol."

Hunter returned to the desk, a soft drink in one hand, his Scotch on ice chinkling in the other. He handed the ginger ale to Marshall.

"I'm sure you know, Marshall," he said, his tone more serious, "that by virtue of your position as Chief of Psychiatry you automatically sit on the executive committee. They meet at noon on the third Friday of the month. You'll be joining the other heads of the hospital's clinical services. The committee makes most of the important decisions regarding the medical staff."

Marshall nodded, then offered, "Chris called me last week and wanted to meet before my first meeting and brief me on some of the hospital politics."

Hunter's salt and pepper colored brows arched with interest. "He did, did he? And what did you two discuss?"

"He had a late afternoon emergency so we never met."

"Have you rescheduled?"

"Not yet."

Hunter nodded then paused for a moment as if to process this bit of data. It was almost as if he had said, 'good.'

"What's more, Marshall," he continued, "there's an even more crucial role here at the clinic I want to discuss with you."

This comment piqued Marshall's curiosity. Sitting up a little straighter in his chair he felt a little anxious.

I just assumed exec was the height of my administrative involvement. Maybe not.

"In case you haven't heard, Nick Cardamone, our chief of laboratory services, was recently 'head-hunted' away from us by the Mayo Clinic. This leaves an extremely important vacancy in the scheme of things."

"Where's that?" Marshall asked almost reflexively.

"As the medical staff's representative to the board of directors. As you might imagine, Marshall, it's a position which calls for an individual with outstanding professional credentials, a sense of strong personal integrity, and a commitment toward doing what's right and proper."

Hunter paused, leaving Marshall hanging. A certain sense of modesty had him doubt Hunter was considering him the job. But if he wasn't, then why was he telling him all this? To run the other candidates by him?

"Aren't you curious as to why I'm sharing this with you?"

"Extremely."

"Good. Because at the next exec meeting I'm planning to nominate you for that role."

Marshall was shocked. Had he heard his boss correctly? Here he sat, having spent barely six weeks at this world famous medical institution and now the CEO was asking him to run for the board of directors.

"Me?" he finally blurted out. "You're going to nominate me? May I ask why?"

"Certainly," Hunter replied, his expression betraying the pleasure of witnessing Marshall's reaction. "Because I can't imagine anyone better suited for the job." Rising from his chair he strode around to Marshall's side of the desk.

"I find you bright and accomplished, Marshall," he continued. "In your work in the mental health clinics and in your writing you've displayed a deep compassion for the common man. You bring a fresh psychological perspective to the table. And most important, you're a rookie here. You have no history at the institution, which could bias your judgment. There's no ax to grind, no alliances to honor, no favors to repay. You could offer an objective viewpoint to issues concerning the Clinic not swayed by your experience here. In short, Marshall, you're an ideal candidate for the position."

What an incredible honor and privilege, Marshall thought.

He took a moment to absorb the impact of the offer. "Whew. That's quite an acknowledgment, Bertram," he finally said. "Are you sure I'm the right person for the job?"

"I'm certain of it, Marshall. You seem destined to serve this institution nobly and with integrity. I'd stake my reputation on it."

"If you say so," Marshall replied, still not quite believing him.

"Can I assume you'll accept the nomination?"

"Certainly," Marshall declared enthusiastically, still swept up in the moment.

"Good. I'll let the other members know. That should make your election to the position a mere formality."

Marshall nodded, comprehending how much influence the CEO must have in these matters. Then he noticed Hunter checking the clock on his desk.

"Well, Marshall, I have a meeting with my vice presidents at three. I'll be in touch. Remember, Exec is next Friday."

"That's one meeting I won't miss," Marshall informed his boss.

"I didn't think you would," Hunter said, patting him on the back.

They walked to the door together. He seemed about to turn away when he held his index finger up to his lip and paused. Turning toward Marshall he asked, "Have you heeded my warning about Rose Shaw?"

A knife-like pain pierced Marshall's chest. With it the balloon of pride that had been expanding since Hunter's nomination began to deflate.

"What do you mean?" Marshall replied lamely, trying to mask his uneasiness.

"You two haven't struck up anything, have you?"

"No," Marshall lied, his voice a little softer than he'd intended, "beyond a few casual conversations. Why?"

"I just don't want you to get drawn into her silken web. You're too valuable to the organization to be distracted by a woman like Rose."

"Whatever you say, Hunter," Marshall conceded, curious about his reasons for expressing this, the second warning, about Rose. Loath to reveal his growing fascination with this woman Hunter claimed was so dangerous Marshall repeated, "Whatever you say."

chapter nine

probing the subconscious

Marshall eased over to the bookshelf, cupped the candle flame with his right hand, and extinguished it with a puff. He reached over and turned off the CD player. As the soft melodic music ceased the darkened room was bathed in eerie silence. An automobile horn, then an ambulance's siren violated the stillness.

Marshall's thoughts wandered toward this evening's rush hour, imagining droves of downtown workers, desperate to kick off their summer weekend early, choking the inadequate highways leading out of the city. Hadn't his own secretary slipped out over an hour ago, begging off early so she could head down to the shore?

That's all the better for me, he thought. *There's less chance for some unexpected interruption.*

He peered through the shadowy lamplight at the comely figure recumbent on the leather recliner. In the soft yellow light that seeped out from under his Tiffany desk lamp, he could just make out her round face. The tense lines around her eyes were slack, as drained of stress. Her auburn hair, appearing ebony in the shadowy light, lightly grazed her shoulders. Her breathing was deep, measured, and regular. She was fast asleep.

Once again he had used a standard induction technique—eye fixation on the flickering candle combined with head-to-toe relaxation. She had responded wonderfully. She was a good subject.

He moved closer, pulled up a straight-backed chair, and positioned it at an angle to her somnolent body. He sat down and regarded her thoughtfully. She looked so innocent lying there, her expression blank, her breathing steady. She was wearing a summery blouse that seemed crowded with too many bright bold colors and her skirt barely covered the top of her thighs. It was a typical Rose outfit, he thought with a smile. On her over-sized feet her white sandals formed a 'v' at the heels. Her calves rested against the footrest. This was another sign of her deep repose.

She seems so vulnerable lying there, he thought, her shapely body drained of anxiety, its defenses denuded. It made him feel omnipotent, she subject to his suggestions, under his tutelage. He'd never taken advantage of a patient in this state before. He knew he never would. He wasn't like Rose's childhood boyfriend. He was a principled professional.

With some effort he shook off these musings and began the process of deepening Rose's state of heightened suggestibility. This was the third time he'd induced her. The first two were mostly introductory in nature, testing her suggestibility, trying some simple exercises while she floated in the early stages of trance. Now, with the help of some post-hypnotic suggestions, it was becoming much easier to take her deeper. Once she was under he guided her through a series of more sophisticated exercises, each one designed to further that end.

Certain she was deeply hypnotized, he sat back and reviewed his notes from their earlier sessions. Based on what Rose had shared with him about her childhood, he sensed that she had been a willful child, headstrong and wild. She tended to resist authority, especially in the form of her parents, but also teachers and other adults in her life. She seemed uncompromising in her determination to have things her own way. This kind of rebelliousness, Marshall knew, came naturally to some children. But there were other things about Rose's childhood that concerned Marshall.

His eyes scanned the yellow legal pad full of scribbled notes, arrows, asterisks and underlines. He searched for a specific item. There it was. Apparently Rose always had trouble getting along with other children. First in the neighborhood and later in school, she had few friends, and tended to be something of a loner. When he had asked her about this, she had minimized its significance, claiming to prefer to do things by herself.

"But it wasn't as if I was always alone," she had hastened to add. "If I wanted someone to do something with me or go somewhere, I could usually get them to agree. I had that kind of knack with people."

Then he lighted on a more telling sign as to what kind of child Rose had been. It had to do with a pet hamster her mother had bought her when she was six. At first Rose had enjoyed watching the little brown rodent running around in his cage, drinking from his tiny cup, eating food pellets from the plastic dish. Then one day, apparently bored with the hamster's monotonous routine, Rose decided to make things more interesting. That's when her mother found her standing on a footstool by the sink, leaning far into the basin, shoving the little creature down the metal drain with the garbage disposal grinding away.

"I wasn't really going to do it," she had assured Marshall after she told him the story. "I just got a kick out of imagining what would happen if I did." Imagining the potential consequences of this action, Marshall shivered.

Another incident, less than a year later, was gleaned from a similar script. It was on a Saturday afternoon. Rose was with her mother at the local laundromat. Wandering out the front door she came upon a gray tabby kitten. Then, while her mother's back was turned, she brought the stray back into the shop, tossed it into a high capacity dryer, and turned on the machine.

Were these acts of rebellion or examples of mischievous behavior by a disturbed child, he wondered.

The idea of clarifying the source of this conduct intrigued him. He considered the age-old question of nature versus nurture. Was it primarily genetics that had shaped Rose's personality? If so, then her environment couldn't be blamed for the way she'd turned out. Nor could it explain the long-range effects of it on her present condition. But if it was her circumstances, her neighborhood, her socio-economic status, and most crucially, her relationship with her parents that had influenced her, than the effect of all this needed to be sorted out. And now, lying near him on the couch, he felt she was most susceptible to candidly revealing some of the intricacies of that world in which she'd grown up.

"Rose?" he said. She flinched at the sound of her name. "How are you feeling?"

"Good," she replied. Her voice, normally dulcet, now low and flat.

"Are you relaxed?"

"Yes," she answered.

"And feeling safe?"

"Yes."

Marshall paused for a moment, checked his pad and decided that his calculations were accurate. Rose was currently thirty-five. In 1976 she would have been eleven. He felt it was vital to his analysis that he get an unedited sense of the relationship Rose had had with her mother. The time right before the accident would be especially valuable. His instinct told him that more than anything else, Rose's childhood relationship with Karen Shaw set the stage for whatever came later.

"Rose, do you remember how old you were in 1976?"

She hesitated before answering. Finally she said, "I was eleven."

"That's right," he agreed, "you were eleven. And I want to take you back to your home neighborhood of Millcreek in the summer of 1976." He paused for a moment, letting her picture the place. "Just imagine that we're sitting in a special time machine with all its fancy dials and levers. I push the 'Go' button and the capsule starts whirring and vibrating. A series of flashing lights are joined by some strange sounds. A couple of minutes later the motion and noise stops. Slowly I reach over and turn the door's latch. With a grunt we push the door open and step outside. Now we're standing outside the capsule in your old hometown of Millcreek. Do you see that?"

Rose's face lit up briefly, a trace of a smile on her lips, the hint of excitement in her posture. "Yes," she said, a little breathless. "Yes."

"That's wonderful," Marshall said supportively. "And what do you see?"

"I see my house," she said, her voice higher, more girlish.

"What's it look like?"

"It's painted light blue with white shutters. There are two windows in the front and my old swing set in the yard on the side."

"Is there a porch?"

"No."

"How many floors are there?"

"Just one."

"So it's a ranch house."

"My mom calls it a cottage," she corrected him.

"And is Mom home now?"

"No, not yet."

"Where is she?"

"At work."

"At the hospital?"

"Yes, at the hospital. She works daylight."

"What time will she be home?"

"Around four o'clock, unless she gets held up with a sick patient."

"What are you going to do until she gets home?"

"Ride my bike, I guess. Or go over to Cheyenne's."

"Who's Cheyenne?"

"My girlfriend."

"What do you do at her house?"

"Listen to records."

"Is that all?"

Rose hesitated for a moment, as if reluctant to say anything further.

"Do you do your homework?" he probed.

"Sometimes."

"What else?"

"We go up into her brother's treehouse."

"Her brother's treehouse? What do you do in there?" She hesitated. "What do you do in there, Rose?" he repeated, this time more forcefully.

"We smoke cigarettes."

He pictured Rose sitting in the treehouse, puffing away. He then recalled how she struggled to walk up Beechwood Boulevard.

No wonder! She was only eleven when she started!

"Does your mother know about the smoking?"

"I don't think so."

"Do you remember when she found out?" Rose paused before nodding.

"Can you tell me when?"

"Near the end of the summer. Right before I went back to school."

Marshall considered this for a moment.

"All right, Rose," he said longing to get a sense of how Karen Shaw related to her daughter. "Let's move forward in time to the day your mother learned about your smoking. What happened on that day?"

Rose hesitated, apparently uncomfortable with this recollection. He coaxed her some more. Finally she relented, beginning by saying, "It was almost dinnertime. I was over at Cheyenne's that afternoon. When I walked in the house I could tell Mom was pissed."

"How could you tell?"

"When I went in the kitchen to say hello to her she didn't answer. She wouldn't even look at me. She just faced the stove and stirred the food."

"What did you do next?"

"I turned to leave."

"What did she do?"

"She said, 'Just one minute there, young lady! Where do you think you're going?'" Rose imitated the inflection of her mother's voice, measured and cool.

"To my room," Rose replied without further prompting from Marshall.

"You stay right where you are. There's something I want to discuss with you."

Marshall watched as Rose started to squirm. Then she began to tremble.

"I found these in your bookbag this afternoon."

Marshall knew Rose was recalling her mother holding up the pack of cigarettes.

"But Mom," she whined. "They're not mine."

"They're not? Then whose are they?"

"They're Cheyenne's."

"Then what were they doing in your bookbag?"

"She gave them to me to hold."

"Why would she do a thing like that?"

"So her parents wouldn't find them."

"Liar!"

Rose shouted this out with vehemence. Suddenly her face jerked to the right as if she'd been slapped.

"What do you think I am, Rosebud? Stupid? I've been around the block a few times, too, you know. I'm onto you and your little delinquent friends. They smoke and now they've got you doing it. Don't lie to me and tell me you don't. I can smell it on your clothes. I can see it on your teeth. Here, let me smell your breath."

Rose pressed back into the cushion of the recliner. She squirmed again, rotating her head from side to side, as if avoiding her mother's grasp.

"Yep. I knew I was right. You think I'm stupid, don't you little girl? You think you and your friends can pull a fast one on me? But the truth is, you're the stupid one. Don't you realize how dangerous it is for you to do something like that? It's a filthy, dangerous, disgusting habit. And I'll have none of it. Now get your little butt up to your room. When you father gets home—*if* he gets home—I'll call you for dinner. After that just plan on spending all your free time there for the next week. As far as I'm concerned, young lady, you're grounded!"

Marshall could sense Rose's upset. Her lip quivered and her face took on a hurt, angry expression. He was anxious to know what was going through her mind at that time.

"Rose," he said softly, "what did you think about your mother's punishment."

"I'm pissed!"

"Did you want to get back at her?"

"Sure."

"But what could you do? After all, you're only a young girl."

"Oh, I can do plenty, mister," she retorted, her expression smug and defiant.

"For instance?"

"For instance," she mocked, "I could go outside and let the air out of her tires. That would make her real mad when she goes to leave for work in the morning. Or, if she keeps me grounded for too long, I could go to her room while she's sleeping and use my lighter—I still have my disposable Bic, you know—and set her mattress on fire."

Marshall cringed. Despite his need to maintain a professional posture, he blurted out, "You'd do something like that? She could get hurt. You could burn the house down."

"No I wouldn't," she replied matter-a-factly. "She'd be fine. The house would be *fine*. Daddy keeps an extinguisher in their bedroom closet. He'd put out the damn fire."

"But why would you do something that spiteful?"

"To prove that I'm not someone she could fuck with."

Marshall leaned back trying to absorb what he'd heard. He jotted down some notes. After glancing at his watch he realized it was time to bring her back to the present.

"Rose," he instructed with gentle firmness, "It's time for you to relax again. That's right, relax. Let the images from home fade away. Let them fade away. Imagine yourself back in the time machine, sitting in front of the control panel, programming the computer to take us back to the present. There, the button is pushed and the capsule begins to whir and vibrate. The flashing lights come and then go. Then everything quiets down. I open the door and we're back."

Rose seemed relieved. The strain in her face slackened and she appeared peaceful and relaxed. He lightened her trance by having her imagine walking up a broad staircase, reassuring her that when she reached the top she'd feel awake, alert, and refreshed.

While guiding her through this process he experienced a mixture of satisfaction and concern. On one hand he'd uncovered a traumatic experience out of Rose's past, one, which had upset the young girl, but certainly nothing that earth shattering. Most children experiment in forbidden territory and survive the wrath of their caregivers once discovered. Smoking is certainly high on the list. And Rose's mother, if his patient's recollection could be trusted, had acted appropriately, if not a little harshly, to her daughter's behavior. And Rose, for her part, had been appropriately upset with the reprimand and subsequent punishment. Here was an instance of a young girl testing her limits. He wondered about some of the others.

"Nine," he counted, "almost awake now, adjusting to your surroundings, recalling the room and the time of day.

"Ten. Eyes open, wide awake now, alert and refreshed."

Rose's beautiful hazel-green eyes fluttered open and she looked around. Marshall parted the curtains and raised the blinds. Soft early evening light poured into the room.

"Well, how'd I do?" she asked.

"Splendidly," he replied. "You responded very nicely to my suggestions."

"What did I talk about?"

"Don't you remember? You described an experience from your past, when you were eleven years old and your mother caught you smoking."

"I did? Let me see. I think I remember. She was pretty mad."

"She sounded so. She grounded you for a week."

"It wasn't the last time."

"Can you recall other things that made her angry with you?"

"A few. Yes, several in fact."

Marshall checked his watch again. He would've loved to continue this session a while longer. But they'd been at it for close to two hours already. And even if Rose was 'fresh, awake and alert,' Marshall on the other hand felt tired and drained. The intensity of their session following a long day at the hospital had taken its toll. Besides, it was almost seven. He hadn't eaten since lunch. And Sally wanted to meet him for a light dinner at Sweet Basil's in Squirrel Hill at eight. His inquiry into Rose's past would have to wait.

"Between now and our next session I want you to reflect upon those instances. We can discuss them in detail then."

"All right, Marshall," Rose said sweetly. He walked her to the door. "So you really think this helped?" she asked.

"Very much," he reassured her. "We can use it again sometime if you run difficulty with some of your recollections. At the very least it got us on track."

"That's great. I can't wait for our next session."

"Neither can I, Rose."

chapter ten

purely for amusement

Marshall felt trapped under the pavilion of an outdoor amphitheater. Thousands of gyrating teenagers surrounded him. A haunting repetitive melody bathed the crowd. Reflexively his body began to sway. The full moon turned orange-red. Cones of light washed over the congregation then receded. Musicians dressed in shorts jammed on the stage. *The Grateful Dead?*

The hazy air reeked of marijuana. He needed to void. The sea of hippies, bare-chested or clad in tie-dyed shirts, performed surrealistic dances. Cluster after cluster rotated in stilted circles forming sinusoidal oscillations with tattooed arms. He struggled through the throng, bouncing like a billiard ball off dozens of smelly bodies. Rotating arms, swaying hips, stomping feet formed his gauntlet. Mustiness emanated from their shirtless torsos. Heat radiated off their skin. He could almost taste their sweat.

Vertiginous from the revolving motion, seasick from the undulating background, he panicked. Hazy darkness engulfed him. Terror percolated. He felt lost and abandoned without hope of escape. Suddenly a murky white light appeared in the distance.

Desperate for resolution he felt drawn to the illumination. Approaching, it took on shape and form. A woman, sensuous and bewitching, danced in place, radiating inner light, pale, fluorescent, harsh but with a circumferential softness. She swayed to the musical strains.

Timidly he ventured closer, fascinated by long, soft, flowing hair—a silk kimono. She was easily the most beautiful creature he'd ever seen, her complexion flawless, captivating and angelic, possessing an earthly quality that made her radiate fertile desire.

Helplessly he felt drawn to her. They stood toe to toe. His body mirrored hers, swaying back and forth in a perfect harmony. Their spirits mingled across the narrow chasm on a concrete surface surrounded by hordes of gyrating deadheads.

He gazed on, drunk with desire and crazed with lust. Inching closer, drawn by her magnetic beauty, he was aroused and stimulated, seduced by her mesmerizing motion. Desperate to hold her, craving to possess her, he reached out his arms. About to embrace her body, it underwent a harsh transformation. The perfect face crystallized into a latticework of chiseled angles. Her soft, sensuous body waxed awkward, rigid and stiff. From her occiput arose a pair of scaly thorns. Her eyes, once abysmal and inviting, turned coal black. Suddenly he confronted a demon from hell.

Consumed with a terror, crazed to insanity he wrenched his eyes from the creature and fled, wondering if he'd just confronted Satan herself.

Marshall screamed. At first his voice sounded hoarse and raspy. Then the shriek turned loud and shrill. Sweating profusely, his breaths were rapid and shallow, his heart racing. Peering around, he appreciated where he was and forced himself to relax. Remnants of the dream persisted, which was enough. He prayed it would never visit him again.

The sky was azure, the humidity low, and the temperature in the upper seventies when he finally left the apartment later that morning. It was the kind of weather he'd reveled in while vacationing with Bernice in Vail. For a moment he waxed nostalgic, recalling the time when his marriage had supportive this kind of indulgence, back when he'd felt a semblance of contentment, if not outright happiness. But that was another time in another place.

Sally was waiting for him on the porch when he pulled in front of her small brick Squirrel Hill house on Caton Street. She bounced lightly down the steep staircase, her summer dress festive, her fine blonde hair catching the sun. After sliding into the passenger's seat, she leaned over and gave him a friendly kiss on the cheek.

"It's been a while since we've been together," she commented brightly. "I've missed you."

"Me too," Marshall agreed, "Hunter's party seems like ages ago. Going to the hospital day at Kennywood was a great idea. This should be fun."

They made small talk as he took Beechwood Boulevard to the Homestead High-level Bridge then turned left onto Route 837. Just past the Rankin Bridge Marshall's pulse quickened a little as their destination came into view. Ever since childhood he'd loved amusement parks. But he hadn't been to one in years. Reveling in this sense of heightened anticipation, he joined the row of cars veering off the main road into the sprawling parking lot.

"Which pavilion are we in?" Marshall asked as they had their hands stamped and paper bracelets wrapped around their wrists.

"The flyer said one through three," Sally replied. "Hunter's expecting a big crowd. They sold almost five hundred tickets."

The hospital group occupied a trio of spacious, barn-like structures tucked neatly within a grove of trees near the southeast corner of the park. Under one section of Pavilion I, a large group of people was playing bingo. Behind the reception desk, out by a grove of maple trees, an Asian-looking artist sat before an easel and was painting caricatures of some of the hospital employees. A second, tall and gaunt with a dirty blond ponytail, was doing face painting. A long line of children and their parents had queued up, waiting to be made-up.

Lunch, they learned, would be ready in another half-hour. When Sally heard this she suggested they check out the park.

"Sounds good to me," Marshall agreed. "What'll it be, Sal? Rides or a stroll around the grounds?"

Grabbing his hand and giving it a little tug she said, "Why don't you let me show you?" And soon she was leading him through a knot of people meandering in the walkway between two rows of rides.

"The Jack Rabbit was the first coaster my father ever took me on," Sally related as they strolled along. "It was such a thrill speeding down those drops then screeching around the curves. And I survived. I really survived. My mother and sister were waiting for us by the carnival stands. When the ride was over I ran over to them feeling proud and excited."

"We were all weaned on that one," Marshall confessed, warming to her story. "I know it hooked me on these things. Why don't we see what kind of line the Thunderbolt has?"

The maze was full when they got there. Patiently they inched along surrounded by an assortment of teenagers and young children dressed in an odd array of soccer team shorts, T-shirts, cutoffs, tie-dyes, sleeveless tops, sandals, and tennis shoes. Marshall noticed a group of young males with long unkempt hair, tattooed bodies, and pierced ears. They were joined by some adolescent girls with rings and small rods in holes in their ears, navels, and tongues.

I guess each generation seeks creative new ways to make their statement, he decided. He shared this observation with Sally.

"Thank goodness my kids have remained pretty tame," she shared. "And when they do get a little out of hand I just keep reminding myself that it's only a stage and eventually they'll grow up and join the mainstream."

"Even though I don't have any children of my own," Marshall commented, "I know what you mean."

The Thunderbolt was everything Marshall remembered it to be. He found the climbs drenched with anticipation and the descents breathtaking. Several of the unexpected dips felt exhilarating. While tightly gripping the safety bar, he glanced over to check if Sally was all right. From the rapt expression on her face he could tell she was having a great time.

With windblown hair and pounding hearts they staggered down the exit ramp. Lunch was in full swing when they returned to the pavilion. After filling their plates they joined a family of five at a long rectangular table near the northern edge. Marshall recognized one of the home care nurses. Sally greeted her by name then formally introduced them. Carol Buckman, in turn, presented her husband, an architect with a local firm, and their three children, two boys, twelve and nine and their youngest, a seven-year old daughter. The little girl proudly showed Marshall the colorful cartoon characters that had been painted on her two freckled cheeks. The two boys, wearing identical Pirate baseball caps, grudgingly revealed temporary tattoos of some popular action figures.

Marshall was famished. He found the barbecued chicken tasty and the pasta filling. By the time he'd started on his dollop of potato salad he was starting to feel full. Eating in silence he seemed content to eavesdrop on Sally and Carol discussing the recent changes in home care reimbursement and how it was affecting the mechanics of their department.

He reached for his beverage cup. When he glanced back in Sally's direction, he noticed that she was staring over his right shoulder with an annoyed expression on her face. Then she seemed to catch herself and forced a smile. Someone was standing behind him, Marshall deduced. As he turned to investigate, he heard Sally say, "Oh hello, Dr. Shaw."

"Hi Sally," Rose replied. Marshall craned his neck and glanced up. From this vantagepoint, her broad friendly grin and bright sparkling eyes were distorted. "And how are you, Dr. Friedman?" she asked peering down at him.

Before he could reply, Sally inquired, "You two know each other?"

"We met at Dr. Hunter's party," Rose reminded her. "Don't you remember?"

"Oh," Sally said, her voice trailing off. "That's right."

"Mind if I join you?" Rose asked, still facing Sally

With some effort Marshall tore his eyes away from Rose. Glancing across at Sally he saw how she was struggling with her composure. Then, as if she finally rediscovered her manners she said, "Why certainly, Dr. Shaw. Please do."

Rose forcefully inserted herself between Marshall and one of Carol's sons. Initially she sat so close to him that he could feel her bare thigh against his pant leg. Eventually she created a bit more room. For a long time after that, no one said a word.

"What a beautiful day for an outing," Rose eventually commented as she reached past Marshall for the water pitcher. Her scent was familiar. Her right breast peeked through the armhole of her sleeveless blouse. The combination of sensations had him stirring. "And look at the turn-out," she continued, as if unaware of her effect on him. "It's such a thrill being part of a place that can get this kind of turn-out from its employees. Don't you think so, Dr. Friedman?"

Marshall thought it sounded odd being addressed formally after they'd been on a first name basis for so long. "Most definitely," he replied, feigning enthusiasm. "Ever since I arrived at the Hunt I've met nothing but friendly, dedicated people."

"Well that's certainly the case in my department," Rose concurred.

Marshall glanced at Sally, trying to assess how she was coping with Rose. But by now she'd resumed her conversation with Carol and seemed oblivious to them.

Rose swallowed a mouthful of food then asked Marshall, "Do you like the rides, Dr. Friedman?"

"Uh, why, sure," Marshall replied. "The coasters are my favorites."

"I like them all," Rose declared. "In fact, going to amusement parks is one of my favorite ways of vacationing. I've been to several in California and Florida. When I was a kid we used to have one just a few blocks from my house. It was called Waldameer Park, near Presque Isle. My friends and I used to go there two, maybe three, times a week."

"Isn't that near Erie?" Marshall asked, condemned to play the straight man.

"That's right," Rose confirmed. "Were you ever there?"

"No," Marshall replied honestly.

"Well, it's a great place to grow up," Rose confided. "Maybe I can show it to you sometime."

This comment prompted a scowl from Sally who apparently was only creating the pretense of being deep in conversation. A moment later she looked away.

"Maybe you could," Marshall agreed, trying to sound as noncommittal as possible.

"There's one thing about amusement parks," Rose continued, almost finished with her desert. "I hate to go on the rides myself."

"I know what you mean," Marshall said. "It's something you have to share to enjoy."

Rose nodded then turned to Sally. "Mrs. Steiner, pardon me for interrupting. But since you came to Dr. Hunter's party with Dr. Friedman, I assume you're his date today, too. If that's so, would you mind if I borrowed him for a little while? That way I won't have to go on the rides alone?"

Sally looked up, an embarrassed expression on her face. Then quickly regaining her composure, she replied, "Dr. Friedman and I came together, Dr. Shaw, but we're not dating, we're just friends. Feel free to 'borrow' him for as long as you like." Then staring at Marshall, she added coolly, "Is that okay with you Marshall?"

Feeling trapped, Marshall stuttered, "I guess i-i-it's okay with me. Actually, I was looking forward to checking out a little more of the park."

"Good," Rose announced swinging her legs over the bench and standing up. "Then you can do it with me, Dr. Friedman."

There was nothing Marshall could do to change his fate. After gathering his trash, he stood up and hurried after Rose, who by that time was almost to the entrance of the shelter.

They made their way along the broad promenade. On the manmade lake multicolored paddleboats floated lazily in the olive green water. High above them, on something called The Skycoaster, pairs of patrons were strapped together, hoisted hundreds of feet in the air, then released to swing back and forth, their only support, a long braided cable.

Marshall noticed how the park had become much more congested. The carnival stands, amusement rides, arcades, stage shows, and fast food eateries were now all choked with people.

"You were pretty rude to Mrs. Steiner back there," Marshall commented.

"You mean Sally. What makes you say that?"

"The way you barged in on us. Couldn't you tell you upset her?"

"I don't know what she's so pissed about. It's a free country. And remember I was invited to this shindig too. I work at the Hunt and I happen to be a physician there."

"I know all that, Rose. But you could've been more polite."

"I *was* polite!" Rose exclaimed then crossed her arms. "And besides, what's she got to be mad about? Is she afraid I'll steal her boyfriend away?"

"Boyfriend?" Marshall asked. "What do you mean by that?"

"Oh, you know Marshall. Everyone thinks you two are an item."

"What kind of 'item'?" he asked, knowing full well what she meant.

"That you're sleeping together, that's what."

"But, just like Sally said, we're just friends," he insisted.

"Does she *really* know that?"

Marshall paused to consider this for a moment. "I hope so," he said candidly.

After that they walked along in silence. Eventually Rose snuggled up to him, took his arm, and asked in a gentler tone, "Do you think Sally knows about us?"

"Knows what about us?" Marshall snapped.

"That you've taken me on as a patient, Marshall."

"Oh that. I don't think so."

"Good."

They slipped back into a disquieting silence. He felt the pressure of her body against his side. This helped soften his icy mood. Glancing up to see where they were he noticed the intertwining cables and girders of *The Steel Phantom*. Off to the right a fanlike spray of water rose high out of a remote rectangular pool. *Another water ride,* he guessed. But before he could check his map Rose steered him to the left.

"Oh look!" she cried. "Lets do that!"

"The merry-go-round is for children, Rose," he protested. "I bet there isn't a kid over ten on one of those wooden ponies."

"So what," she retorted. "Back at Waldameer, we used to always go on the carousel with our boyfriends. It was fun. It was romantic."

Although he thought the notion ridiculous, Marshall could appreciate how, to a lonely and impressionable young adolescent, this scenario would appear extremely romantic. But Rose was an adult, wasn't she?

Oh well, he said to himself, not anxious to get into another tiff.

A few moments later they were standing on the circular platform. Rose hurried over to a golden palomino and using the stirrup worked her way onto the plastic saddle. Marshall stood beside her, grasping the metal pole and feeling ridiculous. The Wurlitzer piano played the theme song from The Sting. The wooden surface began to rotate. Marshall, swept up in the gentle motion, thought about the ornate carousel in that vintage movie. After a time the carousel slowed to a stop. Rose asked if they could to do it again. Marshall agreed, happy to perpetuate her romantic fantasy.

On their way to the next attraction they stopped for ice cream. Rose ordered a twist with sprinkles. For the first time in longer than he could remember, Marshall asked to have his cone dipped in chocolate syrup. After he paid for their treats they moved along, both licking away.

The day had become considerably hotter. As the sun beat down on them, tiny droplets of melted ice cream dribbled through cracks in the chocolate shell of his cone. Without asking, Rose leaned over and helped him catch the narrow white streaks. At one point the their tongues touched. For several moments afterward, Marshall's tingled.

Rose wanted to go on the Ferris wheel next. Marshall, knowing it was futile to protest, agreed. The wait was brief. Soon they were being hoisted up in a cup-like basket swinging back and forth with the motion of the wheel. They went for several revolutions without stopping. Finally they paused at the very top of the arc, easily the highest point in the park. Marshall pointed out landmarks. When she complained about having trouble seeing one, he leaned over, draped his arm around her shoulders and pointed it out again. When the massive wheel resumed its revolution he left his arm there. Rose eased closer and rested her head on his chest.

Back down on the midway they came to a row of booths offering conventional carnival games. Each of the barkers tried harder than the next to get them to 'take a chance.' When a young boy in the last booth called out that there was a 'winner every time,' and Rose noticed the stuffed panda bears sitting on the top shelf above the playing area, she said imploringly, "Marshall, win me one of those. Please!"

After examining the layout he grasped the object of the game. About ten feet from the edge of the booth were a row of plastic clown faces. From the hat of each clown protruded a deflated balloon. When the attendant gave the signal the contestants used conventional squirt guns to send narrow streams of water into the clowns' mouths. The faster the water entered, the faster the balloons rose. Whoever exploded his balloon first won a prize. Further victories allowed you to trade up.

Although the effort seemed juvenile, Marshall agreed to play. Battling against eleven other contestants, it took him eight contests and about a half-hour to win enough times so they could take one of the giant stuffed animals home. Finally, when his cherry red balloon exploded the fourth and final time, Rose's face lit up. Jumping up and down, she leaned over and hugged him tenderly. Then, when the teenage boy handed her the black and white panda, she gathered it up in her waiting arms and gave Marshall a sloppy kiss on the cheek.

Marshall checked his watch. They'd been gone nearly two hours. He knew Sally would be cognizant of his extended absence and not too happy about it. But Rose coaxed him on.

"One more ride," she cajoled. "Please?"

"Which one?"

"Let's go over there," she said pointing vaguely to a corner of the park tucked away near a more wooded area. After passing the Grand Prix, the Whip, and the Scooter, they stopped at a small maze that serviced the oldest ride in Kennywood Park.

It was The Old Mill, a water ride familiar to most of the nation's traditional theme parks. As they stood in line, inching their way toward the platform, Marshall hummed a Bruce Springsteen's song, 'Tunnel O' Love.' When it came their turn, Rose paused and let Marshall pass into the rickety rowboat first. He checked his balance, then carefully sat down on the far side of the front bench. Expecting to see Rose stepping in beside him, he glanced over and noticed that she had stopped to say something to the young girl running the ride. Finally she set her stuffed panda in the rear seat and joined Marshall in the boat. He asked her what she had said to the teenager.

"I asked her if we could have the boat to ourselves. This way there'd be room for the bear."

"Good thinking," he commented.

A lever was pulled and the antique craft started to float. Rounding a gentle curve it slipped under the gray wooden facade and a moment later they were plunged into murky darkness. A few yards farther along the boat's underside slid onto a rubber runner and was hoisted up a gentle incline. At the top it was released into a narrow stream of water.

Within the pitch-black tunnel Marshall noticed the sound of lapping water. In the distance he heard the happy shrieks of young children. They rounded a curve and an eerie light, multicolored and iridescent, loomed in the distance. A preternatural scene from the Wild West appeared. It featured comical skeletons dressed up as cowboys presiding over the lynching of an old bearded prospector.

Rose giggled as they floated past, then leaned against Marshall and placed her hand on his knee. Around the next bend was another scene from the Wild West. A trio of young prospectors was panning for gold in a tiny stream by the woods. Hidden behind a stand of trees was a pair of claim jumpers, their Colt forty-fives drawn. At the crackle of imitation gunfire, Rose jumped.

More scenes of similar ilk floated by. Musty darkness passed briefly into shaded daylight as the boat moved from one large section of the mill to another. Soon they were once again bathed in shadows. Marshall leaned back and patiently waited for the next scene to appear. As he did he felt Rose's hand migrate to the space between his thighs. Obligingly he spread his legs. Gently, she cupped his groin. With a mixture of surprise and delight he shifted closer, curious to discover what was coming next. It didn't take long to find out. Her other hand slipped behind his neck and she pulled his mouth against hers.

The kiss began soft and tender. Slowly, relentlessly, he felt the pressure increase. Slipping her tongue between his teeth she explored his mouth. He felt himself becoming hot and hard.

The boat glided around another bend, floating by a scene which Marshall ignored. Out of the corner of a partially closed eye he noticed that another boat was just entering the bend behind them. Embarrassed, he pulled away and sat back. Glancing over at Rose, he searched for some clarification. All he got was a devilish grin. They were plunged into utter darkness again. Her hand remained between his legs. Now she began stroking in earnest.

Marshall, swept up in a wave of incredible pleasure, abandoned himself to the experience. Darkness engulfed them. Was it the lack of Wild West displays or the fact that his eyes were shut? He cracked them a sliver. A rectangle of hazy light loomed ahead.

On the edge of awareness he knew this marked the end of the ride. He hoped he would climax before they reached at the exit.

Rose seemed willing to urge him toward his goal. With what seemed like practiced adeptness, she caressed him gentle but firm. The pressure in his pants heightened. Just as they reached the exit, Marshall, with a tiny yelp, erupted.

Pinned against the edge of the moat by a wooden runner the weathered rowboat stopped abruptly. Marshall, sweaty and spent, glanced self-consciously at the people in line. Rose, in contrast, seemed cool and collected. Gingerly she stepped out of the craft then reached over to gather up her panda from the rear compartment. After that she offered Marshall a helping hand. He gratefully accepted it, hoping none of the onlookers had noticed how his other hand was furtively shielding his crotch. Once on the platform he grinned sheepishly then hurried down the ramp and out onto the crowded midway.

chapter eleven

glimpsing the future

Marshall strolled hand-in-hand with Rose, eyes on the ground, beset by a nagging sense of embarrassment. Then Rose giggled and he lightened up, appreciating the humor in the situation, especially the juvenility and sheer spontaneity of it. His boxers felt damp and uncomfortable. A downward glance confirmed that his khaki shorts had stained. He caught Rose's eye and pointed at the discoloration. She grinned back, thoroughly enjoying her complicity in this escapade. Marshall scanned the immediate vicinity and noticed a men's room. He suggested to Rose that he clean up in there.

"Don't be long," she admonished. "We should be getting back."

Glancing at his watch he noticed that it was almost five o'clock. Once inside one of the stalls, he used a clump of toilet tissue to soak up much of the stickiness. While dabbing himself, he mused how it had to be twenty-five years since anything like this had happened to him. Not since his sex-crazed adolescence, while riding a bus or passing through the cosmetic section in one of the local department stores, had he been stirred into this kind of eruption. Now, well into his middle-age years, he was impressed that Rose had rekindled this adolescent propensity.

He concluded his business and left the stall. Upon exiting the facility he considered sharing some of these personal recollections from his childhood with Rose. This would suggest an intention to be more intimate with her. However, when he reached the place he'd left her, Rose was gone. A cursory search of the immediate vicinity confirmed that fact.

Disappointed and a tad worried he made his way back to the picnic area. Perhaps she'd returned to the pavilion and was waiting for him there. He spotted Sally sitting on a bench under the shelter next to Bertram Hunter and his wife, Maggie. He looked around for Rose and didn't see her. A part of him was actually relieved. He knew Sally wouldn't be happy about how long he'd been gone. And if Rose was still around, the combination of irritants might provoke another altercation.

"The Prodigal Son returns," Sally said sarcastically. "And where have you been all this time, Dr. Friedman?"

"Oh, going on the rides."

"Sally tells us that it was none other than Dr. Rose Shaw who spirited you away, Marshall," Bertram Hunter interjected, arching his eyebrow. "Is that true?"

Marshall, feeling like a teen-ager caught breaking one of his father's rules, replied meekly, "Yes."

"Hmmm," replied Hunter. "And where is our talented geneticist now?"

"Of that I'm not sure," Marshall replied honestly. "I stopped to use the bathroom and thought she was going to wait for me. When I came out she was gone."

"That's too bad," Hunter said, not sounding that upset. "I was looking forward to seeing her again."

Marshall sat down next to Sally who mentioned that the three of them were discussing what to do about dinner.

"How about you, Dr. Friedman?" Maggie Hunter asked. "Have you made any plans?"

"Well, actually, no. I hadn't thought that far ahead."

"Hunter and I were thinking of stopping at the Georgetown Inn on our way home. The food is good and the prices reasonable. And the sunsets from Mount Washington are spectacular. Would you and Sally like to join us there?"

Marshall glanced over at Sally, still uncertain about her mood. Without a moment's hesitation she nodded in agreement.

"We'll be happy to come along," Marshall translated.

"Good," Mrs. Hunter said, daintily clapping her hands. "Bertram, hand me your cellular and I'll see if they require reservations."

"What time, Maggie?" Sally asked.

"Oh, probably not until around eight."

"Good," she replied. "Then if you and Hunter will excuse us, Marshall and I are going to take stroll around the park."

"You go right ahead, my dear. Hunter and I still need to work the crowd a bit. I declare, this event feels almost like one of our dinner parties."

"I'm sure it does," Sally agreed. Then to Marshall she instructed, "Come on, Dr. Friedman. Now it's my turn to offer you to a little amusement."

Marshall thought the park appeared less crowded as he and Sally made their way in a westerly direction. Glancing over at Sally, he sensed she seemed a little introspective. He searched for some way to break the ice.

"So what did you do while I was away?" he asked lightly.

Sally glanced up at him, looking like he'd summoned her back from somewhere far away. "Oh, Carol took her daughter over to Kiddieland and I joined them. We stood around while she went on the rides. You know, Marshall, I'd forgotten what a thrill it was being around a five-year-old who's having that much fun. It brought back memories of when Jared and Stephanie were that small."

"Do you miss it?"

"Sometimes," she replied, drawing the word out. "I suppose I do. At least at moments like that."

"Would you ever consider going through it again? I mean, having another child."

Sally turned slightly to face him.

"That's an intriguing question, Marshall. Why do you ask?"

"Just curious, I guess. I've never had any kids of my own. Sometimes I wonder what it would be like. Did you enjoy it enough the first time to go through it again?"

Sally paused. Finally she declared, "Yes, Marshall. With the right person, I'd definitely have another child. In my opinion raising children is one of the most gratifying experiences a person can have."

Marshall thought he understood and nodded.

Sally guided him under an archway that led to a section of the park Marshall didn't immediately recognize. Off to his left was a large rectangular pool dominated by two parallel rows of fountains that sprayed cascades of water high up into the air. Toward the far end a long steep ramp connected to a circular corridor that hovered a hundred feet above the surface. As Marshall peered absently in that general direction, a boxy-looking rowboat, carrying a dozen people or so, stood poised at the top of the ramp. A moment later the boat started its slippery descent, rapidly accelerating into a brisk slide. As it plunged into the pool a V-shaped curtain of water enveloped it and a chorus of boisterous shrieks erupted.

They continued along past a flying ride called the Roll-o-Plane then the Pitt Fall. Finally they reached a row of concessions stands and carnival booths near the far end of the park. Near an old-fashioned shooting gallery, Sally paused and said with a mixture of excitement and relief in her tone, "Oh good! I was hoping she was still in business."

"Who's that?" Marshall asked innocently.

"Madame Olga." Sally pointed to a small curtained booth tucked away in this most remote corner of the park. "She's a tarot card reader. I've consulted her several times in the past. I think she's great. I wanted to bring you to see her, Marshall—to have your fortune told."

Marshall considered her idea. On one level, he thought this kind of stuff was a bunch of bunk, thoroughly contrived and rigged, like those phony mentalists he'd seen in nightclubs and on TV. On another, however, the notion of having his cards read intrigued him. This would be his first reading. Bernice had attempted to get him into a boardwalk booth when they were in Atlantic City a few years back, but he'd refused. More recently, however, after researching the fields of mysticism, spiritualism, and the world beyond the senses for his book, he'd become less skeptical.

"How about it, Marshall?" Sally persisted. "Don't you want to get a glimpse of the future?"

"Maybe," Marshall hedged. "And if I agree, what should I expect?"

"You mean in the booth? Not that much. Madame Olga will probably start by having you sit down in a chair across a small table from her. Then she'll ask if you want your palm read or the cards. I always go for the cards. I think they reveal more. Then she'll ask you a personal question about yourself. She'll base her reading on that."

"Sounds pretty simple to me. Are you going to do it?"

"Of course. But I want you to go first."

"Why?"

"I'm curious to see what you think."

"All right."

They walked over to the booth. A small signed pinned to one of the maroon curtains indicated that Madame Olga was in. Under it was written, 'Please step inside.'

"Make sure you tip her," Sally instructed. "The amount depends on how reliable you think the reading is, not necessarily whether you like it or not."

Marshall glanced back at her and nodded. With a wry smile he entered the darkened booth. Once inside his nose was immediately accosted by the tangy-sweet odor of incense. As his eyes adjusted to the muted light he looked around and concluded that this was actually the vestibule to another room. A bolt of coarse fabric was stapled to one of the walls. He reached out and stroked it. Then, just as he was about to sit down on a musty smelling sofa, a short stocky woman poked her head out from between a second set of curtains.

"Sir. Come," she beckoned graciously, her smile warm and maternal. "Please do not be afraid. I, Madame Olga, am quite harmless. Come and sit with me."

Her accent sounds eastern European, he decided as she took his arm. *Hungarian, perhaps. Maybe she really is a gypsy.*

"I will do your reading now," Madame Olga announced. "Together we will explore the future. Your future."

Marshall hesitated. Finally, he allowed her to coax him into the inner room.

A circular table and two cushioned armchairs filled the tiny enclosure. Madame Olga settled herself in one of the chairs. The other, she indicated, was for Marshall. A dark red oilcloth covered the table. Upon it rested a white candle and a large crystal ball.

In the flickering firelight Marshall examined his hostess. She was easily in her mid to late fifties, he decided, with gray-black hair and a wrinkled, weathered complexion. Her costume reminded him of the garb worn by the gypsies in the movie, Thinner, based on a Stephen King novel. There was the long pleated silk dress, full bodied and colorful, dozens of silver bracelets on her wrists, and around her neck a layer of beaded necklaces. Two large gold hoops dangled from her pierced ears.

"Would you like your palm read?" she inquired pleasantly, "or shall I shuffle the cards? It will be ten dollars for each, fifteen if you choose both."

"What about the crystal ball?" Marshall asked innocently.

"That, my good man, is just for effect."

"Oh," he replied, smiling at his foolishness. "I'll try the cards."

"Very well."

The mysterious old woman slid out a drawer under her side of the table and withdrew a deck of oversized playing cards. She divided them in half, shuffled, then had Marshall cut the deck. As she shuffled the two halves, folding them over each other, Marshall observed her hands. Despite their ancient gnarled appearance she was dexterous and skilled. He pictured her working a high stakes blackjack table at an Atlantic City casino.

"How old are you, sir?" she inquired, her tone businesslike.

"Forty," he replied without hesitation.

"And have you a question for me? It will help focus the reading."

"I was warned you might ask me that." Her eyebrows arched with amused interest. "Let's try, will I find romance in my future?"

"An interesting inquiry," Madame Olga commented, "and one I think the cards will help us answer."

She held the shuffled deck in her left hand and flipped over the top card. Even though it was facing away from him, Marshall made out the picture of a cherubic cupid suspended above a man and a pair of women. Squinting, he read the caption. It said, The Lovers.

"Could it be possible that you were born in the month of June, sir? Our first card represents the astrological sign of Gemini."

"Umm," Marshall said. "Interesting. Actually, my birthday is June seventeenth."

She nodded, looking satisfied. "This card," she explained, "symbolizes harmony and the association of opposites. It suggests emotional intensity and focuses on love and attraction. It also predicts that a decision will soon have to be made."

Marshall immediately thought of Rose. Could the card be referring to the potential for an intensely emotional relationship with her? And it involved love and attraction. Yes, all this sounded favorable, right in step with what he was hoping she'd say. Then he imagined what kind of decision he would have to make.

While he dwelled upon this, Madame Olga flipped over another card and set it on top of the first, rotating it exactly ninety degrees. Marshall cocked his head so as to make it out. The card showed two mongrel dogs howling at the moon. In the lower half of the scene a lobster was swimming in a dark blue pool of water. The card was labeled, The Moon.

"Ah," Madame Olga continued. "Although love and romance appear to be in your future, the path there will neither be straight nor smooth. Expect the unexpected. You will hear inner voices warning you of danger from the unknown. But, by the same token, guard against letting your imagination run away from you."

Although Marshall nodded, he was confused. Her comment seemed vague. He tried to imagine a scenario that would incorporate these disparate predictions. But Madame Olga's hands distracted his reflections. In rapid succession four more cards appeared positioned roughly at the main compass points around the first two.

"Here we have a quartet of cards which speak of upheaval and strife," the seer reported solemnly. He glanced up and noticed how the furrows in her forehead had deepened and her eyes seemed black as coal. "They involve several aspects of your life." Then, without elaborating, she looked up at him and inquired, "May I ask you, sir, are you a professional?"

A bit leery of the question, Marshall replied candidly, "Why, yes, a psychiatrist, in fact. Why do you ask?"

"Your original inquiry referred to love and romance," she reminded him. "Judging from the initial cards it appears likely. But before you reach the emotional gratification you seek, you will be forced to climb a mountain of conflict. During that time you will experience a crisis. It will occur at the interface between your personal and professional lives. There," she said tapping a grimy fingernail on a colorful card positioned to the left of the original two. "Do you see The Tower?"

He nodded, studying the picture of a cylindrical brick structure being struck by a bolt of lightning. Its crown-like top blew off and its occupants toppled to the ground.

"This card reveals how destructive influences will create chaos in your life. Perhaps an accident or even a shocking event will occur. It will make you prey to misery and destruction. You will be faced with a difficult decision. There will be an argument and possibly a breakdown. You will feel the need to escape from the negative influences in your immediate environment and seek refuge for reflection and renewal. You will need cogent advice. It will come from an unexpected source. This, as you may imagine, will be a difficult time for you."

He nodded, acknowledging her prediction and feeling uneasy about what it implied. But before he could dwell on it further, she pointed to another card. Instead of facing Madame Olga, this one was upside down. Marshall read the caption. Called the Star, it was a picture of a naked girl kneeling by a stream with a cluster of bright stars sparkling in the sky above.

"Normally this card signifies a bright future filled with tranquillity and peace," the older woman told him. "But in a reversed position it unfortunately predicts aimlessness laced with a feeling of deep sadness."

This reading was getting pretty gloomy, he decided. A pang of despair sliced through Marshall's chest. If what this woman was saying came true, he fretted, he was headed for some uncertain times. This was certainly not what he'd expected when he let Sally to persuade him into going through with this. Fortunes were supposed to be upbeat and optimistic, weren't they?

At least the ones I fish out of Chinese cookies usually are, he thought.

As if reading his mind, and Marshall was certain that Madame Olga could do precisely that, the old woman announced, "but Doctor, let me reassure you that all is not lost." Four more cards had appeared faces up on the table. "Regard these images. They suggest that you may benefit from the counsel of close friends or family. These are the relationships which will enlighten you. That, in addition to the rejuvenating properties of independence and solitude, will help you discover the answers you are seeking. And from there all your energy will flow into a series of new beginnings."

Marshall sighed with relief. Now things were starting to sound more encouraging. But what could these new beginnings be? And with whom? Was she referring to the start of a completely new relationship? Or the rekindling of an old? Before he could interrogate Madame Olga further, the old crone announced: "My final prediction is that you will experience a satisfying outcome to your crisis complete with transformation and spiritual rebirth."

She pointed to the final card nearest to her that was labeled, Judgment. Three figures were peering up at an angel who was blowing a trumpet above them.

"This card, my good doctor, predicts an end to suffering, the regeneration of spirit, and the fulfillment of new beginnings," she declared triumphantly. Marshall nodded.

He paid the fee and added a generous tip. He then left the booth with a thankful smile on his face, as if snatched from the abyss of a fate much worse than death.

"Well?" Sally asked. "What did you think?" She was seated at a small round table under a striped umbrella, sipping a soft drink through a straw. Marshall squinted back at her, his eyes adjusting to the light.

"I must admit it was a little unnerving in there."

"Why?"

"Your gnarled old seer seems a little too pessimistic for my tastes. She predicated all kinds of crisis, conflicts, misery and destruction for me."

"My word! It sounds like you're about to preside over the fall of the Modern Age."

"Hardly that monumental," Marshall assured her. "And it's only fortune telling. I'm not sure I believe in all that mumbo-jumbo anyway."

"I bet you would have if she'd told you only good stuff."

"Maybe," he conceded. Nursing the can of Coke she'd gotten him, he asked, "So, how about you?" gesturing with his head back toward the Tarot Card booth. "Going to try your luck?"

"I already did, earlier this afternoon. While you and Rose were romping around the park."

"Oh," he replied, a little embarrassed. "What did you find out?"

"Mostly good stuff," Sally confided. "The kids are in fine shape. They're both going to be successful. She did warn me that Jared has a tendency to take on too much. If he continues doing that during college, he might be in for some rough sailing. Stephanie, on the other hand, is headed for a career in photography or advertising."

Marshall nodded, impressed with the specificity of Sally's predictions. "How about you personally?" he asked curiously. "What's in store for my dear friend, the administrator of nursing?"

"A life of success and tranquillity shared with the man of my dreams."

And although she said this without mirth or sarcasm, Marshall couldn't help get the feeling she was teasing him.

"Is that so?" he commented. "And who, might I ask, is this knight in shining armor?"

"Of that I'm not so sure," Sally said evasively. "Once I wake up, Marshall, I never remember my dreams."

chapter twelve

exploring discipline

Marshall met Rose at his office on the following Wednesday evening for another therapeutic session. Her dreams were becoming more disturbing, the imagery more graphic, the actions more violent. On Monday night, a particularly frightening nightmare had triggered a migraine headache that had lasted almost thirty-six hours.

Before the hour began Rose apologized for her sudden departure from the amusement park on Sunday. "I'm really sorry I abandoned you like that, Marshall," she said sounding earnest. "But since you came with Sally I felt awkward going back to the pavilion with her still there. So while you were cleaning up I thought it best that I split. That way you had less to deal with."

Marshall considered this explanation. "When you put it like that," he conceded, "I suppose you did what was best. And thanks for thinking about me."

The drawn curtains blocked the rays of a mid-summer orange-red sun. The Tiffany lamp on Marshall's desk provided the room's only illumination. Rose sat on the couch across from Marshall. He rolled his leather desk chair around to be closer to her.

With Marshall's prompting Rose described the latest version of her recurring nightmare. The woods, the eerie suspense, and the woman in the white cloak were back. This time, however, when the mysterious specter raised her deadly butcher knife the heart she stabbed was Rose's. Standing transfixed in her dream, stunned by the act, Rose waited for the pain and the flow of her blood to start.

"Sounds pretty gory to me," Marshall admitted. "Any idea what it means? Who do you think the woman is?"

Rose paused before replying. "It might be my mother," she finally said. "Mom used to wear a white uniform to the hospital. The cloak could be reminding me of it. But why would she stab me like that?"

"I don't know yet," Marshall admitted. "What do you think?"

Rose took a moment. "Could she be trying to kill off some part of me she doesn't like? You know, like a surgeon removing a tumor or a diseased organ."

Marshall, tenting his fingertips, nodded in agreement. He asked Rose to give him a moment. Walking over to his file cabinet he unlocked the bottom drawer and pulled out a manila folder.

"From what you revealed while under hypnosis," he told her, "you and your mother weren't the best of friends. She seemed like a pretty strict disciplinarian, committed to having you modify your behavior—at least regarding your smoking when you were a pre-teen. You, on the other hand, didn't deal with punishment well and began imagining some pretty dramatic ways of getting back at her."

"I did," Rose said, appearing interested. "What did I say?" Marshall checked his notes. He told her about the imaginary acts of revenge, like bleeding her mother's tires or setting the mattress on fire. "I said those things!" she exclaimed.

Marshall nodded. "And before we concluded you hinted about other things you two had fought about over the years, behaviors of yours that your mother didn't feel were appropriate or proper. Do you remember any of those?"

Rose seemed to consider this. Marshall remained silent, his patience in these settings a virtue that had served him well through the years.

"My most vivid recollection," Rose finally related, "was how we were always fighting about how much independence I was allowed. She insisted I stay close to the house. I wanted to get away. I wanted to ride my bike around Millcreek or even go out on the Isle."

"Presque Isle?"

"Uh-huh," Rose confirmed. "I hated being cooped up in that tiny house. The Isle was so close. There were all these neat beaches and woods. I made friends with the fishermen."

"And you were how old at that time?" He tried to picture the scene.

"Around nine or ten."

"So your mother didn't want you leaving the neighborhood?"

"That's right," she admitted

"Did she try and stop you? Did she ground you like when you were caught smoking?"

"Worse."

"Worse?" What could be worse, he wondered.

"Yes. She locked me in my room. It made me feel like a prisoner."

"What did you do?"

"I broke out through my window," she declared. He could hear the proud defiance in her voice. "After all, Marshall, it was only a one-story house."

"What did your mother do when she found you missing?"

"She made my father put iron bars on my window."

That seemed a little radical to him. Curious what her reaction to this imprisonment was he asked, "And how did that make you feel?"

"It made me hate her even more."

I bet it did, he thought. Aloud he asked, "What did you do about it?"

"What could I do? I was only ten at the time."

Marshall remained silent for some moments, making notations on his steno pad and reflecting on her comments. "Where was your father through all this conflict and punishment?" he finally inquired. "What was his role in disciplining you?"

"Oh Dad just went along with her. He was her flunky. He'd do anything she told him to."

"And how did that make you feel?"

"It made me mad. And it should have. After all, he was always saying how I was his 'little princess, his best girl.' If that was so, the least he could do was stand up for me once in a while."

"Is that all? Did you have any other feelings for your father other than betrayal?"

"I suppose I felt sorry for him. I got this sense he was weak. He never stood up for himself or told us what he thought was right."

Rose paused. Marshall left her alone with her thoughts. Instead he considered the gory dream and wondered what key it held to her distress. He pondered a less literal interpretation of the nightmare. Perhaps it wasn't that Rose's mother had tried to kill her, but had instead stifled her to the point of cutting off her independence. *But a knife to the chest,* he questioned? That did seem a little extreme for a woman to conjure up, even one who was extremely bitter over being confined. He recalled the two paperbacks on dream interpretation he'd just purchased at the medical school bookstore. He made a note to review them more thoroughly. Glancing over he noticed that Rose was regarding him.

"Were there other instances where you and your mother came into conflict?" he asked.

"Dozens," Rose confirmed.

"For instance."

"Well she loved to punish me for not doing my homework or coming home with grades she thought were not up to something she called 'my potential.'"

"What would she do to you?"

"Take away my stereo for a few days or not let me watch TV."

"Pretty standard," he commented.

"Not to me."

"Why not?"

"It just wasn't!" Rose snapped back. Marshall noted this reaction on his pad.

"How did it make you feel?" he probed.

"Pissed off."

"And about her in general?"

"To be perfectly honest with you, Marshall, there were times when I really hated her. I would sit there in my room and fume. Those must've been the times I imagined stuff I could do to get back at her."

"Like the tires and the burning bed?"

"Worse."

"Worse?"

A brief, asymmetric grin crossed Rose's lips. Had he caught a certain fiendishness there? This suggestion of pure evil made him shudder.

"Once I checked with one of the older kids in the neighborhood. My friend told me his family belonged to a Mafia. I asked him if I could hire a hit man to knock her off."

"What came of that?"

"Nothing, of course," Rose replied lightly. "I was just being stupid. And besides I could never afford it even if they took me seriously."

Marshall nodded, for the moment believing her, but reserving the right to remain skeptical. He suspected that Rose was a determined, strong-willed woman with personality traits which had been present early in her development. Like everyone she had impulses. But was she actually capable of following through on these impulses, especially ones with such dire consequences?

Not ready to become confrontational he said, "Well that's just about enough for now." Reaching over he cranked the lamp up a notch. "I think we're making progress. Let's set up another appointment."

Rose nodded. He waited for her to rise. Instead she looked him squarely in the eye and asked, "Marshall, how come you ask so much about my mother."

"Well," he replied slowly, "her death occurred at what I perceive as a pivotal point in your psycho-social development. How you reacted to that incident or what you've repressed about it is probably crucial to some of the psychological manifestations you are experiencing now." Rose nodded. "Would you like to tell me more about your father?" he asked. She nodded again. "Like what?"

"Like, despite the way he related to my mother, I still loved him dearly. We were extremely close. After Mom died I saw how devastated he was. I felt like I had to make up for the loss. It was my job to take care of him."

"But I thought your aunt took over that role?"

"With the cooking and cleaning, maybe."

He sensed where she was going. "But not emotionally?"

"No," Rose replied pointedly. "It was up to me to give him the love and affection that my mother couldn't."

"And did you?"

"As well as I could."

"That's wonderful," Marshall said.

She hesitated for a moment, then added, "He's still living in Millcreek, you know. But he's all alone now. My aunt died about six months ago."

"That's too bad," Marshall said sympathetically. "How's he managing?"

"Not that well," Rose admitted. "In fact last week I received a call from his social worker. He was in the hospital a month ago, in Hammet, where my mom used to work. After she died, he really started hitting the bottle. Now he's got end stage cirrhotic liver disease. A visiting nurse checks on him twice a week. She told the social worker that he's getting to the point where he can't take care of himself anymore. She thinks he should be placed. That means a nursing home or some such thing. She wants my input."

"Well?"

"Of course I'm going to help. I'm driving to Erie this weekend to meet with them. They have this detailed care plan they want me to review."

"Going there would be very supportive of you. I'm sure he'll appreciate it. Is there anything I can do to help?"

"Yes," Rose replied without pause. "Come with me."

It was Marshall's turn to hesitate. "To Erie?" he asked, trying not to sound surprised. "With you?"

"Yes. I know it's kind of sudden. And it's probably more than I can expect at this point in our relationship. But it's important to me, Marshall." She took a breath. "I guess what I'm asking for is moral support. In a short time we've become pretty close. I fell safe around you, like someone I can trust. You seem to have my best interests in mind. That's why I want you to be there when I tell my father that he's not well enough to live in his own home anymore. With you there, I know it would be easier for me to do that."

Marshall remained calmly attentive during her explanation. In contrast, his insides were in turmoil. He took a moment to consider the possibility.

He had nothing to keep him tied to Pittsburgh for the weekend. And he couldn't deny his growing infatuation for Rose, how he desperately wanted to get to know her better. A weekend away with her would give him the perfect opportunity to do so.

But what will the accommodations be, he wondered? *What tyoe of sleeping arrangement did she envision—and where?*

These, he realized, were minor details compared with the decision whether to actually go. His assent would implicitly take their relationship to a new, more intimate level. Could they deal with the ramifications of such a move? Was he ready to take that chance?

After all, I'm still married, he cautioned himself. *If word leaked out, what would people think? If I end up getting a divorce, how would those proceedings be affected? And then there's Sally, the nagging unknown in my life. How would she react to the news? I guess what I'm asking myself is, am I ready to take a chance with Rose?*

His impulsive reply was, "Sure, I'd be glad to go and offer whatever support I can."

"That's super, Marshall," she replied with a sigh. "Can I call you tomorrow? We can go over the details? I plan to be on the road by five on Friday. Does that work for you?"

"I think so. I'll check my office schedule and let you know."

"Good," she said with a nod.

"Can I walk you to your car?" he asked, not ready to let her go.

"No," she replied, now on her feet. "I still have work to do in the lab. But thanks for the offer. We'll talk."

"All right," he said and escorted her to the door. Before she stepped into the hallway she paused for a moment, leaned over, and gave him a kiss on the cheek.

"Thanks," she said with genuine warmth and affection. Then she was gone and he was left him with a confusing sense of emptiness in the center of his chest.

chapter thirteen

back to the future

It had been years since Marshall had ridden in a convertible with the top down, and never had he been a passenger in a fiery red sportscar with an attractive woman at the helm. But here he was, his thinning brown hair caught in the breeze, his arm crooked out the window frame, streaking up the Interstate in a Pontiac Firebird.

It was Rose's idea to leave work together. Now, at four-thirty in the afternoon, with Marshall's Mercedes still in the parking lot, they were on the road. And from the lack of congestion on the highway, they had beaten the rush hour traffic in the process.

It was warmer than Marshall had expected, but not as stifling as it had been the last two weeks. The late afternoon sunshine had a hazy quality to it, the air less humid but still definitely August-like. Although he preferred the calm climate control of his luxury sedan on afternoons like this, feeling the wind on his face and the sun beating on his bald spot was not unpleasant.

He glanced over at Rose and grinned. Sitting there with the heel of her hand atop the steering wheel, her white scarf wrapped loosely around her head, and a colorful silk blouse flapping in the breeze, she certainly looked the role. Her wrap-around sunglasses reminded him of a pair of aviator shades he used to wear. As if sensing his gaze, she turned her head slightly and gave him a warm smile. The roar of the wind blasting through the cab made conversation impossible.

Once on I-79 they streaked past miles of hills, meadows, and woodlands, each stretch interrupted briefly by housing communities, farms, and a smattering of industry. Near the town of Zelienople, Marshall shouted over the din that his sister used to live nearby in Beaver Falls.

About an hour later Rose detoured from the main road and took them to Conneaut Lake. At a quaint little restaurant, they dined on open-faced roast beef sandwiches, mashed potatoes and gravy. During the meal Rose shared about the Saturdays during her high school years when she'd drive down from Erie with some of her friends, ride amusement park rides, get stoned and then fornicate in the woods by the lake.

"Have you ever made love on coke, Marshall?" she asked so innocently that initially he thought of the popular soft drink.

"You mean, on cocaine?" he clarified.

"Of course, that's what I mean. Well, have you?"

He shook his head, no.

"Well, it's quite a rush," she declared. "You should try it sometime."

He noted the sparkle in her eye.

From Conneaut they took Route 18 north passed acres of checkerboard farmland intermingled with miles of unspoiled fields, meadows, and woods. When they merged onto Interstate 90 the rural road became major highway. Then at Exit 5 Rose turned onto Sterrettania Road. Heavily populated residential communities seemed randomly interrupted by tidy suburban parks, small strip malls and then larger shopping centers. At the intersection with 26th Street they entered a complex commercial district with sprawling shopping plazas extending like spokes in both directions.

Without hesitating Rose made a sharp left onto 26th. A half-mile later, she turned right onto a small street called James. Suddenly they were out of the huge commercial district and into the bowels of a modest, highly residential neighborhood, its grid of narrow streets characterized by rows of cottage-style homes.

Marshall glanced over at Rose and guessed from her distant, nostalgic expression that she was reliving something more remote, more sentimental that today's Millcreek with its small, flat, well-kept lawns and backyards cluttered with aboveground pools, prefabricated tool sheds, and modest playground sets.

Midway up the next block, Rose slowed the Firebird to a crawl then turned left into a narrow concrete driveway. She parked behind a late-model gray Skylark with a deep dent in the trunk compartment and broad bands of orange-brown rust rimming its wheel wells. Beside them stood a small, lonely-looking cottage, its blue tin siding pale and tarnished, its slate gray roof missing some shingles. Marshall noticed that the front of the house had three windows, no porch, and only a single cinderblock step leading to a white screen door.

Beside him, in the eerie silence of the stalled car, Rose sighed deeply then announced, "Well, we're here."

As Rose pulled it toward her the screen door creaked loudly. "Dad!" she called, poking her head through the front door. "Dad, are you here? He's gotta be here," she said to Marshall. "Where else would he be?" Marshall offered her a supportive smile. "He spends most of his time in the day room. That's where he probably is."

Without further ceremony she marched into the house and through what, to Marshall, appeared to be a common living-dining room. He noticed the maroon threadbare sofa surrounded by two end tables and a chipped, stained coffee table. A basic shelving unit filled up most of one wall along with a wooden door which was shut. He turned his attention to where he was going.

It was almost eight PM. Neither of the lamps was on. One false move and a chair leg could send him tumbling. He followed Rose into the kitchen, which was little more than a narrow corridor covered in soiled linoleum with cabinets and shelving on one side, and a sink, stove and refrigerator on the other. He heard the sound of canned laughter nearby. Rose's father was probably watching some prime time situation comedy. This must be where the day room was, back off the rear of the house. Rose disappeared through an open doorway. Marshall closed ranks, stopping just under a square-shaped portal.

"There you are!" he heard her cry in a lighthearted, distinctly insincere voice. He looked inside and saw the shadowy figure sitting lifelessly in a Lazyboy recliner at the end of the narrow enclosure. The room seemed to be about half the length of a Pullman railroad car and about the same width. Brighter than the rest of the house, it looked through a row of windows out onto the back yard. Garish light emanating from the old-fashioned console television. A thin, gaunt man with a prominent Adams apple stared at the screen.

"How are you, dad?" Rose asked her father. She leaned over and flipped on a switch. The ceiling fixture responded with a burst of bright yellow light. The old man squinted, then winced momentarily, before resuming his impassive expression. It seemed obvious to Marshall he was ignoring them.

Rose gave her father a kiss on the cheek then crouched down in front of him. "We've come to visit you, dad," she said sweetly. "We'll be spending the night. I have a meeting with Mrs. Lester tomorrow. She thinks you should go into a nursing home. I'm not sure if I agree. After I talk to her, we can decide."

Marshall, who had taken a couple of steps into the room, was impressed with her candor. There was no rambling preamble here, no piffling pleasantries or dithering digressions into trifling comments about family and friends. He saw that Rose could be a no nonsense person. He watched her reach up and take her father's hand; a lifeless bundle of tendons, nerves, and muscles set upon one of the armrests. In the artificial light Marshall appreciated the prominent bony knuckles hiding under the sallow wrinkled skin speckled with tiny reddish-brown spots, those spider angiomata characteristic of end-stage liver failure.

"I've brought a friend along with me, Dad," Rose said to the indifferent face. "His name is Marshall Friedman. He's a physician, a psychiatrist, at the hospital I work at in Pittsburgh. Would you like to meet him?"

Again the old man offered no response. Marshall hesitated, not sure what to do next. He wondered if the old man misinterpreted Marshall's presence here. Maybe he thought Rose had brought him along to help with the nursing home decision. Perhaps he expected to be psychoanalyzed, which, of course, was ridiculous. But given the man's self-imposed catatonia, he had no clue what his thoughts or feelings were.

Reluctantly Marshall eased over to where Rose was standing. He bent his five-foot-ten inch frame and held out his hand. Mr. Shaw ignored him, or didn't see him, or just didn't care. Instead he just sat there as if mummified, with his back straight, his occiput against the headrest of the recliner, his legs together, and his feet flat on the floor. Standing this close to Frank Shaw, Marshall couldn't help but notice that the man emitted a particularly poignant odor. Involuntarily, he wrinkled his nose and turned away.

Rose must have noticed his involuntary reaction. "Marshall, why don't you get the bags out of the car," she said, standing up and placing a gentle but firm palm to the small of his back. "When you return I'll show you where you'll be sleeping."

He nodded, murmuring, "Sure." He turned and left, glad to have this brief respite.

It wasn't until after ten that Marshall looked up from where he was sitting on the sofa and saw Rose drag herself into the living room. He set his Michael Crichton novel down on the end table. She sat down heavily beside him then slipped off her shoes and tucked one foot up under her other thigh.

"Well, he's finally settled in for the night," she said. There was a hint of irritation in her tone. "I made him some hot oatmeal which he finally ate. He probably hasn't had anything else all day, although the social worker assured me that he gets Meals on Wheels."

Marshall sat there and let her talk. He couldn't tell if he was hearing compassion or disgust. He hoped it was the former. In a spontaneous gesture of support he reached over and squeezed her hand. She barely responded.

"How the hell is he going to continue living by himself?" she asked, almost rhetorically. "Damnit, Marshall, I practically had to lift him out of that recliner onto the bed bodily. He can't weigh more than a hundred and twenty pounds. He really is dying, Marshall."

He waited for the tears. All he saw was a cool concern in Rose's pretty eyes.

"The cirrhosis seems pretty far advanced," he offered, trying to remain objective.

She nodded. "But he's really adamant about staying in this house. He doesn't want to leave. It's his home. He said that if he's going to die soon he wants to be here."

"That's understandable," Marshall commented. "But is it safe?"

"I doubt it. The visiting nurse and home health aide are in and out twice a week. And I'm not about to pay for a live-in companion or even a private duty nurse."

"What about you, Rose? Would you consider taking care of him for a while? It probably won't be that long."

"I've considered it Marshall, believe me. But my research project is at such a critical stage. And the vote on the department chairmanship is coming up next month. If I took a leave of absence, I could just as well kiss that position good-by. Once this work-related stuff is settled, maybe I could help out."

"That may be too late."

"Then it will be too late."

The harshness in her voice bothered him. Maybe she wasn't so warm and compassionate after all. But she was faced with some tough questions, wasn't she? Hadn't she told him that after her mother's death her relationship with her father had been close? Was she abandoning him now or just doing her best under the circumstances? He sensed that she was a dedicated research scientist. Given that, he could appreciate her reluctance in putting her career on hold. What would he do in her shoes? He wasn't sure. But whatever her decision, it was his job to support her.

"Come over here," he said warmly, reaching his arm out along the edge of the sofa. She slid over and snuggled by his side, setting a warm cheek on his shoulder. With his cheek set against her soft auburn hair he detected the faint aroma of her shampoo.

Some time later Rose softly called his name. His eyes fluttered opened and he oriented to the sound. She, in turn, was regarding him with an amused smile on her lips. It was then that he realized he'd dozed off.

"I must be more tired than I thought," he commented groggily.

"I can understand that," she said, patting him gently on the cheek. "It's been a long day for both of us." Leaning forward she gave him a kiss on the lips. "Why don't we turn in? I'll show you your room." He nodded. "This way then," she said. "You'll be in my old room. It's on the far side of the kitchen."

He picked up his overnight bag and followed her back through the kitchen. They entered a darkened room on the other side and without pausing she crossed to the window and flipped on a lamp by the bed.

The bedroom came to life. Longer than it was wide, it ran parallel to the day room and shared a common wall with it. At one end a narrow casement window with bars on it looked out on the part of the yard that was to the right of the house. A second door, its white paint chipped and cracked, interrupted the right-hand wall. This, Marshall assumed, led to a closet or the bathroom.

A burgundy comforter covered the narrow single bed. A navy blue bedruffle hung down to the threadbare carpet. Covering the walls were posters of rock groups and movie stars. A plywood bookshelf and Rose's desk were lined up against the right-hand wall encroaching on the available space and making the room feel claustrophobic. He knew he was too tall for the bed and imagined his feet hanging over the end when he lay down.

But the place did seem tidy and clean. That was until he absently ran his fingertips along the desktop and made four cigar-shaped streaks in the thin layer of dust. Rose noticed this.

"There's really no one to clean in here," she explained. "And since I left for college, it's seldom used."

"Oh, that's okay with me. I don't usually notice that sorta stuff."

"Set your bag on the desk. There are fresh towels and washcloths in the bathroom. I'll be on the other side in my parents' room if you need anything."

"We share a bathroom?" Marshall asked.

"It's the only one in the house."

"I guess I'll knock before I use the toilet."

"If I'm worried about you seeing something you're not supposed to, I'll lock the door from the inside. But I doubt that will be necessary." With that she leaned forward, kissed him on the cheek and added, "Remember, if you need anything, I'm right next door. See you in the morning."

"Great," he replied. "Sleep well."

After Rose left Marshall stood there for a moment wondering if she was uneasy about hosting an adult male friend in her childhood home with dear old Dad in the next room. But then again, he couldn't imagine Rose being uneasy about anything. Either way, if they were going to be intimate this weekend, it would have to wait.

From his overnight bag he extracted a pair of shorts and a T-shirt, then settled comfortably in the narrow bed with a foam pillow propped up behind his back. He returned to his novel but the poster on the wall above across from him caught his eye. It was an ad for a rock concert by The Ramones, a band Marshall was unfamiliar with. He wondered if it was a favorite of Rose's from her teenage years.

This drew him to the other posters to the walls. The groups had strange names like the New York Dolls, Iggy Pop and the Sex Pistols. Another by the side of the bed displayed four musicians in black leather costumes their faces were grotesquely made-up. The group's name was KISS.

Were these musicians the spokesmen for teenager Rose? Did they reflect her angry, isolated adolescence, crystallized in a loud, violent counterculture? He tried to imagine the turbulent ideas and agitated emotion in her post-pubertal body.

Marshall walked over to his overnight bag and removed a pair of pants and shirt. Under the pretense of looking for a hanger, just in case Rose walked in, he opened the closet and checked out it contents. On a short pole hung about two dozen items, jeans and cotton pants, shirts, mostly flannel and denim, a couple of dresses, only one skirt which was long. Lined up on the closet's wooden floor were hiking boots, old tennis shoes, snakeskin cowboy boots, and two pairs of black pumps. In a cardboard storage box tucked off in the corner Marshall found board games and about a dozen movie magazines.

Standing back up he was eye-level was a shelf that was mounted above the rack of clothes. A row of shoeboxes was piled there with names written in neat block letters on side panels facing him. Richie Balaban, Chris Cogenhaur, Gary Perlmutter. Below each name was a set of dates. He took down one of the boxes, the one labeled with Richie Balaban's name, and noted that his stretch of time was from March 3, 1980 to July 7, 1980. Easing back on the bed, Marshall investigated the contents of the box.

What he found was a teenage girl's mementos: stacks of photographs, letters, cards, and notes written in sloppy cursive. There was a coin from the Erie County Fair and two unexploded firecrackers. The snapshots Marshall found interesting. Most were of a not unattractive fair-haired young man dressed similar to the rock musicians in the posters with a black leather vest, a denim shirt, frayed jeans held up loosely by a chain belt, and wrists adorned by thick metal bracelets. Richie even had tattoos on his arms and chest.

Marshall recognized Rose in a couple of the pictures. Outside her pale blue cottage-style house, she posed next to a large Harley-Davidson motorcycle. Another displayed her in a two-piece bathing suit at some beach, the green-black water behind her, a lighthouse off to the left. On the back of the photo was written, 'Presque Isle #9.'

He studied the image of Rose as a sixteen-year-old. Despite the short dark hair and chubby figure, she didn't look that much different from her adult version. But despite the similarity, the picture bothered him. It was the expression on her face that made him feel uneasy. Hard and defiant, she wore a scowl that brimmed with disgust and impatience. Maybe she was having a bad day? Or had the person who was taking the picture made her angry? How much of the time had she spent angry in those days?

He skimmed the notes and letters. From what he could tell, Rose and her boyfriend Richie had become a couple for a while, spending evenings and week-ends together, going to concerts and movies, or hanging out in the parking lot of the nearby bowling alley. Out on the Isle they had sex frequently and with a frenzied, lustful bent. Rose's diary went into great detail this part of their relationship.

Then, an incident occurred at the junior prom that exploded the emotionally charged relationship into pieces. The evening had started off memorably enough, with a romantic dinner at a local seafood restaurant followed by a ride to the high school's gymnasium in Richie's father's Cadillac. Then sometime during the party, after a few dances with her, Richie slipped out of the gym, ostensibly to smoke a cigarette with some of his buddies in the faculty parking lot. When he didn't return right away Rose went looking for him. What she found was her boyfriend necking with one of the sophomore girls.

A heated argument ensued during which Rose fired a long series of accusations and insults at him. Richie didn't take the censure well and their fight escalated into a pushing match. When the dust finally settled Rose was driven home by her girlfriend's date in a ripped soiled dress, her hair in disarray, her pride severely wounded.

The disappointment and hurt was chronicled in Rose's subsequent journal entries. Once Ritchie started to date this new girl Rose abandoned any hope of getting him back. Instead she focused on revenge. In one entry she outlined a plan to steal her aunt's Warfarin, a pharmaceutical grade rat poison, and slip it into his beer at the next party.

Another entry described ways she could sabotage his motorcycle, like cutting the brake cables or pouring salt into the gas tank to ruin the engine. She also imagined several ways of getting back at the sophomore girl, ranging from rumors about her sexual orientation to pushing her over the balcony at the next rock concert.

Beware the woman scorned, Marshall thought as the hair on the back of his neck bristled. *But she wasn't even a woman at that time—just a girl.*

He picked up another picture of Rose standing next to the Harley. In this one, the motorcycle's tires were flat. The scornful expression on Rose's face was gone. In its place was triumph. Her right hand hanging limp by her side was holding what looked like a steak knife.

It looks like she'd actually achieved a measure of revenge on poor Richie, he concluded, *and had the chutzpah to document it on film.* Flipping the picture over, he noted that 'All's well that ends well!' was neatly printed on the yellowing Kodak paper.

Feeling exhausted by this immersion into a segment of Rose's turbulent past, Marshall returned the shoebox to the shelf. He hesitated then took down the other two. Inside he found similar sets of memorabilia. The course of Rose's relationships had a repetitive pattern. They each began with excitement, hope, and enthusiasm. Then something happened and the boy lost interest. In Chris' case another female came into the picture. Gary, on the other hand, left town abruptly, disappearing without warning or explanation. And from what Marshall could tell from Rose's entries, each time they left she was devastated.

Marshall settled back under the maroon comforter, the boxed chronicles safely back on their shelf, and lay there for some time reflecting on the vulnerable young girl who had been repeatedly hurt. Did all the vindictiveness that followed represent the dark side of Rose's personality that he needed to bring to the surface? Given its depth and breadth he hoped he could control it when it did. With that grim notion preoccupying his thoughts, he flipped off the light and went to sleep.

Some time later Marshall was deep in the midst of a lurid dream with sinewy figures in black leather masks and capes playing distorted instruments upon a dimly lit stage and adolescents in cutoffs and biking vests dancing to the loud dissonant music. The doorknob turned with an eerie creak. He awoke with a start. The next thing he knew another body was under the covers facing him.

"I couldn't sleep," Rose said softly. "I hope you don't mind."

"Of course I don't mind," he said, his voice still heavy with sleep.

She was wearing a sheer nightgown with a v-neck, its hem only reaching to her mid thigh. She pressed up against him, her thigh burrowing between his, her soft full breasts flush against his chest. He felt himself stirring. Seconds later he was aroused.

Well, this is a pleasant surprise, he said to himself, savoring his excitement. *And just imagine, I thought I'd have to wait.*

His arms were around her. She nestled close then moved her face so that her lips brushed against his. She settled her head on the pillow. Their cheeks met. He could feel the tiny hairs around her lips like cropped threads of a cashmere sweater grazing his skin. He moved slightly and discovered a soft irregular mole near the corner of her mouth.

He was pulsating now, his breath short. He hadn't been this aroused for years, perhaps ever. She shifted her head slightly. Their lips met, barely touching, lingering for several delicious moments until she pulled back.

He knew she was ready. He took his right arm from around her shoulders and worked it into the crevice between her thighs. Through the nightgown and underwear he could feel moisture there. He raised the hem with his fingertips and walked up her leg toward her crotch.

"Marshall," she whispered softly into her ear. "Not tonight, dear. Just hold me."

For a second he was taken aback. Had he done something wrong? Hadn't she wanted him to take the initiative? Then he relaxed, recalling her dilemma.

"Not with Dad so near," she warned. "I just need someone to hold me tonight."

"I understand."

Then she removed her leg from between his, wriggled free of his arms, turned so that her back was pressed up against him and was soon asleep. Marshall, despite their aborted lovemaking, felt satisfied. Contentedly, he followed suit.

chapter fourteen

presque isle

A staccato knock on the door woke Marshall. His eyes opened to a partly cloudy Erie morning. Slipping his spindly legs out from under the covers he got up and opened the door. Rose greeted him wearing a bright yellow blouse, khaki shorts and tan sandals.

"Sleep well?" she asked brightly.

"Uh-huh," he replied, vaguely recalling that just a few hours ago she'd been under the covers with him. Or was that a dream? "How about you?"

"Like a log."

She breezed by him into the room and raised the Venetian blinds. With a grunt she lifted the window allowed a waft of warm humid air drift into the room. Marshall smelled fresh cut grass mixed with a seashore scent that must've been blowing inland off the lake.

"How soon can you be ready? There's practically nothing in the fridge to eat. I'm heading over to the mini-market on the avenue. Wanna take a walk?"

"Sure. I'll be ready in fifteen minutes."

Twenty minutes later they were strolling along the curbless street heading in an easterly direction. The clouds parted and an irregular patch of morning sky peeked through. Marshall checked his watch. It was nine-thirty. They passed clusters of young children playing, some on the porches, others riding bikes. Above, a low-flying aircraft roared.

"That's the third jet plane I've seen this morning," Marshall noted. "They all look like they're coming in for a landing."

"Erie International's a couple miles west of here, just on the other side of the railroad tracks."

"That must be pretty convenient."

"It would be, if we ever went anywhere."

Twenty-fourth Street ended at Midland. They continued up a concrete driveway, by a large yellow ranch house across two back yards and another house before emerging on the next street over.

"A friend of mine used to live back there. Her father was transferred to Cleveland just before I left for college so they sold the place. Now I'm not sure who owns it. The mini-market is on the next block. And that's Cannondale Park," she added pointing across the street. "I spent many a summer there before my mother finally let me bike out on the Isle."

The sprawling park reminded Marshall of the playgrounds of his youth, the swings, slides, and jungle gyms giving way to tennis courts and baseball fields. A pair of rusting batting cages stood diagonally across from one another.

Glancing over at Rose, who was silently strolling beside him, he sensed how she seemed a part of the fabric of this lower middle-class neighborhood. Marshall pictured himself integrated into this scenario, a family man with a wife and children nestled in some residential community living the life he'd only imagined.

He had no children of his own. Life with Bernice in Manhattan, with the traffic, the crime, and the unbridled tension was not conducive to a conventional family life. But he was back in Pittsburgh now, in a city of neighborhoods with friendly people and manageable terrain. Picturing himself as a man with a family seemed somehow easier.

Then he paused to take an objective look at what he was considering. Was he actually imagining a future with a woman he scarcely knew and had never slept with? Was that ridiculous, or what?

And for godsakes, Marshall, he admonished himself. *At least you should follow through with the divorce before fantasizing about a whole new life.*

They purchased provisions at the Stop-N-Go. Back at the house Rose made eggs with toast, hash browns, and sizzling strips of bacon. It was such a basic breakfast and the likes of which he hadn't had for months. And it was delicious.

Mr. Shaw joined them at the dining room table. Despite Rose's series of questions, he ate with slow deliberateness and said nothing. Before she left for her meeting with the social worker, they helped the old man back into the day room.

Rose left for her meeting. After she returned around noon they packed.

"Ready for some fun?" she asked as he walked into the living room. "We'll stop here later and see that dad gets his dinner. Now it's time to head for the beach."

With the Firebird's canvas top down, Rose drove along Route 832 toward Presque Isle State Park. The road curved to the right before merging seamlessly with Peninsula Drive. Marshall consulted a map he'd picked up at the Stop-N-Go and noticed that the topography of the Isle resembled a goose with its long neck curving southward back toward the mainland. Dense woodland was crisscrossed by hiking tails and dotted with dozens of small lakes. The beaches were along the perimeter.

"The beaches are numbered," Rose informed Marshall. "My favorite has always been number nine. It's also called Pine Tree. It's big and has the best surf. And there's this charming little lighthouse where I like to eat my lunch."

Marshall thought of the snapshot of Rose in the Richie Balaban memorabilia collection but kept the association to himself. Ten minutes later, after twisting along the narrow perimeter road, Rose pulled into a large parking lot. She cut the engine and announced that they'd arrived.

Pine Tree Beach stretched for about two city blocks and was composed of equal parts sand and small stones. From the edge of the parking lot Lake Erie's blue-black water appeared about seventy-five yards away. Marshall scanned the beach where hundreds of bathers were lying under a wide variety of colorful umbrellas or sunning on blankets, towels, beach chairs, or boogie boards. He turned left and noticed that the crowd thinned out in that direction. About five hundred yards away stood a white lighthouse. Tapping his arm, Rose directed him in that general direction.

They trudged about fifty yards. "Here's a good spot," Rose indicated in a clipped voice. He couldn't help but notice her labored breathing. She bent over and clutched her chest. He asked what was the matter, but she waved him off and sat down on a nearby boulder. After composing herself, she told him where to position the blanket. By the time he had the four corners secured with his sandals and their lunch bag, Rose was already rubbing oil onto her arms and legs.

"Could you get my back?" she asked him.

"Sure."

He squeezed a handful of the emollient on his palm and began working it into her skin. Rose's colorful one-piece bathing suit exposed her back down to the waist. Up the front, two Lycra bands supported her breasts, before knotting behind her neck. The crevice between her breasts all the way down to her navel was bare. The effect, he decided, was extremely sexy.

"Mmmm," she hummed. "That feels wonderful. You've got great hands, Dr. Friedman. You should've been a surgeon."

"Thanks," he said, "but I couldn't stand the stress in the OR. Your muscles seem extremely tight. Is that from your meeting with the social worker this morning?"

"I suppose so," she replied, "although I thought things went well. We decided that he needs to be placed, but not right away. We're looking for a way to keep him in the house for a little while long."

"How long's 'a little while'?" Marshall asked.

"At least a month. He has a health plan from the ceramics factory that supplements Medicare and will cover a home health aide three days a week. I'll spring for some private duty help the other days. But I can't do that indefinitely. Home Care will check on him twice a week. But before the fall he'll probably be in the Veterans' Home."

"He's not going to like it."

"I know. But that's too bad. He should've thought of that while he was pickling his liver all those years."

"Ouch!" Marshall said, reacting to the harshness of her comment. Rose must have thought it was the sun.

"Do you want me to get your back?" she asked.

"If you have something stronger than that Crisco I just used on yours."

"There's some SPF 15 in my bag."

"Good."

He turned away from her and soon felt a ribbon of cool cream slither down his spine. Her big, strong hands caressed him, smoothing then rubbing the tanning lotion into his hairy back. At first he tensed up, then relaxed, as she worked the balm deep into his muscles.

"That feels incredible," he told her, his chin sinking lower into his chest. "If I didn't know better I'd think you did this for a living."

"Maybe I did," she replied playfully.

Lying supine on the blanket, with his eyes shut behind his sunglasses, Marshall surrendered himself to the lassitude of the August afternoon. As the soothing warmth of the summer sun baked his moist skin his mind started to drift. Shouting children, scolding parents, barking dogs, and the monotonous regularity of the surf faded into the background. He imagined a parade of beautiful young women clad in skimpy colorful bikinis, strolling along the sand, their unsteady footing exaggerating the sway of their nubile bodies.

"Something's got you excited," Rose commented. He flinched, startled by the sound of her voice. Raising his eyelids a sliver he noticed that she'd propped herself up and was practically hovering over him.

"What?" he asked, trying to recall her comment.

"Whatever you were dreaming about, it seems to have had an effect. I was just wondering, that's all."

Abruptly the bulge in his bathing suit became evident to him too. Feeling a bit embarrassed, he told her about the bikini clad women.

"Interesting scene," was her only comment. Anxious to change the subject, he suggested they take a dip in the water. "Good idea," she agreed. "After that we can have lunch over by the lighthouse."

On any other day Marshall would have considered the food Rose had brought along basic and uninteresting. Today it was some of the best he'd ever tasted. Ravenously he consumed two hefty corned beef sandwiches, a double portion of potato salad, a handful of chips, and two packages of Twinkies.

Afterward they lingered at the picnic table, watching the surf and savoring the solitude. Two other couples were sunbathing nearby, but the scattered boulders and rolling sand dunes kept them pretty isolated. Marshall picked up a piece of wood, about the size of a maestro's baton, and started to play with it. Bleached to a powdery white it was as smooth as if scrubbed with sandpaper.

Rose stood and gathered their trash, disposing it in a can by the base of the lighthouse. After returning their picnic basket to the beach site, she suggested they take a walk to work off the meal.

The Sidewalk Trail started directly across Peninsula Drive. They slipped under the wooded canopy into the cooler shaded air. Maples, pines, oaks, and junipers bordered the concrete path, species indigenous to northwestern Pennsylvania. Marshall took a deep breath and relished the musty, oddly fresh scent of wet wood. He noted how the surface was concrete. Rose explained how the first lighthouse keeper, needing a path to Misery Bay where he docked his boat, had paved it.

"There's a monument to Commodore Perry there," Rose told him. "He fought the British in 1813 in the Battle of Erie. Most of the ships were built from local timber right in Misery Bay. A replica of the boat, The Niagra, is docked in Erie harbor across the sound from Presque Isle. There's a really great seafood restaurant I plan to take you to tonight for dinner."

"I'd like that," Marshall told her.

The area around Misery Bay was packed with tourists. They strolled over to the memorial, which looked like a miniaturized version of the Washington Monument. Commodore Perry's story was documented on a series of panels bolted to the base of the concrete structure.

"So the bay's name refers to the hardships that the men suffered during the winter following the Battle of Lake Erie," Marshall paraphrased.

"That's right," she agreed. "It's a place I can relate to."

By the time they returned to Beach Number Nine, the sun-soaked afternoon was beginning to wind down. Marshall estimated that the number of bathers had dwindled by three-quarters. He set his alabaster stick on the blanket and squinted up at the sun, now fading to a pale shade of yellow. The sky was milky white.

Rose came over and suggested a swim. Once in the water she challenged him to race out to one of the rock formations positioned like a granite battleship about two hundred yards from the beach. Although she started out fast, she faded just as quickly and he won. A half-hour later, after they'd frolicked in the surf for a while, they emerged from the bubbling surf.

Back by the dune Rose started gathering up their stuff, suggesting that they call it a day. And as had become his habit during much of this weekend excursion to Erie, Marshall submissively agreed.

chapter fifteen

before bed and breakfast

Their romantic dinner by the lake in a charming little seafood restaurant at the foot of Holland Street became another chapter in what, for Marshall, was turning into an idyllic weekend. Seated in the shadow of a reconstructed version of the post-colonial brig, Niagara, they dined on lobster and king crab and swapped anecdotes from their past. Across the water the sun turned from a pale yellow disc into a glossy orange sphere before dipping behind the shadowy woodlands of Presque Isle.

An hour earlier, after taking their post-beach showers in Rose's house in Millcreek, they had bidden farewell to Mr. Shaw. Standing on the threshold to the day room he heard Rose tell her father he would be permitted to remain in his home a while longer. From the dubious expression on the wrinkled old face Marshall wasn't sure he appreciated what she'd said. Or perhaps he just didn't believe her.

Then, Rose left the day room ahead of Marshall. For some reason Frank Shaw's expression brightened. He caught the Marshall's eye and with a bony right index finger gestured him near. Fascinated by this bit of animation and even more curious to see what the old man wanted, Marshall complied. Edging over to the lounger, he leaned forward until his ear almost touched the man's dry cracked lips.

In a hoarse whisper the old man said, "Be sure to take care of yourself."

Marshall regarded this as a piece of lighthearted advice, a casual comment one might make to another as they part company. It was another form of, 'Have a nice day.' But, as he was about to respond in kind, Marshall noticed a frigidly candid look in the old man's rheumy eyes, an honest expression tainted with apprehension and loathing. Involuntarily, a shudder passed through Marshall's lanky frame. This was no polite pleasantry, he realized. This was an unbridled warning.

But what could he possibly be warning me about? Marshall wondered, as he picked up his overnight bag and left the rank smelling room.

They left the restaurant and headed up the coast on East Lake Road. After passing through a heavily industrialized portion of Erie they skirted around Lawrence Park then continued through the residential tree lined streets of Harbor Creek. About ten miles north of downtown Erie, Rose slowed the Firebird before making a sharp left. A two block long access road led to a large three-story wooden structure. It was a stately manor with a broad deep porch, a gravel driveway, ornate porticos, and brown shutters. Marshall peered out his window and noticed an elderly man sitting on the porch rocking in a chair and smoking a pipe.

"This is the old Pitcarin mansion," Rose replied before Marshall could ask. "The family was the largest scrap metal broker in the county until the late fifties. The most recent generation wasn't much into the business and eventually the oldest brother sold the house to the Gettys. That's Mr. Getty sitting on the porch. One of his cousins lives in Millcreek. He and his wife Mary bought the place the year after I left for college and made it into a bed and breakfast. I've been here for meals but never stayed overnight. I figured this weekend would give me a chance to try it out."

Marshall nodded and smiled. After stretching his long legs, he popped the trunk and tended to the luggage. A few minutes later he joined Rose up on the wood-paneled porch.

"Elmer," she said to the proprietor, "I'd like you to meet a friend of mine. His name is Marshall Friedman and he's a psychiatrist at the medical center in Pittsburgh where I work. Marshall, this is Mr. Getty."

"Nice to meet you," Marshall said, shaking the older man's thin bony hand. He looked like a slightly younger, healthier version of Rose's father, thin but not scrawny with sharp, chiseled features. "Rose started to tell me a little about the mansion while we were in the car."

"Well, hard to call it a mansion, son," Elmer Getty corrected, his voice low-pitched, deep and clear, "but there's sure plenty to tell about it. After you two get settled in maybe we can set a spell in the living room and I'll share some stories with ya."

"I'd like that," Marshall told him.

They went inside. A corner of the spacious living room had been sectioned off into a reception area. Behind a tall narrow counter stood an antique cherry wood roll top desk and a small squat table cluttered with a few small business machines. A partitioned sorter, like an oversized spice rack, was mounted on the wall, its square slots labeled with a dozen or so room numbers.

While Rose attended to the registration process, Marshall surveyed the rest of the room. It seemed dark but not gloomy with high ceilings and the walls papered in a pastoral design. The furniture, he decided, could have been culled from the local antique stores. Returning his attention to the registration desk, Marshall heard Elmer Getty tell Rose, "Top floor room straight ahead, just like you requested. Enjoy."

"I'm sure we will," Rose assured him. But it was toward Marshall that she directed her glance. Was that a mischievous sparkle he detected in her hazel green eyes?

"You'll have to hike up the two flights," Mr. Getty said apologetically. "I never got around to installing that elevator my older guests keep harpin' about. Much too expensive for a small operation like this."

"No problem, Mr. Getty. We can manage."

Marshall took this as a cue and gathered up their luggage. By the foot of the staircase he paused by a full-sized replica of a golden retriever. The canine had been mounted in a sitting position, its head cocked to one side, its long tongue lolling out past the hinge of its jaw, a friendly, almost human, expression in its inanimate eyes.

Rose paused about three steps up the first flight of stairs, noticing what had caught Marshall's attention. She called over to the proprietor, "This looks a lot like Blue, Mr. Getty."

"It is Blue," he replied.

Marshall was impressed by their room's antique charm. The arched ceiling had exposed wooden beams and the papered walls displayed equestrian scenes replete with horses, stables, and farmhouses. A huge rectangular window dominated one wall and below it was a padded window seat with upholstery in the same design as the curtains. There was a sturdy wooden armoire, a broad chest of drawers and a sitting chair up against the other wall. But more than anything the room space was dominated by a classic style four-poster bed with a chenille spread and a half dozen pillows and bolsters arranged tastefully upon it. As Marshall set his overnight bag down on the Oriental rug that partially covered the hard wood floor he could just imagine some of the romps which had taken place within this romantic room.

"It's just the way I imagined," Rose said after she finished looking around. "They even have one of those old-fashioned tubs in the bathroom. You know, the kind with four legs that look like claws."

She assigned Marshall a few drawers in the chest and they emptied their bags. After lining up her toiletries up on the bathroom shelf, Rose came out and found Marshall standing at the foot of the bed. Without preamble she draped her strong arms around his thin neck, stood high on her sandal-clad feet, and gave him a firm kiss on the mouth. Stirred by the passion and excited about what would come next he started to swell. But she broke the contact and suggested they go downstairs and sit with Mr. Getty for a while. He deflated.

"I want to hear some of those stories he promised to tell us," she explained.

Not even attempting to feign enthusiasm he said, "All right."

They returned to the first level where their host was relaxing in his easy chair reading the paper. The colonial-style lamp gave the room a shadowy, almost somber feel. In the background Marshall recognized the twangy, melodic strains of a country western love song. Rose sat down next to Marshall on the sofa and took his hand. They waited for their host to acknowledge them.

After a few moments, without putting the paper down, Marshall heard him ask, "Coffee?"

"None for me," Rose replied. "How about you, Marshall?"

"No, thanks."

"After-dinner drink?" Elmer Getty asked, this time folding the newspaper and setting it on his lap. "There's a few of those fancy liqueurs everyone's always raving about in the cabinet. The Missus always insisted that we stock that kinda stuff for the guests. I myself never developed a taste for them. Too damn sweet. I'll take my Canadian Club any day." Marshall noticed a half-full bottle of the popular whiskey on the table by Mr. Getty's elbow.

"Elmer," Rose said moving her hand to Marshall's thigh, "I haven't seen Mrs. Getty since we got here. Is she away?"

"You could say that," Mr. Getty replied. "Mary passed two years ago. Died suddenly of something the doctors called a ruptured cerebral aneurysm. It was late one night while she was sittin' up in the bedroom watchin' the CMA awards on TV."

"That's too bad," Rose told him. "I'm sorry to hear that."

"She was a wonderful woman, my Mary," Elmer Getty said. "Gentle as the day was long."

"I bet you miss her."

"Can't help it," he acknowledged slowly.

They sat around in a cloud of silence for a few more minutes. Rose began massaging the inside of Marshall's thigh and soon he was hard as a rock. Totally distracted from the homey setting he found himself desperate to know when they would finally go up to their room.

Rose, on the other hand, seemed intent on seeing this session through. She finally broke the lull by asking Mr. Getty about those interesting stories he'd promised to share with them. The old man first regarded her intently, then nodded.

"All right," Mr. Getty said in his characteristic drawl. "See that couple pictured on the mantel." He pointed a long bony figure toward the fireplace. "That there is Bess and Charlie McCormick. They celebrated their seventy-fifth right here last fall. The Today Show used a copy of that photo the morning after they spent the night here."

"That's charming," Rose said. Mr. Getty beamed with a kind of vicarious pride.

"But I guess the event that stands out in my mind the most," the old man continued, "was when Tom Ridge, after he won the race for governor in ninety-four, rented out the whole house for the weekend. His entire campaign team stayed here with their wives as a little prize for working so hard to get him elected. He's from around these parts, you know."

"Of course I know, Elmer," Rose said sweetly. "I'm from these parts, too. But Marshall doesn't know the story, so why don't you fill him in on the details while I go up and get ready for bed."

Marshall, her teasing making him almost crazed with desire, was about to protest. But a purposeful glance from her hazel green eyes reminded him that it would be rude to cut the old man off just when he was about to relate his proudest moment.

So instead of begging off Marshall mumbled graciously, "I'll see you upstairs."

Rose leaned over, gave his crotch another firm squeeze, kissed him lightly on the cheek and whispered, "You know I'll make it worth your while." As his lustful eyes followed her shapely frame up the narrow staircase, he began to pulsate even harder.

chapter sixteen

passion play

With his heart pounding wildly Marshall approached the third floor landing. A shimmer of yellow light peeked from under their door, which was odd because the room had no fireplace. Tapping lightly on the door he waited for Rose to respond. It opened to a darkened chamber hauntingly illuminated by dozens of candles, the apparent source of the penumbra he'd seen coming from under the portal.

Marshall stepped into the room just as Rose emerged from the shadows, clad in a sexy black lingerie ensemble, consisting of a frilly bra and matching bikini briefs. There was a pair of silver bracelets on her wrists and black spiked heels on her feet.

The effect was both disarming and arousing.

"Welcome, Marshall," she greeted him, her voice soft and husky. She gently took his arm and escorted him to the bed. "May I help you with your clothing?"

"Uh," Marshall stammered, still awed by her appearance. "Sure."

Rose left him by the bed and shut the door. Marshall heard a soft click followed by the thump of the deadbolt lock. There'd be no further disturbances tonight, he realized. She returned to the bed and began unbuttoning his shirt. As her nimble fingers traveled down the expanse of his chest his eyes were glued on hers, their hazel green color transformed into a glistening onyx by the shimmering candlelight.

Once his shirt was undone Rose caressed his hairy chest. Using the fleshy part of her soft palms she made broad sweeping motions titillating his breasts and leaving elliptical bands of goose bumps on his skin. After her final arc Rose slipped her fingertips into the armholes of his shirt and an instant later the garment rolled off his shoulders and slipped to the floor.

His pants, a pair of loose-fitting khakis he'd changed, came next. With the belt loosened she eased down his zipper. Finally, with her free hand she reached inside his boxers and liberated his engorged member.

"I'm glad you're as excited as I am," she commented, her voice delicate and enticing. A playful smile danced lightly on her full, painted lips. As Marshall's knees nearly buckled all he could do was nod.

Rose helped him onto the mattress. The chenille spread was gone. She eased him along the blanket until his head rested against a pair of pillows that were propped up against the broad heavy headboard. Once supine she removed his loafers, socks, pants, and briefs. Next she asked him to position his arms and legs in a spread-eagle position. As he extended his limbs she joined him atop the bed, balancing unsteadily on her knees, leaning over and massaging much of his body.

"Comfortable?" she whispered into his ear, nuzzling her face under his jaw, nibbling kisses along the side of his neck. His hoarse voice failed him again. He just nodded. "Good," she said and withdrew.

He rested for a moment while she slipped off the bed and began undressing herself. He found her movements slow and sensuous. His semi-tumescence rapidly reached full mast.

Delicious moments passed. His arousal became nearly irrepressible. Rose, apparently sensing his condition, leaned over and pinched the tip of his erection. It relaxed.

She lay down on the bed next to him. The touch of her skin felt electric. He turned to face her. Their lips met in a deep passionate kiss. She reached down and fondled him, the caresses sending shudders down his spine. Fueled by the intensity of his desire, he was immersed under cascading waves of pleasure. A feeling that could only be described as pure ecstasy washed over him. Then she disengaged.

He felt abandoned—but only briefly. Her ministrations resumed. They began as a sensation of warmth, followed by moisture, mixed with a gentle rhythmic motion. Like a damp velvet glove sliding over his erection, Marshall felt Rose's lips sliding ever so slowly along the length of him. He peered down and in the muted glow of the amber candlelight he watched in amazement as Rose Shaw brought him to an incredible climax.

He wasn't sure how long he'd been asleep. It couldn't have been long. The flickering candles still offered the room its only illumination. They seemed to have plenty of tallow left. He was resting on his side now, covered by the spread. Rose was lying there too, facing him, her eyes open, a proud smile on her radiant face. When he saw her there and recalled the wonderful crescendo, he smiled back. She reached over. With the palm of her hand she caressed his cheek.

"My turn?" she asked.

"It would be my pleasure," he replied, his voice dry and raspy.

And for next hour or so Marshall dedicated his entire body and soul to making passionate love to this amazing woman. And in the process, for the first time in more years than he cared to admit, he enjoyed the delights of a polyorgasmic night.

chapter seventeen

the slate beach

Marshall couldn't remember when he'd slept so well, at least not since he'd left Manhattan. And as a bonus he awoke the next morning to a pale gray sky and the broad naked back of Dr. Rose Shaw. As he watched her chest swell with the rhythm of her repose, he reflected on the previous night. Ostensibly he'd achieved a level of pleasure rarely experienced before. The notion filled him with optimism and the promise of a rich and satisfying future. Was this the soulmate for whom he'd been searching? Certainly it was too early to tell, but there was definitely potential here.

As if roused by his thoughts about her, Rose stirred. First she rolled onto her back then raised her right arm lazily in his direction. He reached up, cradled her palm in his, and brought her hand to his lips. She emitted a low-pitched moan, turned her head, and gave him a sleepy, slit-eyed smile. Then she eased around, setting her chest against his and pressing her thigh against his groin. Gently she moved her leg up and down until he was hard. They made love again.

Later, when he reminisced about this incredible weekend in Erie, and he tended to reflect upon it frequently in the weeks to come, Marshall would take particular delight in recalling this early morning intimacy. He would appreciate it for its tender and measured rhythm, their respectful, intelligent exploration of each other's bodies, the attention to detail, and the gradual crescendo that culminated in a delicious climax. Rather than the lust-laden ecstasy of the night before, he wondered if that morning-after interaction would set the tone for their subsequent time together.

The aroma of eggs and coffee sifted all the way up to their room. Breakfast was being served. By ten o'clock they'd showered and headed downstairs. From midway along the first level staircase Marshall surveyed the dining area. He was amazed how different it looked in the lakeside daylight. Reaching the bottom of the staircase he paused to pat Ol' Blue on the head.

Three other couples were already seated around the long cloth-covered table. A freckle-faced teenage girl with a shock of carrot-colored hair showed them to their seats. By the time their coffee and juice had arrived they were ready to order.

Marshall sipped from his glass of cranberry juice and eavesdropped as Rose chatted with a slender ash-blonde woman at the head of the table to her left. The elderly woman and her husband, a large, ruddy-faced gentleman, were from nearby Meadville, forty miles south of Erie. They had chosen a weekend getaway at the Gettys as their forty-fifth anniversary celebration. After breakfast, they would be driving to Buffalo where their eldest daughter was hosting the family for a dinner party in their honor.

Marshall watched Rose interact with the amiable couple and was fascinated by how, in a matter of minutes, she'd discovered that, in addition to all this, the couple had a second daughter in Hamilton, Ontario, and their son, Richard was a captain in the Navy. His ship was docked in Newport Beach, Virginia. As Myra, the matriarch, expressed a heartfelt desire that her 'boy' would be permitted to fly up for the celebration, she casually gave Rose's hand a squeeze.

The young waitress interrupted Marshall's musings to see if he wanted more coffee. Already feeling wired from his first cup, he declined. He rarely drank coffee in the morning and never caffeinated. His rigid daily routine, he noted, had been violated once again.

As if a flower had settled on his skin, he felt Rose's palm softly light upon his outstretched hand. He turned to face the sparkle in her beautiful eyes, now more hazel than emerald in the daylight. She smiled broadly. His heart quickened, dazzled by how beautiful she appeared.

"Are you finished dear?" she asked sweetly. He warmed with the endearment. Glancing down at his plate, he noticed it was empty, but barely recalled consuming the meal.

"Sure."

"Good. There a special place by the lake I want to show you. Let's take a little walk. It'll help us work off breakfast."

"I'm game."

She rose to her feet, said good-bye to Myra and her husband then took Marshall's hand. Heading through the kitchen, they found Mr. Getty at the sink rinsing off the breakfast dishes.

"Great omelet, Elmer," she complemented him on their way past. "I love the way you mix in the cheese with the veggies. Nobody does it better."

"Thanks, Rosey," Mr. Getty said, barely looking up from his work. "You were always one of my biggest fans."

The screen door slammed as they stepped off the back porch and onto a dirt path that crossed the lawn. A couple hundred yards further, on the far side of a small wooded area, they emerged upon a small grassy field. Off to one side Marshall noticed a swing set, sliding board, and jungle gym. It was a small local park of some sort. Beyond the far edge the ground sloped downward. In the distance he could see a stretch of the lake.

Rose took his hand and led him toward the water. Near the center of the grassy field they paused for a moment by a rock the size of a small boulder. Without saying anything Rose pointed to a brass plaque bolted to one face. Marshall saw it and read the inscription.

>HALLI REID PARK
>NAMED FOR THE FIRST WOMAN
>TO SWIM ACROSS LAKE ERIE
>STARTING AT
>LONG POINT, CANADA AT
>6:00 P.M. AUGUST 8, 1993,
>SWIMMING 26 MILES
>TO ARRIVE AT
>FREEPORT BEACH
>10:30 AM AUGUST 9. 1993

"You know I was here when Halli reached this shore," Rose told him, "along with about a thousand other people. It was an amazing feat. Quite inspirational to tell you the truth." She slid her arm in the crook of his elbow and guided him down toward the water. "And it came at a time when I was a little desperate for inspiration," she continued. "I was home visiting Dad for a couple weeks in the summer, bored with my work in that genetics lab in Baltimore, and uncertain where I was heading next. It was a turning point and I wasn't sure what I wanted to do with my life. Sometimes I believe that seeing Halli accomplish that mark gave me the incentive to go after the job at the Hunt."

They paused at the edge of the field just before it sloped down toward the water. Marshall pulled her close to him and gave her a kiss on the top of her head. She looked up and kissed him back on the lips. It was the kind of tender moment, Marshall realized, that had been missing from his life. Choked with emotion, his chest ached and swelled.

The line of his gaze rested upon the beach along the water's edge. Instead of the sandy expanse he'd expected, stones, piles of sticks, and what looked like shingle-sized slabs of rock littered the narrow jagged stretch of shoreline. A little surprised by the nature of this unique terrain he walked over to take a closer look. Squatting down, he picked up one of the slabs.

Turning back to Rose he asked, "What *is* this stuff?"

"It's slate."

Intrigued by the notion he replied, "A slate beach?"

"Yep."

"How'd it happen?"

"It's apparently indigenous to the area, a reflection of the shoreline's rocky shelf."

"Interesting," he said with a slight nod. "I've never seen anything like it before."

"It is unique," she agreed. "Here. The stuff's all over the place. Let's walk a little farther up the coast and I'll show you. But be careful, it can be slippery, especially where it's wet."

Walking hand-in-hand, they began negotiating the flat rocks, stepping tentatively with Rose slightly ahead, leading the way. Marshall could feel the soles of his loafers slipping slightly on the glistening surface. They continued northward along the shoreline for about two hundred yards where a broad shallow creek interrupted their progress.

The tributary seemed to emerge from the woods to the east. Marshall checked the flow and noted it was brisk. The creek-bed had a slate floor too with broad rocky slabs stacked one atop the other like giant irregular stairs.

"Slip off your shoes," Rose suggested.

He glanced over at her. "You mean we're going to cross this thing too?"

"Yes, why?"

"Is it safe?"

"Of course it's safe. I've done it hundreds of times."

"If you say so."

Trusting her, Marshall removed his shoes and stepped gingerly into the broad shallow stream. Rose, her sandals hooked over her index finger, followed closely behind. He found the clear water cold, but refreshing. The broad steps, mostly flat and slick, harbored subtle ridges that helped anchor his footing, kneading into his soles like the knuckles of a masseuse.

When's the last time I did something this juvenile? he asked himself. *Decades. Or is it just spontaneous and natural? And does it really matter? I'm having fun.*

They reached the far side of the creekbed and clambered up the short steep hillside. Turning toward the lake Marshall noticed that here the slate beach appeared smoother, less cluttered, with a few larger boulders scattered among the stones and kindling. Rose seemed headed toward a pair of spherical rocks nestled among the shale about ten feet from the water's edge. She led Marshall over to them.

"This was where I used to come when I was a teenager," she told him as they sat down next to each other on the adjacent rocks, each the size of a large medicine ball. "I'd drive up after school to study or do homework. What I ended up doing was read movie magazines or write in my diary. It seemed so peaceful and isolated. I knew no one would bother me here."

He could appreciate her sentiment. The area was remote, if not desolate. The pale gray sky, like a high ceiling, extended out for miles before it blended imperceptibly with the dark foreboding water. Marshall peered out toward the horizon and spotted a cigar-shaped freighter. Heading north to south across it his field of vision, he watched it undulate amid the choppy waters. Nearby, noisy gulls scanned for fish.

"Do you bring your keys with you?" Rose said, startling him slightly.

"Keys?" he repeated. "As a matter-a-fact, I did. Why?"

"Give them to me and I'll show you."

He reached in his pocket then handed her the ring.

"What's this one for?" she asked, holding up his apartment key. He told her. "And this?" It was to his office. "And this is obviously to your car." There was a Mercedes logo on its base. "How about this one?"

At first he didn't recognize this last member of the ring. It had been a while since he'd needed it. Then he remembered.

"Oh, that's to my place in Manhattan."

"Good."

Rose reached over and picked up a thin slab of slate, about one foot-square. It had a smooth surface and rounded edges. She set it in her lap, held the key like a pen, and began etching lines on the surface. At first he had trouble figuring out what she was creating. Then he saw an engraved heart take shape surrounding a bunch of letters. Intrigued he shifted his attention from the rock tablet to Rose's face. On it she wore an intense expression, her eyebrows pinched, her forehead furrowed, her tongue protruding slightly.

She looks like a schoolgirl in a penmanship class, he decided.

After she finished her scratching, she took a moment to appraise her work. Then she handed it to him. "Here," she said proudly, "this is for you."

He accepted her gift and studied it. On the slate, within a crude valentine, Rose had written, "Rose Loves Marshall, 8/14/00" in irregular block letters. Through the heart she'd inscribed an arrow.

The tenderness of the gesture moved him. At first he didn't know how to respond. Then, almost without thinking, he said, "Thank you, Rose. I love you, too."

Marshall, swept up by this wave of emotion, set the slab down on his lap and held out his arms. Rose slid into them, flowing toward him like a warm summer breeze. They hugged fiercely then kissed with a passion that he had now come to expect from her. After they parted she set her head gently upon his shoulder.

He gazed down at the slab of slate and studied Rose's schoolgirl engraving. "Can I take this with me?" he asked, picturing it in a wrought iron holder on the mantel.

"I was hoping you'd let me leave it here," Rose countered. "I want to bury it in a place only the two of us knows about. Then years from now we can come back and dig it up. It'll remind us of today."

Marshall loved the idea, its romantic sentimentality touching his heart and making it ache all over again. He thought back on times when, as a schoolboy, he'd carved his initials and those of some girl he liked in the bark of one of the trees in Frick Park. Years later, while strolling along the paths in those same woods, he would inadvertently come across the memorial. The appreciation of it would instantly awaken a flood of pleasant memories about the childhood crush.

Rose took the slab, slid off the boulder, and knelt down behind her boulder. He watched as she removed a couple layers of shale. Into the shallow hole, like a rudimentary time capsule, she set the slate valentine.

"Now it's like we've been joined together and returned to the earth to be nourished and sustained," Rose said solemnly, peering up at him from her squat position. There wasn't a hint of sarcasm in her voice.

Marshall recalled a chapter toward the middle of his book, *When Good Men Go Bad.* In this particular section he had explored the notion that within the planet Earth resided the ultimate source of human energy, sustenance, and contentment. It was a concept he'd come to embrace. Now, perched on a boulder on a slate beach north of Erie, Marshall peered down upon Rose's radiant visage. Moved by the conviction in her tone and how her notion of earth-energy intermingled with his own true beliefs, he acknowledged that in this remarkable woman he had finally found a soulmate.

chapter eighteen

a conflict of interest

"So how did you like your first board of directors meeting, Marshall?" Bertram Hunter asked. The CEO stood at his waist high liquor cabinet mixing himself a drink.

"It was quite an experience," Marshall remarked from his seat by the desk. "There was such a broad diversity of the people sitting around the table. They really do come from all walks of life."

"I should say so," Hunter agreed, walking back over to his own chair. He handed Marshall a glass of pop. "Let me see now. We've got a city councilman, two corporate lawyers, several prominent businessmen, an economist, a celebrity, a few administrators, an industrialist, and of course a physician. It's a bright, accomplished, strongly opinionated group that seems to have the welfare of this institution as its highest priority." Settling in he added, "And it's a real privilege having those people around to help me make decisions about the clinic."

"You know, I've been a Steelers fan all my life," Marshall shared. "When Andy Russell walked in I was tempted to ask him for his autograph."

"Art Rooney Sr. was on the board until he died a couple of years ago. And regarding Andy," Hunter commented, tipping his glass toward Marshall, "If you think he was a great linebacker, you should see him manage a portfolio,"

"That just may be a valuable endorsement, Hunter. I've pretty much ignored my investments since getting here. Maybe I'll give Andy a call and see what he thinks."

"Good idea."

They sat sipping their drinks. Marshall absently glanced past Hunter out the large window behind the desk where he noticed an old woman in a tattered raincoat pushing a shopping cart along one of the windy paths of the city park. Seeing this homeless person made him appreciate how fortunate he was to be who he was at that moment. He glanced at the pyramidal-shaped mantel clock on one of the bookshelves. It was seven-thirty PM, an hour after his first board meeting ended.

"I'm glad we finally approved that new research building for the genetics department. I've been lobbying for that project for nearly eighteen months now."

"Judging from the architect's model it's going to be impressive," Marshall commented. "Five stories tall and a hundred and fifty thousand square feet of usable space. That's a huge chunk of work space."

"Just like I mentioned during my presentation to the Board," Hunter reiterated. "Once that building's finished we'll have the largest research facility of its kind anywhere from the NIH in D.C. to the Mayo Clinic in Rochester, Minnesota. And if you believe the pundits genetic engineering and molecular biology are the next great frontiers of medicine."

"And a great place for us to be at the start of a new millennium."

All this was pretty heady stuff, Marshall thought, being part of an institution that ranked up there with some of the top medical centers in the country. He looked across the large desk and expected his boss to be beaming with pride. Instead Hunter was hunched over with his hands folded on the desk.

My, he looks awfully tired, Marshall assessed. There were bags under his eyes and a pasty cast to his usually tan vibrant complexion. *He's lost some weight too. This job must be taking its toll.* Hunter straightened up and began massaging his chest. The gesture alarmed Marshall. *Maybe it's just a little indigestion. But then again, Sally did mention his heart? I wonder....*

"Exec's scheduled for the Friday after Labor Day, Marshall," Hunter said, leaning back and setting his head against the chair. "Several of the department head positions will be up for reappointment. Chris Jeffries submitted a list to me a week ago."

Marshall suddenly felt apprehensive. Had Hunter arranged this informal session to tell him his chairmanship was not going to be renewed?

"That's right," Marshall said trying to sound calm. "Jeffries is the new president of the medical staff. Any surprises? On the list I mean?"

"If you're worried about your chair, Marshall, you can stop right now. I went out and recruited you specifically for that position. And so far you've done a great job." Despite himself, Marshall emitted a sigh of relief. "But there are a couple spots that aren't as definite." Marshall inched forward waiting for Hunter's next comment. "Now that we have approval for the new genetics building," Hunter continued, "whoever chairs the Medical Research Department is going to wield a tremendous amount of power. Judging from the size of the expansion its budget will probably rise into the eight-figure territory. That means we need an extremely competent person to run things over there. I'm talking about someone who's dependable, highly motivated, and with impeccable credentials."

"Who's chief now?" Marshall asked.

"Trevor McCormick, but he's planning on an early retirement next year. He's been playing the research game for thirty-five years now. And he turned sixty last spring. Also, politically speaking, he tends to be somewhat conservative in his approach to research, more comfortable with clinical pharmacology projects and coordinating large multicenter trials. Jeffries thinks we need someone with more biotech savvy. Someone who has real hands-on experience in the lab. Someone on the cutting edge of that new genetics frontier we were just talking about."

"Who does that put in line for the job?" Marshall asked again.

"Why Rose Shaw, of course," Hunter replied. Marshall nodded. Then before he could comment Hunter continued, "Who I think is a great choice. She's bright, forthright and has started to publish the kind of research we're after in some very reputable journals. Trevor tells me that he's very impressed with her work.

"However, Marshall, you must realize that we're talking about a job that calls for more than a scientist working in a lab. We need someone who's comfortable functioning in an administrative capacity, who can interact effectively with the people in the department. It requires a person capable of devising and executing the kind of research plans which may ultimately have an institute-wide effect. And perhaps, most important of all, someone who can be depended upon to relate to the media and the public in a manner which will support the high standards and outstanding reputation of the Clinic."

"And Dr. Shaw? Do you feel she has these qualities?"

"Ah," Hunter replied, his hesitation ever so slight, "I believe so. But it's vital that I know for sure. At least as sure as possible." Marshall nodded, instinctively appreciating the CEO's concerns and hoping he could support him as he went through this period of soul searching. "Which is the main reason I asked you to stop by the office after the board meeting. I have a little project for you."

Marshall sat up straighter. "A project?" he asked both intrigued and a little apprehensive. "What sort of a project?"

Hunter hunched forward again, but this time his eyes were wide open and his expression solemn. "As you might have sensed during your short time here at the Hunt, Rose Shaw is a person who provokes strong reactions in people. Either you like her or you don't. And from what I can gather from my informal conversations with other members of the Executive Committee, they seem split roughly down the middle regarding her appointment. If we put it up for a vote, and it comes down to a tie, I'll be faced with casting the deciding vote. Thus, Marshall, when I walk into that meeting in early September, I want to have as much information on our candidate as possible."

"Which is understandable," Marshall concurred. "But how can I help?"

"You're the Chief of Psychiatry. You're quite well acquainted with personality dynamics. Who, more than you is better qualified to assess the psychological competency of a candidate for chairperson of an influential hospital department? Oh, sure, there are all kinds of psychological tests I can submit her to. But what I need is someone I trust to interpret them, someone who can assess the results in light of the demands of the job. That will give me a comprehensive profile of our candidate's personality strengths and weaknesses. Then I can go to exec and cast my vote responsibly. But for that I need some degree of confidence."

"Does that mean you have doubts about her?" Marshall asked.

"No, not really. Rose's record since coming to the Hunt has been exemplary. Her research is top notch and she seems to do her job in a competent, efficient manner. The project she's working on now is the kind of groundbreaking stuff I was referring too earlier. It should help set the tone for future projects here. But, and here's the bugaboo, three months ago, when she first applied for the department chairmanship, I felt obligated to go back and review her original employment application. What I found there were some inconsistencies, problems between what she recorded she'd done, and what we found out when we tried to confirm things."

"Inconsistencies?" Marshall repeated. "Like what?"

Before replying Hunter paused to rub his chest again. "I'd rather not delve into the specifics with you now, Marshall," he said evasively. "If you take on this job, I want to remove all bias from your evaluation. I'd rather you go in fresh. You know, with a clean slate."

Some clean slate, Marshall thought ruefully, flashing back on the weekend he'd spent with Rose in Erie and the two nights he'd slept with her since. But to his boss he only commented, "Of course I understand, Hunter. When would you need the report?"

"At least a week before the meeting. That'll give me some time to review it myself. And if I think it's warranted I'll be able to circulate the findings to the other members of the committee. After all, they're entitled to the same background data as I am. This way everyone can make an informed decision when she comes up for vote."

Marshall nodded, just beginning to appreciate the onerous task he was assuming. Contrary to what Hunter believed, he *did* have a strong bias. How couldn't he? Which meant he should disqualify himself without further discussion. But to do that would be to admit to Hunter that he and Rose were seeing each other. And this was something he wasn't ready to reveal. After all, he was still married. He had his reputation to consider. If their affair was brought to light, he had no idea how the hospital administration would regard it.

"All right," Marshall said, trying to mask whatever reluctance he felt toward the task. "I'll have it back to you two weeks from tomorrow. That'll give you a week to review and distribute it if necessary."

"Capital, Marshall. I knew I could count on you."

Hunter stood up walked around the desk and patted his staff psychiatrist on the back. Marshall, sensing the meeting was coming to an end, rose too. The CEO walked Marshall to the door, a fatherly arm slung around his shoulders.

"Now let's blow this joint for the night," he suggested jovially, "and get some well-deserved rest. Tomorrow's another long day for me. And, I suspect for you, too." Marshall stepped through the doorway. "Thanks for taking this on, Marshall. You're really showing yourself to be a team player."

"You're welcome, Hunter," Marshall replied.

As he turned to walk away he noticed the CEO rubbing his chest for a third time in an hour.

chapter ninteen

the profile

Marshall found he had plenty to think about during his twenty-minute ride home that evening. *Thank goodness I didn't make plans with Rose for tonight,* he sighed as he pulled onto the Parkway East. *I'm not sure I'd be able to act natural with her now that I have Hunter's little 'project' to do. How in the world am I to handle this evaluation?*

The most authentic course of action, he decided, would be to perform the assessment as requested. He was certainly competent enough to acquire, process, and formulate the data into a comprehensive report for the boss. But did competency imply objectivity? Probably not. And he seriously doubted his ability to be objective.

So what? he declared to himself. *So what if I'm not objective?* From what he already knew about Rose, he was pretty sure she could handle the job. Any bias he had toward her didn't really matter as long as she was qualified. Did it? And besides, if he were anticipating a long and intimate relationship with this woman, wouldn't one of his roles be championing her in the face of new challenges. This would be an opportunity to rehearse that role.

But, on the other hand, could assuming such a cavalier attitude ultimately compromise Hunter and the institute? After all, the CEO had, in good faith, brought him to Pittsburgh. He'd recognized Marshall's talents and accomplishments and rewarded him with a prestigious position full of power and influence. Now he was an officer of that institute and was being asked to use his expertise to perform a vital function designed to serve the clinic's best interests. Would his conscience allow him to compromise the integrity of that enterprise? Probably not. But if not, then how was he going to complete this undertaking that he'd already agreed to? Sadly he realized he didn't know.

Marshall arrived home, no nearer to a solution than he'd been when he left the hospital. Absently he sorted through his mail, tossed some leftovers into the microwave, and changed into a T-shirt and a pair of shorts. He flipped on the television but couldn't find anything that held his attention for more than a few minutes. Finally he settled for the Pirates game, but didn't pay much attention to the action.

I'm not even sure I can let her know what Hunter's up to, Marshall realized. *If I do and then go and perform the evaluation she may withhold information or try to prejudice my evaluation of her personality. Certainly, if the way she played me in bed on Saturday night is any indication of how talented she is, I'm sure she could play some psychological tricks on me too. Plus, I don't want her to suspect Hunter is questioning her competency. It may upset the apple cart. She might even blame me for having to perform the evaluation. And that would put a damper on our relationship. After all, as the song goes, "We've only just begun."*

The baseball game ended just after ten. Marshall got ready for bed. He watched ER for a while, its fast paced, medically oriented plotline distracting him from his musings. Finally, when the news came on, he tried to sleep. But before dozing off he pictured the next day's schedule and assessed how busy his Friday would be. As he anticipated the ten o'clock conference he had to give to the psychiatry residents, an idea occurred to him.

"That's it," he cried softly to himself. "That's how I'll get around it."

With this welcome realization he drifted right off to sleep.

Marshall regarded the young man sitting across from him. For some reason his young psychiatry resident reminded him of Captain Billingham from the popular sixties sit com, McHale's Navy. He had the same the round face, thin lips, a button nose, and full head of neatly combed jet black hair. He also knew that Dr. Don Owen was less than five and a half feet tall. He pictured an officer's cap on his head and grinned.

"Thanks for stopping by, Don," Marshall greeted him. "I know you're usually out make rounds about now, but I hoped you might have a few minutes to spare after the conference."

"No problem, Dr. Friedman," the resident said, his voice high-pitched and lyrical. "Most of my people are in group right now. Jake Fisher's facilitating the session so I'm actually free until after lunch."

"Good," Marshall said, absently fingering a corner of the manila folder set on his blotter. "Then we can talk." Before the ten o'clock conference Marshall had spent nearly an hour reviewing his residents' folders. After comparing and contrasting records he'd chosen Owen.

"How's the training program coming along? I rarely get to talk to you guys about it."

"Just fine," Don replied. "It took me a while to learn the routine. But it's been almost two months now and I feel like I've been here for years."

"That intense?" Marshall commented, aware that Owen was the hardest working and most conscientious of his first year group. From the charting he'd done on his patients, Marshall inferred that this young psychiatrist was amazingly astute for someone at his level of training.

"At times, yes."

"Is there any room on your plate?"

"My plate?" he repeated, looking confused. Then he apparently understood what Marshall was getting at and brightened up. "I suppose so," he replied, "why?"

"There's a special assignment I want you to consider."

"An assignment?"

"Yes."

"What's it about?"

"Well, let me give you some background first," Marshall began. "Each year around this time the chairpersons for most of the hospital departments face reappointment. It's a routine process that's usually just rubber-stamped by the Executive Committee during its fall meeting. However, whenever there's a fresh appointment, the committee can request a full psychological assessment of the candidate before they vote for approval. It's a type of safeguard against electing someone who's not fit for the job. Follow me so far?"

Don nodded, leaning forward in his chair, a Daytimer open on his lap, his gleaming white teeth absently gnawing on the tip of a ballpoint pen.

"This year there's a vacancy in the Medical Research Department. Dr. Hunter has asked me to perform a psychological assessment on the leading candidate for the job. It's Dr. Rose Shaw. Do you know her?"

Don shook his head.

"I didn't think so. It would be unusual for your paths to cross. Anyway, what I'm asking you to do is lay the groundwork for the report. You know, do the history, perform a psychiatric exam, administer a battery of personality tests, then come up with an assessment. I'll take that information, interview Dr. Rose myself, then integrate all the data into a final report."

Don nodded again. "It sounds like doing a standard intake history and physical," he commented, "with the psychological testing added on. That should be no problem, Dr. Friedman."

"I was hoping you'd say that, Don," Marshall replied encouraging the young man with a broad smile. "And I really appreciate your enthusiasm. Now let me offer you a word of caution. Since Dr. Shaw is quite a bit different from your typical clinic patient, evaluating her may prove challenging. Stick with it and you might get a taste of what you'll come across in private practice. If you end up in general practice, that is."

"The truth is, Dr. Friedman, I really haven't given it much thought," Don conceded. "But I agree, this sort of interview would present a unique opportunity. Does Dr. Rose know about this?"

"She will in a day or two."

"And when do you need the assessment turned in?"

"No later than two weeks from today, if you can swing it."

"No problem. Could you let me know when it's okay to set up our meeting?"

"Of course, Don," Marshall said rising from his chair. The young man followed suit. "And thanks again for taking this on," Marshall added, starting toward the door. "I know it might look like scut work, but I truly believe it's a genuine learning experience. Let me know what you think after you turn in the report."

"Sure will, Dr. Friedman," Don said as he left the office. "And thanks for having the confidence in me."

"I know it's well placed, Don," Marshall said and softly shut the door.

chapter twenty

we've only just begun

Rose handled the news of the upcoming psychological evaluation better than Marshall had expected. In fact, she seemed to regard the exercise as a challenge.

"If Hunter doesn't already know what makes me tick, nothing your little resident finds out will enlighten him. I've got nothing to hide, Marshall. And if standing under a psychiatric microscope is what it takes to nail down this chairmanship, then that's what I'm going to do." And that was that.

They were sitting in Station Square, a turn of the century railroad station now transformed into an indoor mall, having a quiet dinner at a place called Tequila Junction. Marshall liked the upscale Mexican restaurant, its food tasty, the service attentive, and the atmosphere smartly casual. As they sipped margaritas a small band of cheerful musicians, clad in white cotton shirts, black bandoleer pants, and felt sombreros, weaved their way around the room playing lighthearted Central American ballads.

After their meal they browsed the shops. Rose stopped in The Limited and brought some shorts and a bright red top then coaxed Marshall into one of the men's stores where she picked him out a pair of ties and a silk shirt. Ice cream cones at the corner sweet shop followed.

On their way toward the parking lot she suggested they stop at Jellyrolls, a karaoke bar nestled toward the far end of the mall. After claiming a small table for two near the center of the floor, they watched in amusement as a series of young adults, most in their early to mid twenties, picked a favorite song, stepped up to the microphone, and delivered their selection with full electronic accompaniment. Midway into his second beer, Rose unexpectedly suggested Marshall give it a try.

"Me?" he asked incredulously. "You want me to go up there and *sing*? No way."

"Why not?"

"Because I have no intention of making a fool of myself in front of a room full of strangers."

"Did those people who just sang make fools of themselves?"

Marshall considered her question. "Well, not really," he conceded. "Actually some of them were pretty good."

"So what makes you think you wouldn't do as well?"

"That's simple. Because I can't sing."

"Neither could they—at least not well. And I bet there's practically no one in this room who can. But they're willing to stand up, give it a try, and have some fun in the process."

Marshall regarded this notion. The last time he'd performed in public was twenty-five years ago, as a member of the high school glee club. This karaoke stuff was different. He'd have to stand up there alone in front of a crowd of people with a microphone in his hand and the spotlight trained directly upon him.

"Go, Marshall," Rose commanded. "It'll be fun."

Although every fiber of his rational being insisted he stay put, there was something about the way Rose said this that had him rise to his feet. As soon as the other patrons saw him start toward the stage they reacted with a burst of enthusiastic applause. This encouragement felt like a fresh breeze lifting him up and setting him on stage.

A ponytailed young man by the platform wearing a denim shirt and suede vest shook Marshall's hand. He introduced himself as Ray the Deejay, then checked if Marshall had a special song he'd like to sing. Since up to just seconds earlier he had no idea he'd be on stage, Marshall said no. Ray offered him the book of the available selections. Marshall leafed through it, eventually coming up with what he decided was a perfect choice. He took the mike and introduced an early Neil Diamond tune called *Cracklin' Rosie,* dedicated it to his date, who he introduced by her first name. The crowd erupted in another round of excited applause.

After the spirited instrumental intro, Marshall focused on the TelePrompTer and began singing the catchy upbeat song. At first he felt tentative and self-conscious, but seemed to gain confidence with every phrase. By the last verse he was standing with the microphone held high in his right hand, head thrown back, delivering the lyrics just like he recalled seeing Neil do during a late seventies concert at the Civic Arena. Hitting the last note just right, he was rewarded with another roar of approval from the patrons. When he returned to his seat Rose leaned over and kissed him on the cheek.

"That was fabulous, Marshall," she raved. "If I didn't know better, I'd think you were a professional."

"The shower's the only place I belt out my tunes," he confided. "Meanwhile, how about you? Isn't it your turn now?"

Without hesitation Rose replied, "I believe it is, Marshall. I'll go after that young man there."

A few minutes later Rose stepped confidently up onto the stage, took the microphone from Deejay Ray, and in a husky, slightly off-key voice performed the Carpenters' classic, *We've Only Just Begun.* During the entire time she sang, her gaze never wavered from Marshall's.

They rode the Duquesne Incline, a small cable car that ran up the steep hillside from the Southside to Mount Washington. Exiting the station, they held hands to cross Grandview Avenue, then continued on to the fourteenth floor of the Trimont where Rose's condominium was located.

Rose's unit was nothing like Marshall had imagined it would be. Expecting rich earthtones with antique furniture and bold paintings in ornate frames, he was almost blinded by the burst of white. From its blonde carpets to the bleached wallpaper and almond-colored furniture, the unit was a study in brightness. The chrome and glass bookshelves also seemed to fit the scheme. To Marshall's eye, the place appeared pure, unblemished, and almost antiseptic—the antithesis of which he thought its owner imagined herself to be.

Is this her way of purging the part of her that was linked to a more soiled past? he wondered. *Perhaps. Does that invalidate the warm, sensitive part of her personality I love? No, that's still there. I experienced it first hand in Erie.*

Rose offered him a drink. He was tempted to refuse, citing that he'd had too much alcohol already. But she insisted, explaining how she hated to drink alone. There was an imploring look in her hazel green eyes. Her dexterous fingers marched gently up his arm. And as had become the custom during their brief courtship, he found it impossible to refuse her.

They sat beside each other on the white leather loveseat, their shoes off, their stocking feet propped up on the coffee table. The music in the background sounded melodic and soothing. Marshall felt relaxed and settled. Despite the starkness of the color scheme, it seemed easy to unwind. The sofa was soft and inviting, the carpet plush, the lighting subdued. He enjoyed the notion that they could be here together, on a date of sorts, and not feel compelled to fill every moment with frenetic activity. They could just hang out. It portended good things to come.

Just as Marshall began to doze off Rose snuggled up to him. He put his arm around her shoulder and she leaned her head on his chest.

"Would you like to stay?" she inquired softly.

"I was hoping you'd ask."

"Good, I was hoping you'd want to."

She remained next to him for a few minutes longer. When the CD finally clicked off it seemed to be the signal to stir. She disentangled herself from his embrace then kissed him lightly on the neck before heading off to the bedroom.

He waited for her to invite him in. A couple of minutes later she did. He stood up and approached the partially closed door. Opening it wider he peered inside and noticed the queen sized mattress set on a low platform and flanked by two nightstands. An integrated headboard, two long chests of drawers and a rectangular mirror completed the ensemble. All the pieces were finished in the same almond color.

Rose seems to be taking this purification rite a little too far, he reflected.

But then again, perhaps there was some internal consistency he was casually dismissing here. He made a mental note to pursue this with her in therapy.

Rose was still in the bathroom when he entered. A moment later she appeared at the doorway draped in a white terry-cloth robe,

"How about a nice hot shower first?" she suggested.

The idea had never occurred to him. But now it sounded wonderful. He couldn't remember the last time he'd bathed with a woman. More than a decade ago at least, with Bernice, at her parents' home in the Hamptons, for convenience, not eroticism. Then snapping out of his reverie, he focused on Rose grinning at him from the doorway. The alcohol-induced languor from the living room had dissipated, replaced by the excitement of delicious anticipation. This, he imagined, was going to be a blast.

The over-sized shower stall was equipped with two heads. A separate Jacuzzi tub filled the opposite corner. Marshall sensed that the bathroom was important to Rose, disproportionately large, ultra modern, well stocked, and well appointed. Porcelain bowels fit seamlessly into sparkling white marbled counter tops. The second commode, on closer inspection, was a bidet. What a stark contrast to the narrow functional bathroom in her childhood house, he thought. Hadn't Rose been forced to share that room with her parents?

As Marshall stepped into the enclosure, two steady streams of hot water converged upon him. He slid the glass door shut and noticed the large frosted rose sculpted into its pane. He approached his hostess. The steam engulfed them in a misty swirling cloud. It felt like he was walking in a dream. Rose, however, was real enough, rubbing up against him, her slippery skin simultaneously firm and soft. Possessively he ran his palms up and down her sides. She turned and leaned back against him. Shutting his eyes he focused on his tactile exploration of her many curves and crevices, imagining himself a blind man using physical clues to formulate a visual image of his subject.

From a dispenser on the wall Rose plopped a dollop of scented lotion on her cupped palm. She soaped him. Weak-kneed, he luxuriated in the sensation, her large hands making smooth brushstrokes across his tingling skin. Dreamily he imagined himself poised on the edge of the cliff, ready to jump into some ecstatic oblivion. Then she paused. It was now her turn. At first he didn't comprehend, he so wanted her to finish. Then he appreciated her desire and, with a shake of his head, like a dog coming in from the rain, he snapped out of it. Applying the soap to her warm wet body, he heard her swoon. Then she eased up against him. The pressure on his groin intensified his arousal.

Just as he was about to climax she had them rinse. After drying off she led him into the bedroom and they made love in her queen-sized bed. First he allowed her to attend to him. She did so with what Marshall imagined as an ideal mix of tenderness and passion. It was his turn to minister. He approached the task with relish, searching for triggers, carefully gauging her reactions, pleased with himself when he ignited her sensitive spots. It felt just as satisfying giving pleasure as receiving it. The preliminaries melted into the main event, their individual rhythms merged into one. Soon, accompanied by two syncopated cries of joy, they climaxed together.

As he dozed off—and it wasn't much after that—Marshall sensed himself basking in the radiance of total contentment. And just like when Rose had sung to him from the stage before they left the karaoke bar, he had the sense that his new life had just begun.

chapter twenty-one

dear marshall

During this time, Marshall often fantasized about achieving personal and professional actualization while savoring the joys of his blossoming romance with Rose. The last thing he expected was a major intrusion from his past on his designs for the future.

Sitting at the desk in his study, he held a letter in his hand. It was just past eight on Monday evening. His workday had been especially stressful, filled with hospital rounds, a clinical psychiatry conference which he presented, his one o'clock departmental meeting, then three hectic hours of outpatient work in the medical office building. About midmorning Don Owen left a message that Dr. Shaw had agreed to meet with him. Then Hunter's secretary delivered a preliminary agenda for the upcoming Executive Committee meeting. Attached was a handwritten note thanking him for helping out with the credentialing process.

Sally stopped by just before noon and asked about lunch. Although he was pleased to see her he had to decline the invitation. His deskwork had piled up to the point where he had no other choice than to work through. By six, tired and drained, he finally finished. He left the hospital, stopped for a bite a nearby German restaurant, and arrived home a half-hour later. The letter in Bernice's neat familiar cursive was waiting for him.

The perfumed stationary was the same style as he frequently picked up for her at a Lexington Avenue specialty shop near his Upper Eastside office. He held the parchment paper up to his nose and detected Palomo Picasso, his wife's favorite perfume.

August 26, 2000

Dearest Marshall,

I hope this letter finds you well. I know it seems a bit unusual to write with the phone so close, but there's much I need to share with you and I was worried that without a written agenda I would forget the key points.

I've recently returned from a two-week cruise of the Greek Isles. The ports were absolutely idyllic. The perfect weather made the touring incredible. The people were warm and hospitable and we even docked at Mikanos for a day—you know, the island John Fowles wrote about in The Magus. I remember how much you loved that novel with all its psychological manipulations and sexual innuendo. The island is as lovely and charming as he described almost forty years ago.

With Mom and Dad back in the city, I decided to return to Manhattan, too. When I first entered our condo with the curtains drawn, the windows sealed, and all the furniture draped in white sheets and plastic, it seemed cool and lonely. But now that I've been back a few days I'm getting used to being home again.

I expected to miss you more once I got back to our old home. And I suppose that for a while, away from the hordes of people on the ship, the orchestrated excursions, the fancy meals, and extravagant shows, loneliness had the best of me. But the feeling was short-lived. Now it's faded completely leaving me with the notion that we've reached a crucial juncture in our marriage.

Before you left for Pittsburgh, you called this move a trial separation where we could use the time apart to evaluate our true feelings. After that we'd see what the future would bring. In all honesty I believed you. I thought you were right. We both had nagging concerns about the 'rut' our relationship had slipped into, the routines, the lack of spontaneity, the concomitant waning of emotion and desire. But, by the same token, I truly believed that this was just a phase we were passing through—that all we needed was time and distance to discover we wanted and needed each other more than ever. I pictured us stepping back from an elaborate painting we'd gotten to close to in order to appreciate its beauty and vision.

Unfortunately, I was wrong.

What I discovered, Marshall is that the longer I remain separate from you, the more comfortable I am with the *notion of not having you in my life. Rather than this 'trial separation' generating anxiety and longing, it has actually provided me with a sense of freedom and exuberance. Now that you've moved away I feel more liberated and alive than I've felt in years—like the filters that were before my eyes have been removed and now I can appreciate the world in living color.*

Please don't take this the wrong way. I'm not blaming you for what's happened, nor am I implying that you were responsible for our muted existence. I suspect that I, like you, became a victim of a relationship that had run its course, that had lost whatever vitality it had at its inception. And I think—correct me if I'm wrong—that we've both fallen out of love with each other, but we were too stupid (or too proud) to acknowledge it. So instead of making the tough choice to move on, we plodded along, insulated by the routine and sacrificing our aliveness in the process. And now that the weight of the relationship has been lifted, we are both free to live more fully again.

Marshall paused, amazed at the perspicacity in her assessment. He too, for years, had felt the burden of their marriage. And more recently, with it hidden in the shadows of his Pittsburgh existence, he too, had appreciated a rebirth of aliveness. But up until that moment, so immersed had he been in this new life, that he hadn't taken the time to examine the question as carefully as Bernice apparently had. How ironic, he thought.

Who's the true analyst in the family? he asked himself.

Returning to the letter, now having read it twice already, he reviewed her conclusion and appreciated its significance.

I hope you grasp and concur with what I'm saying. Because if you do, Marshall, it will make what I'm going to write next that much easier to accept. I've spoken to our friend, Leslie Levy. I've explained how I feel. He said he understood. At my request he's agreed to draw up the necessary legal papers (if that's what we want, he says). I'm sorry to say this, but it is what I want.

I'm anxious to hear your reaction to all of this. I know it may seem sudden and somewhat definite. Then again it may also be something you would have pursued on your own if you had only mustered the courage (which I suspect would have been difficult for you since you pride yourself on being such a nice guy). But, whatever the reason, I'm still interested in your response. Please write or call. It would trouble me greatly if our subsequent interactions were exclusively through our respective attorneys.

*Yours with love,
Bernice*

As he set the scented paper down for the third and final time Marshall said, *Whew,* to himself. *She's offered me my unconditional release before I even requested it. I wonder if this is what I really want? It seems so sudden. But with Rose in the picture, it's also remarkably opportune. I wonder how Dr. Shaw's going to react to all of this?*

He spent the rest of the evening in a sort of mental cruise control. A series of television programs scrolled past his eyes, but his thoughts kept returning to Bernice's letter and its implications.

Living on his own in Pittsburgh these past couple months he had started to feel detached. He appreciated, of course, that he was still married. But it was more a cognitive reality than an emotional bond. Bernice, after all, was four hundred miles away. And although their marriage still existed like an imaginary cord keeping him tethered to Manhattan, the cord was starting to fray. Now, unexpectedly, his wife was prepared to sever it. And what's more, she sounded determined to follow through.

When he viewed this situation candidly, he realized that he wouldn't fight her on the matter. She had apparently made up her mind. And although he'd resisted arriving at the same conclusion himself, he was sure that with Rose's help the transition into the post-marriage world would be seamless. He wondered how he should handle the nuts and bolts of the divorce.

Did he need a lawyer of his own to represent his particular interests or could he trust Leslie, a longtime family friend, to make sure that the settlement agreement was fair and amiable? Was it necessary to take a trip to Manhattan where he could finalize things in person? That, he suspected, would be the most civil thing to do. It would show that he was a mature adult intent on handling an awkward situation in a polite, amiable fashion.

And to get some real closure I wouldn't mind seeing Bernice one last time, he conceded.

But then again, a contact of this nature might make things harder, he realized. It wasn't unusual for him to counsel patients and their families to make clean breaks when faced with withdrawing life support in a situation where death was inevitable. If this divorce was inevitable—and it certainly appeared to be—then perhaps it would be wiser to make his own break clean.

Then he had an intriguing thought. Maybe Rose could join him in New York. He'd plan a getaway weekend after the Exec meeting so they would celebrate the committee's decision to elect her head of the research department. After finalizing his divorce he would be free to openly pursue his relationship with Rose. This, of course, implied that Rose would be around as the new chairperson a position that required Marshall's endorsement. And while immersed in this swirl of overlapping agendas he finally fell asleep.

chapter twenty-two

the evaluation

The next morning Marshall hoped that work would distract him from dwelling on Bernice's letter. And it did for a while. Then Sandi Coles left a message and instantly Manhattan was back in his musings.

His literary agent seemed in good spirits when she picked up on the second ring. The sales on his book had picked up, she reported. Revenue from it was currently in the black.

"That new marketing strategy Bernice's father set in motion seems to be working," Sandi related. "I got a call from Mr. Caruso yesterday. He's the shoe manufacturer who heads the group of businessmen that bankrolled your book last spring. He reviewed the numbers we sent him and was pleased. In fact he now regards you as, 'a favorable low risk investment.' He was wondering whether you have any more books up your sleeve. I told him I thought you were working on something new."

Marshall was both surprised and encouraged by this information. At least his writing career seemed secure for the moment. He told Sandy that he had some ideas about a sequel to *Why Good Men Go Bad,* but hadn't started working on anything yet.

"Well there's no time like the present," she suggested. "And on a more sour note," she continued, "I also got a call from Bernice. But before I stick my foot in my mouth, have you heard from her?"

"The letter came yesterday," he confirmed.

"Did it say what I think it did?"

"You mean, about the divorce? Yes it did."

"Good. Ah, uh, I don't mean it's *good*. But it does let me share what else she related without it coming as a surprise."

"I bet her father's pulling out of the self-help book business," Marshall predicted.

"That's a tactful way of putting it, Marshall. Now that you two are splitting, he doesn't feel it's appropriate for him to support your writing career."

"Even if I'm a low risk investment?" he asked somewhat rhetorically.

"Even with that," Sandi agreed. "Anyway, I'm glad we got that out of the way. So how are things going otherwise? How are they treating you out there in the Boonies?"

"I can't complain. Everyone's been extremely supportive. Actually, I'm starting to like living in my home town."

"That's great, Marshall. Once your new project gets underway invite me out for a visit."

"Why wait until then?" Marshall asked, booting up his computer and started searching for the 'games' folder. The conversation was drifting into pleasantries. He was getting bored. "Pittsburgh's a great place," he offered lightly. It was her next question that refocused his attention.

"What do you think of that guy Bernice met on the cruise?"

"Guy? What guy?"

"The stockbroker from New Haven?" The pause told Sandi she'd said too much. "You mean she didn't tell you about him in her letter? I just assumed.... Oh, Marshall. I'm sorry."

So that's why she's so anxious to dump me, Marshall thought bitterly. *All that analytical mumbo-jumbo was just a smoke screen for her true motivation. She's screwing someone else!*

"No, Sandi," Marshall admitted. "I didn't know. I guess that helps explain why her plans seemed so sudden."

"I suppose so. I feel sick that I was the one who told you."

"No harm done, Sand," Marshall said, magnanimity muted by the realization that he was 'screwing' someone else too. "To be honest with you, I'd rather know."

"That's good," Sandi said with relief in her voice. "Well, I'd better be going. I have a twelve-thirty appointment in West Chester and traffic's a bear this time of day. Fax me a synopsis and a chapter outline of this new book of yours once you have it."

"Sure, Sandi. I will. Bye."

Later that morning Marshall's secretary brought him Bob Owen's psychological profile on Rose.

Great, he thought, relieving her of the document. *It's Thursday already, just eight days before the Executive Committee meeting. Hunter wants the official version on his desk by Monday.*

Marshall's intention was to have the report retyped on departmental stationary, give Don credit for his efforts in the acknowledgment section, then affix his own signature to it. But after reviewing the resident's unexpected assessment, he reconsidered his plan.

It wasn't the quality or scope of the work that upset Marshall. Owen had done a competent, comprehensive job. Included were a battery of some of the most modern and sophisticated psychological tests available to the clinical community. It was Dr. Owen's final conclusion that gave Marshall pause.

Marshall reviewed the report for a second time. He scrutinized every phrase, checking the material for content, logical progression, thoroughness, and clarity. His resident's effort had been exemplary. Marshall re-screened the psychological tests. He found the responses consistent with the summary sheets that accompanied them.

All the major testing modalities were there; the Minnesota Multiphasic Personality Inventory-2, the Myers-Briggs, the Rorschach Ink Blot, the Thematic Apperception Test, and even the Keirsey Temperament Sorter. The last, he knew, was very contemporary and used Jung's theory of psychological constructs to identifying various personality types. He rechecked the conclusions in each category. With a growing sense of alarm he noted a high level of consistency. On the last page Bob documented his conclusions.

Final Impression: Antisocial Personality Disorder

Dr. Rosemarie Shaw appears to suffer from a deep-seated antisocial personality disorder, also known as a psychopathic or sociopathic personality. From her history and the results of the comprehensive psychological testing she seems to demonstrate a clear-cut pattern of irresponsible behavior lacking in moral and ethical constraints. This predicts a high probability for recurrent conflicts with society at large. Her behavior during childhood and adolescence, which included truancy, delinquency, and substance abuse, is consistent with this conclusion. Although there is no pattern of unlawful behavior, there is the suggestion of job failure, inability to sustain long-term relationships, aggressive behavior in confrontational situations, and sexual promiscuity (the latter two more apparent from the testing than the history). Her response pattern, specifically on the projective testing, suggests a lack of anxiety or affectation in situations which seem to warrant a more emotional response. Her charm and wit appear to be highly developed. That was evident during the interview process.

Treatment recommendations:

Individual psychotherapy or cognitive behavior therapy should be beneficial if a sense of trust is cultivated. Group sessions may also be of some value although long-term prognosis is guarded-to-poor.

Even after his third review of the report Marshall was still stunned by his resident's assessment. After all, wasn't he in the process of analyzing Rose himself? Wouldn't these therapeutic sessions hinted at her sociopathy? And what about the intimate time they'd shared together? Who, better than he, was equipped to assess the strengths and weaknesses of Rose's personality? Don Owen had to be wrong. Marshall was sure of it.

Perhaps it was the way the young resident had phrased his questions. Marshall knew only too well that when interviewing a patient the physician's inflection and choice of words could adversely affect the patient's responses. This, in turn, would skew the entire process. But on the other hand, that same degree of latitude wasn't available in the psychological testing process. He couldn't imagine how the objective tests would have been misinterpreted. Except maybe the Rorschach. Those inkblots offered some room for subjective interpretation and misinterpretation. Maybe the weight of all this subjectivity was enough to throw off the entire assessment, at least from the young resident's point of view.

The bottom line was that here he sat with the report Hunter had commissioned and now he was stuck with it. The deadline for delivery was only three days away. He had neither the time nor the energy to trash the resident's offering and create one of his own. And what about the patient? He tried to imagine how grueling it must have been for Rose to go through the evaluation process in the first place. He was pretty sure she would never agree to endure it again. So knowing this he returned to the question he'd posed to himself after reading the report the first time.

What am I going to do now?

The next evening, while strolling down one of the hospital basement's labyrinth of hallways, Marshall was still plagued by that same nagging question.

It's quite a dilemma. If I modify Owen's report in Rose's favor my professional integrity will be in jeopardy. If I turn it in as is, Rose will probably lose her bid for the chairmanship.

This untenable position had preoccupied him for nearly thirty-six hours. Rose, he knew, was pretty vindictive. His clandestine peek into her adolescent memorabilia established that fact. If she lost the vote next week, she would almost certainly blame him for her failure. And this might strike a mortal blow to their fledgling relationship.

But beyond that, there was this implicit negativity about his girlfriend's personality. Who, he wondered, was the real Rose? Certainly not an anti-social psychopath with violent tendencies. But no angel either, he realized. Perhaps, if he shared the results of the evaluation with her, listened to her reaction, then added this to the mix, it would help him decide how the final report to Hunter should be phrased.

It was Friday evening. They had a dinner date. Rose, he'd learned, was in the midst of the final stage of one of her major projects. For convenience she asked him to meet her at the lab. Marshall's apprehension was laced with excitement. This was the first time he would be visiting Rose in her work environment. It was the side of her he'd only heard about. Their professional meeting followed by a quiet romantic dinner should segue nicely into what he wanted to discuss with her. Finally, once the unpleasantness of the psychological evaluation was out of the way, they may, with some luck, salvage the evening. The prospect made him tingle with anticipation.

He approached the part of the basement that housed the research labs. Parallel rows of exposed pipes and ducts stretched the entire length of the long hallway. A cacophony of hisses, rumbles, and kachunks distracted him. His brown penny loafers swished along the polished concrete floor.

He knew this was the forgotten section of the hospital, where top scientists shared space with a gross pathology lab, the contaminated organ processing unit, the hospitals blood product storage dispensary, maintenance, engineering and, of course, the morgue. If Hunter had any plans of showcasing their state of the art research, he mused, he obviously couldn't do it in this dungeon.

A pale light guided him toward a heavy metal door. Upon its frosted glass window was printed BIOGENETICS AND BIOPROSTHETIC RESEARCH AND DEVELOPMENT, TREVOR MCCORMICK, DIRECTOR, in neat block letters.

He knocked on the door. There was no answer. He knocked again, this time louder and called out Rose's name. His voice echoed down the long deserted hallway.

He tested the knob and to his surprise it turned. Cautiously he pushed the door open. Inside was a half-dozen or so black stone tables piled high with glassware and racks of test tubes. The shelves were full of reagents and other chemicals. Small indescript machines seemed positioned everywhere.

All this equipment but no workers, he observed. *Despite what Rose said, there doesn't seem to be much going on.*

He crossed the room to a door on the opposite side and knocked again.

"Yes?" spoke a familiar voice from inside. "Who's there?"

"It's just me," he replied, "Marshall."

A deadbolt slid open and so did the door. Rose greeted him with a smile.

"Hi," she said. Leaning over she planted a tender kiss on his cheek. "I'm glad you're here. Things are going better than I expected. I'll be done in a few minutes."

He nodded his approval. She wore a lab coat with her name stitched in red cursive over the breast pocket. Under it she had a low-cut black cotton dress on.

Rose busied herself at a desk in the corner. Marshall meanwhile assessed this inner lab. Rectangular in shape, it was smaller than the first one, with two blacktop tables set flush against the whitewashed walls. The sound of humming motors and bleeping monitors suggested that important work was in progress. A pair of electric generators were set on one of the tables and a half-dozen oxygen tanks, like upright torpedoes, stood in the corner.

It looks like an intensive care unit for experimental objects, Marshall decided.

As if appreciating his confusion, Rose said, "Here, come with me. I was actually working over there inside the genetic engineering lab."

"Genetic engineering?" he replied, intrigued. "The term sounds so futuristic."

"Yes, doesn't it. Come, you'll see."

They entered a nearby room. This one appeared spotless, with stainless steel tables and metal chairs, harsh white fluorescent lighting and a host of high tech equipment all around. Various sized glass cubes were perched on the counter tops, each supported by its own set of tubes, pumps, motors, and drains. Sophisticated monitoring equipment was also mounted at each station.

Like appreciating nuances of shape and size once your eye adjusts to the muted light in a darkened room, Marshall began to note the specifics of the objects around him. Housed in some of these glass cubes were clumps of rubbery or fleshy-looking material, indistinct and barely resembling anything in his limited experience. Others, to his amazement, contained more familiar items. And to his amazement some looked like rudimentary body parts—a finger, an outer ear, an eye, a nose—not unlike the block dissections preserved in formaldehyde in the gross anatomy lab during his freshman year of medical school.

"What *is* all this stuff?" he asked. "Did the path lab run out of storage space or something?"

"No, silly," Rose replied. "They're experiments."

"In what?"

"In cloning."

The word gave him pause. It was the last thing he'd expected her to say. It conjured up all kinds of images from science fiction and fantasy. Hadn't the process been in the news lately? Something to do with sheep.

"Are you serious?"

"Of course I'm serious. We have, incubating in these cubicles, a living chronicle of the work I've been doing since I arrived at the Hunt in 1995."

Gripped by a certain respectful deference, Marshall approached one of the glass containers. "Wow, Rose!" he exclaimed. "This stuff is fascinating. How in the world is it done?"

"Trade secret," she replied with a playful smile. "What do you think?"

"It's amazing."

"I thought you'd like it." She paused for a moment, as if letting him absorb as much of the ambiance of the setting as he chose. Finally she asked, "Ready for dinner?"

Snapping out of his personal version of *The Twilight Zone,* he said absently, "Sure. Let's go."

chapter twenty-three

burning desire

They sat at a cozy little corner table in a seafood restaurant just a block from the Trimont. Through the opaque glass a panoramic view of the city presented itself with a skyline awash in cascades of white and yellow lights.

Before their main courses arrived they shared a plate of sliced vegetables. Marshall stared transfixed as Rose placed a large carrot stick in her mouth, licked then withdrew it slowly, without biting down. Next she pinched a cherry tomato between her thumb and index finger, set it delicately on her curled tongue, and rolled the small sphere through her puckered lips. The bulge in his pants suggested that this foreplay was having its effect. Marshall loosened his tie and undid the top button of his pinstriped shirt. Rose smiled mischievously. She seemed to be savoring his reaction.

Their entrees came. They ate and talked, mainly reviewing some of the upcoming social events they'd planned to attend. Then, when Rose mentioned a health fair her lab was sponsoring next month, Marshall recalled one of his main agenda items for this evening.

"By the way," he commented, trying to sound as nonchalant as possible, "Don Owen submitted his report yesterday. Suffice it say, it wasn't what I expected."

"Oh really," Rose replied, taking a bite of her fish. "This salmon is delicious, Marshall. You should try it the next time we come here. I just love the sauce." She swallowed. "And what did your little resident have to report?"

Marshall, as tactfully as he could, summarized Dr. Owen's findings. While speaking he made a point of studying Rose's reaction. He was amazed at how composed she seemed, regarding him intently, apparently fascinated by the results. At one point she actually stopped eating, her knife suspended in the air like a conductor's baton. He related the resident's final assessment and treatment recommendations. Rather than her expression shifting from one of rapt attention to alarm or even anger, he caught the devilish twinkle in Rose's stunningly beautiful green eyes. Then her face blossomed into a broad mirthful smile.

Astonished by her reaction he stammered, "You mean you're not upset?"

"Upset?" she replied with a chuckle. "Of course I'm not upset. Why should I be? To be honest with you, I'm pretty proud of myself."

"Proud?" he repeated.

"Yes, that I pulled it off."

Floundering in a sea of confusion, Marshall stuttered, "p-p-pulled what off?"

"Portraying myself as a social outcast with violent tendencies. Isn't it obvious that I was playing a little game with your resident, Marshall? I wanted to see if I could make myself out to be just the opposite of what I really am. I answered all those questions so it made it look that way. I guess I succeeded."

"You mean, you *wanted* him to diagnose you as a sociopath?"

"Something like that."

"But why?"

"To see if I could do it. And to show you how ridiculous your little psychological assessment was Marshall. And how insulting, I might add."

Marshall was stunned. From what Rose was saying, she'd chosen her responses in such a way as to make herself appear like a she had a personality disorder. Which meant that the entire evaluation was fallacious. Just like a liar beating the lie detector machine, she had successfully corrupted the results of her own personality evaluation.

She's even brighter than I thought, Marshall marveled.

"So you modified your answers in a way that would totally invalidate the evaluation?"

"That's right."

"But I'm supposed to turn that report into Hunter before the Board Meeting." He could almost hear the whining in his voice

"I suspected as much."

"Then, what am I suppose to do?'

"Whatever you like, Marshall. Whatever you like."

They left the restaurant and strolled the short distance to the Trimont arm in arm. The night air cleared most of the confusion from Marshall's head. In its wake he found himself concerned about how the disclosure of their concomitant subterfuges would affect Rose's mood.

On the elevator up to her unit, Rose turned to him, patted him gently on the cheek and said, "Marshall, believe me, I understand how you had to do what Hunter asked. He's your boss and you're the head of psychiatry. I also realize that you have a certain bias when it comes to me. So how can I blame you for sending your little resident to do the job?"

He gave her a wry smile and said, "So you understand?"

"Of course I understand. And I hope you're not mad at me for toying with young Don like that," she continued. "Actually it was a lot of fun. So now that that's out of the way," she added giving him a hug, "how about if we concentrate on enjoying the rest of the night? Now that I know what kind of battle I'm in for with the Exec Committee, maybe I can spend some of that time trying to lure the Chairman of the Psychiatry Department into my corner."

"And how do you propose to do that?"

"Oh, you'll see."

Once inside the alabaster palace—Marshall's nickname for Rose's condo—she relieved him of his blue blazer and hung it up in the coat closet. By the time he'd settled down on the leather sofa she was back from the kitchen with a two glasses and a bottle of wine. She set down the tray and poured.

"A toast," she suggested, offering him a glass.

"Of course," he agreed.

"To us," she said the goblet just above eye level.

"To us," he repeated, their tap making a musical clink.

"Remember staying at Mr. Getty's place in Erie?" she asked sitting down beside him.

"How could I forget?"

"Did you enjoy that night in our room?"

Their maiden night of lovemaking came back to him in a rush with the anticipation, the brief foreplay and ultimately, their shared pleasure. Involuntarily he began to stir.

"Immensely. Why?"

"Do you remember some of the things we talked about the next morning?"

"Vaguely. Why?"

"Have another glass of wine. I'm going to get the room ready. Then you'll find out."

After Rose left, Marshall sipped his wine and thought about the intimate conversation she'd referred to. He pictured that lazy Sunday morning, lounging around in bed, sharing intimacies, secrets, sexual preferences, and flights of imagination. There *was* one particular story he'd related about an evening during the waning months of his marriage to Bernice.

They'd been out to dinner with the Levys. The foursome stopped at an art gallery after a delicious dinner at a restaurant in Tribeka. After emptying four glasses of champagne he was feeling amorously frisky.

The notion of impending arousal returned. He smiled almost wolfishly to himself. He recalled the cab ride home and how Bernice's head had been leaning on his shoulder, her eyes closed, her face looking beautifully serene. He had traced the line of her face with the tip of his finger, from her coifed hairline, past her eye, her cheek, and the corner of her mouth. With a growing sense of excitement he reacalled how the rest of the evening had played out.

The cab pulled up to their building. As the doorman approached he placed a gentle kiss on her forehead. Bernice stirred. She appeared confused, then embarrassed.

"I guess I dozed off," she confessed. "Those parties are more draining than I realized."

"That's all right. You had your little beauty rest."

Once inside their unit Bernice checked with their live-in housekeeper before heading off to the bedroom. Marshall had a snack, set the security alarm, then joined her.

With the windows cracked and a bouquet of cut flowers splayed lazily from the Oriental vase on their dresser, their bedroom emanated a sweet, refreshing odor. The comforter was turned down and the pillows fluffed. Marshall brushed his teeth, washed his face, and then joined his wife under the covers. But instead of reaching for the remote he leaned back on the pillows, stared blankly at the ceiling, and anticipated the rest of the evening.

Bernice had her hair brushed back and was wearing a flimsy white baby-doll nightgown. Devoid of make-up he couldn't help noticing the tiny lines around her eyes and lips. She saw him staring and asked, "What?"

"Oh nothing," he replied innocently, then leaned over and kiss her cheek.

She commented about the pleasant evening they'd just spent together, then reached toward her nightstand, picked up a copy of *Town and Country* and leafed through it. At eleven-thirty he eased down flat and turned off his lamp. A few minutes later she set down her magazine and doused her light. Then sliding backwards toward him, she tucked her body against his. They frequently slept this way.

Although her breathing soon became more regular Marshall sensed that Bernice was still awake. Turning on his side, he reached his arm around and hugged her waist. Inching his hand under her nightgown, he grazed her the downy skin on her belly. He reached her left breast and began fondling it. She moved closer and reached an exploring hand behind her back.

"I guess you've got more on your mind than sleep tonight," she commented softly after her fingertips found his crotch. "Let me get this thing off."

She peeled off her nightgown and faced him. He was already out of his briefs. The touch of her breasts against his chest made his skin tingled. They kissed, her familiar lips full and soft. He eased her backward and caressed her breasts some more before sliding his hand toward her kinky mound. She responded with a soft moan. Marshall, intent on concentrating on what he was doing, was surprised to find his mind wandering.

Here I go again, he thought ruefully.

Every time he started to make love to his wife, for some unfathomable reason he became distracted and detached. Tonight he expected that the heightened self-esteem from his literary success and a few glasses of champagne would translate into wave of unbridled passion. But the nature of his accomplishment and the lingering effects of the alcohol seemed to be creating the opposite effect. That spontaneous arousal that had swelled to his wife's familiar touch withered.

She reached over to check on his arousal. Then, with a hint of concern in her husky voice, she asked, "What's wrong?"

"I'm not sure. Maybe it's the champagne."

"Oh that," she said and sounded a little relieved. "You're probably right. Let's see if I can help."

She tried fondling him. Responding to her practiced hand he began to stir, but couldn't sustain the erection. Knowing that he had to do something to avoid a total meltdown, he resorted to one of his favorite fantasies. He visualized a voluptuous blonde dominatrix, clad in black leather standing before him, her ample breasts, like two ripe melons, generously exposed. Chains, like garland, encircled her wrists and neck. She had long hair and emerald green eyes. In her black-gloved hand she wielded a nasty looking whip.

He attempted to incorporate Bernice into his fantasy, dressing her in a similar outfit and imagining her standing directly above his prostrate body. He visualized being blindfolded and his hands bound behind his back. He imagined what she could do to him, exposed this way.

The fantasy helped. He stirred again.

"Now that's better," Bernice commented.

Foregoing any further foreplay, he eased his wife onto her back and mounted her. She guided him in. He held back as long as he could, waiting for her arousal to build. Her moans gave way to a series of staccato yelps. He released. Moments later, feeling sated but oddly deflated, he rested atop her. Then he rolled onto his back and fell asleep.

Was that the story Rose had referred to? He glanced at his hand and noticed it was trembling. His heart began pounding forcefully. He was more apprehensive than he thought.

Before Rose, he'd never shared his fantasies with a woman before—not even with Bernice. And now it sounded like they might act one out.

A few minutes later Rose beckoned him, not from hers, but from the second bedroom, her study, with its desk, a filing cabinet, bookshelves and a computer workstation. Along one wall a large window looked out toward the city. Tonight, however, the slatted blinds were drawn and all of Rose's utilitarian items were shrouded in eerie darkness. A row of thin white wax candles mounted in sconces along another wall provided the room's only illumination. Marshall thought he detected the haunting aroma of cinnamon and pine.

"Over here, Marshall," Rose called from the far end of the room. As his eyes adjusted to the darkness he detected her shadowy profile standing about ten feet away. "Please stand in front of me," she requested, her voice soft but authoritative. Almost reflexively he complied.

She was wrapped in a long white robe, her arms folded across her chest, her head was cocked slightly to the right. *She looks amazingly beautiful tonight,* he decided, appreciating the creaminess of her complexion in the flickering candlelight. Her auburn hair, loose and thick, splayed casually on the terry cloth robe. Her eyes, dark, lustrous, and emerald green, fixed his gaze.

"Remember that fantasy you shared with me the morning after we made love at Mr. Getty's? About the woman in a black leather suit who utilized her feminine power to dominate you?" The question was asked simply. As she spoke she started unbuttoning his shirt.

"Uh," he replied, his throat uncomfortably dry. "Of course."

"Would you like me to act out that fantasy with you tonight?"

By now she had already worked her way down to his belt and zipper. A host of tantalizing possibilities popped into his head, images which triggered a cascade of involuntary physiologic reactions. Droplets of perspiration beaded on his forehead. He started panting. By the time he said, "Sure," his entire body was trembling with excitement.

"Excellent," she replied. "Then let's begin."

Before undressing him further, she stepped back and untied the belt that held her robe in place. The edges parted. She slipped it off her shoulders. Underneath she was wearing a split leather top which concealed some of her breasts but exposed all of her cleavage. The two sections of the top met just below her navel and were connected by black elastic straps to a pair of thigh-high mesh stockings. She wore spiked black leather boots on her feet. Thick silver bracelets and a heavy chain choker completed the ensemble.

"Is this what she might have worn?" Rose asked with devilish sweetness. Paralyzed with anticipation, all he could do was nod. "Shall we continue?"

He stood stark naked before her. From behind her back she produced a riding crop. She reached out and lightly brushed the instrument over his chest and arms. Gooseflesh popped up everywhere. Involuntarily he shivered.

"Cold?" She asked, mockingly.

He nodded.

"Good," she replied with unexpected harshness. "I'll warm you up soon enough. Now come with me into the next room and lie down on the bed."

A few moments later Marshall was on Rose's bed. Nudging his thighs with her riding crop she made him assume a spread-eagle position. Then she asked him to close his eyes and relax. Trembling with excitement, he felt both anxious and aroused. What would come next? This might be his fantasy, but it was Rose's show. She was the puppeteer. He was the marionette.

Before he could grasp what was happening she slipped a pair of soft cloth restraints around his wrists. Soon his arms were secured to the corners of the almond colored platform bed. Just as the significance of this development began to sink in, she did the same thing with his ankles. Suddenly, Marshall was lying naked and supine, his arms and legs outstretched, his hands and feet restrained. He no longer had control of the situation. He was totally at Rose's mercy.

This sobering realization sent another shudder through his bare body. This submissive physical exposure gave him an uncomfortable sense of vulnerability. Almost simultaneously he felt a body-tingling thrill. She hovered above him. He gazed into her gleaming eyes.

"There's one more thing before we begin," she said.

Marshall asked, "What's that?" His voice sounded like little more than a croak.

"You'll see."

He waited, apprehensively. Balanced on her knees again, Rose worked her way up toward the headboard. Leaning over she draped a swath of black fabric over his eyes. Abruptly the room was plunged into darkness.

Marshall panicked. Anchored to this bed completely naked, deprived of his sense of sight, he was gripped by this total loss of control. At first he balked, insisting that they stop this silly game and start acting like mature adults. He was ignored. Next he raised his voice and resorted to idle threats. Before long he was thrashing about like a trapped animal straining at his restraints. Eventually, exhausted and defeated, he settled down, his anger giving way to acquiescence.

He waited. Time passed. Exposed, blind, restrained, and vulnerable he desperately wanted to know what was coming next. Robbed of his sight, his other senses began to sharpen.

He heard the whoosh of Rose's heels on the carpet. Then, like a boat rolling over a swell, the mattress shifted and she was by his side again. Her perfume suddenly filled his nostrils. Opium again. Another odor mingled with the perfume then overwhelmed it. It seemed tangy sweet, spicy like incense. His eyes darted wildly under the blindfold.

Suddenly his sense of touch was stimulated again. But, in contrast to the pleasant aroma of the incense and perfume, this sensation was noxious and harsh. Without warning, on the inside of his right thigh he experienced an amalgam of pain and heat. The hot, stinging sensation was so sudden and caustic that he yelped.

"Ow!" he cried. "What was *that?*"

Her response came in the form of another dab of searing fire, this time on the inner aspect of his left thigh. He yelped, then braced. A series of stinging droplets, one after another showed down upon him, tracing a rough circle along the inner aspect of his thighs and genitals. He realized these were globules of candle wax dripped on his sensitive skin.

First he resisted. Then slowly he seemed to accept the pernicious sensation. With this acceptance he started to discount the discomfort and focused instead in on what could only be described as a distorted sense of pleasure. Soon, to his utter amazement, he began to crave the pain. Excitement and arousal mingled with the searing heat and once again his manhood was throbbing.

Suddenly the shower of molten ceased. A pregnant pause followed. Stroking—delicate, gentle fondling—along the length of his erection came next. He felt Rose's practiced fingertips brushing his penis, petting him like a kitten, caressing him from testicle to tip.

Moments passed, but only a few. His arousal became irrepressible. Poised at the summit, he was ready to explode. Rose apparently sensed his condition and pinched the tip of his erection. It relaxed, aborting his release.

A few tantalizing moments of anticipation followed. She started playing with him again. This time Marshall went berserk. Squirming to the limits of his restraints, writhing and bucking, he plunged into the crashing waves of pleasure. A feeling of pure ecstasy washed over him, way beyond anything he'd ever experienced before, and beyond anything he'd imagined possible. And just when he was certain it couldn't get any better, it did.

Warmth became moisture, then gentle friction. Like a damp velvet glove sliding over his arousal, Rose's lips glided along his length. A hand reached behind his head. The blindfold slipped off. He peered down across the expanse of his chest and abdomen. In the muted glow of the amber candlelight, he watched Rose Shaw bring him to climax.

chapter twenty-four

heartsick

"Marshall!" Rose admonished. "Stop snooping in my medicine cabinet." She was standing at the doorway to the bathroom back in her white terry cloth robe.

"What do you mean, 'snooping?'" he replied defensively. "I was just looking for a disposable razor. Besides, what's all this stuff for anyway? Lasix, Digoxin, Vasotec, Verapimil? Aren't they heart medicines?"

She walked over and stood beside him. Caressing his stubbly cheek with her palm she said, "They are heart medicines. And they're mine."

"Your heart?" He asked with genuine surprise. "At thirty-five years old? What could possibly be wrong with your heart?"

"Unfortunately," she replied, "a lot."

She's gotta be kidding, Marshall thought to himself. Then seeing the expression on Rose's face he realized that this was no joke.

Abruptly he flashed back to that afternoon when they'd met for their first therapy session. They'd taken that stroll up Beechwood Boulevard toward after their picnic lunch behind the Pittsburgh Center for the Arts. But it hadn't been a leisurely stroll for Rose. She struggled with the grade, gasping for breath, her skin turning damp and ashen? They had to stop more than once. Her fingernails were dusky and curved.

Come to think of it, he reminded himself, *don't the pulmonary specialists call that clubbing? I just assumed it was a telltale sign of cigarette smoking. What if it reflected some underlying heart disease? Oh my God!* he cried inwardly. *Her heart!*

"What could be wrong with your heart, Rose?" he asked, trying to remain calm. His own felt like a conga drum in his chest. "How serious is it?"

"I'm afraid it's pretty serious."

The conga drum was joined by a giant rubber band that began constricting his chest. Despite appearing healthy and vibrant the new love of his life had some serious cardiac condition.

Abandoning his calm facade he demanded, "Could you be more specific?" while dreading what she would say next.

"I was born with a condition called Epstein's Anomaly," she told him in a voice that remained even-timbered and under control. "Have you ever heard of it?"

"Vaguely," he replied. It sounded familiar but he couldn't remember any details.

"Well," she said slipping her arm in his and guiding him back to the bed. "In layman's terms, it's a malformation of the tricuspid valve which is displaced downward. That makes my right ventricle rudimentary and creates unrestricted backflow across the valve into the right atrium. I also have a persistent hole between my two filling chambers called a patent foramen ovale. Here, let me show you."

She took a piece of stationary from the desk drawer and drew him a diagram.

"The hole was patched at Hopkins when I was in medical school there. The pediatric cardiologists were beginning to use inflated balloon techniques at that time so it really wasn't considered surgery. But they said it was too dangerous to do anything about the valve. They gave me ten to fifteen years."

"And?" he asked, too shaken to be more specific.

"To some extent they were right. Now I'm nearing the end of that stretch. My last echo showed further enlargement of the right ventricle along with progressive pulmonary hypertension. I'm tiring much more easily these days and I'm always getting winded. These, unfortunately, are all signs of advancing right-heart failure, which, I'm told, is pretty ominous. Sometimes my heart goes out of rhythm and I get palpitations. The medications help control the symptoms but can't reverse the disease."

"Rose!" he cried, raking his long fingers through his thinning hair. "This is horrible. How long? Really?"

"At this point, I can't be sure. When I moved to Pittsburgh in ninety-five I hooked up with a female cardiologist at Mercy Hospital who specializes in congenital heart disease in adults. During my last visit in July she said I'd be lucky to see forty."

"But that's less than five years away!" he blurted out, unable to hide his desperation. "There must be something they can do? Some operation? Some procedure?"

"There are a few procedures," she conceded, "but they don't change the prognosis much. And the morbidity is high, which means I could end up worse. Any intervention could compromise the time I have left. So, I've decided to go on as long as I can with the original equipment."

"But, if *something* can be done to help you live longer?" he pleaded.

"It's all too risky, Marshall. I'll take my chances with what I have."

"Oh, Rose!"

He was sitting on the edge the bed. He offered his arms and she slid into them. He clutched her firmly to his chest, the pressure of her warm soft body against his skin feeling achingly agreeable. How much longer would he have that beautiful body available to him, he wondered? How much longer could he savor her touch?

It's not fair! he balked. *I just met her. This is a vibrant young woman in the prime of her life. I'm planning a future with her. Now she's going to be snatched away like a convict on death row. And there's nothing I can do to change it.*

Lying there with her head on his shoulder he felt limp, deflated, and utterly helpless. They remained entwined for a long time. Absently he stroked her auburn hair, intermittently grazing her scalp with his lips. He murmured his love for her and felt her tremble in reply. Fluid brimmed around his eyes. He considered a tissue but remained still. Salty fluid tickled his cheek.

Then he heard Rose chuckle.

"What?" he asked, unable to imagine what she found humorous in all this. "What's so funny?"

"Well," she replied, reaching over and handing him a tissue from the box on her nightstand. "If I'm voted chairman of the research department, and if your resident's psychological assessment is accurate, then the Hunt will only have to deal with a psychopath in that role for a few years."

"Oh, Rose," he wailed. "Don't talk like that. It sounds so morbid."

"I know, Marshall. But, unfortunately, it's true."

chapter twenty-five

a not-so-rosey past

The Seika pyramid-shaped clock on the bookshelf by the window chimed the hour. Marshall saw that it was already noon. Checking his desk calendar, he noted that he had nothing until one.

"I actually have time to take a lunch hour," he announced to the empty room. Rising a little wearily to his feet, he informed his secretary of his intention, then set out for the second floor cafeteria.

Once inside the cavernous main dining area, he groaned when he saw how crowded it was and made a hard left into the more intimate, better-staffed doctors' dining room. The hostess escorted him to an empty table by the far wall and handed him a menu.

His waitress, a short buxom woman with steel wool-like hair tied back in a loose bun approached. As she did he happened to glance over her right shoulder. He recognized the slim profile, soft blonde hair, ankle-length skirt, and royal blue silk blouse partially hidden by the white clinic coat. Marshall stood and informed his waitress that he'd decided to switch tables.

"I didn't know they let nurses eat here," he commented amiably.

Sally glanced up from her journal, peered over her reading glasses and replied, "Marshall. Why, hello. If the nurse is an administrator they do. How you've been?"

"Can't complain," Marshall said. "Mind if I join you?"

"Suit yourself. Just let me finish this paragraph."

While Sally concentrated on her magazine article Marshall ordered a club sandwich. Then he leaned over to see what Sally was reading. There was a diagram of the heart occupying half of one of the pages.

"Studying?" he asked.

"No, not really. Just getting updated. Hunter's been experiencing a lot of chest pain recently. He went to see Chris Jeffries on Monday. He's scheduled a cath for Tuesday. He thinks it's time for that bypass the boss' been avoiding for so long. Hunter wants Jeffries to do one of those minimally invasive procedures that are getting more popular." She pointed to the article she was reading. "I thought I'd see what the nursing literature has to say about them."

"He *was* rubbing his chest a lot the last time we met. I thought it might be his heart."

"He should've had the surgery years ago. But Hunter's such a proud, stubborn man. I know he thought if he ignored it, it would go away."

Marshall nodded. Regarding Sally he couldn't help but notice how attractive she looked in the subdued dining room light. He had decided to approach her now, but expected the interchange to be awkward. After all, hadn't he virtually ignored her since the hospital day at Kennywood Park? But to the contrary, it seemed like she wasn't holding a grudge.

"How've you been, Sal?" he asked cheerfully.

"I can't complain, Marshall. Work here and my kids at home keep me pretty busy. How about you? I haven't seen you around much these days. Is it business or pleasure that's keeping you away?"

"I guess you could say a little of both."

"How so?" Sally replied. "You know I called the Friday before last. Maggie offered me a pair of tickets to the City Theater for their Saturday night performance. I was hoping you were free."

"I'm sorry I missed the call."

"You really should get an answering machine, you know."

"I've been meaning to."

"Were you away?"

Marshall debated answering the question truthfully. Up until now no one was officially aware of his relationship with Rose.

I guess if I should tell anyone, he reasoned, *it should be Sally.*

"Actually, I was away. Rose Shaw asked me to go to Erie with her for the weekend. Her father's ill. His social worker was pushing to send him to a nursing home. She wanted Rose's input. It gave her a chance to visit."

"But why with *you*, Marshall? Why would she ask you to go? I thought you hardly knew each other."

"That's not exactly true, Sal. We've been seeing each other."

Sally didn't reply right away. Eventually she murmured, "Hmmm."

"You don't look surprised."

"I'm not."

"Why not?"

"Because I suspected as much."

"And apparently you're not pleased."

"Actually, Marshall, I'm concerned."

"Concerned? What's there to be concerned about?"

"Rose Shaw, Marshall. I'm concerned about you and Rose."

The pangs of guilt he'd been feeling turned to annoyance.

"Why on earth would you say that?"

"Because I don't trust Rose Shaw, Marshall," Sally replied curtly. "That's why."

Marshall started to process this response, resisting reacting too harshly. He'd expected Sally to bristle at the notion of his relationship with Rose. But this brazen attack on his girlfriend's character was completely unexpected. There was nothing in his experience of Rose that suggested she was untrustworthy.

Taking pains to keep his tone soft and measured he asked, "Why do you say that, Sally?"

"It's just a sense I have, Marshall, based on certain things I've heard."

"You've heard 'things'?" he repeated. "You mean gossip?"

"No, not really gossip. You might call them strong rumors—about things Rose might have done before coming to Pittsburgh."

"That sounds a little vague," Marshall said. "What's the difference between gossip and rumors? Has anything been substantiated?"

"Partially."

"Partially? Now what's *that* mean? You know, Sally, I think you'd better tell me what you've heard about Rose."

Sally paused. "All right," she finally agreed. "But before I begin, let me know how specific you want me to be."

"Specific? Be as specific as you can. What else would you be?"

"What I tell you may put a damper on that blossoming love affair of yours."

"Is that so? Well, don't you worry about my 'love affair'. I'm a big boy. I can take whatever you're going to tell me."

"But if some of this stings, I'm truly sorry."

"Don't be," Marshall shot back, angry at being coddled. "Speak up. I'd really like to hear what you have to say."

Sally nodded solemnly and began her story. It was a tale that began in 1990, five years before Rose came to work at the Hunt when she was fresh out of medical school working in a privately funded research lab in downtown Baltimore, owned and operated by a biogeneticist named Peter Davis.

"I remember Hunter mentioning the place in the mid-nineties when I sat in on the Credentials Committee," Sally said. "It was called the

Davis Biomedical Research Laboratory. The people there were making quite a name for themselves with their innovative work into gene decoding. In fact, Davis was a National Science Award finalist for his work on DNA mapping. And somewhere I'd heard he was one of the first scientists to do gene transfers in living subjects."

"Well, if a prestigious place like that recruited Rose, doesn't that imply she had pretty impressive credentials?" Marshall pointed out.

"You'd think so," Sally agreed. "But there's more. It seems that after Rose had been working at the lab for less than a year Davis suddenly divorced his wife. Two months later he married Rose. Rumor has it that she'd been having an affair with him during her senior year at Hopkins."

This disclosure caught Marshall off guard. Rose had never mentioned being married before. He'd just assumed she'd always been single—which he now realized was pretty naive of him. However, the idea of her having an affair with a married man did surprise and upset him.

"Rumors again," Marshall retorted. "How could you know about such a thing?"

"It came out in the subsequent investigation."

"Investigation? What investigation?"

"The one into Davis' supposedly accidental death three and a half years later."

"Accidental death?" he echoed. "What happened?"

"His car skidded out of control on an icy road near their home in suburban Baltimore. It was three in the morning. He was driving to the lab."

"That's horrible. But why did you say 'supposedly' accidental?"

"Because when one of the insurance investigators checked their garage, he found a puddle of hydraulic fluid on the floor. Rose collected two million dollars in insurance money. The company tried to implicate her in the accident."

"You mean they think she did something to cause it? That sounds a little far-fetched." Marshall felt a mixture of anger and defensiveness. It was like these allegations were being leveled directly at him. "Was anything ever proven?"

"The investigation was ruled inconclusive," Sally replied, her voice soft and placating. "Rose was exonerated."

"Which doesn't surprise me one little bit."

"Why do you say that?" Sally asked.

"Because the Rose I know would have never done a thing like that. She couldn't have. And I happen to know her pretty well."

Sally winced at this statement. "Probably not," she agreed. "But I'm just relating what the committee discovered when they did their background check."

Marshall recalled his own application process for employment at the Hunt. The interview with Hunter had been a mere formality. His references, one of which he knew for a fact was never submitted, had been accepted without reservation. His credentials were never verified or challenged.

"Sally, why would the committee investigate Rose so thoroughly? Why would they even think to look into her background?"

"Because the story was impossible to ignore. When Rose applied for the job here, we requested the standard letters. By convention, one of her references had to come from the chief clinical researcher at her lab. He was a guy named McCafferty. Apparently he and Davis had been good friends. In the 'comments' section of his reply he mentioned the investigation into his boss' death."

"That was a rotten thing to do," Marshall remarked.

"I know. But apparently Rose hadn't made a lot of friends when she worked at the lab."

"That may be so. But like you said, nothing's ever been proven."

"No."

"Which makes sense."

Sally frowned. She obviously didn't agree with his conclusion.

"Is that all?" Marshall pressed.

"That was the major item. There were also some minor discrepancies in her original application for employment. We couldn't confirm all the work experience she claimed to have. And a couple of the awards and citations she said she'd earned couldn't be authenticated. That sorta thing."

"Sally," Marshall said, "despite all this suspicion and concern about Rose's sordid past, Hunter still hired her."

"Yes, Marshall," Sally admitted, "Hunter hired her."

"With what you've told me about her background, why would he go and do a thing like that?"

"If I recall correctly," she replied slowly, "he said he had a gut feeling about her. He liked her dynamic personality and strong temperament. He thought she had a winning attitude and expected she would give the research department a much needed shot in the arm."

"And the committee valued his opinion. After all, he does seem to be a pretty good judge of character."

"Yes, that's true."

"Then in that case, I guess I've got nothing to worry about."

"I suppose you're right, Marshall," Sally conceded. "You have nothing to worry about."

chapter twenty-six

the vote

Marshall had only been in the boardroom a few times, but each time he entered its venerated confines he stood in awe. The rich woodwork, the huge oblong desk surrounded by eighteen heavy oak chairs, the thick burgundy draperies tied back to expose tall rectangular windows, the deep pile carpeting, and the gallery of portraits on the walls conferred upon it an air of stately sophistication. The business of the institute was conducted within these sacrosanct walls. And now he was privileged to both witness and participate in it.

He had arrived a few minutes early, cradling a cup of coffee and watching the other members of the Executive Committee stroll in. All the departments of the hospital would be represented. Also scheduled to attend were the president of the medical staff, two administrative aides, and the chief financial officer. By 9:10 A.M. everyone who was coming was seated. One chair remained conspicuously empty. Then, in what Marshall regarded in a somewhat officious manner, Chris Jeffries stood up, banged his gavel twice, and called the meeting to order.

"First I want to take this opportunity to welcome everyone back to the table," he began graciously, his tall, angular frame impressive at the far end of the table directly across from Marshall. "You can see, the chair to my left is vacant. As all of you must have heard by now, Dr. Hunter suffered a major heart attack on Wednesday evening. He is now on life support in the coronary care unit. In fact, I want to thank all of you for adjusting your schedules to accommodate this earlier start time for the meeting. This will allow me the flexibility to chair the meeting then participate in our CEO's bypass operation and valve repair after he returns from the cath lab later this morning."

A hum of mumbles and murmurs circulated around the room. Some of his colleagues nodded grimly, acknowledging Dr. Jeffries' expression of gratitude.

"Although I know Dr. Hunter would have preferred to be here today, from what I could tell from my limited interactions with him, he finds postponing discussion on the business of running this hospital unacceptable. Thus we will proceed without modification during his absence. The first agenda item is the fiscal state of the institution. For that report I turn the floor over to our chief financial officer, Mr. Luchtenstein."

A short, middle-aged man with dark glasses and an old-fashioned paisley bowtie stood by his seat. He cleared his throat then directed the group to one of the handouts in their packets. While the committee members leafed through the pages, he delivered The Hunt's comprehensive business report.

At first Marshall found much of this information interesting. But eventually the repetitiveness of the figures took its toll and not even the CFO's unusually high-pitched voice could focus his attention. Involuntarily his eyes kept drifting to the empty seat to the president's left.

No, this was not the first Marshall had heard of Hunter's near-fatal myocardial infarction. Had he been home on Wednesday night, he would have received the news directly from Sally. She'd left a message on his new answering machine around nine. Marshall, meanwhile, had been in Rose's condominium, handcuffed, on his knees, and stimulated to distraction by a woman acting the role of his fantasy mistress. He subsequently learned of the tragedy upon arriving at the work the next morning.

From the moment Marshall entered his office he knew something was amiss. Two departmental secretaries huddled by the coffee machine conversing in hushed, intense tones. He sensed the ominous mood. Breaking his pattern of never offering more than a perfunctory greeting, he asked Bonnie if anything was wrong.

"Haven't you *heard?*" she asked, wide-eyed. "Dr. Hunter's had a massive heart attack. He's in intensive care. They're not sure if he's going to make it."

The shock of this announcement vibrated through Marshall like a jackhammer. His own chest tightened and he caught his breath.

"What?" he asked dumbly. "Are you sure?"

"Of course I'm sure," Bonnie replied indignantly. "My friend's a CCU nurse. She worked night shift and was there when he came in. He's on a respirator and one of those balloon pumps. Right now they're giving him a fifty-fifty chance. They think he must have ruptured his mitral valve too—whatever that means."

Despite his relative ignorance about cardiac emergencies, Marshall assumed Bonnie meant that Hunter had suffered a heart attack and the part of the apparatus that held his mitral valve in place had broken loose, causing a sudden rush of blood back toward the lungs. Once documented and stabilized, this condition would require emergency surgery. He would probably go right to the catheterization lab to confirm the diagnosis. Marshall dashed out of the department and headed for the coronary care unit.

"So you see," Mr. Luchtenstein was saying in summation, "the hospital is in an extremely favorable financial position. We're three million over budget from our clinical services, two of our minor construction projects are nearing completion, and we're planning to break ground on the new research building in March. The financial backbone of the institute, The Heritage Foundation, has benefited from the recent bear market to amass assets exceeding a quarter of a billion dollars. Thus, barring any unforeseen disasters or overzealous, highly leveraged buyouts, we should be in excellent fiscal shape well into the next century."

The CFO sat down. Jeffries rose to introduce Mr. Abe Martin, who delivered the Board of Directors report to the Executive Committee. This was followed by a series of departmental reports, most of which were brief and of little consequence. In due course he was polled and offered no report. When the acting chairman of the thoracic surgery department rose and delivered a long-winded description of some new, highly technical equipment recently acquired for the OR, Marshall thought of Hunter.

Hadn't Sally been reading up on minimally invasive open-heart surgery in anticipation of Hunter's elective bypass operation? he recalled. *It looks like the old man had waited too long. Much too long.*

When Marshall had arrived in the coronary care unit the scene was what he like to call, 'organized chaos.' Nurses, doctors, and technicians scurried around in a myriad of directions, most heading for or emerging from one of the dozen or so patient cubicles which radiated like spokes from the modular nurses station. A parade of mobile equipment rolled to and fro before him. Some, like the portable x-ray and sonography machines, stomach suction pumps and respirators, he recognized. Others were completely foreign. This was, after all, alien territory to him, as familiar as the surface of Mars.

I can't remember the last time I did a psych consult in CCU, he reflected ruefully.

A cursory survey of the unit and a few brief inquiries to the staff helped him locate Hunter's room. It was the oversized cubical adjacent to the sliding doors through which he'd just entered, labeled, appropriately Marshall decided, Number One.

When Marshall walked in he found the room already occupied by a nurse adjusting the regulators on the IVAC machines, a perfusionist seated by a sophisticated pump at the foot of the bed, a respiratory therapist making changes on the respirator by the head of the bed, and a hemotech withdrawing some bright red blood out of a plastic tube coming out of the patient's groin. With some sidestepping and a few mumbled apologies Marshall managed to locate an unoccupied corner of the congested cubicle.

Had Marshall not known Bertram so well, he wouldn't have recognized the man—that's how different he looked. His face, distorted by an endo tube extruding from his mouth, looked bloated. His white hairy chest was shaved and pocked with cardiac monitor tabs. Several IV sites violated his arms and a latticework of tubing, resembling a tangle of transparent worms, snaked along his skin.

Hunter, Marshall acknowledged, resembled a typical ICU patient. What had only two days earlier been a vital, dynamic, energetic chief executive, had devolved into a grotesque caricature of himself.

"Is he awake?" Marshall asked, hoping he'd spoken loud enough for the nurse to hear.

"When he's not sedated," a fair-haired young woman commented without shifting her attention from the complicated array of IV bags and dispensers. When she was finished she glanced over. "He really hates the tube. When he fights it his pressure goes through the ceiling."

"Are they taking him to the lab today?" he asked.

"Dr. Carter isn't sure. He said if he can keep him stabilized for the next twenty-four hours, the procedure would be less risky. They just did the echo and the tech says it doesn't look like he ripped a chordae."

"Which means the valve is competent," Marshall translated, more for himself than the nurse.

"That's what they think. Which makes the operation less of an emergency."

"And the more stable he is when they go in, the better his chances," Marshall completed the train of thought.

"That's the theory."

"Now we've reached the new business portion of the meeting," Jeffries informed the committee. "And without further ado I think we should proceed with the first item, choosing a new chairmen for the Biomedical and Bioprosthetic Research Department."

This introductory remark riveted Marshall's attention upon Jeffries. When he finally tore his eyes away from the head of the table he checked the pile of papers on the table before him. After shuffling through the first half dozen or so he came upon a familiar three-page report. Soundlessly he separated Rose's psychological assessment from the remainder of the papers and placed it on top of the pile.

"Now normally this would be a routine appointment with little discussion," Jeffries continued. "But with the construction of our new five-story 150,000 square foot research and development complex, a structure almost exclusively devoted to genetics and molecular biology, this position takes on enormous scope and influence. Thus, in accordance with our bylaws in such matters, we've decided to make the appointment an agenda item and put the candidate's name up for a vote."

Jeffries introduced Rose into the proceedings. He then directed the members of the committee to the biographical sheet in their packet. While the others sorted through their papers, Marshall took a moment to once again review the psychological profile. The first two pages, he noted, were exactly as Don Owen had submitted with the history, physical, and what were collectively called the 'objective personality tests.'

"You also have in your packet," Jeffries was relating, "a copy of a psychological profile performed by Dr. Friedman and submitted as further data in order to assist you in casting your vote. By the way, thank you, Marshall for taking the time and effort to contribute your expertise to this process." Marshall blushed, nodded, and then waved meekly. Then he glanced toward the bottom of the second page. He noted where he'd modified the results of the 'projective tests', specifically the Rorschach, so that they came out in Rose's favor. The final assessment was also Marshall's invention. So, despite the fact that Don Owen had performed the evaluation and submitted the initial report, the finished product was Marshall's.

As he attempted to justify, in his own mind, his unorthodox, unprofessional actions, a conversation he'd had with Rose over lunch a week earlier popped into his head. In the wake of Sally's accusations about Rose's previous wrongdoing, Marshall had been having second thoughts about supporting Rose's nomination. He decided to confront her about the charges.

"I can't believe she's dredging up that story about Peter again," Rose growled while stabbing at her salad with a fork. "It's fucking ancient history, Marshall! And none of her damn business." Marshall, shocked by her irate tone, didn't comment. "I suppose you want to hear what really happened?"

"It would set my mind at ease," Marshall admitted. "The truth is, Rose, at this stage of the game, I'm anxious to know everything there is about you."

"That's so sweet of you to say, Marshall," she said. The acrimonious edge to her voice indicated otherwise. "The truth is—I never did anything wrong. It was an accident, pure and simple. It was a cold snowy night in the middle of February. Peter, my husband, was called to the lab. His head researcher, an old fart named McCormick, was working on decoding a critical portion of the human DNA genome. True to form he'd run into a snag with one of his sequencing experiments and needed Peter to help him out. Peter couldn't resolve the problem over the phone so he went in. This, you have to know, wasn't unusual. He was bailing McCormick out all the time. Where we lived in Woodlawn wasn't that far from the lab. He could be there in fifteen minutes."

"But this time there was an accident?"

"Yes," Rose confirmed, "a bad one. Our house was at the crest of a long windy road. It had snowed earlier that evening, lightly, but enough to leave a fine coating on the street. By midnight it was a sheet of ice. Peter only made it about a half-mile down when he hit one of those curves and skidded. The car went through the guardrail and crashed onto the switchback twenty feet below. The coroner concluded he was killed on impact."

"That's so horrible."

"More than horrible, Marshall. It was the worst night of my life. I had to go down to the morgue and identify the body. Peter's head must've gone through the windshield and his face was so messed up I could hardly recognize it. But, of course, I knew it was him."

Her tone, which had up until now had remained even and under control suddenly, became louder and shrill. "And the bastards from the insurance company claimed I did it," she said, seething. "They said I killed him for the insurance money."

"That was one of the things Sally mentioned," he said keeping his own voice measured. "What was that all about?"

"Oh, one of those damn insurance investigators thought he was Columbo or something. He stopped by the house right after the funeral—while I was in my grieving period—and started grilling me about our relationship; you know, why did I marry Peter in the first place? Did I really love him? He made a big deal about the fifteen-year difference in our ages—as if it really mattered. The asshole even wanted to know about our sex life."

Marshall reached over and patted her hand. He wanted her to know he was on her side.

"Marshall," Rose continued, "if I was a man I would have punched him right in the face. I tried to throw him out. But he wouldn't go until I let him check out the garage. So I did. I had nothing to hide. Then, a week later, some police detective from the local precinct came by and insinuated that the accident was really a homicide. Apparently there was a puddle of brake fluid on the garage floor. That dick from the insurance company said I sabotaged Peter's car."

"I'm no lawyer, Rose, but that sounds like pretty flimsy evidence to build a case around."

"It was, Marshall! When the detective had the forensic lab check the fluid, they discovered it came from *my* car, not Peter's. Which makes more sense since it was found on the part of garage where I parked. But by then the reporters had gotten hold of the story and my reputation was shot."

"So that's when you decided to leave Baltimore?"

"Soon after."

Marshall nodded. He could see she was upset—her forehead lined, her eyebrows furrowed, the corners of her eyes blackened by mascara-tinged tears. She raked her thick fingers through her hair. Marshall reached out and took her hand.

"You believe me, don't you Marshall?" she pleaded. "You believe I didn't do anything wrong?"

"Of course I believe you, Rose. I know you could never do something like that."

"Good," she said, lifting his hand to her lips.

By the end of that luncheon Marshall knew what he had to do.

Sitting at his spot around the boardroom table Marshall reviewed, with some satisfaction, the modifications he'd finally made in Dr. Owen's psychological assessment of Dr. Rose Shaw. Fortunately there was enough ambiguity in the results of the subjective section for Marshall to modify his resident's report.

As the members of the committee were given a few minutes to review his submission, Marshall flipped to the final assessment. Silently he read the report and compared it to the original.

Impression: Normal Psychological Function

Dr. Shaw appears to exhibit normal psychological function in the routine history, physical examination, and psychological testing. She possesses a strong personality type, which is characterized by high motivation, independent thinking, and advanced leadership skills. Although the results of the objective psychological testing suggest a trend toward self-serving, unconventional behavior patterns, the responses on the subjective evaluation modifies this impression. Her comprehensive profile suggests individuality, strong personal drive, creativity, and intellectual superiority. This is reinforced in the Kiersey Temperament Sorter where the subject fulfills the portrait of a 'promoter' or someone who is 'concrete in speech, utilitarian in achieving goals, directing and expressive.' In short, the subject appears to be a woman of action.

He had deleted the section called *Treatment Recommendations*.

As Marshall reviewed his creation, a shudder of guilt spread over him. He felt like a character out of Orwell's *1984*, changing the future by modifying the past. Rather than using a knife and glue, he had utilized his computer to cut and paste.

He knew Owens's original report would have destroyed Rose's chances of getting the position. But he had no obligation to turn in Owen's work. After all, when it came down to it, it wasn't really the resident's report, was it? Hunter had asked Marshall to work up the profile himself. He, thus, had final responsibility for its authenticity. And had he done the evaluation himself, he knew that he would have come up with something more closely resembling the document in its modified form. So, in that respect, he was being genuine.

He patted the breast pocket of his blue blazer and felt the fullness within, a bulge created by the pair of round trip airline tickets to New York City. *And besides,* he rationalized selfishly, *if Rose loses the vote, we'll have nothing to celebrate.*

The balloting began. One of the administrative assistants, a woman named Janet Prizlak, began calling out names. There were sixteen voting members in the room. The poling was being done roughly according to seniority. Since Marshall was the newest member of the committee, he would cast his ballot last.

He diligently kept track of the tally. After thirteen members had voted, the count was seven to six in favor of Rose election. The chief of radiology, a man who had been brought over from the University hospital in the spring, was polled. He said nay. Marshall wondered what he had against his girlfriend. The acting chairman of thoracic surgery was next. He said yea. Marshall breathed a sigh of relief. If Marshall voted for Rose, she would have a nine to seven majority. If he voted against her it would be tie. Since half the committee wanted her, even without him, he felt further justified in throwing his hat in her corner.

"Dr. Friedman?" Janet asked.

Marshall took a deep breath, unfolded his hands and laid them flat on the table before him. "Yea!" he declared.

"What's the count, Janet?" Dr. Jeffries asked.

"Nine to seven, in favor of Dr. Shaw."

"Then that does it, gentlemen and ladies. Dr. Shaw is the new chairperson of the research department."

A hum of reactions erupted. A staccato rap of the gavel silenced the group.

"But before we go on, there is one last vote regarding this matter that I'd like to submit. As you know, earlier this morning, I stopped in the CCU and visited with Dr. Hunter. His sedation was just wearing off and when he saw me he stopped fighting his tube. I tried to communicate with him for a few minutes. From the expression on his face I could tell he understood what I was saying. He knew I was going to this meeting. Before I left the room he gestured toward a pair of envelopes which were on his server. I finally realized that he had intended for me to bring them here."

He held up two mustard-colored manila envelopes. They were of the type commonly used to send memos around the hospital.

"The one I have here is Dr. Hunter's absentee ballot. I purposely held it back until everyone else cast theirs so Dr. Hunter's vote wouldn't influence you other committee members. And besides, according to protocol, the CEO only gets to vote in the case of a tie. So his vote would have been last anyway."

A hum of voices broke out around the room. Jeffries waited for them to quiet down. Marshall reflected back on a morning, just five days ago, when he'd handed Hunter Rose's modified psychological profile. Later that day, the CEO had informed him that he was satisfied with the assessment and even mentioned that he fully expected the committee to approve Rose. So, the logical conclusion was that Hunter had voted for Rose.

"The other envelope," Jeffries continued, "is for Dr. Friedman." At the mention of his name, Marshall felt his throat tighten. He really hated having the spotlight trained on him so much. Jeffries handed the second envelope to Janet who walked it around to Marshall. Instead of checking its contents he took it from her and set it down on the table. "Now," the medical staff present continued, "let's see what have we here?" Like a presenter of an academy award, he glanced at the piece of paper and with a grim frown, nodded. "Well, from what I can tell from this marker, Dr. Hunter has voted, 'nay'." He held up the piece of stationary. It had an arrow written in bold black ink pointing away from the letterhead.

"So people, the tally is amended as follows: nine for and eight against. Dr. Shaw still carries the day."

Marshall sat in a stall in the bathroom. He took a deep breath and ripped open his envelope from Hunter. He dumped out a scrap of paper which fluttered down onto his lap. Picking it up he noticed that it, too, had symbols on it. But instead of an arrow, there was a pair of X's, standing right next to each other. What Marshall saw was,

XX

He considered them for a while. He had no idea what they meant. But he really didn't care. Whatever its significance, he rationalized, the cryptic message didn't change anything. The election was over. Rose had gained her position. Her future was secure. He could finalize his divorce now, which would allow him to integrate his future with hers. After that they would have her abbreviated lifetime to celebrate.

chapter twenty-seven

moving on

When Marshall returned to the hospital on Monday morning he found it difficult getting back into the swing of things. The place looked the same. The staff went about its business in a usual manner. But things seemed different. Perhaps it was because, for the first time in almost ten years, he was single again.

The evening before he'd flown back from a weekend in New York. Although he'd accomplished what he'd set out do, it had been nothing like he'd planned. The adjustments had begun early Friday afternoon right after he'd informed Rose of the committee's decision to elect her chairperson of the department.

Rose had garnered the news with a modicum of excitement. But her smug confidence suggested that she'd expected the result. Her attitude caught him off balance. Then when he checked if she was ready to leave for the airport, he almost stumbled.

She asked if he would make the trip without her, citing some last minute work that she had to finish in the lab by Monday. "The main reason you're going to New York is to finalize the divorce," she reasoned. "I don't have to be there for that."

Marshall, blindsided by this rejection, stuttered, stammered then implored her to review the demands of her job and see if she could do the work and still accompany him. She countered with, "Now that I've been entrusted with this new position, my work has to take priority over my social life. We'll both have to make sacrifices, Marshall." She tried to mitigate the blow by reassuring him that she would make it up to him as soon as possible. She hinted about future trips to exotic places where they could rehearse their erotic role-playing. But he wasn't consoled. Instead he felt dejected and annoyed, ruefully appreciating how being her champion had its unforeseen costs.

Sitting at his desk he twirled a pencil between in his long fingers and searched for inspiration. Morning intake rounds began in ten minutes. His mind, however, was miles away, reflecting on the importance of the weekend that had just past. Despite Rose's absence, his excursion to Manhattan still represented a defining moment in his relationship with her. Coming directly on the heels of her narrow victory at the exec meeting, the finalization of his divorce from Bernice provided Marshall with the liberty to consider his immediate future. With Rose set in Pittsburgh as long as her heart held out, and with his own position at the Hunt relatively secure, his life fanned out before him like a yawning vista of tantalizing, if not limited, possibility.

He thought about Bernice. He had to give her credit for being both gracious and accommodating during such an emotionally charged time. All he'd done was make the trip. She'd orchestrated the rest. Before Saturday, it had been two months since he'd seen her. He wasn't sure how she'd react, how they would interact. In the end it turned out just fine.

Marshall noticed how light the downtown Manhattan traffic was early on this Saturday morning. It felt good being back in the city again, gliding down Fifth Avenue, surrounded by familiar landmarks, buildings, and stores. When he passed Saks, then Bergdorfs he considered the gifts he'd like to bring back for Rose, who was probably slaving away in her Pittsburgh laboratory.

The cab zipped by Doubleday's bookstore where Sandi had scheduled one of his book signings last spring. Hell, it seemed like years ago. Where had the time gone? Now he had a meeting to discuss his *next* book scheduled with her that afternoon.

He stepped out in front of the Empire State Building. Leslie Levy's law firm leased a suite of offices on the twentieth floor. Marshall always enjoyed his visits to this local landmark. It gave him a chance to ride up to the observation deck on the hundred and fourth. Playing wide-eyed tourist once again, he took a special elevator to the building's zenith. Standing on the platform, he leaned against the Plexiglass and absorbed a panoramic view of the most populated city in the country.

Just after nine o'clock, Leslie met him at the door with a handshake and a pat on the back. Marshall smiled amiably. "How you doin', big guy?" his old friend asked as they started down a long hallway. "It's great seein' you again. Too bad it had to be on such an unfortunate occasion. I always thought you and Bernice were in it for the duration."

"Things change, Leslie," Marshall commented frankly. "And so do people, I suppose. We had nine good years together."

"I guess you did," Leslie agreed. "Anyway, we're set up next to my office in the conference room. You know the one, down the hall and to the right."

Of course Marshall was familiar with Leslie's suite. He'd been there a dozen times before. As he strolled down the long corridor he thought about some of those experiences.

My God, Marshall mused, *we have been through a lot these last ten years. And so have our friends. Ah well, that was then and this is now. It's time to move on.*

Hesitating ever so slightly, he pushed the cherrywood door open and peered inside. Although it was just after nine, he was the last to arrive. He looked for Bernice and noticed her sitting at the end of the conference table adjacent to a fair-haired young woman in a powder blue sweater. Leslie followed him into the room and introduced her as one of the firm's secretaries who would function as both witness and recorder for the proceedings.

Marshall nodded, hopeful that all this would be little more than a formality. After all, didn't most couples execute their no-fault divorces by mail? But he was pleased that Bernice had suggested they do it in person. It offered him a sense of closure.

Bernice, he decided, looked exceptionally attractive this morning dressed in a black business suit with a white blouse opened wide at the neck. From his vantage point by the door he noticed her shapely legs and the casual manner with which she sat back a little from the conference table. He especially liked the way she tucked her jet-black hair neatly behind her ears, exposing much of a complexion that boasted a healthy tan. A lingering effect of her Greek Isles cruise, no doubt. Feeling self-conscious, he approached, leaned over, and gave her a peck on the cheek.

"Hi," she said, studying his face. "Thanks so much for making the trip. It's not like you live around the corner."

"Don't mention it. It's a great excuse to visit New York again. Just riding in the cab down here was a treat. I didn't realize how much I missed being in the city."

"There's a lot to miss, Marshall."

After they were all seated, Leslie called the meeting to order. As Marshall had hoped, the legalities proved to be little more than a formality. Without children there was no child support. Bernice was independently wealthy, so alimony was a non-issue. Then when it came time to discuss the settlement agreement, he learned that Leslie's people had come up with a fair assessment of their accumulated wealth. The suggestion was made that they split their assets right down the middle.

Bernice wanted the condo, the furniture and the artwork. Marshall, in turn, would receive compensation for his half of the real estate and its valuables. The Mercedes, an uncontested gift from Bernice, was his to keep. Beyond that there was no further property left to divide.

Before they concluded, Leslie reviewed Marshall's options regarding their mutual investments. After some deliberation, Marshall decided to liquidate his portion of the holdings, anticipating reinvesting the capital with a brokerage firm in Pittsburgh. Leslie, in turn, offered to draw up the necessary papers and send them along. Finally, as an unexpected gesture of her good will, Bernice agreed to forfeit any rights she had to royalties from his first book. After that the divorce papers were signed and witnessed.

With the formalities over, Marshall felt eager to depart. He glanced nervously at Bernice, who seemed to appreciate his anxiety. Leslie, as if appreciating the solemn nature of this moment, gathered up his papers and asked his secretary to join him in the adjacent room. The divorced couple was suddenly alone.

Marshall stood at his seat for a moment, then eased the heavy chair under the table. Bernice approached him.

"I guess this is it," she said, her voice barely audible

"I suppose so," he replied, steeped in the awkwardness of the moment.

"Time to move on."

"Yep," he agreed with a nod. "Time to move on."

She glanced down, as if uncertain what to say next. Then she gazed into his eyes and commented, "We had a good run, Marshall. Didn't we? I mean, it wasn't a waste of time, was it? Any regrets?"

"It was great while it lasted, Bernice," Marshall reassured her. "We were awfully young when we met. Maybe too young to get married. We probably weren't mature enough to know what we really wanted. But we chose well. I have no regrets."

"That's good," she replied, her head bobbing in staccato nods. She looked relieved. "That's good," she repeated.

He held out his arms. She didn't resist. After the hug she rested her head against his cheek a moment longer than protocol might dictate. Finally they parted. Holding her at arm's length, Marshall said simply, "I've gotta to go."

She nodded again, emotion evident on her face. He suspected that she was close to tears.

"Do you have someone waiting?" she asked.

"Not here."

"Back in Pittsburgh, then?" He nodded. "So you really are moving on."

"I suppose you could say that."

"Well, so am I," she countered, a little too emphatically.

"I know. Sandi told me."

"He's a nice man, Marshall," Bernice volunteered. "He works as a stockbroker for Prudential Securities. We met on the cruise. He's been divorced for eight months now. We're taking things slowly."

This was more than Marshall wanted to know. But he kept his uneasiness to himself. *She's entitled to confess,* he conceded, *if that's what she thinks she's doing.*

"I wish you all the happiness in the world, Bernice," he said, trying not to sound patronizing. "Really."

"I know you do, Marshall. And I you. You're a good man, an honest man. I've always admired that in you. It's what attracted me to you in the first place. If nothing else, stay that way."

"That's sweet of you to say, Bernice. And I will."

There's nothing more to say, Marshall thought.

He glanced at his watch. He saw that Bernice noticed the gesture.

"I know, I know," she said. "You have to go." She took his hand. "I'll walk you to the elevator. I have some matters separate from the divorce to discuss with Leslie." They walked down the hallway and waited for the car. "Enjoy your weekend in New York," she said. "I hope your friend is nice."

"Thanks," he replied with sincerity. "By the way, I'm meeting with Sandi Coles in Central Park this afternoon. Should I give her your regards?"

"Of course," Bernice agreed.

Their hands parted. He turned and stared deep into her eyes.

"Be happy, Bernice. If anyone deserves it, you do."

"Thank you, Marshall. I will."

chapter twenty-eight

where do we go from here?

With the pressures of the executive committee vote and his divorce proceedings behind him, Marshall felt compelled to focus on more pressing and ultimately, more distressing matters. Topping that list was Rose's fragile health. In the whirlwind of activity in which he'd been immersed these last ten days, he hardly had a chance to consider it or its ramifications. Now, sitting alone at his desk in the department, he grappled with the notion that this incredible woman, so attractive, intelligent, and professionally driven, harbored such a serious congenital heart problem. His first impulse was to deny its validity. But she'd described her condition to him in earnest. Its existence was difficult to refute.

In a kind of obsessive stupor he reviewed then reassessed the subtle signs and symptoms Rose had exhibited over the last couple months. He kept replaying in his mind their stroll up Beachwood Boulevard when she'd been forced to come to a panting stop. Then there was the afternoon on the Presque Isle when Rose had difficulty negotiating the stretch of sandy beach on their way to the lighthouse.

There were other instances too, seemingly insignificant at the time, but now taking on more magnitude, walking in the park or climbing the red-carpeted steps in the downtown music hall when Rose had to stop and catch her breath. And she always refused to do anything too physically taxing, like play tennis or ride a bike. He'd always sloughed these objections off as being unimportant, assuming she was merely out of shape and didn't want to show it. Now he knew differently.

The duskiness of her features and the clubbing of her fingers should have alerted him. These, he knew, were not the signs of a normal healthy middle-aged female. Even a psychiatrist with a limited background in general medicine should have appreciated that. But he hadn't. And as a consequence her revelation had come as a complete surprise.

Now he was better informed about her condition. Last week, during a short break in his busy schedule, he slipped over to the hospital's medical library and checked out what the major cardiology texts had to say about Epstein's Anomaly. Then he had the hospital librarian perform a Medi-search for him. She delivered a pile of papers, more material than he could ever hope to review. And for good measure, late one evening he'd surfed the Internet for hours, hoping to discover some less conventional, possibly experimental treatment that would offer Rose a shot at more precious years than she could currently expect. Nothing even vaguely appropriate showed up.

Yep, Rose had been straight with him. It was not unusual for infants with this type of congenital abnormality to survive into their twenties and thirties. But only a rare individual could expect to enjoy a normal lifespan. Once symptoms occurred the short-term prognosis became guarded. The two most ominous signs were right-sided heart failure and rhythm problems. Rose already manifested both.

Later that day, while walking over to the clinic building for his afternoon of office patients, he thought back on those earlier psychoanalytic sessions with Rose. He wondered if knowing of her heart disease would compel him to modify his preliminary conclusions. Originally he'd regarded her as an energetic, adventurous young woman, who, as a child, had been throttled and confined by a rigid, old-fashioned, and domineering mother. But now the classic battle between the overprotective mother and the rebellious pre-adolescent took on a whole new dimension. He had focused on Karen Shaw's compulsion to control the innate curiosity and audaciousness of her daughter. Now he suspected that it was Rose's weak heart that must have forced her mother to set extremely narrow limits. He recalled the smoking incident when Rose was nine. Naturally this dereliction assumed greater significance.

Ensconced within this morass of re-evaluation and introspection, Marshall's felt his own heart reach out to Rose. Like a benevolent guardian he wanted to tuck her under his wing and protect her from the harsh reality of the two worlds she inhabited, the hostile one without and the diseased one within. He sensed a part of his very nature being revitalized, the aspect of his personality that longed to rescue and shield. It was what his own therapist, when he'd gone through analysis so many years ago, had nobly labeled his 'hero complex'.

But ironically, at the moment that he longed to be with Rose the most, she seemed the least available to him. He phoned her after returning from New York and several times at work the next day. He left messages with her secretary and on her answering machine. He was assured that she'd get back to him directly. But it wasn't until late Monday evening that she finally returned his calls.

She was terribly sorry for being unavailable. But with her new position, a demanding reality had emerged. She was now negotiating the transition from researcher to chief with no end to the items she had to address. Today, for instance, and for days to come, she would be sequestered in meetings with the outgoing chairman, others reviewing research plans, updating data bases, verifying deadlines, revising schedules, and documenting the details of both new and old projects. Tomorrow a representative from the building committee was scheduled to meet with her leading to many more hours spent pouring over blueprints and architectural models, studying hypothetical floor plans and three-dimensional computerized mock-ups, hoping to optimize the space available while creating an environment which would foster both productivity and camaraderie. The evenings, she warned Marshall, were crammed with appointments and conferences, with marketing specialists, product representatives, and technical experts all designed to make the new research building the quintessential facility of its kind in the nation. And because of her fragile health she was hesitant to include an active social life to the mix.

Although he was annoyed and frustrated that she hadn't made room for him in her busy schedule, he said he understood. A rigorous schedule could be very draining, even for someone at the zenith of health. For Rose it could be physically damaging. Appreciating her dilemma he forgave her for not making their relationship a priority. Before they hung up he did extract a sincere promise that they would get together for a while on Saturday. She wished him goodnight with a reaffirmation of her undying love for him.

Not even the pale gray sky and blustery autumn breezes could put a damper on Marshall's elevated spirits Saturday morning as he drove along Grandview Avenue toward Rose's Mount Washington condo. Anticipating their day together he bristled with excitement.

They would take a scenic drive eastward toward Latrobe along wooded rural roads where the autumn leaves were already changing. Before lunch they could stop at one of those rustic little state parks and take a leisurely hike along one of the numerous nature trails. After eating a bag lunch he'd let Rose rest for a while. Later they'd stop at Nino's, a charming Italian restaurant nestled in the friendly community of Mount Pleasant, for dinner. Lastly, if the mood struck them, they could spend the night at one of the local bed and breakfasts or head back home.

He parked his Mercedes in the guest lot across from the main tower. It had been eight long days since he'd kissed Rose good-bye at the hospital before leaving for the airport. No wonder his heart was palpitating. He had every right to be excited about seeing her again.

The uniformed guard buzzed him in. Marshall strolled up to the reception desk and asked to have Dr. Shaw notified of his arrival. While the broad-shouldered young man sifted through a pile of notes on his desk Marshall thought to himself, *I've gotta get myself a key to her place. This nonsense about checking in then being announced is a pain in the ass. It makes me seem like a common guest.*

The guard glanced up. "Did you say your name was Friedman?"

"That's right."

"I've got a message here for you from Dr. Shaw."

Suddenly feeling a little flustered, Marshall said, "You do?" Then he took the beige-colored envelope from the guard and mumbled, "Thanks." Nodding he turned and went over to one of the chairs near the front windows.

> *Dear Marshall,*
>   *Please forgive me for not phoning. Something came up and I've been forced to leave town. Sorry I spoiled our day together. I was really looking forward to our afternoon in the country. I'll make it up to you as soon as possible. Call you when I get back.*
>   *Love, Rose.*

Marshall's shoulders sagged, and then his face fell. He'd been so looking forward to this time with Rose. What could possibly have come up? Burdened with this uncomfortable sense of disappointment he set his hands on his thighs and stood up. As he walked back to his car he speculated on the nature of Rose's emergency. Perhaps it had something to do with her heart.

Maybe she isn't going out of town after all, he fretted, *but is getting more symptomatic. She mentioned that her cardiologist worked out of Mercy Hospital. Maybe she's there.*

And if it wasn't her health, what else could be so important as to break their date? Could it be her father? Perhaps he's taken a turn for the worse and she's in Erie. That made some sense to him. At least it was another possibility to check into.

"Oh, well, Dr. Friedman," he said aloud. "It looks like you have the remainder of this balmy autumn day all to yourself."

Using his cellular he called Mercy Hospital and learned that no one by the name of Rose Shaw had been admitted. He also tried St. Francis, West Penn, Shadyside, and the University hospital. No one by that name was an inpatient. Mr. Shaw's number was at home. He'd have to wait on that one.

Now, left on his own, the day was laid wide open before him. His week at The Hunt had been extremely hectic. Preoccupied by his investigation into Rose's cardiac condition, he'd fallen behind on everything else. What better way to spend a dreary Saturday than to catch up on his work? And visiting the hospital would give him a chance to see Hunter.

Despite his earnest intention to check on his boss, Marshall had been barely able to step foot inside his cubicle all week. The gravity of the CEO's post-operative condition, made worse by a serious of unforeseen complications, had prompted a bevy of specialists and technicians to engage in one intervention after another. This management schema presented a physical barrier preventing Marshall from entering the room.

But this is Saturday, he reasoned. *The dust must have settled by now. At least enough so that I can steal a few precious moments with the man.*

Thus, Marshall returned to the Hunt and worked in his office for the rest of the morning. Just before noon, he took an ursine-like stretch of his thin arms, rubbed his tired eyes, rose to his feet, and set off for the fifth floor of the Tower Building.

As he patiently stood in the nurses' station waiting for the RN to hand him the chart, he noticed how quiet things were. Only a smattering of critical care specialists mulled around, perched before the bank of cardiac monitors, charting on the patients, or performing routine treatments in the cubicles. Many of the dozen or so rooms were vacant, their post-operative heart patients transferred to a lower level of care.

"Dr. Hunter's still in room one, Dr. Friedman," related Corinne, a full-figured young woman with a mop of lifeless brown hair. She wore pink OR scrubs and a pair of soiled tennis shoes. "The endo tube's still in so he's pretty sedated. But with the blood gases we got this morning the pulmonary tech thinks we can extubate him before dinner."

"That sounds encouraging," Marshall commented. Hunter had been on the respirator for almost ten days now. "How's his mentation when he's not sedated? Is he oriented? Does he understand commands?"

"Best we can tell," replied Corinne, her manner crisp and professional. "He's moving all four extremities and follows instructions pretty well. But he really fights the tube, so we keep him snowed."

"Makes sense to me. When do they think he'll be transfered?"

"Hard to say," she commented. "He's still on that balloon pump. But they're talking about the HeartMate. If he can be stabilized on that, maybe two or three days."

"The HeartMate?" Marshall asked. This sounded like some cardiac support group.

"It's one of those left ventricular assist devices, a mechanical pump that's implanted in the abdomen with a controller. It's powered by an external battery pack worn outside the body."

Corinne handed him a picture from the manufacturer's in-service packet. It depicted a diagram of the heart inside the chest. There was one large bore tube running from the aorta and a second from the tip of the heart both connected to a small circular pump implanted inside the body. A third tube, smaller in diameter, ran from the pump across the skin line to a square box labeled, 'system controller.' The final part of the complicated device was a battery pack attached to a strap draped over the patient's shoulder.

"They call it a bridge to transplantation," she added. "I've actually treated a few patients who've survived with it in place for a couple of months. They say the Cleveland Clinic has the largest series to date, almost three hundred and fifty."

"So they're serious about transplanting him?"

"Seems that way," she confirmed. "There's not much of an alternative, is there?"

"No, I guess not," Marshall said softly. "Can I see him?"

"Be my guest."

Even devoid of all the professional personnel, the room seemed small. Perhaps it was the extra equipment, Marshall thought, noticing the miniature respirator, the old-fashioned suction pump, the adjustable tray-like server and the squat machine by the foot of the bed that he assumed was the balloon pump. Appreciating the nature of this last apparatus drove home the gravity of Hunter's situation. The man's once vibrant and exuberant existence literally rested in the hands of these cold, inanimate, mechanical devices, instituted to assist a heart that didn't have enough power to meet the body's most basic needs.

Hunter, Marshall noted, looked much like he did the morning after his heart attack. The color of his skin was pasty, his face still distorted by the endo tube, his chest rudely violated by incisions and monitoring tabs. His hair, thin and disheveled, seemed grayer than Marshall recalled.

And his legs, spread with his feet pointing outward, were mottled and marred by lacerations.

A large bore catheter emerged from his shriveled member and a set of thinner IV tubes entered his inguinal area. Marshall noted that the urine in his Foley bag was cloudy and concentrated, roughly the color of apple cider. He wondered about Hunter's kidneys. Probably not doing great, he decided.

"Sad, isn't it?" asked a disembodied voice from the doorway. Without turning around he knew to whom it belonged.

"Very," he replied softly. "And depressing as well. Do you think he'll make it?"

Sally walked up and squeezed his arm. "I hope so, Marshall," she said. "He's such a tough guy. He's got a strong will to live. If anyone can survive this thing, he can."

"But the odds are against him."

"More than he realizes."

They stood that way for a while. Marshall gradually sensed the details of Sally's presence next to him, her height in relationship to his, the clean smell of her hair, the angularity of her body. It felt oddly comforting having her so close.

"How's Maggie holding up?"

"Not well, I'm sorry to say," Sally admitted. "She did okay with the heart attack and bypass surgery. I think she'd been expecting that for a while now. And she might appear like a fragile Southern belle to the outside world, but there's a core of strength running right through her. But this past week, with day after day of complications and setbacks.... Well, Marshall, it's starting to take its toll. She's been sleeping in the waiting room almost every night, then taking all her meals in the cafeteria. When I saw what she looked like this morning I told her to go home. One of the techs drove her. I was afraid to let her drive herself."

Sally reached up and dabbed the corner of Marshall's eye with a tissue. She'd come prepared.

"Do you have any plans for lunch?" she asked. There was a hopeful, although somewhat pessimistic tone in her voice.

"As a matter of fact, I'm free all afternoon."

"Would you like to take a walk by the river? There's a nice little restaurant near the stadium I've been dying to try. It's a bit of a trek from here, but I was looking forward to the exercise."

"Sounds fine to me," he replied, suddenly glad for an excuse to leave this gloomy setting. "My jacket's in the office. I'll meet you in front of the hospital in ten minutes. Okay?"

"I'll see you there."

chapter twenty-nine

by the allegheny

Marshall noticed how choppy the dark green river water looked as he and Sally ambled down the concrete path between the Ninth Street Bridge and the Alcoa Building. Stirred by gusty winds, thousands of white caps played on the surface of the Allegheny.

They reached a narrow asphalt pathway and turned parallel to the river. Marshall commented about the Riverside Run, a ten-kilometer race whose course stretched from Three Rivers Stadium to Washington's Landing. "I saw the pamphlet at the Rivers Club. But I haven't jogged for distance since I moved here from New York, so I decided against registering."

Sally nodded, sweeping her hair back off her face and securing it with an elastic tie. Marshall flipped up his jacket collar. Across the river dozens of ultra-modern office buildings and department stores were crowded into Pittsburgh's famous Golden Triangle.

They walked in silence, passing a series of office buildings near the Seventh Street Bridge. Sally pointed out a young male photographer standing on the grass near the river filming a flock of the mallard ducks swimming by the massive black stone stanchion. A pair of in-line skaters darted past and broke his concentration.

The path widened. As it broadened it seemed more desolate, adding for Marshall a sense of emptiness that melded seamlessly with the lingering depression that had plagued him since visiting Hunter earlier that day. How much of this was also due to Rose's absence? He was worried about her. He wondered where she had gone. He was spending time with Sally. But it was with Rose that he really wanted to be.

Sally said something. "What?" Marshall asked. It had been so long since they'd spoken, he'd missed the question.

"How's Rose?" she repeated.

"Good," he replied. "She's good. Why?"

"I'm surprised you're not with her today. Is she working?"

"As a matter-of-fact we were supposed to spend the day together. We planned a drive out to Westmoreland County to see the leaves change. But when I got to her place this morning there was a message for me. Something came up. She had to leave town."

"I hope nothing's wrong."

"I hope so too."

"Didn't you say her father was ill?"

"Uh-huh. That's what I thought too. I'm was planning to call Erie when I get home."

"That's a good idea."

They walked along for a while. Marshall noticed a set of abstract art sculptures to their right, their colors washed out by the flat autumn light. He glanced over at Sally. She was studying her feet so he let it pass. The balmy breeze caught her ponytail and sent it flying. Marshall thought she looked melancholy. His relationship with Rose probably made her uncomfortable. Why in heaven's name had she brought it up in the first place?

"You know Rose isn't well either?" Marshall commented.

"Yes," Sally revealed, "I did. In fact, that's one of the reasons I wanted to talk to you."

"Really?" Marshall replied feeling genuinely surprised. "How much do you know?"

"I know that Rose has Epstein's Anomaly and she could be dead soon."

"That's pretty blunt," Marshall said.

"It's the truth, isn't it?"

"I suppose it is," Marshall conceded. "But I'm still hoping there are things that can be done to postpone that brutal reality."

"Such as?"

"Like repairing the valve or creating a shunt to make the blood flow more like normal."

"Isn't it too late for that? I thought those procedures were usually performed during childhood."

"The truth is, Sally, I'm not sure what's possible. A lot hinges on whether there's evidence of advanced right heart failure."

"Is there?"

"I think so. Her fingers are cyanotic and she seems really short of breath at times."

"Which doesn't sound good, Marshall," Sally replied, her tone more sympathetic. "I'm so sorry for you."

"Not as sorry as I am for her."

"That's understandable," she agreed patting him on the back. He glanced up and noticed the new PNC Park up ahead. "I'm not that hungry yet. Could we sit for a moment?"

"Sure."

They found a concrete bench that faced the river. On the water a tug pushed a pair of barges toward the Point.

"What about transplantation?" Sally finally asked.

"It hasn't come up in my reading. But I guess it's a possibility."

"Isn't it ironic," she commented, "that suddenly there are two people in our lives who both desperately need heart transplants."

"Yes," Marshall agreed, "in a society where donors are at a premium."

"Not a very optimistic prospect."

"No," Marshall agreed again, "it isn't."

Another pregnant pause in the conversation. An elderly couple strolled by and smiled at them. It was as if Sally was waiting for them to pass before she continued.

"Marshall?" she said inquiringly, "did Rose ever tell you why Hunter recruited her to work at the clinic?"

"He thought she'd be an asset to the genetics research program," he offered.

"Yes, that," she agreed. "But more specific."

Marshall couldn't imagine what she was driving at. He thought about his lone visit to the Biogenetics laboratory and pictured the odd set of specimens incubating in the Plexiglass containers. "You mean her cloning experiments?"

Sally nodded a little more animatedly. "Do you have any idea what she's *really* working on down there?" she asked.

"Besides fingers and ears and that kind of stuff?"

"That's right."

"No, what?" Marshall replied curious where this line of questioning was going.

Sally paused again as if considering how much to share with him. Gently she placed her fingertips on the back of his hand. For some reason the gesture seemed patronizing. He withdrew his arm.

Sally frowned and said, "It so happens Marshall that when Hunter brought Rose Shaw to Pittsburgh in nineteen ninety-five, it was with a very special purpose in mind. He knew about her work in genetic engineering and DNA transfer and that the Strauss lab was pioneering the work in the field of cloning. But he wasn't interested in creating items as simple as noses, ears or even fingers and hands. He wasn't even interested in growing whole animals like sheep or bulls. Hunter had a more specific—and I guess you could say more personal—reason for recruiting Rose. He wanted her to clone him a new heart."

"A *new* heart?"

"Yes, Marshall, a heart. It's not so farfetched. He knew his own was badly diseased. And it was only a matter of time before it would fail. He dreaded the idea of undergoing bypass surgery and suspected that since he was approaching sixty he was too old to be a viable transplant candidate. He also has O negative blood, making it very unlikely that he'd ever find a serologic match. So he realized that if he wanted to be around long enough to see his grandchildren grown, he would have to do something desperate."

"But I didn't see any hearts when I visited Rose down there in the lab."

"That's because that particular project is not on display. The work takes place in her secret lab hidden deeper within the research complex."

"A secret lab?" Marshall repeated incredulously. "Com'on Sally. If what you say is true, this is starting to sound pretty weird. You know, almost science fiction*ish*. Are you sure about all this?"

"Of course I'm sure, Marshall. I've been privy to the project since its inception. I even donated blood for the initial genetic typing experiments. The only thing I'm not sure of is whether there's still a human heart being cloned in that lab."

"Why?"

"Because President Clinton banned any further research into human tissue cloning in ninety-seven. That's when Hunter blew the whistle on the project. And now that he's sick enough to need it, I almost wish Rose had continued with her research."

"Even though it would be illegal? And besides, what's Rose have to say about all this? Does anyone know for sure if she's ignored the directive and kept the project going?"

"She's been queried. But you know Rose. It's impossible to get a straight answer out of her."

Marshall considered this for a moment. "Well *someone* must know about this little project," he contended, "someone who could clear up the mystery?"

"That would make sense wouldn't it? But besides me, Hunter and of course, Rose, only a couple of lab techs and Chris Jeffries knew about the project in the first place. And from what we can gather from various rumors, there *is* still something going on in that secret lab."

Marshall was still stuck on something Sally had just said. "Jeffries knows?" He asked. "Well if he knows," he continued, not waiting for her answer, "that would make him the likely operating surgeon if one was needed. And I bet he's hoping a heart still exists so he can implant it. The publicity alone would make him a celebrity overnight."

"Even if it's illegal?" she asked, almost mocking him

"I'm not so sure he'd care about that."

After the briefest of pauses she added, "Well, I spoke to Chris yesterday and he doesn't think it still exists."

"Do you believe him?"

"That's what he says."

Marshall took a moment to process all of this. If there was in fact a cloned heart hidden in some secret lab in the Hunt, eventually it would have to surface. And the most likely person to produce it would be its creator. Certainly, given the opportunity, Rose would clear up this mystery. And he didn't appreciate what Sally was suggesting when she implied Rose was withholding this vital organ—especially if it was Hunter's.

"Let me ask you something, Sally. Are you insinuating that Rose has done something disreputable here?"

"I'm not insinuating anything, Marshall," Sandy retorted. "The truth is, I don't know what the hell Rose has done. What I *do* know is that she was contracted to do human tissue cloning experiments. Then she was told to stop the project. Now no one knows if she has."

"If something as sophisticated as that does exist," Marshall offered, "do you really think Rose could keep it a secret?"

"If it exists," Sally replied slowly, "I bet she'd find some way of concealing it, especially if it had to be nurtured until it was ready to be implanted inside *her own* body."

This assertion caught Marshall off guard. "What's *that* suppose to mean?" he asked. "Do you think she's created a heart for herself?"

"That's exactly what I think." Then before he could protest she added, "It seems to me Marshall, that despite your affair with her, you don't know Rose that well at all. I didn't want it to come to this, but I think it's time to be frank. Rose Shaw is not that sweet little scientist you're in love with. She's a vicious, self-serving sociopath. She's interested in one thing and one thing alone—herself. And it doesn't matter who she destroys in the process of serving that interest. So, you see, it wouldn't surprise me one iota if she's still using the clinic's resources to clone a heart for herself, even though it's illegal. That, Marshall, would be completely consistent with who I suspect her to be."

"You know what, Sally, you're sick!" Marshall shot back. "Rose is nothing like that. She's kind and considerate. Oh, she might be ambitious and a little driven, but who in her profession isn't? And if she's preoccupied with her survival, how can you blame her? For God sakes, the woman only has five years to live. Wouldn't you be a little desperate, too, if you were in her shoes? My guess is, Sally, that that tirade of yours simply represents an overt expression of the jealousy and envy you feel toward her. And for that I feel sorry for you."

"Don't feel sorry for me, Marshall," she snapped back at him, her bluish-gray eyes ablaze. "And what's more, don't give me that psychoanalytical claptrap. I know what I'm talking about. I've known Rose a lot longer than you have. And despite your unsolicited assessment of my personality, I can actually be a lot more objective about Rose than you can, Marshall. After all, I have a lot less to lose if I'm right."

"Well, damn it, I'm going to prove you're wrong, Sally. I'm going to show you all."

"I hope you do, Marshall. I hope you do."

An uncomfortable silence hung over them. Marshall hoped he hadn't said too much, but knew he had. Sally, as if reading his mind, broke the impasse.

"But don't you see, Marshall," she said, her tone more conciliatory, almost placating. "It would have been so easy for her to utilize the institution's resources to realize her own personal needs. And if she has, she's double-crossed Hunter and seriously jeopardized the institution in the process."

"But," Marshall countered, his voice also calmer now, "didn't Hunter conceive of the project in the first place to realize *his* own selfish needs? Wasn't he simply using Rose to ensure his own survival?"

"Perhaps. But he knew enough to stop it. I don't think Rose has that kind of integrity."

"Is that so? So we're talking about integrity here? Well why don't I go to Rose and try to clear up the mystery?"

"That would be splendid. You could go and see if you can learn the truth. And, if she's still growing a cloned heart down in her secret lab, and it still has Hunter's genetic compliment, get her to produce it. Then, despite the illegalities, maybe we can find some way of using it to save him."

"I can do that, Sally. But it's more likely that when I do learn the truth, there will be no heart and you'll have to concede that Rose isn't the monster you've made her out to be."

"On some level I hope you're right, Marshall. More for your sake than mine, I hope you're right."

chapter thirty

domination

The next morning, when Marshall visited Hunter he found him extubated but in no condition to have an intelligent conversation, so he spent the rest of the day anticipating Rose's return. About five o'clock she called from the airport. Her plane had just landed and she was waiting for her luggage at baggage claim. She'd been in Minneapolis interviewing grad students to work in the lab next year. She invited him to her condo for dinner and "whatever". He hung up the phone overwhelmed by a mixture of excitement and relief.

Rose greeted him draped in a short pink terrycloth robe. Her make-up was off and her auburn hair seemed wet and slick. It appeared like she'd just stepped out of the shower.

"Hi," she said, giving him a hug. As he warmed to the pressure of her body, she kissed him full on the mouth. This rush of sensuality disoriented him. After they parted Rose stepped back, smiled at his reaction then took his jacket. Setting it on the arm of the recliner she commented, "Oh, Marshall, I've had such a long day. I hope you don't mind but I thought I'd shower before you came over. How about a drink?"

"Uh, sure," he replied, still tingling. "Maybe a Coke or something." She headed off to the kitchen. "I can't believe how much work this new job is turning out to be," she called. Returning to the living room, she handed him his soft drink and plopped down on the sofa. In her hands she cradled a glass of wine. "It really bums me out that we don't have more time together. But I can't do anything about it."

"I know that," he said graciously. "I understand what you're going through. It's just that I really miss being with you."

"I miss you too, Marshall," she agreed and tenderly stroked his cheek. "But now that you're here, let's see if we can pick up where we left off."

"Sounds good to me."

He sat there, sipping his drinks and letting the mood envelop him.

"Hungry?" she asked.

"Famished."

"Mind if we order out? I'd rather not start putzing around in the kitchen."

"Of course. I couldn't expect you to cook dinner right after returning from being out of town for the weekend."

"Thanks. What are you in the mood for? Casual or fancy?"

"You mean for dinner? Oh, casual's okay."

"Good. Could you give Pizza Outlet a call while I get ready? There's one over on Grandview. I'm pretty sure they deliver."

"What do you like on your pizza?"

She told him then turned and left for the bedroom. As her shoeless feet slid along the white carpet Marshall noticed how the fullness of her calves tapered into a pair of taut tendons. Just this limited glimpse of her shapely legs gave him a thrill. He couldn't wait for the rest of the evening .

The pizza arrived fifteen minutes later. Marshall set down the copy of *People Magazine* and answered the door. He paid the delivery girl, set the box down on the dinette table, and called Rose. She instructed him to get some plates from the kitchen and start without her. He was in the middle of his second slice when she called him into the bedroom.

The pale room was illuminated by a white Lalique lamp set stylishly on one of the nightstands. Marshall looked for Rose and noticed her sitting hunched over a make-up table in the far corner. He walked over, expecting to see her applying lipstick or eyeliner, or whatever women do when they made themselves up. He stood behind her and was treated to a whiff of her perfume. He felt a rush of excitement. As if sensing him there, Rose reached behind her and cupped the back of his neck. She eased him forward and gave him another kiss on the lips.

"I know you've already started eating," she whispered into his ear, "but I thought I'd have an appetizer first. Care to join me?"

He looked around but didn't see anything even vaguely resembling food. Then he appreciated what was laid out on the make-up table and gasped.

"Is that what I think it is?"

"What do you think it is?"

There were two parallel lines of white powder arranged on the surface of the almond colored table. Beside them was a four-inch piece of tubular glass, roughly the bore of a drinking straw.

"It looks like cocaine to me."

"That's what it is."

"You're not going to do that stuff, are you?"

"I sure am. Why shouldn't I?"

"Because it's a drug, Rose. It's an illegal substance." He knew his argument sounded lame. But it was all he could come up with for the moment.

"So what, Marshall. We're adults. We're entitled to do anything we want."

"But it's a crime."

"That's true," she agreed, "but who's gonna know? And besides," she added before he could reply, "once you've had some you'll know it's worth the risk. Have you ever done snow, Marshall? If you have you know what an incredible rush it gives you. Like every nerve in your body is primed and ready to be stimulated." She took his hand and pulled him down so that he was on his knees beside her. Peering deep into his eyes, she implored, "Come on, Marshall. Give it a try with me. You can't imagine how good it makes you feel."

Although he had some resolve in the matter, he sensed that his resistance was wavering. He'd experimented with marihuana as an undergraduate at Pitt, then occasionally during medical school. But since then he'd stayed clean. And although he'd had a couple opportunities he'd never considered doing cocaine. Oh, sure, after talking to some of Bernice's high society friends and analyzing the experiences of several of his patients, he had experience with the effects of the stuff. The sensations while under the influence were apparently incredible. And from what he could tell, as long as one didn't have heart disease or a seizure disorder, it was pretty safe.

But Rose *did* have heart disease, he suddenly recalled. "What about your heart?" he asked plaintively.

"It's never bothered me before."

"Well there's always a first time," he reminded her. But she brushed him off with a flick of her hand. Suddenly her confident bravado had him off balance. And as he teetered between acquiescence and condemnation, she snuggled her face into the crook of his neck and slipped her hand between his thighs. "Please Marshall," she cooed. "It'd be so much fun. I don't want to get high alone."

"All right," he capitulated. "But you'll have to show me how."

"Oh that's the easy part," she told him.

Twenty minutes later the tingling and irritation inside his nostrils had finally passed. But the rush of sensation was just beginning. Like a blast of cool air coursing through his head the languor of this lazy Sunday evening evaporated. He felt like his brain was on full alert. He looked around expectedly, his senses honed to a sharp hue. He felt hungry for stimulation, anxious to process any incoming input. And Rose seemed ready to provide some.

She left him sitting upright on the side of the bed, his eyes darted back and forth, his racing heart pounded forcefully in his chest, pulses of nervous energy coursing through his system like flashes of heat lightening. The painting across from him, an impressionist's landscape, seemed to explode in an eruption of soft pastels. He was totally engrossed in this visual spectacle when Rose tapped him on the shoulder. She moved into his field of vision and he finally noticed her. She was dressed in a black leather halter-top which barely covered her breasts. Her skirt was so short that he saw where the garter belt attached to her fishnet stockings. In a pair of black leather boots with three-inch heels she literally towered over him.

"Marshall," Rose said holding out her hand. "Come with me."

He followed like a child into the other bedroom. This room was almost dark. Protruding from the far wall was a row of narrow white tapers, each in its own ornate iron holder. Rose guided him over to the near wall and had him stand with his back against the smooth surface.

"How do you feel, dear?" she asked pleasantly.

"Fantastic," he replied, still pre-occupied by the rush of energy pulsating through his body. "And very horny," he added with a sly grin.

"I thought you might be," she said, with an amused smile. "We'll deal with that soon enough. But now I want to play a little game with you. After what you've shared with me about your fantasies, I think you'll enjoy it."

Feeling curious and intrigued, Marshall waited to see what Rose would do next. He watched as she walked over to a small chest that was pushed up against another wall. She pulled open top drawer and withdrew a few unusual looking items. One resembled a riding crop with a cluster of leather strands attached to a short round handle. This was followed by two pairs of shiny handcuffs and a thin foot-long chain with alligator clips attached to each end. There were other things in the drawer. Marshall recognized a ping-pong paddle, knives in leather sheathes, and what looked like a pair of clothespins connected by a thin chain.

Holding the handcuffs and riding crop Rose returned to where he was standing. Bending over and leaning forward she drizzled the leather strands between his outstretched legs. "Still excited?" she inquired.

Through his khaki pants the touch of the crop sent shivers into his pelvis. He nodded enthusiastically.

"Good," she said. "Then why don't you get out of those bothersome clothes so we can maximize your pleasure."

He felt so excited by this prospect that his mouth literally watered. Willingly he complied with her request. A few seconds later he was standing completely naked.

"That's good, Marshall," she said approvingly. "Now, just so you remain completely exposed and pretty much at my mercy I want to attach these things to your wrists."

She held out the handcuffs. Working dexterously she snapped one half of each pair to his wrists and the other half to hooks that protruded from the wall behind him. He'd noticed these metal supports when he walked in but had no idea what they were designed for. By the time this was apparent he stood secured to the wall.

"Now that I have you powerless, Marshall, let's take a moment and see how sensitive you are to my touch." She brushed the leather crop along his right thigh, then every-so-lightly between his legs. The caress felt incredibly intense. Once again he was aroused. Rose noted his reaction with approval. "Let's see how responsive you are to the touch of my other instruments of pleasure." She stroked him again. "You'd like more of this, wouldn't you? It's yours if you continue to obey me. Resist, however, and the opposite may very well be true. Which," she added with a malevolent chuckle, "you might enjoy as much. Understand?"

"Yes," he heard himself saying, his voice hoarse and dry.

"The proper response is 'yes, Mistress Rose'," she instructed.

"Yes, Mistress Rose," he replied before he could grasp what he was saying.

"Good!" She exclaimed and looked very pleased.

"Now on your knees and face me!"

The handcuffs pulled at his arm sockets. She knelt in front of him, her breasts out of the halter-top. She had him lick them. Their soft fullness made him so aroused he almost exploded. Then, just when he was becoming engaged, she pulled back. Indicating that it was time to mirror her pleasure with his pain she took the chain with alligator clamps and attached one end to each of his nipples. He cringed at the noxious sensation. She stretched the chain. He arched his back to avoid the pain. It had started out as a sharp ache, but was now unbearable. He began to whimper. She told him to cry 'mercy' and she would stop. Otherwise she would assume he was thrashing around in the throes of pleasure and continue. Obediently he cried, "Mercy!"

The white Berber carpet felt rough against the skin on his knees. Rose stood up and placed a high-heeled boot up against his cheek. He extended his neck. She tapped on his head with the crop.

"Do not look at me until I tell you to, little slave boy," she crooned. "Next I want to show you how to greet me properly. The way you do that is to kiss my boots. That's right set your lips on the rich shiny leather, slave boy and rub your grubby little nose up against it. Picture my beautiful legs inside, longing to be caressed. Now kiss my boots, Marshall. Kiss them, one after the other. Feel the softness against your lips. Lick them. Lick them up and down. Coat them with your saliva. That's my boy, Marshall. That's my little slave boy."

His instinct was to resist. But the closer his nostrils got to the boots, the sweeter the leather smelled. And before he knew it his nose was up against the pliant material. He inhaled deeply. His lips came in contact with the leather. The taste was bland and perhaps a tad bitter. Almost on its own his dry parched tongue protruded. He started licking.

On some rational level he imagined what he must look like. He expected his mind to register humiliation and disgust. But when he appreciated the waves of excitement coursing through his body, the rush of uninhibited sensual pleasure spreading to every pore, he knew he was hooked.

"That's good, Marshall, my obedient little slave boy. Continue licking a little higher. Rise beyond the top of the boot and up onto my stockings. That's it, walk that tongue of yours slowly up my white milky thighs. That's it. That's it! Higher and higher until you reach the tangy sweetness between my legs."

He did what he was told, brandishing his tongue like a scabrous brush, a darting probe, seeking then locating the briny folds between her legs. Suddenly his cheeks were pressed tightly against her inner thighs. He could sense the tension in her muscles. She began to moan, then gasp repeatedly, each breath catching in her throat, the sounds like a trumpet, spurring him on. His lingual manipulations became more animated. Her moans grew louder. Her reaction intensified his own excitement. He felt himself climbing a pre-climactic staircase.

"Ah. Ah. Ah!" she cried hoarsely. "Stop, Marshall! Stop! Not yet. Too soon."

He barely heard her. He felt the crop slip under his chin and pry his face away from her folds. Startled by the interruption, he stared up at her, dumbfounded. She, in turn, gave him one of those wide, beaming smiles. He felt warmed, as if she'd turned a heat lamp upon him.

"You're such a good submissive, Marshall," she praised. "You follow instructions very nicely."

He returned the smile, proud of himself, glad that he could please her like that. Patiently he waited on his knees, curious what she would have him do next. The idea of being at Rose's mercy thrilled and excited him. Suddenly he felt the crop again. It grazed his back, slithered down his spine, and then crossed his naked buttocks. A moment later it nestled between his legs and began stroking his dangling manhood. Instantly he was hard again. Then she attached the leash.

In retrospect, when Marshall looked back on what he came to regard as an incredibly humiliating and dehumanizing experience, the thing that symbolized it most was the leash. While he stood there in his submissive four-point position Rose snapped a rhinestone-studded collar around his neck. She then attached a narrow leather strap to it. Pulling taut on this leash, she made him lift his head and crawl across the room on his knees. After covering a few yards, while his breath was repeatedly cut short by the pressure of the collar against his Adam's apple, the surface abruptly changed from being rough and knobby to soft and fury. A few steps more and the leash became lax. Marshall's head, relieved of the tension, sunk down until his chin came in contact with a portion of Rose's bear skin rug.

"Now, Marshall," Rose instructed, "it's time to roll onto your back."

He was about to protest, but he'd played along this far. The truth was that much of the experience had been incredibly stimulating. Certainly there was more of that to come after this humiliation.

"Spread your legs."

Rose was beside him now, balancing on her own knees, leaning over his prostate body. A moment later she was upon him.

This, he realized, was his reward. Like concentric circles rippling from a stone breaking the surface of a lake, ripple after ripple of pleasure radiated from his groin. Almost uncomfortably erect now, the engorged vessels seemed about to burst. He moaned. He wanted no mercy this time. Instead he undulated under her ministrations, rising then slipping, approaching then receding, each time edging closer to the abyss.

Then, abruptly she stopped. He opened his eyes and gave her a confused, disappointed look. His reaction, however, lasted as long as it took her to mount him, like a cowgirl on a bronco. And just like that cowgirl, she rode him, balancing on squatting legs, rising to the point of disengagement then plunging, the descent punctuated by a subtle twist. The moisture of her internal fluids lubricating the piston-like motion.

It didn't take long. Amid a paroxysm of shuddering pleasure he climaxed. When it was over and he lay supine and immobile, somewhere on a remote edge of his consciousness he appreciated that he was more satisfied than he'd ever been before in his life.

chapter thirty-one

more cardboard boxes

When Marshall awoke the next morning he was distracted by the lingering effects of a series of lurid, erotic dreams apparently spawned by the sado-masochistic sex play from the night before. He licked his dry lips and detected remnants of Rose's briny taste. His nose hairs retained her particular smell. Opening his eyes he recognized the room with its purifying whiteness. But, when he reached over in search of her voluptuous body, he encountered rumpled sheets and a dented pillow.

Unfazed, he stretched his limbs and shuffled into the bathroom. While straddling the teardrop-shaped toilet bowl he called for Rose in a voice still heavy with sleep. He got no response. Rinsing his hands he went searching for her. In the living room he found the white curtains pulled back and a swatch of pale yellow sunlight filtering into the room. The mantel clock said seven. There was a yellow Post-it note on the kitchen counter.

> Had an early meeting. Didn't want to wake you. Hope you had fun last night. Call you later.
> Your loving Mistress, Rose

I guessed as much, he thought. Then, appreciating what she called herself, he felt his groin tingle. *And* yes, *Mistress, I did have fun last night.*

Back in the bathroom he showered, then helped himself to one of Rose's disposable razors. After applying some moisturizer, he checked his face for nicks, brushed his teeth, and decided that he was ready to tackle the day.

The whereabouts of his clothes was his next problem. He couldn't remember if he'd undressed in the bedroom or the study. He checked the smaller chamber, the one that doubled as Rose's dungeon. With a built-in desk, metal filing cabinets and a sophisticated computer station, it appeared innocently functional to him in the daylight. The wall hooks, however, were still there. At the sight of these, images of being restrained, humbled, and humiliated rushed at him. But he also recalled the incredible delights that came next. It took some time to shake off the odd sensation. Finally, emotionally composed, he returned to the living room and noticed his jacket on the arm of the recliner, but nothing else.

There was a long clothes closet in the master bedroom hidden behind a series of mirrored doors. Sliding open the pair on the left, he exposed half of the interior. Inside were dozens of dresses, business suits, blouses and tops. His khakis and blue oxford shirt were not part of the collection. He was about to check behind the second pair of doors when he glanced up and noticed a long wire shelf stretching the length of the closet. Atop it were hats, carry-on suitcases, storage boxes and stacks of sweaters. Nestled in the far corner a pile of shoeboxes caught his eye. Just as he was about to dismiss these as part of Rose's clothing collection, he had an odd sense of déja vu.

Was this another version of the storage system he'd stumbled upon in Rose's Millcreek bedroom two months earlier? He suspected this was so. Old habits tended to persist.

Taking a closer look, he noticed that the boxes were piled three high. Each had a label. He pulled out the bottom container and read: Gideon Crawford, September 30, 1987–June 4, 1989. This must be someone Rose knew during medical school, Marshall decided. He sifted through the pile of memorabilia and a faded color snapshot. It portrayed a handsome young man with a shock of brown unkempt hair and a thin serious mouth. His brown eyes were bright and mirthful. Sporting a Hopkins Medical School sweatshirt with *Class of '89* embossed across the front, if this was Gideon, he must have been an upperclassman, since Rose had mentioned that she had graduated a year later, in '90.

Along with the photo Marshall found invitations to two weddings and a bar mitzvah, postcards from Atlantic City, San Diego, and Vail, ticket stubs from various sporting events, local plays, the ballet, and one from the touring company of *Cats*. Other items in the box included a round trip plane ticket stub in Rose's name to Orlando, Florida and a yellowing newspaper article from the Suburban East section of *The Baltimore Sun*.

Marshall picked up the article and skimmed it. It announced Gideon's graduation from medical school and contained a list of the young man's academic accomplishments. Finally, it reported that he planned to enter a surgical residency at UC San Diego in the fall of 1989. But there was something else in the Sun article caught Marshall's attention. It was a notation toward the end of the last paragraph that Gideon Crawford's uncle was Peter Davis, founder and director of the Davis Biomedical Research Laboratories.

That couldn't be a mere coincidence, Marshall reasoned. One relationship apparently provided a link to the next. He wondered if the contents of the other shoeboxes would help clarify this supposition.

Replacing the lid, Marshall returned to the closet and took down the box with Peter Davis' name written on it. The dates December 22, 1989 to February 14, 1995, were also printed in neat block letters on the white label.

So it's true. Rose had *known Peter Davis while she was still a medical student, which makes the rumor about Rose and Davis having an affair during her senior year at Hopkins plausible.*

Only a few items were saved in this second box, several less than Marshall had expected. One, he noted, was a flyer announcing the 1989 Hopkins' medical staff Christmas party. A second was a torn American Express credit card receipt from a place called the Berkshire Arms in downtown Baltimore, dated March 23, 1989. Two yellow-tinged newspaper clippings were also inside the box, one documenting Davis' divorce from his wife in June of 1989, a second announcing his engagement to Rose. This last notice was dated two months after the first.

To Marshall these items were milestones, not momentos; records of events, not sentimental keepsakes. And rather than clarify matters for Marshall, they seemed to muddle the picture even more. If Rose was as romantic as he knew her to be, where were the tokens of her lover's esteem, the cutsy pictures of the two of them together, the fanciful souvenirs?

With a shake of his head, he set this small pile aside. Then he noticed a letter-sized manila envelope that seemed stuffed with a few more items. It intrigued Marshall that the name of a Baltimore law firm was on the return address. Reaching inside, he pulled out a copy of Rose's employment contract with the Davis Lab. Next came a program from the annual meeting of the National Society of Biomedicine and Genetics. Peter Davis had been the keynote speaker. The last item was an over-sized paperback book from the popular *For Dummies* series. This particular one was called *Car Maintenance for Dummies*. Flipping through the pages he noticed that the parts on hydraulic braking systems were highlighted. His chest tightened. The significance of this discovery struck him. He recalled the investigation into Davis' death. Was this circumstantial evidence that Rose had killed her husband?

Now don't be silly, he admonished himself. *This is just more of that inconsequential crap that Rose was bitching about. Davis was probably an amateur automobile mechanic and the book belonged to him.* But despite this convenient rationalization Marshall still had trouble shaking the uncomfortable feeling that there was something evil afoot.

He replaced the items and was about to continue his search when he heard the staccato high-pitched beeping of a pager. Although the sound was muffled it sounded familiar. Using its chirping he located the device clipped to his pants which were hanging next to Rose's winter suits on the left side of the closet. His shirt was there too. He checked the number on the digital display. It was his office looking for him. The clock radio on Rose's nightstand said eight-thirty. His sleuthing had taken over an hour. He phoned the hospital, lied to his secretary Bonnie that he'd overslept, and would be in by nine-fifteen.

The rest of his search would have to wait. Wistfully he took Davis' shoebox, placed it on top of Gideon's, and carried both back to the closet. Reaching up he took down the third then balanced the three containers in his outstretched arms. With it at eye-level he glanced at the label on this last shoebox. When he read the name he almost dropped the pile on the floor. There, printed in the same neat black block letters, was BERTRAM S. HUNTER. The corresponding dates were November 6, 1996 to June 15, 1999.

Oh my Lord! thought Marshall. *Rose and Hunter! And it lasted almost three years! No wonder Hunter seems to know so much about Rose. He had plenty of 'quality' time to find out. But she's never let on about it, always acting so cool and composed when they're together. And Sally must know too, beause Sally knows everything about Hunter. Wasn't she the one that mentioned an alternate solution to Rose's heart problems? Well, now it appears that there's more than one reason I have to have a chat with Dr. Bertram Hunter.*

Reluctantly, Marshall set the stack of boxes on the shelf, dressed, and left the condo. On his ride down the elevator he reflected upon what he still had to do. If Hunter was finally capable of talking, he'd find out what the old man knew. He also needed to establish once and for all if Rose was cooking up anything in her mysterious secret lab. Despite their having spent the entire night together, he'd been so distracted by their bizarre lovemaking that he'd forgotten to ask her about the cloned heart. Now he felt more compelled than ever to find out whether it existed, and, if it did, whose genetic complement had spawned it.

Emerging from formal lobby into the glaring autumn sunlight, Marshall resolved to have all his questions answered—and answered soon.

chapter thirty-two

clearing the air

Marshall finally got his chance to visit with Dr. Hunter late Monday evening after the patient had improved enough to be transferred to a low-level monitored bed on the Tower Building's seventh floor.

After a light dinner in the cafeteria Marshall finished some deskwork, then set out for the stepdown unit. Casually strolling along deserted hospital corridors, he recalled similar evenings during his medical internship when he'd passed through cavernous hallways at Philadelphia's Presbyterian University Hospital. Now, like then, his footfalls echoed hauntingly off clear glass display cases. In this pensive mood he reached the bank of elevators. As the brightly lit car arrived, he wondered how his conversation with the CEO would go.

When Marshall entered, Maggie Hunter was sitting in a recliner by the bed. She glanced at him over the rim of her reading glasses and raised a cautionary finger to her lips. Her glance directed Marshall toward the bed where he saw Hunter dozing semi-erect with a newspaper spread across his lap. After Marshall approached, Maggie offered him her cheek.

"Has he been asleep long?" he whispered.

"About forty-five minutes. Since the evening news ended."

"Should I wake him?"

"Sure. In fact, let me. Now that you're here, I can head home. I arrived at noon, which makes for a long day."

"I know what you mean."

"Bertram, dear," Maggie whispered into her husband's ear. The old man stirred then opened his eyes. "Marshall's here. He's come to pay you a visit."

Hunter turned a dopey stare from the source of the sound toward Marshall. His bushy eyebrows arched and his dry lips formed a half smile.

"Oh, Marshall," he said, his voice heavy from sleep. "How're you doin', my boy? I must've dozed off there for a moment." He slipped his wristwatch out from under the thin hospital blanket. "Oh my. I've been out for nearly an hour." Turning to Maggie, he added, "I'm so sorry, dear. I haven't been very good company, have I?"

"Don't be silly, Bertie," she said, stroking his face. "I'm just thrilled you're coming along so well. And, besides, Chris says you need all the rest you can get. I'm quite content to sit here and keep you company." Marshall saw his appreciative smile. "Marshall's here now, so I think I'll go. It's getting late and you know how I hate to drive in the dark." Marshall looked out the window and saw that the sun had indeed set, leaving a pewter sky swathed in purple in its wake. "I'll come back tomorrow around lunch time."

Hunter reached out and grasped his wife's wrinkled hand. She leaned toward him and they kissed. Marshall found the scene touching. He hoped his relationship with Rose would eventually be blessed with such warmth and affection. A moment later Maggie departed.

The private room, now occupied only by him and his boss, suddenly seemed uncomfortably quiet. Marshall pulled over a straight-backed chair and sat down near the bed.

"So how are holding up, sir?" he inquired. "You've been through quite an ordeal, haven't you?"

"More than you can imagine, Marshall," Hunter agreed. "And none of it was any fun."

"I would think not."

"But the rough stuff's over for a while. And Chris implanted this little device yesterday afternoon. He says it should take the strain off whatever heart muscle I have left." Hunter patted a solid object concealed by his gown. Marshall recalled the diagram of the left ventricular assist device Hunter's nurse Corine had shown him. "In fact, I might even be going home in a few days."

"That's wonderful," Marshall commented supportively. "So that's a HeartMate under there," he added.

"That's what they call it. They say it's the premier bio-medical invention of the decade. Without it I'd probably be dead."

"It's your bridge to transplantation," Marshall said metaphorically.

"Well, at least it's my ticket home and my lifeline until some compatible donor decides to cash in his chips. Which is pretty much of a crapshoot these days, if you ask me."

"That sounds awfully pessimistic, sir," Marshall commented, "especially for someone who's usually so upbeat."

"With what I've gone through already," Hunter confided, "the idea of having a transplant—with all its concomitant risks and complications—is tough to imagine. It exhausts me just thinking about it. You might think

I sound ungrateful, but I almost hope it takes a while to find one. Maybe I can even live out my life with this baby and not have to go through another operation at all." He patted the hidden battery pack again.

"I think you'd be forced into a pretty restricted lifestyle, sir. Which, in all due respects, is not the Hunter way."

"I suppose you're right, Marshall," Hunter agreed.

A silent interlude ensued. They regarded each other, but not directly. Marshall found the lull awkward and discordant, sitting there primly in his pressed blue blazer and jacquard tie. In contrast Hunter rested beside him in a wrinkled hospital gown hiked up so high that someone standing at the foot of the bed could easily see the his privates.

You check into a hospital, Marshall observed wryly, *and out checks your dignity.* Marshall finally broke the ice. "Sally and I were discussing your condition the other day," he commented. "She mentioned some alternative treatment for the heart disease."

"Besides transplant? Did she say what that alternative was?"

Marshall nodded. "It sounded a little fantastic to me, but she said it had something to do with cloning—a cloned heart that you commissioned Rose Shaw to grow for you."

"She told you about *that* alternative."

Marshall paused for a moment. "So it is true, then?" he finally said.

Hunter seemed to be considering his answer. "Yes, Marshall," he finally admitted. "What Sally told you is true."

"And she also implied that it's probably not a possibility any more."

"That's essentially right."

"Why not?" Marshall inquired, hoping to hear the answer from Hunter's own lips. "Didn't the project work out?"

"No, Marshall, the project was quite successful."

"Then what on earth happened?"

"I stopped the research two years ago when experimental study into human tissue cloning was banned in the United States."

"So that ended it."

"You would think so."

"You sound skeptical."

"I am skeptical, Marshall."

"Why's that?"

"Because I've got this sneaking suspicion that Rose Shaw disobeyed my directive and continued her research. I believe she's gone and cloned a new heart for herself."

"For herself?" Marshall repeated, trying to sound surprised. "But why would she do a thing like that?"

"I can only speculate on her motivation, Marshall. My gut feeling is that she feels her medical need supersedes mine."

What's so bad about that? Marshall thought but resisted saying aloud.

A cloud of silence descended upon them once more, this one more oppressive, more suffocating than the first. Marshall imagined them poised on opposing sides this disputed issue. Hunter seemed to sense his posturing and commented, "I guess, Marshall, since you're so involved with Rose, it's only natural that you would see it her way."

"I can't deny I have an emotional bias. But, except for what Sally told me, I really don't know the details, Hunter. I think it would help me to understand the ramifications if I learned how this all came about."

"That's fair enough, Marshall. Do you have some time? It might take a while."

"I have all night," Marshall indicated, "if that's what it takes."

"All right, son." The older man shifted slightly on his backside, then reclined deeper into the pillows. "I suppose it all goes back to the purpose for which Rose was recruited to work at the Hunt. Her expertise in biogenetics certainly made her an attractive candidate. But more so, it was the fact that her training gave her very valuable, cutting-edge insight into the field of tissue cloning." Marshall, though he knew all of this, was pleased to hear Hunter reiterate it. "Her skills had been honed at Peter Davis' Lab in Baltimore, one of the first research centers in the U.S. to actively pursue such projects. Had Davis lived and Rose stayed on there they would have probably cloned a non-human animal long before the Europeans."

"I toured Rose's lab downstairs," Marshall interjected. "She showed me some of what she's been doing there."

"Then you know what I'm referring to," Hunter said approvingly. "Did she happen to show you a heart?"

"No. As a matter of fact, she didn't."

"That doesn't surprise me, either," he said with a weary sigh. "As you must know by now, Marshall, that heart was supposed to be mine. In fact, my primary motivation for recruiting Rose was selfish. I wanted her to pilot a cloning program that would harvest the organ I desperately needed to survive."

"So it's true," Marshall said. "You *were* planning to be the first human to have his own cloned organ implanted."

"That's right," Hunter confirmed. "And if it succeeded, I would have achieved the lease on life I've been desperate for, not to mention a permanent place in the annals of medical history."

"But why you sir?" Marshall asked naively. "Why take the chance? Why be the first to undergo this kind of experimental surgery, with its actual and potential risks?"

"Why not me, Marshall?" Hunter counted. "Why not the founder of one of the most prestigious medical centers in the country, an institution that sponsors some of the most avant-garde research performed anywhere in the world. Who better than me should take the product of this innovative research and have it implemented? Imagine standing beside some of the real pioneers of medicine, men who've put their health and lives on the line to benefit their field of study."

Hunter leaned his head back and closed his eyes for a moment. When he opened them again, he regarded Marshall and asked, "Have you ever heard of Werner Forssmann, Marshall? He was a German house officer who, in 1929, was researching ways of delivering medications directly into the heart. In order to test his hypothesis he threaded a plastic tube into his left antecubital vein and advanced it until the tip entered the heart. Then he walked over to the radiology department and had an x-ray taken. And from that bold beginning the field of cardiac catheterization was born. Is it such a great leap of faith to see me in a similar role where cardiac cloning is concerned?"

Marshall recalled having seen a picture in his sophomore year of medical school of that very same x-ray, depicting a silhouette of the heart with a wormlike foreign body floating in the right ventricle.

"No, I suppose not," he conceded.

"I didn't think so either."

The piece of paper Hunter had sent him at the Executive Meeting came to mind, the one that displayed the pair of x's. "And you think that Rose has actually double-crossed you by keeping the project going?" he suggested.

"That's right," Hunter confirmed. "And as I mentioned to you, Marshall, not only did Rose disobey me, but she deceived me as well. She agreed to stop the project then went ahead and utilized the resources of the institution—the resources I provide her with—to continue the work."

"And you felt," Marshall confirmed, "that by informing me of that deception through a cryptic message at the Exec Meeting, it would give me the impetus to vote against her bid for chairperson of the research department?"

"That was my hope, Marshall," Hunter confirmed, sinking deeper into his array of propped-up pillows. "I knew the vote would be close. Most of the committee members were squarely in one camp or the other. Only a couple of swing votes were left. One, of course, was mine. Another was yours. And as I weighed my options, I knew that if I voted against Rose it would seriously jeopardize my marriage."

This confession confused Marshall. Then he recalled the shoebox with Hunter's name on it in Rose's closet.

"Are you alluding to the affair?" he asked.

Hunter paused, surprise in his weary eyes. "So you know about that, too?"

"Yes," Marshall replied, tactfully offering no more.

"How did you find out?"

"It's pretty tough keeping secrets around this place," Marshall commented vaguely.

"I suppose you're right," Hunter said with a sigh. "And yes, Marshall, it was my affair with Rose that gave me pause."

"So Maggie didn't know about it?"

"She didn't know then."

"How about now?"

"Now things are different," Hunter confessed. "Let's just say that since I've fallen ill, we've had plenty of time to talk. And compared to what I've been through as a patient in this hospital, confessing my moral transgressions was a breeze."

"How'd she take it?"

"Like the proud Southern lady she is."

"Good," Marshall said. He recalled the elderly couple's tender parting just a few minutes earlier. "And you said the other swing vote was me." Hunter nodded. "But what made you think I'd vote against Rose when you knew how much I cared about her?"

"Well, first, Marshall," Hunter replied, "I was hoping the results of the psychological assessment would influence your opinion."

Marshall frowned at the mention of the doctored report. He wondered if Hunter had noticed his expression. "But the report was favorable," he rejoined, his voice meeker than intended.

"We both know, son, that that report you submitted was a fraud."

"What do you mean by that?" Marshall retorted defiantly.

"Stop trying to cover up what you did, Marshall," Hunter countered. "You know how much personal experience I have with Rose. That's why, after your sugar-coated report crossed my desk, I felt compelled to make some discrete inquiries. Suffice it so say that it was pretty simple for me to learn that Don Owen had really performed the psychological evaluation. When I checked with him, he was only too happy to tell me what he'd discovered. You must admit, Marshall, the discrepancies between his conclusions and yours are striking."

Feeling guilt weighing him down, Marshall could barely hold up his head. Hunter had him dead to rights. He had wrongfully modified a sanctioned medical report and submitted it as an official document. And almost as soon as the subterfuge had been enacted it had been discovered. But more significant than that, in the process of protecting the reputation of his lover, Marshall had deceived a good man who had been his recruiter and supporter. Now, if Hunter chose to withdraw that support and dismiss him on the spot, Marshall had no recourse but to concur.

"But if you knew," Marshall asked, a hint of desperation in his voice, "why didn't you call me on it?"

"Believe me, Marshall, I was about to," Hunter conceded. "But unfortunately my heart attack came along, making it impossible for me to communicate with anyone."

"I suppose that's so."

"Until the meeting," Hunter added.

"When you tried to warn me?"

"Yes."

Marshall thought about this, recalling the executive committee meeting and the vote to elect Rose chairman. "But even if I was able to figure out that coded message referred to the cloning project, did you really think it would change my mind?"

"You already knew the results of Rose's original psychological assessment. That alone should have raised some question about her competency. Then, if I'd been successful in communicating her self-centered deceptiveness, it might have been enough to get you to vote against her. Given the condition I was in, it was all I could think to do."

"You ended up voting against her," Marshall related.

"Yes, but it wasn't enough."

"And you tried to warn me," Marshall repeated, more to himself than his boss, "but I failed to decode the message."

"Which is unfortunate, not only for me, but for the institution as a whole." Hunter sighed, his expression grim. Marshall knew it mirrored his own.

The CEO began to fidget, finally resting his head back against the headboard and shutting his eyes. "I'm getting pretty tired, Marshall," he admitted, his voice starting to falter. "This HeartMate is good, but not that good. I still need a fair amount of rest."

"I understand, sir," Marshall said, starting to rise. "But one thing before I go. Do we know for sure if there is a human tissue heart in the secret lab?"

"No, not really."

"Don't you think you should have some proof before we start crucifying Rose?"

"I suppose that's fair, Marshall. But in my current condition, I've no way of securing that proof. And besides, on a more practical note, even if the heart's mine, I couldn't take it now. It would be criminal."

"So let me get this straight. If there's still a human tissue heart down there, its very existence has far reaching implications for the reputation of the Hunter-Neuman Clinic. Is that accurate, Hunter?"

"Yes, Marshall. It is."

"So destroying it is somewhat of a priority?"

"I should think so."

"Then, if you've been so anxious to have this matter handled, why haven't you done something about it yourself? Why haven't you marched down to Rose's lab and learned if she has, in fact, been cloning a human heart? Then we would have all known for sure."

"Because I truly believed the project had been curtailed. It's only recently that I've given credence to rumors to the contrary. And before I could confirm them, I got sick."

Marshall listened to his boss and wanted to believe him, but didn't. He had another theory, a more plausible explanation, but given the fragility of his boss' condition, he hesitated putting it on the table. Instead he offered, "All right, Hunter. Since we do have to clear up this matter, what would it take?"

"For starters, how about finding out if the organ actually exists," Hunter suggested the obvious. "And if it's not down there in the lab—and I wouldn't put it past Rose Shaw to have hidden the damn thing somewhere outside the hospital by now—then try to find some documentation that it exists. She's a scientist. She must have a log of some sort where tissue samples and experimental procedures are recorded. Then cross match the medical record numbers with the hospital's computerized patient database and come up with some answers."

"I can do that," Marshall told him.

"Good," Hunter, appearing relieved. "I'll be anxious to learn what you find out."

"With that settled I guess I'll be going. Be well, sir. I hope you have a rapid recovery from this point on."

"Thank you, Marshall. That's very kind of you." Hunter then leaned over and opened his nightstand drawer. From his wallet he withdrew a thin piece of plastic, roughly the size of a credit card. "Before you go, let me give you something."

"What's that?" Marshall took the item from Hunter. He turned it over in his hand and noticed the magnetic strip on the back.

"It's a key to a private lab within the research department."

"You mean to the one where Rose is working on the heart cloning project?"

"That's the one."

"Who else has access to that room?"

"Besides Rose, no one."

"That's what I thought."

And with that Marshall pocketed the card, shook the old man's hand, turned, and left the dimly lit hospital room.

chapter thirty-three

sleuthing

It was with some trepidation that Marshall returned to the labyrinthine hallways of the clinic's sprawling basement late Monday evening. Beside him the large parallel pipes hissed and clanged. Beneath him his leather soles slapped rhythmically on the linoleum floor. Part of him hoped he'd come upon the security guard making rounds, just to know another human being was in the vicinity.

Another long hallway and two turns later he arrived at the frosted glass door that led into the Molecular and Biogenetics Research Lab. He tried the brass knob and found it locked. Using the standard metal key Hunter had also loaned him he opened the door.

It's nice to have friends in high places, Marshall thought as he slipped through the narrow portal. *Especially if you want to get into locked departments in the middle of the night.*

He debated whether to turn on the light switch.

The glow might draw the guard to the department, he reasoned. *But on the other hand, if I start stumbling around in the dark, there's an even greater chance I'll disrupt something and make a mess. Why didn't I bring a flashlight? I'm more a novice at this sleuthing stuff than I thought.*

Using the muted light that filtered through the door glass, he felt his way past a coat stand and two metal desks until he reached the entrance to the main lab. Not sure whether the key Hunter gave him would work on the inner chamber door, Marshall was relieved to find this portal was already open. Once inside he flipped on the switch and instantaneously the room was flooded with a white fluorescent illumination. Aided by this harsh light Marshall recognized much of what he saw. This was where Rose had greeted him, then introduced him to some of her cloning projects. The Plexiglas cubes, pipette racks, beakers, pumps, and oxygenators looked pretty much the same. But now he knew there was more here than met the eye.

Both Sally and Hunter had mentioned the existence of a secret lab. It was apparently concealed within the larger confines of the research complex. Rose required ready access to it so it was probably located nearby.

When it came right down to it, the 'secret' lab wasn't that secret. In fact, once Marshall knew what he was looking for, its entrance was pretty obvious. After scanning the wallspace, much of it obscured by tables, shelves, refrigeration unit, filing cabinets and the like, he headed toward one of the far corners of the room. There, nestled between two metal desks was a thick metal door. Embossed on the nameplate was, TOP SECRET, AUTHORIZED PERSONNEL ONLY. To the right, recessed in the doorframe, a rectangular box was bisected by a narrow vertical slot. Marshall slipped the cardtrol out of his breast pocket and with the magnetic strip away from him slid it through the narrow crease. A tiny green light blinked on. He heard a click. Grabbing the lever-like door handle, he rotated it clockwise. The door released.

This detective work is getting easier, he mused with a satisfied smile. *Having the right keys sure helps though.*

A rectangle of silver light poured through the partially opened door. Marshall fumbled around near the entrance but couldn't locate anything that resembled a switch. Opening the door wider he finally noticed a large metal desk pushed up against the right-side wall. Upon it was a small reading lamp with a green plastic shade. He walked over and pulled the metal chain. Instantly a section of the room was illuminated in an eerie yellow light.

And then he saw it, on a pedestal near the center of the room, housed within a cube-shaped Plexiglass container. Supporting the specimen was a sophisticated array of devices; an electric generator connected to a wire leading into one of the chambers, several small bore rubber tubes delivering then draining both clear and amber-colored fluids, and a bubble oxygenator which must be supplying vital gases to the amazing, life-sustaining milieu. The living organ reminded Marshall of a disembodied brain he'd seen in the science fiction movie, *Donovan's Brain,* perched passively on a stainless steel table with wires and tubes running in all directions, monitoring and ruling an entire world from deep within the rocky core of some alien planet. But this wasn't a brain. It was a human heart, full-sized and pumping away. Marshall glanced at the monitor set beside the cloned organ on the counter. The squiggly complexes marched across the screen at a rate of sixty beats per minutes.

Fascinated by the awesome spectacle he took one complete rotation around the beating organ. He took note of the chambers, the major vessels, the coronary arteries, and the veins. He made out the complex network of nerves that, like a delicate spider web, coursed along the surface. Truly, he'd never seen anything so amazing—or more bizarre—in his entire life.

And if Hunter's contention was correct, this cloned piece of human tissue had the potential to be implanted into a human being's body and actually *work*. The notion was mind-boggling. And the fact that this particular heart may be destined to save his beloved Rose's life made the whole thing all the more wondrous. But wasn't this all conjecture who the cloned organ was designed to benefit? That's what he was there to clarify. So, with a shake of his head, he tabled his sense of amazement and began searching for incriminating evidence.

Near the reading lamp on Rose's desk was a flatscreen monitor and a computer terminal. He slid out the keyboard tray and tried the same sequence of keystrokes it took to turn on his own unit in the Psychiatry Department. With a sense of satisfaction and relief he heard the motor start to whir and the familiar Windows logo came into view. While he waited for the unit to boot he checked the desk drawers. Except for the narrow one on the top right, they were all locked.

Disappointed but not deterred, Marshall rummaged around in the only section available to him. Finally, stored in a wooden matchbox off to one side he found what he was looking for. With this key he gained access to the rest of the drawers.

But what should I look for now? he asked himself.

Hadn't Hunter suggested that, in regards to utilizing samples of human tissue, there must be a record-keeping system where the biologic specimens were cross-referenced with the donor's medical identification number? At Bellevue, until about five years ago, the medical record number had been used. More recently the social security number had come into vogue. Since coming to The Hunt, Marshall had identified his patients exclusively through the latter. After spending almost fifteen minutes sifting through a pile of medical journals, another of Xeroxed research articles, some biomedical company advertisements and literature, telephone and medical society directories, and slide cases, he finally found the research log near the front of the lower left-hand drawer.

It was a narrow notebook with a denim cover and blue-lined pages. He turned to the first page. CARDIAC CLONING PROJECT was written there in Rose's neat cursive. The inception date was September 23, 1996.

Bingo! he congratulated himself.

He turned the well-worn pages and found several hundred entries listed. Each page was divided into five columns. The columns were labeled, Number, Donor, Specimen, Date, and Experimental Destination. From the third column Marshall noted that different kinds of source material had been used in the experimentation: skin, blood, muscle biopsies, nerves, and arteries. Notations in the final column signified whether the specimen was being grown in tissue culture whole, or being diced up for things like genetic mapping, nucleotide sequencing, and regulator protein characterization. Although Marshall had heard some of these terms in passing, most of this terminology and what it connoted was vague at best to him.

Suffice it to say, he told himself, *I've found the documentation I'm looking for.*

By now the computer was fully booted and humming. Returning to the log Marshall focused on the Donor column, noting that there were a couple dozen individuals listed. Finding a pad and pen he wrote down the specific numbers. Next, on the computer, he opened the Star Navigator system that would allow him to search the clinic's vast database for information about any patient whose records had been entered into the computerized history of the institution.

Since there were both six and nine digit numbers in the Donor column, Rose's log apparently predated the hospital switching over to the social security medical record system. When he pulled up the names that corresponded to the numbers he found some duplication, indicating that some donors were identified both by their medical record and social security numbers. When it came down to it only seven different individuals had donated biologic material to the Cardiac Cloning Project. Included in this list were three people Marshall failed to recognize. The ones he knew, and which gave him pause were, Bertram Hunter, Sally Spenser, Chris Jeffries and, of course, Rose Shaw.

So Chris Jeffries donated tissue to this project too, Marshall mused. *I wonder if he was just helping out or was this a little hedge against his future too?*

But how, he wondered, could he tease out which specimen was used to produce the cloned heart that was pumping away just three yards from him? Whose genetic material did it contain?

As fate would have it, finding this piece of the puzzle turned out to be relatively simple. When Marshall went back to the logbook, he noted that partway into it a sixth column had been added to the recording process. This column, however, had no label. But, at the end of some of the entry lines, recorded in that last column was a small asterisk. Marshall, curious about the asterisk's significance checked the front of the log for a key. There was none. Then he flipped to last page. There, on the very bottom, like a footnote indicator, he learned that the asterisk referred to the harvesting of unfertilized mammalian eggs. Then he flipped back to see which entries had been highlighted with the asterisks. Not particularly surprising was the fact that all of these had been associated with specimens donated by Dr. Rose Shaw.

So Hunter was right, Marshall conceded.

Sitting with his head propped up on his cupped palm, he reflected upon what he knew of the cloning process. He recalled the brief nine-minute video he'd downloaded from the Internet a week earlier.

A British scientist had discussed the process of mammalian cloning calling it nuclear transfer. It occurred when an unfertilized female egg was harvested in the lab. Then, all of its genetic material was extracted. Next, after an intact cell from an adult animal was obtained, the cell and egg were placed in close proximity. Utilizing a brief electric spark the genetic material from the cell migrates across the membranes from the adult cell to the unfertilized egg giving the egg all the information it needed to produce a complete organism.

Not only did Rose use her own biologic tissue to clone herself a heart, Marshall concluded, *but she must have also used her own eggs to grow it in too.* The very idea made him shudder.

He shut the log and gingerly set it back in the left-hand drawer. He ripped off the top sheet of the notepad folded it neatly, and slipped it into his breast pocket. He then returned the pad to the drawer.

Then a more uplifting thought occurred to him. *But it also means,* he realized, *that even if it's contraband, if Chris manages to implant it, Rose'll be around for many years to come.*

Buoyed by this distinct possibility, he secured the lab. Mindful of carefully retracing his steps, he made certain that everything was left the way he had found it. Finally, like a prison guard who, after making rounds, gets to leave the dungeon, he ascended from the bowels of the building and rejoined the mainstream of civilization on the clinic's first floor level.

chapter thirty-four

stiletto

Marshall stood at the kitchen counter shredding a head of lettuce when he heard the doorbell. He wiped his hands, walked into the living room, and pressed the intercom.

"Who is it?"

"It's me," came a familiar voice. He buzzed her in. A few seconds later Marshall watched Rose climb the steps to his second floor apartment with a rolling overnight bag bouncing behind her.

She paused and waited for her lungs to catch up. "Hi, there," she said through labored breaths. "I don't walk steps that much anymore. I forgot how tough it is for me."

"Here, let me," he offered.

"Thanks, Marshall," she said, rewarding him with a kiss on the cheek. Her breath, musky and faintly minty, gave him a stir. "I'm really glad you were staying home tonight. This should be fun."

Rose had called his office earlier that day, indicating she was scheduled to meet with the architectural firm handling the design of the new research wing at their Shadyside office later that afternoon. She suggested they spend the evening together—"if you don't have any plans, this is." She even offered to bring dinner. He was thrilled with the idea, went one step further, and told her he'd cook.

Once inside his apartment he took her raincoat and hung it up in the closet. Then pointing to the carry-on, he asked, "So what's this all about?"

"As if you can't figure that out," she said with a coy smile. "I'm spending the night, if that's all right with you."

Without attempting to conceal his delight he replied, "Of course it's all right."

She smiled again, this time a warm, bright one.

He went over and sat down on his leather sofa. He expected her to join him but instead she started strolling around his apartment, inspecting books and knick-knacks on the bookshelves, then commenting on his paintings. At first this perfunctory examination of his things made him uncormortable. After all, this was only the second time she'd visited his apartment. But eventually her familiar scent, the facility with which she made herself at home, and merely the fact that she was *Rose* dissipated his anxiety.

Dinner was another story. Despite the short notice, he did his best to add some spice to the evening. On the way home he'd stopped at Pier One and bought a pair decorator candles with wrought iron holders. From a State Store he took the salesman's advice and purchased a bottle of Napa Valley Merlot, from the Pride Mountain vineyard, circa '95. The staples came from a gourmet market on nearby Walnut Street and the tablecloth was borrowed from a neighbor. Lastly, although he didn't possess any fine crystal or china, thanks to a serviceable set of Bernice's discards, his everyday dishes proved more than adequate. Thusly prepared, he escorted his guest to the small circular dinette table by the kitchen.

"Oh, Marshall," Rose said, "this is lovely. You shouldn't have gone to the trouble."

"No trouble at all," he replied gallantly.

He started them off with a fresh salad of mixed greens and tomato slices. He suspected having the bottled dressing on the table looked tacky, but he had no small containers. Rose didn't seem to notice. The main course came next, a dish he'd learned to prepare a while ago containing Raman noodles mixed in a wok with stir fried vegetables sautéed in tamari sauce. By smacking her lips and commenting on its succulent taste, he knew Rose enjoyed the fruit of his effort. He modestly deflected the acknowledgment but couldn't hide the blush.

Despite just completing a long day's work, he noticed how radiant Rose looked, her green eyes sparkling in the candlelight, her hair tied back and clipped. He wondered if she'd freshened up before coming over. He was pretty sure she hadn't changed, her black business suit a little wrinkled and there was a smudge on the collar of her white cotton blouse. Perhaps she'd stopped at a friend's place on the way. The thought of friends brought Steve Heller to mind. They'd run into each other at the hospital earlier that day. In the course of their conversation Rose's name had come up.

"Oh, by the way," Marshall said, "I spoke to Steve Heller at the hospital this afternoon."

"Steve Heller?" Rose asked innocently. "Who's he?"

"An old friend of mine. I'm sure you've seen him around. He's interim head of the anesthesiology department."

"That's nice. How is he?"

"Fine. The last time we spoke was at Hunter's July Fourth picnic. Since it's been so long we decided to go into the coffee shop and chat. While I was updating him on friends and family I told him we've been seeing each other. That's when he mentioned that he saw you at the airport last weekend."

"He saw me? It must've been in passing. No one like that came up to me."

"He was going to, but felt a little awkward. You were off in the corner of the waiting area talking to someone."

"Is that so? And who was I with?"

"Chris. Chris Jeffries."

Rose paused—just briefly—but long enough to ratchet up the tension that was rapidly filling the space between them. "Chris was with me. What's so unusual about that?"

"Was he seeing you off?"

"No," Rose retorted, "as a matter of fact, he was coming with me."

This pronouncement and the haughty manner with which it was delivered cut him to the quick. "He went with you?" he repeated. "But why? I thought you were going alone."

"I needed his help, Marshall," Rose explained, her tone tempering a bit. "As I mentioned to you when you called last week, my department is budgeted for another research assistant. I can recruit either a Ph.D. or someone out of a medical residency program. A local headhunter gave me the lead on three suitable candidates, all from the Midwest. Rather than asking them to come to Pittsburgh, I decided to fly to Minneapolis and interview them on their home turf. I wanted to see the types of facilities they trained in and get a sense of how sophisticated their research was. When I told Chris about it he was kind enough to offer to come along. As president of the medical staff, he is a *defacto* member of any search committee, you know."

"If you wanted company, why didn't you ask me?"

"Believe me, Marshall," Rose replied, "I considered it. But I knew this wasn't going to be a pleasure trip. I was scheduled solid from the moment I arrived on Saturday morning to when we left for the airport Sunday night. You and I wouldn't have had a moment to play. So it seemed senseless inviting you along."

He considered this explanation, trying to see the situation from her point of view. To her way of thinking, she was being considerate, looking out for his well being, anticipating his frustration at being a third wheel in an unfamiliar setting with no one to hang out with. Gradually his annoyance abated and with it the pain in his chest.

"But it thrills me that you're so jealous," she said with a playful smile. "In fact, it makes me all tingly inside. Maybe after dinner I can reward you." This prospect more than mollified him.

An hour later, after desert, coffee and tidying up, they retired to Marshall's bedroom. Once there it was Rose who took command of the scene. First she suggested Marshall undress, then had him lie down on the bed. While he complied with her simple request she went out to the kitchen and poured them both another glass of wine. Upon returning she sat down on the bed next to him and proposed a toast.

"To a long, happy life together," she said, clinking his glass. Marshall, worried about all the alcohol at dinner and the effect it would have on his performance, hesitated. But Rose, in a gentle but firm manner insisted. Not wanting to jeopardize the mood with another disagreement, he emptied his glass.

Rose then stood up and moved to the foot of the bed. Slowly, deliberately, she started to undress. While removing her suit jacket and cotton blouse she began swaying back and forth. Next she unfastened the latch on her skirt and eased the zipper from her waist. She slipped it down over her hips and the length of her upper thigh. While she sensually exposed herself to him, Marshall gazed transfixed.

Sinking deep into a fascinated stupor, he imagined himself a sultan titillated by his favorite concubine. But despite the arousing display, his eyes, for some reason, started to lose focus and his eyelids became uncomfortably heavy. Vaguely cognizant of his wavering concentration, he willed himself to remain awake, refusing to be denied the spectacle of Rose's striptease by something as silly as sleep. But resist as he might his mind clouded over and he stopped concentrating on the show. Giving his head a violent shake, the fog cleared. Rose had removed her skirt by now and was clad in a pair of silk panties and a strapless bra.

She began to sway provocatively, easing her arms around her back, removing the clasp from her hair, then shaking it out in a graceful sweeping motion. Next she unlatched the clasps on her bra, one after another, easing the tension so that more and more of her ample breasts were revealed. When the lower latch came loose, the ends gave way, and the flimsy support fluttered to the floor.

But as much as Marshall wanted to see what came next, he was denied the remainder of Rose's performance. While tracking the descent of the delicate bra from breast to floor, like a window shade descending over a dirty pane of glass, his eyelids fell shut. And unfortunately, for the sake of Marshall's continued enjoyment, they refused to rise again—at least not for a while.

When Marshall awoke it was to candlelight. He'd been dreaming about strolling along the beach at sunset, just at the edge of the water, the sand cool against his face, the sun baking his face and shoulders. Suddenly a sharp pain sliced across the bottom of his foot. He wondered if he'd stepped on a broken shell or a shard of glass. The pain was severe enough to wake him up.

He tried to orient. He noticed the paddle fan hanging suspended in the shadows from a familiar ceiling. He was still in his bedroom. But then, an odd sense of uneasiness gripped him. Just before dozing off, something both entertaining and arousing had been in progress. He'd been watching Rose do her striptease. Where was she now?

He flexed his neck and focused on the spot near the foot of the bed where he recalled she'd stood. Rose was still there. But something was different. She was no longer almost undressed. Instead of standing there in her panties she'd donned one of her dominatrix outfits, complete with leather straps, wrist and neck chains, garters and netting. Her full-bodied hair rested in disarray on her bare shoulders. Her arms were clad in full-length gloves. An image of Tina Turner in the Mad Max movie *Thunderdome* came to mind. He couldn't see her feet but was sure she was wearing those spiked knee-high vinyl boots.

So we're going to play S&M again, he thought, not unexcited. He'd come to crave this aspect of their lovemaking. It was so different from anything he'd experienced with any other woman. And although he was a bit apprehensive of the pain Rose seemed to delight in inflicting, on some level, these noxious stimuli tended to enhance his overall enjoyment.

When he was alone Marshall tended to sleep with his arms outstretched and extended above him. So it didn't strike him as unusual that they were fixed in this position when he awoke. What did unnerve him though was that when he tried to move them, he couldn't. At first he thought they were asleep, transformed into numb limbs, which frequently happened when Bernice had fallen asleep with her head on his shoulder. But this time, no matter how hard he tugged, his arms wouldn't move.

Something was wrapped around his wrists. He craned his neck and peered over his shoulders. Cloth restraints had been wrapped around each of his wrists, their tails trailing off toward the corners of the bed. He tried to imagine what they had been secured to and recalled that his mattress was set upon a metal frame. And of course, Rose had done this, just as she'd tied him up before, working this binding ritual into her little game.

How about his legs? They too were outstretched in a spread-eagle position. He tried to flex at the knees but could only bend a few degrees. He struggled with the ropes. He had to give Rose credit. She knew how restrain someone. Perhaps a sailor had taught her to tie knots? With Rose anything was possible.

Becoming resigned to his station, he flexed his neck enough so he could regard his mistress. Even in the muted candlelight he could make out the triumphant, almost malevolent smile on her face. Then he saw what had caused the slicing pain along the base of his foot. Rose was holding a long thin knife in her hand. Its black handle seemed to blend into the darkness of her gloved hand. But its blade, sharp and menacing, was evident, reflecting yellow candlelight back into Marshall's eyes.

"So you're awake, my pet," Rose greeted him. He didn't like the tone of her voice. It sounded fiendish, almost sinister. "I suppose my striptease wasn't exciting enough to keep you up." He began to protest but she silenced him by jutting a gloved arm forward like a Nazi soldier saluting his Führer. "Do not speak until you're told to, slave boy!" With this forceful admonition, Marshall wasn't sure he was capable of uttering another word, even if he wanted to.

Rose strolled around to the side of the bed and peered down at him withher piercing emerald green eyes. He returned the gaze. Absently, with a satisfied smile on her full lips, she tapped the blade of the stiletto knife on her gloved palm. She seemed to be considering what to do next. Then she nodded.

Rose stooped down. When she stood up again she was holding the set of nipple clamps in one of her hands. Leaning over him, she attached the alligator-like teeth to each of his breasts. Pains shot him through him like a pair of hot pokers. He clinched his teeth and bit the inside of his cheek. The taste of blood filled his mouth.

"You like?" she said in a mockingly. He shook his head "no", then gagged on the blood that had pooled in the back of his throat. He coughed a spray of it into the air. It rained down upon his face speckling it crimson. Rose moistened a tissue with her tongue and wiped off the crusting blood. "There, there, my pet. We didn't want you to hurt yourself. Any pain that's inflicted in here will be from my hand, not your teeth."

This barbed comment made his chest constrict. In this assailable position she could do anything to him, things he knew he could hardly imagine. And it was precisely that sense of the unknown that petrified him.

Leaning over she stroked his sore cheek and whispered in his ear, "You know you've been a naughty boy, my pet." He looked at her, but had trouble focusing with her so close. He inspected the roughened section of his inner cheek with the tip of his tongue and wondered what she was talking about. "You broke into your mistress' sacred domain," she was saying, "and violated it with your unauthorized presence there. Then you contaminated her personal belongings."

The accusation confused him. Was this more of her play-acting? Was she creating this scenario as a backdrop for their game? He had to object, but in the most respectful of ways.

"No, Mistress Rose. I did nothing of the sort."

"Silence!" she barked. "Have I granted you permission to speak? And besides, not only did you speak, but you *lied!*" This last reproach came out like a hiss. Its venomous quality made Marshall cringe. "You lied, my slave boy," she repeated, her tone more lyrical now. "I have proof."

Proof? Proof of what?

He rotated his neck and watched her lift something off his nightstand. It was a piece of paper. She unfolded it then held it suspended in front of his eyes.

"Do you know what this is?" she asked harshly. "It's a list of medical record numbers. It corresponds to subjects who donated biologic material for my human tissue cloning experiments. There's only one place this classified information is documented. And it's in my private lab."

Marshall groaned. She was holding the piece of paper from the notepad he'd used to write down the medical record numbers from Rose's research log. With this stupid piece of paper, she indeed had evidence that he'd been in her lab.

"Do you know where I found this incriminating little piece of paper, slave boy? Of course you do, my little pet. It was tucked neatly in the breast pocket of one of your shirts."

She set the damning piece of evidence down and sat beside him on the bed. Holding up the knife she let him regard it for a moment. Then she slipped the blade between the nipple clamp chain and his chest and flexed her wrist. This movement put tension on the metal chain. Streaks of pain shot from his pinched nipples straight through to his back. He began to squirm, but quickly realized that this simple motion increased the tautness of the chain.

"Stop!" he pleaded. "Please stop!"

"The correct word is 'mercy' slave boy. You must say, "Mercy, Mistress," if you want me to stop."

"Mercy, then!" he cried. "For God sakes, have mercy, Mistress!"

To his consummate relief she lowered her wrist. The chain sagged. His nipples remained sore but the searing pain was gone.

"Why, my little slave boy, were you sneaking around my personal domain? What could have motivated you to invade my sacred workplace and soil it with you worthless presence?"

Cognizant of the nipple clamps, the stiletto knife, and whatever other agents of torture Rose might have in her bag, he carefully considered his answer. In a voice that sounded meek and soft he asked, "May I speak, Mistress?"

Rose's expression brightened. "Yes, my pet. You may speak."

"I broke into your private lab at Dr. Hunter's request. Since he is now suffering from advanced heart diseased, he wanted to know if you were still cloning a heart and if it belonged to him."

Rose nodded. "He could have asked me himself. He is well enough to communicate."

"He tried."

"Not hard enough."

Marshall didn't know how to respond to this. He just nodded.

"And what did your vile search reveal?"

"That there is an experimental heart down there and it is yours, Rose. You deceived Dr. Hunter by using the clinic's resources to clone a new heart for yourself."

"Of course I did," Rose agreed, leaning over him again, this time resting her forearm on his chest so that the tip of the blade grazed his throat. "Does that surprise you my pet? What else would any reasonable person with my congenital cardiac defect and my extraordinary scientific talents do?"

Marshall was afraid to answer, afraid to agree, afraid to take issue with her course of action. The knife was too close, its point too sharp, its wielder too unpredictable. A series of images flew into his head. The photo of Rose as a teenager, a knife in her hand, standing beside a motorcycle with slashed tires. A picture of Peter Davis' automobile careening through the guardrail along an icy road near his suburban Baltimore house. Posters of heavy metal rock groups on the walls of Rose's Millcreek room, their evil painted faces melding seamlessly with the scene in his bedroom tonight. And, most alarming of all, a hazy image of Karen Shaw crashing her car along an Erie highway with twelve-year old Rose in the back seat.

"I'm just as entitled to that heart as Hunter," Rose asserted, a maniacal gleam in her emerald eyes. "Maybe moreso. Those were my eggs we harvested to grow the thing. It was my talent and experience that created the organ in that dungeon of a lab he gave me. And damn it, Marshall, Bertram Hunter is sixty-five years old! He's lived his life. He's accomplished everything he wanted to. Besides, now that Chris has bypassed his diseased heart he'll probably squeeze a lot more precious years out of his than I will out of mine. You know it's different with me, Marshall. I need something extraordinary to happen so that I can live a normal life. I deserve that heart! I deserve it much more than that manipulating fucker, Bertram Hunter!"

Almost paralyzed with fear, he let her rant, acutely aware of how utterly defenseless he was, knowing that one false move, one unexpected utterance, could send that stiletto knife plunging right through his larynx.

And then, for some reason, she relaxed her grip and the tip of the blade receded. She smiled down at him. Not that demonic smile he'd seen just before she attacked him, but a gentler, friendlier expression.

"I know you were just doing what you were told, my pet," Rose told him, her face just inches from his, the odor of the wine still faintly on her breath. "I know Hunter's your boss and you were being his flunky. I know you can't help it, Marshall. Look at you now. Isn't it obvious you can't help it?"

He didn't know what to say. He hadn't been given permission to speak.

"But I can't have you violating my sacred workroom, my personal space, without my permission, without being forced to do penance. And I've come up with an appropriate punishment, a perfect way you can make amends."

He couldn't imagine what she was about to suggest—or decree was more like it. He prayed it didn't involve further pain or humiliation.

Rose shifted positions so that she was straddling him from above him, her knees beside his head, her groin in his face. From this unusual vantage point he could appreciate the kinky tendrils of her pubic hairs and the acerbically fishy odor that emanated from her folds. The matted locks were dark brown and glistening. He sensed her arousal. Then this woman, his patient, his lover, and now his dominating mistress uttered a single command.

"Lick me, slave!"

It was the most obvious request and the last thing he'd expected. Perhaps this setting had started as one suited for erotic adventure. But hadn't it inexplicably transformed itself into a theater of the macabre, a canvas soiled with pain and humiliation? Now, however, thanks to Rose's twisted sense of symmetry, her desire to mete out a modicum of justice, it had come full circle.

He only hesitated for a moment. Then he leaned his head forward and met the thrust of her pelvis toward his face. His nose abutted against her pubis and his tongue sought, then located, like fruit buried inside a thicket, the soft folds concealed within her bush. The odor intensified. The briny taste became familiar. He lapped away wielding his tongue like a dexterous instrument of pleasure. He knew that the better he performed, the more likely it would be that he'd survive this ordeal without further trauma, without further scarring.

From the grunts and groans that emanated from deep in Rose's throat he was sure he'd found the mark. First she rocked back and forth, then gyrated with a slow rotating motion, like a belly dancer responding to a haunting melody. Guttural cries melded with a litany of 'ohs' and 'ahs.' He could almost feel her arousal. Spontaneously it became contagious, almost infectious.

Loathe to respond, recalling the way she'd treated him and not wanting her to triumph again, he deliberately resisted this reaction. But contrary to his will his organ assumed a life of its own. Against his volition he was sucked into the primal mating dance, helpless in the face of his masculine responsivity. Gratefully he accepted his inability to stem the tide of his own biology and succumbed.

Whether it was from a shift in his posture or a change in the way he ministered to her, Rose seemed to sense his arousal. Reaching behind she first fingered his throbbing erection then clutched it firmly in her hand. Next she pinched the glans in a practiced fashion in order to abort his premature eruption. Standing up straighter, she moved her pelvis away from his face, shimmied backward, and positioned herself above him. After guiding his erection inside her, she sank down. For Marshall, the sensation was electrifying.

Rose rode him like a bronco. Rising, then plunging, a cowgirl on her favorite stud, she ratcheted up the tension. Finally, when he couldn't hold back any longer, he arched his back, cried out louder than ever before and exploded inside her. Sometime shortly after that, as he hovered on the very edge of post-coital consciousness, he sensed that she'd followed suit.

chapter thirty-five

by the trimont

"So what do we do now?"

Seated on the edge of Hunter's bed Marshall posed this question. The patient was reclining in a chair by the window. Amber-colored late afternoon sunshine sifted into the hospital room.

"So we now have proof of what I suspected all along," Hunter commented. In this light Marshall thought he looked much better than the last time he'd visited. "The cloned heart exists. And it was grown using Dr. Shaw's denucleated eggs merged with her own genetic complement."

"That's it in a nutshell. So," Marshall repeated, "what do we do?"

"Destroy the damn thing, of course."

"Are you sure?"

"Of course I'm sure. I can't have that contraband lying around. If it's discovered it could destroy the reputation of this institution. It can't be implanted, Marshall. I don't want that woman surviving one more minute than her allotted lifespan."

He could understand the man's concern—even his bitterness. But he was surprised to see how insensitive he seemed to Marshall's feelings. Of course, Hunter had no way of knowing what Marshall felt for 'that woman'.

"You really hate her, don't you Hunter?"

"Shouldn't I?" the older man replied. "She's jeopardized the reputation of an institute I've spent my whole life building. I think that should engender some negative feelings."

"But look at it from her perspective, sir. She did the research. She donated the eggs. She carried the fetus. And, most significantly, she does have a life-threatening cardiac condition that will probably kill her before she's forty. Isn't that enough to justify her actions?"

"Listen to me, Marshall," Hunter began. He set a fatherly hand on the younger man's forearm. "If we're discussing the merits of whether Rose Shaw deserves to beat her fate, then there's something crucial I need to put on the table. And believe me, I say this knowing full well how much you care about her. But hear me out before you decide to stand by her."

Hunter eased over. "Marshall, my son, Rose Shaw is a bad person. First of all, mentally she's not well. At the very least she's a morally corrupt sociopath driven to achieve her self-serving ends. At the worst she's a homicidal psychopath person who'll stop at nothing to succeed."

Hunter's words struck Marshall like a slew of darts. After all, the man was disparaging the woman he, until very recently, loved.

"Hold on, Dr. Hunter," Marshall countered. "I'm the psychiatrist, here. Why don't you let *me* make the diagnoses around here?"

"If you recall, I tried that once before," Hunter pointed out, "and you made a mockery of it. How can I trust you to act objectively now? And even if I'm not a psychiatrist, wrapped in your cloak of authenticity, I think I'm also qualified to voice an educated opinion in this regard. Remember, Marshall, my relationship with Rose Shaw was pretty intimate. Hell, we slept together for over two years. And however incredible she was in bed, it doesn't stop me from seriously suspecting her mental stability."

Hunter paused. Marshall sensed the growing tension in the room. Leaning back, he gave himself some breathing room and peered through the waning daylight at his boss.

"The bottom line, Marshall, is that Rose has to be stopped. She's a dangerous woman and a potential menace to this institution."

Marshall was getting sick of hearing Hunter's opinions, but he resisted the urge to tell him so. Instead he asked, "If I agree to do what you asked and destroy the thing, how do you want me to do it?"

"That's up to you. You know the layout of the lab. You know how the heart's supported. Be creative."

He nodded, and then was about to make some excuse why he had to leave. Instead he commented, "Remember when you told me that one of the reasons you didn't expose Rose was because of your affair with her and the damage she could do to your relationship with Maggie if word got out?"

The older man seemed intrigued by Marshall's question. "Of course I do," he admitted. "Why?"

"I think you were lying."

"Lying? Lying about what?"

"Initially, when I was introduced to this cloning stuff, I admit that I was pretty naïve about the subject matter. Since then I've become more informed. Hunter, you, yourself, told me that after the British revealed the existence the cloned sheep, Dolly, in 1997, President Clinton, by executive order, banned any further research into human tissue cloning?"

"That's right, Marshall. What's the point? We've already covered this ground."

"It means," Marshall continued unperturbed, "that even though you suspected Rose was carrying on human tissue cloning experiments under the auspices of the Hunter-Neuman Clinic, you resisted exposing it, even though coming forth may have mitigated the possibility of criminal charges being brought against the institution."

"That's right," Hunter admitted, "but how does that make me a liar?"

"Because, Hunter, I suspect that the real reason you failed to blow the whistle on Rose was you knew she was still working on a cloned heart and you were under the impression that the heart was yours."

Marshall watched the color drain out the CEO's face. The older man sank back into the easy chair.

"But that's what she told me," he confirmed in a voice that was little more than a whisper.

"That's what I thought," Marshall said smugly and walked out of the room.

Driving home that evening Marshall had plenty to think about. Despite his infatuation with Rose, he still had to reconcile the ugly picture Hunter had painted of her. After what Rose had put him through recently, he sensed she was unstable and capable of doing harm. But was this enough to label her mentally ill or contend that she was intrinsically *evil?* Make no mistake about it, he had his concerns. These concerns, in his psychoanalytic way of thinking, involved the negative experiences she'd suffered through during her childhood and the effect they must have had on her personality development. Was she a disturbed product of her environment? Like her heart, was her brain also congenitally defective? Did this make her sociopathic, or, even worse, psychopathic? Don Owen's psychological assessment seemed to point in that direction.

But Marshall wasn't ready to jump on the bandwagon yet. He sensed a certain lack of data, the absence of a crucial piece of the puzzle, which, once supplied, would give him crucial insight into the core of her being. He hoped Rose would supply that missing data. However, either through repression of childhood memories or by purposefully deflecting his inquiries, until now she'd resisted his efforts to elucidate this history. What had actually happened on that dreary afternoon in Erie so many years ago when Karen Shaw died? It was essential that he find out. Without that information he could neither destroy nor resurrect his love.

Marshall sat alone in his office. It was Friday morning. Inpatient rounds were over. His cadre of residents and nurses were off on their workday chores. Despite a pile of administrative work to do it was almost impossible to stay focused.

He thought about yesterday morning, awakening in his own bed with no sign of Rose. Had the whole thing all been a dream? But there was that raw area inside his cheek, his tender, irritated nipples, and the dried, crusty material flaking off his tumescent penis that told him otherwise. Rose had indeed been there.

I guess it's time to find out what I need to know, he said to himself.

Taking a deep breath he placed the call and was to be put right through to Rose. She sounded cheerful enough. They exchanged pleasantries. Neither made reference to the other night. He mentioned that there was a serious matter he needed to discuss with her. He preferred to do it in person. He suggested they get together that evening. Perhaps a quiet dinner at a Mount Washington restaurant?

Unfortunately, she already had plans. Something about a dinner conference at a downtown hotel. He offered to meet up with her afterward. She declined, citing fatigue from a busy week. He was about to conclude the conversation, expecting contrived obstacles to subsequent suggestions. She surprised him with an invitation for him to stop over for coffee in the morning. Feeling oddly relieved he agreed to stop by around nine.

Marshall approached the impressive high-rise that housed Rose's condo with a sense of grim determination. He contrasted this solemnity with the upbeat mood he'd felt while visiting in the past. But this wasn't a date. It would be more like an interview. And hopefully he'd get the information he needed.

Marshall still felt intent upon offering Rose the benefit of the doubt. She was a creative, strong-willed woman stricken with a cardiac deformity that threatened to take her life. She had an instinctive drive, an overwhelming desire to modify the dreadful hand fate had dealt her. She was not willing, he knew, to march to the gallows without a fight. And if this necessitated a bit of professional deception and an unauthorized appropriation of institutional resources, so be it.

What, he asked himself, *is the real price of adding precious years to a person's life? Certainly less than Rose had extorted from The Hunter-Neuman Clinic.*

Harboring this noble sense of purpose he pulled into the visitors' lot. He parked his Mercedes and locked it. Walking toward the curb, he checked for cars in the street. Out of his peripheral vision he noticed a sporty silver sedan parked in the corner of the lot's first row. But more than the car's sharp sportiness, it was the woman who was being helped into the passenger seat that caught his attention. It was Rose. He called out to her.

She was already seated when he reached the side of the car. He waited for the electric window to slide into its sleeve.

"Marshall!" Rose said excitedly. "You're here."

"Of course I'm here," he replied, "you invited me. Remember?" Bending over he checked to see who was in the front seat across from her. The tall thin frame, the confident, almost arrogant profile was unmistakable,

"Top of the morning to you, Friedman," Chris Jeffries greeted him. Marshall hated that condescending joviality. "Good to see you again. Up here visiting someone?"

"You know I am, Jeffries," Marshall said, his body starting to bristle. Then staring directly into Rose's hazel-green eyes, he asked, "What the hell's going on?"

"Oh, Marshall," she replied lightly, then reached over and set her hand gently upon his. "Chris called this morning and told me about this brand new Jaguar. Isn't it gorgeous? He insisted on taking me for a spin. I told him we had plans, but this is his only day off, so he wouldn't take no for an answer. I tried to call you on your cellular, but I guess you had it turned off."

That's bullshit! Marshall swore to himself. Whenever he was in his car the cell phone was on.

"Don't you think you're being a little rude," Marshall asked, "standing me up like this?"

"Rude?" Rose replied, with what passed for authentic surprise. "No, not at all. This is the only time Chris can take me out. It's you who could be a little more flexible, you know. We'll get together later this afternoon if that's what you want."

If that's what I want! Marshall repeated under his breath.

"What I want," he said aloud, "is to talk to you. There are very important matters we have to discuss. Don't you think you owe me that much, Rose?"

"Of course I do, honey. Just indulge me for a few hours. We'll have our talk later. I promise."

Every masculine fiber in his body encouraged Marshall to stand firm. He was about to open the door, reach inside and drag Rose out onto the asphalt. Chris Jeffries chose that precise moment to lean across the seat and say, "Be a sport, Friedman. I'm not kidnapping your girlfriend. I'm just borrowing her for a couple of hours. Cut her some slack and she'll be glad to reward you later."

What an asshole, Marshall thought. *No way I give in to this bastard. It's time to draw the line.*

But then he began to waver. Was he really prepared to make a scene out here on Mount Washington, in broad daylight, with locals all over the place? Besides, in the scheme of things, was her heading off with Jeffries for a few hours such a big deal? Could he, in all reality, force her to stay behind?

He hesitated a few seconds longer then leaned over again and angrily said, "Bye."

Rose seemed relieved. She reached out the window, drew his head toward her, and kissed him firmly on the lips. Then, gazing up into his eyes she said, "Thank you. I promise I'll make it up to you."

He nodded, recalling the last time she'd promised to 'reward' him. Maybe it wasn't such a bad thing that Jeffries was taking her off his hands. But that still didn't solve his dilemma. He still needed to talk to Rose, or dredge up the information some other way. He took a single step back, then sidestepped out from between the Jaguar and its neighboring vehicle. While coping with a jumble of mixed emotions he watched Jeffries pull his sporty car out of the slip and drive away.

chapter thirty-six

back to the future, again

With grim determination Marshall headed northbound out of Pittsburgh, traveling on Interstate Route 79. He thought it ironic that, like Rose, he was getting a chance to see the autumn leaves of Western Pennsylvania change colors. But despite the rolling still life filled with clusters of dusty brown, pale green, flaming red, and burnt orange, he barely noticed the spectacle.

The reason why was he couldn't stop thinking about Rose. A host of lingering questions preoccupied in his mind. First and foremost was, how did he *really* feel about her? Was it just sexual attraction fueled by raw and sometimes deviant eroticism—or did he truly love her as much as he thought he did? And how did this emotional bond square with the untenable position Bertram Hunter had placed him in, right in the middle, sent to bring her down? And more importantly, how did she feel about him?

He couldn't avoid the conclusion that on some level she'd used him, like she'd used Peter Davis and Bertram Hunter earlier in her career. Marshall wondered if the egotistical Chris Jeffries was next. Did the arrogant thoracic surgeon appreciate the role he was playing in the 'Story of Rose'? Marshall expected that, even if he did, Rose still had a way of blurring the borders between reality and fantasy. Did anyone really ever know, once they were caught in her web, what role they were playing in her life? He seriously doubted it.

One thing's for sure, he conceded, *she went after and got my vote to get the chairmanship.*

This realization made him angry. But his ire quickly abated, acknowledging that political support was a small price to pay to have Rose look on him with favor. And he couldn't deny that he loved having her in her life. Her vitality, her creativity, and her *joie de vivre* energized and enlivened him. She made it a treat to wake up in the morning. That's why it was so hard for him to destroy her. And if he agreed to be Hunter's hammer, he had to be certain there was sufficient cause.

Hunter called her evil, which is a pretty strong indictment. It's hard to believe she's really that bad.

In this self-absorbed fog he sped past the rural boroughs and towns of northwest Pennsylvania. Finally, just past noon, he merged with Interstate 90. A map lay open on the passenger seat. He confirmed that Route 20 was nearby. Another half mile and he would be at the Shaw house.

The exit was upon him. He eased down the ramp and made a left onto Twenty-sixth. Almost immediately he recognized some aspects of the area. He fell in with the traffic, eased past a series of staggered strip malls, crossed the intersection with route 832, then made a right onto James Street.

Marshall stood on the packed dirt stoop and rapped on the front door. While he waited he scanned the now familiar street with its boxy cottages and tiny front lawns. Parked nearby on the rutted asphalt driveway was Mr. Shaw's blue Skylark, its side panel dented and wheel wells caked with crusty brown rust. Its corroded rear axle now rested on a pair of thick gray cinderblocks.

"Yeah, whaddya want?" came the gruff greeting from inside. Marshall glanced up as the old man's scarecrow-like face peered out at him from a between the front door and its warped wooden jamb.

"Why, Mr. Shaw, how are you?" Marshall replied injecting as much joviality into his voice as he could. "It's Marshall Friedman. I was here with your daughter about a month ago."

"Rose, you say?" The gaunt old man replied his expression devoid of recognition. "You say you know Rose?"

"Yes, sir," Marshall persisted. "I'm one the doctors at the hospital in Pittsburgh where she works. We came to see you in the middle of August when the social worker wanted to put you in the Veteran's Home."

"You mean that bitch, Mary Popovich?" Mr. Shaw retorted. "No one's putting me in no damn nursing home."

I didn't think so, Marshall agreed to himself. Aloud he asked, "May I come in?"

"Why do you wanna come in here?"

"I need to talk to you about Rose. I'm worried about her. I think she might be in trouble."

"What's new about that? She's been in and out of trouble her whole life."

"Which is what I need to talk to you about," Marshall persisted, easing forward, hoping they wouldn't have to hold this entire conversation in the doorway.

"Oh, all right," Mr. Shaw finally relented. "But make it quick. There's a ballgame gonna start in twenty minutes."

"This shouldn't take long, Mr. Shaw," Marshall assured him.

The old shut-in opened the door wide enough for Marshall to pass, then closed it with a thud. Suddenly the room was plunged into the same hazy darkness Marshall recalled from his last visit. He waited for Mr. Shaw to lead the way to his day room off the back of the house. After negotiating the pair of steps the old man settled himself into his easy chair. Marshall followed. But without any other chairs in the room, he was forced to lean up against the hospital bed. He silently inventoried the room. Not much was different since his last visit, including that odd blend of rancid odors, the occupant's 'old man's smell.'

Frank Shaw, meanwhile, stared at the television. A pair of commentators discussed the significance of the upcoming game between the Cleveland Indians and the New York Yankees. Both teams were perennial pennant contenders. Marshall suspected that with its proximity to Cleveland there must be thousands of Indians' fans in Erie. Marshall wanted to get down to the reason of his visit. During his two-hour long ride from Pittsburgh to Millcreek, he'd given a lot of consideration to what he would ask Mr. Shaw, rehearsing several different ways of introducing his concerns about Rose to the old man. In the end, rather than offer some convoluted story, Marshall told the truth.

Speaking partially to the television and partially to the old man, Marshall commented, "I want you to know, sir, that my initial interactions with your daughter were strictly professional. In case Rose didn't mention it, I am a trained psychoanalyst. I was hired in the spring to run the psychiatry department at the Hunter-Neuman Clinic. Your daughter Rose came to see me a few weeks after I arrived, complaining about violent nightmares she was having. She asked me if I could help her. I agreed to take her on as a patient."

During this sincere and factual introduction Mr. Shaw continued to gaze at the television screen with a neutral expression on his face, showing no sign of recognition or comprehension,

He might as well be sleeping with his eyes open, Marshall thought.

"Excuse me Mr. Shaw," Marshall said directly at him. "Did you hear what I said?"

The old man turned his head toward Marshall but kept his eyes fixed on the television. "You're the new shrink at the hospital and Rose came to you for help."

"That's right," Marshall confirmed, amazed at how concisely Mr. Shaw had summarized what he'd said. "We had a few sessions together and this helped me get to know her better. We talked about her headaches and then explored her childhood. It seems like Rose must've been a difficult child, headstrong and independent."

Marshall detected a shift in Mr. Shaw's focus of attention. Although his gaze was still fixed on the screen, his ears had perked up slightly and his head was cocked in Marshall's direction

"I also got the impression," Marshall continued, "that Rose and your wife didn't see eye to eye on much. She said she was too strict with her, that she dominated her life. Now, we're talking about the perceptions of a pre-adolescent female here, which would tend to be a little biased. But, on the other hand, when Rose described what she had to deal with, it did appear that she was subject to more restrictions than the average girl her age."

"Is that so?" growled the old man. Now glowering at Marshall he continued, "Why, 'cause Karen wouldn't let her smoke or bike out onto that damn peninsula where her friends got drunk and did drugs?"

This outburst, so unexpected and venomous, startled Marshall. He hesitated for a moment. "Certainly not sir. That type of exposure is certainly dangerous for a child of any age. But I was referring more to the frequent groundings, the lack of playtime, the limited number of friends." Feeling a little daunted he admitted, "You know, I'm not really sure what I mean here. But do the specifics really matter? Isn't it the way Rose perceived her relationship with her mother that's really important here?"

"You're damn right it is!" The older man retorted.

Marshall waited for Mr. Shaw to elaborate. He didn't.

Well, at least I've got his attention away from the baseball game, Marshall noted. *That counts for something.*

"But in light of what I *do* know now," Marshall continued, "that degree of overprotectiveness was warranted and even justified. After I got to know Rose intimately,"—Marshall would allow the old man interpret that any way he chose—"she told me about her heart disease. That helped explain some of the symptoms she'd been exhibiting, symptoms that seemed unusual for a woman of her age. It also put her relationship with her mother in a totally new perspective."

"No shit, Doc!" Mr. Shaw retorted with condescending irony.

Marshall let the outburst pass. Instead he said, "Being a nurse and not a lay person, I'm sure your wife appreciated how sick Rose really was. She must have done her best to protect her."

"Which, let me tell you, mister, was no fuckin' picnic. 'Specially when you're trying to rear a child with the temperament of a buckin' bronco and the wildness to match."

"I'm sure it wasn't easy," Marshall agreed, although he had no idea. "And she apparently did a pretty good job—until the accident."

"Oh, did she?"

"Well, look at Rose. She's turned out pretty well."

"Maybe," the old man said, "and maybe not."

Marshall couldn't imagine what this meant. From what he could tell Rose had been up against mortal odds and was doing remarkably well. But Mr. Shaw's ambivalent attitude confused him. Perhaps he knew something about Rose he hadn't thought of.

"As a result of my talks with Rose," Marshall offered, "I got a sense that the psychological trauma she suffered when your wife died in that auto accident was monumental. The event appears to have been so upsetting that she's completely repressed it. She wasn't even able to recall what happened under hypnosis. And this repression has apparently effected her mental stability."

Mr. Shaw turned and stared him right in the eye. Then he looked away. Marshall sensed that he was weighing something in his mind, considering whether to share it or not. Marshall had seen that expression on the faces of patients he'd treated hundreds of times over the years, surfacing when they were confronted with a thought or realization which seemed too painful to express. As he frequently did with his patients, Marshall assumed a receptive posture. Given enough space the old man might eventually reveal what he was thinking.

Finally Mr. Shaw did breach the silence. "What did Rose tell you about the accident?" he asked in a hoarse voice that seemed a pitch lower.

Marshall had to think about that one. "She told me that your wife was driving along a local highway. That she, Rose, was in the back seat doing her homework. It sounded like they'd been arguing. Then suddenly your wife lost control of the car. Rose was knocked unconscious—or at least she was banged up so much she has no further recollection of the event."

"That's not how it happened, Dr. Friedman," Mr. Shaw replied. Then unexpectedly he struggled then got to his feet. "And if you just wait here for a second there's something I wanna show you."

Marshall was fascinated and intrigued by this development. He tried to imagine what he wanted to show him.

It took Mr. Shaw almost ten minutes to return. When he did he held in his hand a soiled canvas bookbag by its strap. It was the kind of backpack that reminded Marshall of one he'd once owned while a student at Pitt. Mr. Shaw shuffled back to the recliner and settled himself on the seat. He set the bag on his lap then turned to face Marshall.

"I don't know what you think of my Rose," he began solemnly. "I suspect you've become pretty fond of her—being 'intimate' and all that. I guess you might even believe you're in love with her. Well, Dr. Friedman, I have some fatherly advice for you: get over it."

The old man's advice felt like a jab in the gut. A gush of bile regurgitated bitterly into the back of his throat. Whatever Mr. Shaw knew, Marshall was reluctant to find out about it.

"Rose, Dr. Friedman, is what my mother used to call, 'a bad seed.' It was something I suspected early on. Later I knew it for a fact. But more important, Karen knew it, almost from the moment the baby was born. It was something you almost sensed about her from the start."

"What do you mean, 'a bad seed'?" Marshall asked, fascinated by the term.

"It's hard to put into words. Rose was a colicky baby. She never seemed happy. When she wasn't cryin', she was fussin' and spittin'. She never settled down." Mr. Shaw paused, set his head back against the cushion and appeared to be collecting his thoughts. A brief, almost nostalgic, smile passed across his thin dry lips.

"To me she just sounds spirited," Marshall suggested.

"No, Dr. Friedman, it was much worse than that. There were these things that happened when she got a little older. We thought they were just variations of normal. But when we were forced to discuss her with a school psychologist when she was nine, we found out they all meant something."

"For instance?" Marshall asked.

"For instance," Mr. Shaw repeated, "when she was just a tot, not more than four, one of her cousins showed her how to burn up little insects with a magnifying glass. Once she got the hang of it, she loved doing it. Then, when she was six, she liked to catch frogs down by the creek and then torture them to death with safety pins and piano wire."

Now that does sound a bit atypical to me, Marshall conceded.

"Oh, and when she was seven, there was this incident with Karen at the laundromat. The shop was on the corner of Twenty-sixth and St. James back then. Karen was by the machines folding a load of clothes. That's when Rose wandered out back and found a stray kitten sniffing around the dumpster. She picked it up, carried it inside, and tossed it in one of the dryers. Seems Rose thought that was a real hoot."

Marshall was not a child psychologist. But he knew that this sort of behavior in children suggested serious underlying psychosocial problems. Suddenly the results of Don Owen's assessment of Rose assumed greater significance.

"But with her having that heart problem, we found it tough to be strict with her. On some level we figured that she was entitled to as much life as she could squeeze out of each and every day, even if we thought some of the things she did was wrong."

He paused again, a pensive look on his face. "Looking back—and I've done that a lot recently—it seems we were much too easy on her. And seein's how you say Rose thought she was mistreated, that must strike you as a bit ironic. But let me say truthfully, Karen and I tried our best to guide and protect her the only way we knew how."

Marshall nodded, appreciating their conflict and the consequences of their leniency.

"When she was real young we felt unwilling to punish or scold her," Mr. Shaw continued, "which, I suppose, just made her spunkier. Then when she got older, she acted entitled to all that freedom." The older man's expression reflected his conflict and pain. Marshall placed a supportive hand on his arm. "Then she had these friends at school. They were in what we used to call the 'fast crowd.' When I was growing up, Dr. Friedman, it was hard to imagine nine and ten year olds smoking cigarettes and doin' illegal drugs. But not around Millcreek in the seventies. That shit was everywhere. The older kids pushed it on the youngsters. And the little ones got hooked. I guess I should be glad that crack cocaine wasn't around when Rose was growing up, 'cause she wudda more 'en likely gotten into that too."

Marshall shuddered, trying to imagine the scenario.

"By the time Rose was twelve she was completely outta control," Mr. Shaw reported. "And to make things worse, Karen was forced to work the nightshift at Hammet. I had to be at the ceramics plant by seven makin' it impossible to keep track of her. And the more we restricted her activities the more she fought us. We were battling all the time. And nothing came from it but hurt feelings. Most of the fights ended up with Rose flyin' outta the house. Sometimes she wouldn't show up for days."

"Days?" Marshall repeated incredulously. "But where would she go?"

"We wondered the same thing. When we pressed her for answers she told us she'd been hanging out with friends. Later we found out that she was usually on the Isle, sleeping outside in the woods or on the beach wrapped in an old sleeping bag. That was the part that really scared us. I could imagine all kinds of things happen to her. She could have gotten raped or drowned."

"What on earth did you do to control her?"

"We locked her in her room and put bars on the windows. Then we hired us a sitter. She was an older girl from Fairview by the name of Carrie. Her mother worked with Karen at the hospital. She was a nice enough kid, a junior in high school. And to our surprise, Rose took to her right away, although she did call her 'the jailer'."

Marshall nodded. But the old man had turned away, staring at the television screen again, and absently stroking the canvas bag in his lap.

"Carrie taught Rosey good manners too," Mr. Shaw reported. "We knew that 'cause soon after we hired her Rose started to behave. She stopped fighting with us over every this and that. And she even began tryin' harder in school—you know, doin' her homework and gettin' better grades. It was a stretch that must've lasted six months."

The calm before the storm? Marshall suspected. "Then what happened?"

Mr. Shaw hesitated. After a long few moments, he turned to face Marshall with a sad, injured look in his old rummy eyes.

"That's when the accident happened," he replied.

chapter thirty-seven

what evil wrought

Back in his Mercedes, heading southbound on Interstate 79, Marshall tightly gripped the leather-bound steering wheel. While desperate to stretch the distance between him and Millcreek, the multicolored autumn woods pressed in upon him. But he was only peripherally aware of their resplendent splendor, his thoughts, instead, revisiting over and over again the shocking story Frank Shaw had shared with him less than an hour earlier.

"It happened on October thirtieth, nineteen seventy-six," Mr. Shaw said without further preamble. "I'll never forget the date 'cause I see it on Karen's tombstone every time I visit the cemetery. It was the day before Halloween, on what we kids used to call 'mischief night'. The accident happened just as the sun was goin' down.

"Those were the pretty uneventful days," he reminisced. "We'd had stopped frettin' over Rose since Carrie was comin' over after school. She'd help her with schoolwork and push her to get more involved in stuff. She was the big sister Rose never had. In fact, it was Carrie's idea that Rose join the drama club. She told her it was a way she could act out and not get punished for it. That's where she was comin' from the afternoon of the crash. They was havin' rehearsals for the play the school was puttin' on at Christmas time. Carrie would usually pick her up afterward. But with it bein' Karen's day off, she offered to do the chauffeuring."

There was a distant look in Frank Shaw's eyes. Marshall eased forward, now only lightly leaning against the lowered siderail of the day bed.

"Back then we had a six-month-old Chevy Citation—one of those K-cars that were popular in the mid-seventies. I didn't think it was that sturdy and would've gone with a Volvo or an Audi. But Karen liked the styling and the big hatch. She bought it with her own money."

Marshall knew the design.

"It happened right up on Twenty-sixth," the old man continued. "The police claim Karen lost control of the car. When they found her she wasn't wearing a seatbelt. Her head cracked the windshield. The emergency room doctor said she died instantly."

Marshall groaned. "I'm so sorry," he said. Then something Mr. Shaw had just said struck him as peculiar. "What do you mean, 'the police *claim* she lost control of the car'? Did she or didn't she?"

Mr. Shaw slowly turned his thin, gaunt face toward Marshall. "To be honest with you, Dr. Friedman," he replied evenly, "I believe the answer is she didn't."

A baneful chill passed through Marshall's taut frame. "If she didn't lose control of the car," Marshall persisted, "then what caused the crash?"

But instead of answering the question, Mr. Shaw took the green canvas school bag off his lap, held it up, and pointed to an irregular stain on its rear panel.

"Whaddya think this is, Dr. Friedman?"

Marshall studied the black blotch. Reaching over he touched it lightly. Amoeboid in shape, it had a smooth center and crusty edges.

"I don't know," Marshall admitted. "Mud, perhaps. It's probably not ink, not with those rough raised edges." Mr. Shaw who slowly shook his head. The tendons in his neck tensed forming a deep hollow between them. His prominent Adam's apple quivered.

"Then what is it?" Marshall asked.

"Blood, Dr. Friedman," Mr. Shaw reported. "It's dried blood."

"Blood?" Marshall echoed, then realized where the bag had been. "Of course it's blood. This must be the bookbag Rose had with her in car with her during the accident." Mr. Shaw nodded. "Then, it makes sense. There must've been blood all over the inside of the car. Some of it stained the bag. Is it Rose's?"

"No."

"Then it's your wife's." Mr. Shaw nodded again. "But what's the significance of that?"

"If you examine this satchel carefully, Dr. Friedman, you'll notice that the blood didn't come from outside of the bag, it soaked through from inside. And there were also tiny slivers of bone inside too."

"How could you know that?"

"Because I discovered them."

"Then the police must've known about that too." Mr. Shaw failed to concur. "Didn't they?" he asked.

"No, Dr. Friedman, unfortunately they didn't."

"Why not?"

"Because they never knew the bag was there."

Now Marshall was really confused. Every time he thought he glimpsed the truth, he was led down some blind alley. He stopped trying to figure out what happened and waited for Mr. Shaw to elaborate.

"You see, doctor," the old man complied, "the police never knew about this here bookbag because it got shoved under the front seat right after the accident. And I only found out about it a couple months later when Marty Crenshaw, one of my poker playin' buddies, brought it to my attention.

"You see, Marty worked part-time at his Uncle Ted's Auto Graveyard. In the end of January in nineteen seventy-seven—that's three months after the accident mind you—a customer wanted a bucket seat for his seventy-three Citation. Marty, o' course, knew about Karen's Chevy and pulled one out of that wreck. The bag was under the driver's seat. When he found it he figured it was Rose's and brought it over to my place so I could have it back."

"Now wait a minute, Mr. Shaw," Marshall said raising his hand. "You mean the police never searched the car after the accident?"

"Sure they searched it," Mr. Shaw replied, "but not real carefully. Why should they? They thought they were dealin' with a straightforward auto crash. They didn't think they were investigatin' a crime scene. And besides, there was a dead driver and a badly injured young girl to deal with."

Marshall nodded, but wasn't convinced.

"After I checked the bag and figured out what really happened, I had the police report pulled. The cops were convinced it was an accident from the start."

"But it wasn't, was it?"

"No."

"Then what really happened?"

"Can't you work that out for yourself, Dr. Friedman?"

Suddenly the horrible reality of the incident struck Marshall full force. In his mind's eye Marshall saw Karen Shaw driving her new Chevy Citation along Twenty-sixth Street in Millcreek. Behind her, with a set of school books spread open and a flaccid school bag tossed on the seat beside her, was Rose. The pre-teen, fresh from drama club, was acting out her reformed persona by diligently doing her homework.

Then the unthinkable happened. Driving along this county road, which easily supported a speed of thirty-five miles per hour, Karen Shaw lost control of her vehicle. Something unexpected occurred causing it to go careening off the road. It struck a stationary object and the impact sent the driver hurtling into the windshield. Marshall thought he knew what that 'something' was.

"That's right, Dr. Friedman," Frank Shaw said, reading the psychiatrist's mind. "Dear sweet little Rose must've reached down and unlatched her mother's seat belt. Then she picked up the empty school bag and slipped it over her head. It couldn't have taken long. One moment she's driving along a four-lane highway. The next she's blindfolded. A few seconds later she's dead."

"Oh...my...God!" Marshall cried, unable to contain his revulsion.

"It's the only explanation I can imagine, Dr. Friedman. Karen always wore her seatbelt, even when she was hurryin', even when she was distracted. And this was her *day off*. She was relaxed, at ease. And there's what I found in the schoolbag, the blood and bone chips on the inside. The only explanation I can see is that Karen's head was also inside the bag when it hit the windshield."

"But wouldn't the police have been able to tell that when they reached the scene of the accident?" Marshall protested.

"Not if the blood soaked through and stained the glass too. *And not if Rose had the presence of mind to pull the bag off and shove it under the seat.* No, I think the police would have accepted what they found—because that's what they were expectin' to find."

"Whew," Marshall said, slumping back down on the adjustable bed. "And of course you couldn't turn her in. Well, I guess you could have," Marshall corrected himself, "but she *is* your daughter and you'd just lost your wife." The older man remained mute while Marshall digested this gruesome scenario. "Did you ever confront Rose with this information? Did she ever confess?"

"No, I didn't confront her, Dr. Friedman," said Mr. Shaw. "And, no Rose never confessed."

Marshall couldn't help asking, "I wonder why not?"

"It's like I told you, she's a bad seed. In the balance of things she came into this world carryin' more evil than good. Lord knows some people may even call her a monster. But she's also my daughter. And although I didn't feel totally relaxed around her, I still didn't want her put away. Maybe it's because of that heart condition of hers. Call it rationalization, if you must, but I honestly figured she'd die soon enough, of what you folks in your business call, natural causes."

Marshall considered the irony of this way of thinking. "So her mortal illness saved her from being exposed," he concluded.

"I suppose that's one way of putting it."

His mind started to wander, as if repulsed from the grisly story he'd just been told. The baseball game was midway through the seventh inning. Cleveland was ahead five to four. They'd been talking for over two hours.

I wonder if I should offer to get the old man dinner, he asked himself, *or see if he needs anything from the store?*

It would have be the right thing to do, help this shut-in with his barest essentials. It would have also given him a handy excuse to flee that haunted little house as soon as possible. But then he would have to come back. In the end, he just left.

Now driving toward Pittsburgh, on a darkening highway, the sky above the color of orange sherbet, a ribbon of red taillights ahead of him, Marshall recalled that curious warning Mr. Shaw had given him just five short weeks earlier. Just as he and Rose had left the cottage for dinner, their amorous night at the Getty Bed and Breakfast just a few hours away, Frank Shaw had said, "Take good care of yourself, Dr. Friedman."

Now Marshall understood what the sad, old man had meant.

chapter thirty-eight

motivation and opportunity

When Marshall arrived back at his apartment it was just past seven on Sunday evening. By then much of the charge of his emotional reaction to Mr. Shaw's horrible story had dissipated. Thinking more rationally he attempted to construct a coherent analysis of the tragedy that occurred in that middle-class borough of Millcreek some twenty-three years ago.

But, as he worked through the deductive exercise, he found he had many more questions than answers. Some of these, he knew, he could have asked Frank Shaw before he left Erie. But at the time, he'd been so intent on fleeing that all else seemed secondary. Now, safe in the familiar confines of his Shadyside home, he considered calling Rose's father. Instead, he decided to let the old man rest.

Regarding Rose's psyche, he realized it was of singular importance to determine how Rose reacted to her mother's death—or should he call it murder? Had she grieved, felt remorse, or possibly even relief? If Rose had committed cold-blooded matricide, the latter was most probable. And although he was a seasoned professional, well acquainted with scores of gory tales from the distorted lives of his mentally ill patients, he still shuddered when he contemplated Rose's depravity.

Besides, this was personal. Rose was someone for whom he cared deeply. In his fantasies she was going to be his mate, someone whom he envisioned bearing him children. And although, in the discovery of her true nature, he felt delivered from the dangers of an uncertain fate, he still couldn't deny his feelings.

His mental ruminations lasted late into the evening. Scenes from their two intense and passionate months together kept haunting him, sometimes in snippets, and others in lengthy scenarios where he relived passionately intimate moments. He wondered if much of what he had coveted had been mere illusion, much of what he'd experienced been unilateral and only superficially reciprocated. Was he simply another pawn in her chess game, another rung on the ladder of success? Would he ever know for sure?

Before leaving that dreary house in Millcreek, Marshall had had the presence of mind to ask Frank Shaw about his daughter's habits and interests when she was a pre-teen. After the gruesome tale the old man had revealed, this inquiry must have seemed oddly trivial.

While waiting at the doorway, anxious to depart, Mr. Shaw had shuffled away but returned a few minutes later carrying an old cardboard box. Piled inside were a couple dozen books, mostly paperbacks. He set the box down at Marshall's feet. Marshall knelt down and began sifting through the contents. Mr. Shaw stopped him.

"No," he had said simply. "Not here. Take them with you. They're yours now. Consider them souvenirs from a sick childhood."

Marshall glanced up, saw the old man's expression and nodded. Hefting the box into his arms he cradled it to his chest.

"I'll keep the bookbag," Mr. Shaw said simply.

In the privacy of his home, curious whether their nature fit his theory, Marshall investigated the contents of the box. As he'd suspected, Rose seemed to have preferred novels, and mostly science fiction. It intrigued Marshall that Rose's imagination stretched beyond the common interests of a girl her age, far into the reaches of fantasy and fancy. Had she mentally rejected the reality of her own world and sought an allegorical version? Or was she searching for theoretical ideas and concepts to provide her with some novel way to change the hand fate had dealt her?

He wondered when Rose had conceived of her plan to secure a normal lifespan? Was it after reading Aldous Huxley's 1932 novel, *Brave New World,* where the concept of cloning had be introduced? If Rose had imagined the prospect it would have given her hope. Perhaps she'd taken this theoretical concept literally 'to heart' then devoted the rest of her life to bending the forces of nature to create a totally new future.

He then reviewed what he knew about cloning and tried to square it with what Rose had accomplished.

Marshall imagined the scenario where Rose had apparently been both donor and surrogate mother in her egotistic experimental design. Had she subjected her own compromised body to the stress of pregnancy just to produce an exact duplicate of herself? But even if she had and the pregnancy had gone to term, all she would have had was a newborn baby. What about the prolonged growth period to adulthood? But by Hunter's own admission, this was a five-year sprint, not a lifelong marathon. And yet, set there in the Plexiglass case in Rose's lab, Marshall had observed, not an embryonic or infant-sized heart, but an organ of adult size and proportion. How on earth had this feat been accomplished?

Wearily he rose from the living room carpet. Absently he picked up the books and returned them to the old cardboard box. While stretching his aching back Marshall recalled the Medline search the hospital librarian had performed for him a week earlier. He walked into the second bedroom and located his briefcase leaning against the computer station desk. Inside he found a folder stuffed with articles.

He sat down at his desk and sifted through the documents. Some were of a general scientific nature and others dealt with the moral, ethical, and social aspects of human tissue cloning. Marshall was looking for something more specific, more technical.

How can you take a human organ that requires a fixed amount of time to grow into maturity and accelerate that process ten or twentyfold? he asked himself. *What would you use? Human growth factor? Thyroid hormone? Some protein rich concoction? But whatever it was, Rose must've done it.*

Below the pile of articles on general topics Marshall found a handful of papers clipped together with a black clamp. They were abstracts mostly dealing with highly technical topics. Then, just as he was about to set the folder aside, he came upon a title that seemed more cogent to his specific inquiry.

ACCELERATED IN VIVO MATURATION OF EXTRACOPOREAL MAMMALIAN ORGANS.

The abstract, just one extended paragraph in length, described a sophisticated technique where a group of researchers took cloned animals, sacrificed them, harvested their hearts, liver and kidneys, then attempted to not only keep these organs alive, but accelerate their growths curves. Although their results were preliminary, they did seem promising. Marshall wondered whether this was the kind of foundation Rose had utilized to build her own project. Had she been the one who had made further inquiries into the matter?

The scope and breadth of this notion boggled Marshall's analytical mind and left him breathless. Despite what he now knew about her pernicious methods, he couldn't help marvel at Rose's vision and design.

She might even be a genius, contaminated by a vile core—but a genius nonetheless. However, even if he comprehended her motives and condoned her actions, her product was illegal and the work criminal. And this alone was enough cause for him to try to stop it from coming to fruition.

With a deep sense of sadness he knew that the final phase of Rose's project had to be thwarted. And regrettably, with what he now knew about the nature of the work, and because of his intimate, highly personal relationship to its creator, he considered himself the logical person to sabotage it.

Exhausted from a long, emotionally draining day, he set aside his reading materials and prepared for bed. Lying down on his mattress, not even considering reading a book or watching television, he turned out the light. Then, just before Marshall slipped off into a dreamless sleep, he realized how he could accomplish what he had to do.

chapter thirty-nine

in preparation

Early the following morning, motivated by the unsettling information he'd obtained from Mr. Shaw, paired with the conclusions of his own research, Marshall set out to execute his mandate from Dr. Hunter. His first order of business was to head over to the Department of Surgery and find his friend Steve Heller.

Despite being old friends, Marshall rarely got to observe Steve in his professional habitat. So he considered it a treat catching a glimpse the handsome, Brillo-haired anesthesiologist facilitating inductions, rectifying problems with incompatible agents, coordinating complicated procedures, and deftly managing the intricacies of a complex surgical theater. But on this particular Monday morning, Marshall didn't have the luxury of standing around and watching the show. He needed data, the kind Steve could reliably provide. Marshall caught up with him between two of the special procedure rooms. He made his request. Steve was more than glad to help.

Marshall knew that his friend owned a couple of firearms and enjoyed recreational target practice on Saturday afternoons. Using the pretense of the recent rash of robberies and rapes in his Shadyside neighborhood he told Steve that he was frightened for his safety. The anesthesiologist suggested to Marshall what he needed to purchase and where.

After lunch, during a lull between psychiatry grand rounds and the start of office hours, Marshall visited Dr. Hunter. He briefed the CEO on the details of the plan. The old man approved. He said he would do his part. They discussed the timing and execution of the final phase and agreed that Wednesday evening would be most appropriate.

That evening Rose called. It was the first time he'd heard from her since she'd driven off with Chris Jeffries on Saturday morning. She was effusively apologetic for standing him up then failing to get back to him for the rest of the weekend. He patiently listened to her prattle on, appreciating the call for what it was, a ploy to ensure his continued loyalty. He reassured her that he wasn't angry about the mix-up and suggested they make plans to get together soon. He intentionally avoided designating a specific time and place, though, knowing that if he completed his mission, Rose would come looking for him.

His Tuesday morning schedule was unusually light. After meeting with the residents to discuss the overnight admissions, he joined them for inpatient rounds, then took a break. Instead of reviewing reports, writing letters, and answering inquiries he donned his sports jacket, told his secretary he had some errands to run, and left the building.

Marshall was familiar with Wilkinsburg, a small community of on the eastern outskirts Pittsburgh. He often used its main drag, Penn Avenue, on his way to the parkway. It was one of the most dangerous, narcotic-infested neighborhoods in all of Allegheny County, an area Marshall purposely avoided after dark.

But on this early autumn morning with the sun peeking out from clusters of high cumulus clouds, Penn Avenue, bustling with dozens of shoppers, merchants, delivery trucks and service vans, appeared safe and amicable. In fact, Marshall realized wryly, the most daunting part about venturing there today was dealing with the traffic then finding a place to park.

He passed Ladderman's Arms Company before he realized it was there. Turning right at the next intersection Marshall circled the block and found a meter in a public parking lot. After securing the Mercedes with his Club, he made his way past the retail outlets, used car lots, restaurants and shops on back toward his destination.

At the storefront Marshall pulled on the metal door. Locked, it refused to budge. Peering intently through the shaded glass he caught the eye of one of the salesmen who buzzed him.

Once inside, the establishment reminded him of a secondhand jewelry store with its rows of glass cases arranged in the shape of a 'u'. But these were chock full of all kinds of firearms and other hunting paraphernalia. Ladderman's, Steve had mentioned, was one of the finest retail outlets of its type in the area. Marshall had imagined it would be bigger.

Two salesmen were waiting on customers. Marshall took the opportunity to browse. At first he found the very idea of being there intimidating. He'd never held a real gun in his hand, let alone fired one. Oh, there was the shooting gallery at Kennywood, firing ballbearing-like pellets at targets from what amounted to a toy rifle. But that didn't compare to discharging real ammunition from deadly firearms. And this place had the real thing, revolvers, pistols, colts, and berretas, all arranged neatly in the well-lit display cases, clean, polished, and uniformly lethal. And that was not to mention the rack after rack of menacing looking rifles, both hunting and high powered, mounted along the walls. The macabre scene made Marshall cringe.

He was browsing a laminated sheet of paper describing the screening procedures for potential firearm purchases when one of the salesmen approached. From the guy's smile and casual appearance Marshall assumed he was amiable enough. Probably in his late thirties, he had curly brown hair and a mustache with flecks of gray. Noticing his green and blue flannel shirt and his khaki work pants Marshall wondered if he'd just returned from a hunting trip.

"Sorry about the delay," he greeted Marshall in a friendly, easy-going manner. His nametag said 'Ned'. "They promise you a ninety second turn-around time when you punch in all the pertinent info. But sometimes the system drags. Sure beats waiting five days like we used to up till two years ago."

"Sure does," Marshall agreed.

"So what can I help you with today?"

"I'm looking for a gun," Marshall replied with just a hint of hesitation.

As the salesman smiled, Marshall could have kicked himself. What else would he be there for, a new suit? "Well you came to the right place," Ned replied, still amiable. "Did you have a particular firearm in mind?"

Marshall thought back to his conversation with Steve. "Do you sell something called a Browning Hi-Power?" he inquired.

"We sure do," Ned replied, looking impressed with Marshall's choice. "And it's a helluva weapon. Would you like to see one?"

"Yes, I would," Marshall replied with a slight stammer in his voice.

Ned followed the inner corridors behind the counters to a display case situated directly behind where Marshall was standing. Using a key chained to his belt he unlocked the cabinet, reached inside and withdrew a slender revolver from the top shelf.

"Isn't she a beauty?" Ned suggested, holding the small sleek pistol in his large callused hand. He tested its weight on his outstretched palm then stroked it affectionately. "It's very popular model, extremely easy to use. At last count, I figure there's gotta be five million of 'em in circulation around the world." Marshall wondered if that was a lot. "Look how slim and graceful the barrel is," Ned continued. "It's got a double-column magazine with an external hammer and a lock-up similar to the Colt 45. The grip tends to be a little chunky though. But I see you have a large hand so that shouldn't be a problem. My only beef with it is that the sighting plane is low and close to the hand. See that." He pointed to the little notch on the top of the barrel. "But it's a light, accurate weapon with little recoil, so the sighting isn't as critical."

Marshall spent this entire soliloquy staring at the firearm and nodding in agreement. To his untrained eye, it looked slender and guileless, a simple practical device with an economy of design and utility. It was hard to imagine the terror and mayhem it could engender.

"Here," Ned said, "check it out. See what I mean."

He handed the pistol to Marshall who picked it up gingerly. Thoroughly intimidated by this deadly device, he could barely disguise his trepidation. But once he held the firearm squarely in his palm and permitted his long slender fingers to wrap lightly around its grip, he lost some of his apprehension and began to enjoy its feel in his hand. Slipping his index finger into the trigger housing he set it against the curved stem.

"That's a pivoting type trigger," offered Ned, helpfully. "It works a drabber on the right side of the frame that happens to be very intricate and hard to adjust. Our local gunsmith curses every time we send him one to fix."

Marshall tugged on the trigger and felt it pivot smoothly. He imagined performing this action with real bullets in the chamber, feeling the slight recoil, wincing at the earsplitting explosion.

Yes, he admitted grimly to himself, *Steve was right on. This little baby is just what the doctor ordered.*

He asked Ned about how the safety catch worked and the specifics of loading the magazine with bullets. The double-column housing seemed simple enough. The ammunition, Marshall learned, could all be stored in the clip or a bullet could be housed in the chamber. This, Ned explained, made the firearm ever ready. But it also increased the risk of a deadly accident if the pistol was toyed with.

When Marshall indicated he was serious about purchasing the firearm Ned requested some personal information, then recorded Marshall's profile on the order form. He punched the data into his computer and sent it off. As Marshall had learned from the flyer, instantaneously, three different databases were being cross-referenced to see if someone with Marshall's name, social security number and address, had any previous convictions or was ever arrested for a gun-related incident. If there was no match then the store could sell the firearm to him.

While the inquiry was processed, Ned took the time to sell Marshall a bottle of cleaning solution, another full of lubricating oil, along with a special cloth for wiping and shining the weapon. He then handed Marshall a pamphlet with instructions on how to break down and reassemble the weapon. Marshall found the diagrams detailed but comprehendible.

It took less than three minutes for Marshall's approval to return. Ned, appearing satisfied with the process, completed the paperwork, then recommended some ammunition.

"I like the Winchester Silvertips," he told Marshall pulling out a box of the nine-millimeter bullets. "These have a hollow point bullet and an aluminum alloy jacket with lubricant near the base."

Marshall nodded, assuming that somehow this was important information. He, for his purposes, was just interested in obtaining something that would allow him to follow through with his plan. Ten minutes later, with his new purchases boxed and bagged, he stepped through the security door and back onto Penn Avenue.

That was almost too easy, he thought solemnly to himself.

chapter forty

missing parts

Marshall thought about the last time he'd used his doctor bag. It was during his senior year of medical school, that onerous year of clinical clerkships when, with a novice's naiveté, he'd felt compelled to have his vital instruments at hand. Then, when it became apparent that all he really needed was a stethoscope and a reflex hammer, he'd banished this black imitation alligator bag to the corner of the closet.

On Wednesday afternoon, back in his Shadyside apartment, Marshall realized that once again the bag could serve a purpose. After rummaging through a pile of storage he finally located it in a box labeled 'miscellaneous' in the spare bedroom closet. Then, after visiting hours ended that evening, it was with the time worn bag in his right hand that Marshall strolled through The Hunt's second level-parking structure. Casually hefting it, he decided the satchel seems pretty light. The Browning and a box of bullets didn't weigh much.

The security guard at the main information desk checked Marshall's hospital ID, then let him pass. Noting with some satisfaction that the hospital's well-lit corridors were pretty much deserted, he headed for the nearest stairwell. After looking both ways he slipped through the heavy metal door and headed down the steps toward the basement.

Marshall negotiated the series of sharp turns that brought him to Rose's Biogenetic Research laboratory. As he walked within the eerie solitude of the hospital's lower level his footfalls echoed hauntingly off the gray cinderblock walls. He considered his mission and wondered if he would pull it off. He thought about the sophisticated weapon in his satchel and gauged whether the evening he'd spent practicing at that indoor shooting center on Troy Hill had been enough.

Mastering the sleek Browning Hi-Power turned out to be harder than he'd expected—so much to learn and so little time to learn it. He thought about that sleazy gun club on the North Side he'd visited yesterday evening, full of tough looking, gun loving, beer drinking, hunter types. Most, he imagined, had to be card-carrying members of the NRA with color photos of Charlton Heston on their mantles and stuffed animal heads on their walls. How absurd it was that he'd been forced to purchase a membership to the club just to try it. As if he'd ever go back.

I needed a place to train, he rationalized, *and Troy Hill is pretty convenient. So I guess you could call the whole experience a necessary evil.*

The silence in the empty corridor seemed suffocating. Unexpectedly the overhead ductwork clanged. It gave him a start. He felt an impulse to flee the hospital and retreat to the cozy confines of his Shadyside condo. But that sort of respite had to wait. He had a job to do.

Marshall reached the main door to the research department, then paused. From inside his black bag he extracted a pair of thin rubber surgical gloves and donned them with a snap. Next he checked the doorknob and found it locked. Taking the passkey from his pocket, he slipped it into the keyhole. The knob turned and he opened the door.

Inside the room he felt around for the light switches. Finding them, he flipped a couple and instantly the room's recessed lights flickered on. Then he tried the door to the main lab. It was unlocked. Pushing it forward a few inches he peeked inside. The room, illuminated only by this narrow rectangle of white light seemed darker than the first. Marshall found more light switches and flipped them on.

The hum of machinery, a cacophony of dissonant tones from pumps, monitors, oxygenators and other equipment sounded like an orchestra playing a piece by Stravinsky. Marshall checked the black stone counters and saw familiar plastic containers, each housing some odd body part. The bizarre props and weird noises seemed more tailored to a science fiction movie set than an authentic biogenetics lab. Or did it match something Rose had read about in one of her futuristic novel as a teenager?

Refocusing on his mission, Marshall searched for the shiny metal door which led to Rose's private one. He easily found it. Using Dr. Hunter's cardtrol he activated the locking mechanism. A series of beeps was followed by the whirring of machinery. Seconds later the door opened toward him. Marshall reached out and pulled the recessed metal handle.

He stepped into the dimly lit room. *Rose must've left her desk lamp on,* he realized. He tried to recall the exact location of the Plexiglas cube with its precious contents. He seemed to remember a small table, almost like a pedestal, perched in the center of the room, surrounded by a host of support equipment. It was then that he became painfully aware of the silence. *Where's all the noise? Where's all that vital equipment?* Anxiety gripped his chest. Peering into the shadows he discerned the outlines of the pumps and monitors. But when he went over to the cube and looked for the heart, he found to his alarm that it was, indeed, gone.

At first he hoped he was mistaken. Perhaps Rose had found a way to dampen the sounds and the heart was still nearby. He flipped on the overhead lights. The glare seemed so harsh that he had to squint. He stared at the pedestal. No, he hadn't been mistaken. The Plexiglas cube was there. But the precious cloned heart was missing.

Immersed in a whirlwind of distress and confusion he wondered where the vital organ could have gone? Had she simply moved it to another part of the lab complex for further experimentation? His search of the other two rooms confirmed that this was an unlikely possibility. Back in Rose's inner sanctum, he paused by her desk and pondered the situation.

The heart was gone. He assumed Rose had taken it. But what could she have possibly done with it? And why? Then he knew the answer. It was the 'why' that made it so obvious. But he had to find out for sure?

He took a shot and called Rose at home. He didn't really expect to find her there. If what he suspected was true, then both donor and recipient would most likely be in close proximity to each other—and it wouldn't be in a condo in the Trimont. What he didn't anticipate was how explicitly the message on her answering machine seemed to confirm his suspicions.

"This is Dr. Shaw," the recording announced. "Something personal has come up forcing me to take a temporary leave of absence. Dr. William Richardson will handle any work-related inquiries in the research department. He can be reached at..." and the number at the hospital followed.

So she'd taken a 'temporary leave of absence.' But where? And for how long? He reasoned that if she'd been admitted to the hospital it was probably somewhere close. With the risk of damaging it so great he doubted whether she would have taken a chance and transported the precious organ over any protracted distance. He considered some of the other major medical centers in the city and was tempted to call. But would they tell him if she was there? He wasn't a relative or a staff physician. Would she even be admitted under her own name? He decided to check the Hunt first.

He booted up the lab computer terminal and logged into the hospital's inpatient database. When he typed in Rose's name he came up empty. *Suppose she's registered under an alias or some false identity?* If he knew her social security number he could use that as a cross-reference to get her real medical record number. But he didn't. Then he thought of something.

Quickly he found the key to the locked desk drawers. He checked the middle drawer for the logbook but wasn't surprised it was also gone. Rose knew that he'd penetrated her inner lab once. He expected her to eliminate as much of the incriminating paper trail as she could. On the chance that she'd just left it out, he checked for the book on the counter and up on the storage shelves. Although he found boxes of reference material, several loose leaf binders and two rows of textbooks, the donor log was gone.

Delving back into the top drawer he felt around for the notepad. While searching its recesses he recalled how much trouble that little piece of notepaper had gotten him into. Reflexively his left hand went up to his throat. He stroked the spot where Rose had placed the point of her knife. A tiny scab still marked the wound. He imagined what would have happened if Rose had pushed the knife home. He shuddered. Suddenly his fingertips felt the notebook. The gruesome memory from last Friday night dissolved.

There was no writing on the top sheet of the notepad. Although it was probably unlikely, Marshall hoped that no one had used the pad used since the last time he'd been there. From a cup stuffed with writing utensils he picked out a number two pencil. Using the side of its cone-shaped point he spread a thin layer of graphite on the top page of the pad. Last week, he'd used a ballpoint pen to transcribe the entry numbers from the logbook. Now, with the help of the grey-black graphite wash, the ghosts of their impressions reappeared. He recalled Rose's and keyed it into the computer. Under a list of her inpatient activity he found, to his satisfaction, that her most recent admission was yesterday, Tuesday, October 11, under another name.

This bit of data gave Marshall pause. His throat constricted and chest tightened. Unlike when she flew to Minneapolis with Jeffries last month, this time Rose wasn't off somewhere. Instead she was right there in the Hunt, lying in a room above him, admitted under the name of Karen McCurty. Was this her mother's maiden name? he wondered. Wouldn't that add a bit of irony to the situation? And if Rose was indeed here, that must mean the heart was nearby too. But where? Then he thought he knew.

He found Steve Heller's home phone number on a scrap of paper in his wallet. Up until then he'd resisted using Rose's lab phone, concerned that, if an investigation ever occurred into this caper, any calls he made could be traced. But now he had no choice. He punched in the number and held the phone to his ear. It rang and rang, over a dozen times. While he waited he imagined what he would do next, especially if Steve wasn't home.

"Hello," answered a familiar voice. His friend sounded winded.

"Steve, it's Marshall. Thank God you're home."

"I almost wasn't. You caught me on the way out. I was down in the garage."

"This'll only take a minute. I've got something very important to ask you."

"Sure. Fire away."

"When they do cases in the OR that require bioprosthetic parts like a heart valve or arterial graft, where are those items stored?"

"In a climate controlled room adjacent to the OR. They also store the incoming transplants on dry ice there. Why?"

"I was just curious, that's all," Marshall replied, hating to sound so circumspect, but not knowing how much to share with his friend. Before he hung up he had one more question. "I know it's after hours, Steve, but is it possible for you to still get into that room?"

"I don't have a key, if that's what you mean. But it's easy enough to get the security guard to let me in." Steve seemed to hesitate. Then he asked, "Marshall, do you mind telling me what this is all about?"

Marshall knew that if he answered the question honestly it would expand the circle of people who knew about Rose's illegal cloned heart. But he couldn't think of a lie that would make sense.

"Let me preface this by saying that this is highly classified information. If the authorities find out about it, the Hunt's reputation could be seriously damaged."

"Marshall, buddy, what the hell's goin' on here? Whatever it is, you can trust me to keep it to myself."

"I know that Steve. It's just hard. But here goes. Bertram Hunter and I believe that Rose Shaw has illegally cloned a human heart. He sent me to her lab to confiscate it. When I got here, it was gone. I think she might have moved it to that room you were telling me about by the OR."

"Why would she do a thing like that?"

"Clone the heart or remove it from the lab?" he asked Steve.

"Both."

"Well, she has a condition called Epstein's anomaly. It's a serious congenital heart disorder."

"I know what Epstein's anomaly is, Marshall. We put a shunt in a six year old with pulmonary hypertension from it last week."

"Sorry," Marshall apologized. "Anyway, the organ she made was engineered using her own genetic material. Now she's been admitted to the hospital under an alias. And recently she's been buddy-buddy with Chris Jeffries. What I think is that she's planning to have him implant it in her."

"That sounds pretty wild," Steve declared. "But it also makes a lotta sense. It would certainly remove any risk of rejection. And furthermore, it makes the call I just got from the nursing supervisor more alarming. Apparently Dr. Jeffries has asked her to mobilize the cardiac transplant team. He claims that a heart has just arrived for one of his inpatients and he wants it implanted tonight."

"Tonight!" he exclaimed.

"That's what she said," Steve reported.

"And you said you were on your way to the hospital?"

"I didn't say that, but I was."

"Can I meet you in the OR?" Marshall asked, knowing his friend wouldn't refuse.

"I'll be there in fifteen minutes."

chapter forty-one

cardiac arrest

As Marshall left the research complex, he turned off the lights and secured the doors. Once back in the basement corridor he removed his gloves, put them back in his black bag, and reoriented himself. It was one thing to find his way from the steps near the guard's station to Rose's lab. It was quite another to use this labyrinth of intersecting hallways to get from the lab to the main surgical complex.

He spotted an 'exit' sign at the end of the hallway and followed it to the nearest stairwell. Like a character in an action film he mounted the steps two at a time before bursting through the first floor firedoor. He instantly recognized a row of display cases along the far wall.

Good, he told himself. *I'm near the main entrance on East Street in the old building.*

Next he headed northward, straight through a set of intersecting corridors, reaching the bank of stainless steel elevators the serviced the Tower a few moments later. The set of thick metal doors opened soundlessly. Ten seconds later and twenty feet higher he stepped out into the carpeted hallway that led to the wing that housed the hospital's surgical suites. Beyond a pair of double doors the row of operating theaters stretched to the southern end of the building. Facing these were preparation and recovery rooms, special procedure suites, and the staff changing lounges. Ignoring a large yellow signed that warned, AUTHORIZED, PROPERLY ATTIRED PERSONAL ONLY, he slapped the metal disc on the wall and the double doors flew open. Glancing down at his khaki slacks and casual shirt in lieu of scrubs, he thought, *for the moment this is gonna hafta do.*

He hurried passed the main desk. Out of the corner of his eye he noticed a middle-aged woman in green scrubs and a flimsy cloth hairnet charting at the counter.

"Hey, mister!" she called after him. "Where the hell do you think you're goin'?"

Marshall had heard that attitude and crassness were legendary in certain seasoned OR nurses. This caustic greeting suggested that this churlish reputation was not unfounded. Despite being pressed for time and intent upon his mission, he decided that, rather than make a scene with this old battle-ax and attract security to the department, he would present himself at the desk.

He approached the counter, reached into his pocket, and pulled out his hospital picture ID. "I'm Dr. Marshall Friedman," he introduced himself, "chairman of the psychiatry department. One of my patients is in the department being prepped for a heart transplant. I've come at the request of her family."

The nurse seemed to be ignoring his explanation as she scrutinized the laminated badge. "Well, Dr. Friedman," she said generously. "I suppose you're who you say you are. But what did you say you were doin' down here again?"

"Like I told you, I was called by the family of one my patients and told that she's suppose to be have a heart transplantation tonight. They were worried that she wasn't psychologically ready for such an ordeal."

"Ain't it a little to late for those kind of second thoughts?" she asked derisively. But before he could come up with a plausible rejoinder, she continued, "Anyway, what's her name?"

Marshall offered the name he'd seen in the computer next to Rose's medical record number. The charge nurse checked a sheet of paper on the desk and reported, "Well you got the name right, doc. There *is* a Karen McCurty bein' prepped for a cardiac transplant in holding area two. Now what can I do for *you*?"

"Is there any chance I can check on her before you banish me to the waiting room?" Marshall implored, flashing her his most ingratiating smile. "It would be extremely generous of you. And I know Karen's family would really appreciate it if I could offer them an eyewitness report that everything's all right."

"I don't know, doc," the old nurse countered. "It's highly irregular to have anyone 'cept the transplant team to be in the department during such an important procedure. But if she's still in the holding area and seeings you *are* one of her personal physicians, I suppose we can make an exception. But don't go wanderin' back there in street clothes. The surgeon's lounge is right across the hall. Why don't you go over there and put on some scrubs. That's pants, shirt, and shoe covers in case you don't know. Meanwhile, I'll go back and check with Dr. Jeffries and see if it's okay for you to be here."

"That would be great."

"Now I didn't say nothin's for sure doc. I said I'd check."

"I know. And thank you for just doing that."

The veteran RN grunted in reply.

Just as Marshall finished putting on a green v-neck shirt and a pair of baggy cotton pants Steve burst in the door.

"What's the story?" he asked, removing his Pirates jacket in one motion. "Where's Rose?"

"I'm hoping she's still in the holding area. There's an old battle-ax in charge out there. She wouldn't let me go see her until I was 'properly' attired."

"Don't fault her, Marshall. She's just doing her job. Since you're already in scrubs, you go on ahead. I'll meet you in pre-op."

"All right. But hurry up. This is really alien territory for me."

Steve nodded, a grim expression on his handsome face. "I know," he replied.

Marshall left through the thick wooden door and headed down the smooth tiled hallway toward the operating suites. He was so intent on reaching his destination that he failed to notice the charge nurse hailing him as he passed the main desk. "Doc!" she called to his retreating back. "You're too late. Your patient's already in the OR."

"Shit!" Marshall swore under his breath after what she said registered in his brain. Then he reasoned, *at least the procedure is just starting. Maybe we can get to the heart before it's implanted.*

But the problem was, he didn't even know where to look for it. Then he recalled how all the bioprosthetic devices bound for the OR were kept here in the department. He continued down the hallway. On his left he passed three cavernous rooms each with a dozen or so stations situated in horseshoe configurations around a centralized desk. Sophisticated monitoring and treatment equipment were all over the place. There were recovery rooms flanking a large holding area. He tapped another wall mounted metal disc that controlled the electronic doors to the middle room. Inside it was empty. The charge nurse was right, Rose had been moved elsewhere.

A few patients were still being treated inside Recovery I and II. *Stragglers or late afternoon cases from earlier in the day,* he assumed, *probably headed for intensive care or the stepdown unit.*

Across the hall was the row of operating suites. Marshall counted eight of them in four couplets each with a scrub area between. He tried the first four doors in succession. They were all locked.

Besides Rose's operation, it's a quiet night, he concluded. *The ER staff must be holding the line.*

Continuing down the hallway he noticed a rectangle of light sneaking into the hallway from three doors up. Just then a young man in a scrub suit, shoe covers, and a bathing bonnet-like head covering walked out of the room. Marshall was about to ask him in which room the transplant was talking place, when he glanced to his right and saw the sign on the door next to OR 4. It said, BIOPROSTHETICS AND HUMAN TRANSPLANT STORAGE.

Well, they couldn't be more explicit, could they? he observed. *Let's see what's doin' in there.*

But just as he was about to open the door a familiar voice behind him said, "Hey doc, whaddya think you're doin'. This room's off limits. In fact, now that your patient is in the OR, the whole department is off limits to you. So if you would kindly put your street clothes back on and leave I would certainly appreciate it."

Before he could turn and confront her, Marshall heard Steve say. "That's okay, Gladys. Dr. Friedman's with me. I'll take over from here."

"If that's what you want, Dr. Heller," the veteran nurse said hesitantly. Marshall sensed she was flustered. "He never said you were with him. He told me the patient in four is his."

"It is, Gladys. Now go along back to the desk while I handle things. It's all right. Really."

"If you say so, Dr. Heller," grumbled Gladys, apparently none too thrilled about being trumped by the head of anesthesiology. As the charge nurse retreated Steve smiled knowingly at Marshall.

"This is obviously the room you were talking about," Marshall said, relieved that his ally was on the scene.

Steve nodded. "I don't think it's locked," he guessed. "Let's give it a try."

Marshall turned the knob. It gave easily. With a gentle push the door opened. The light was already on.

Inside Marshall looked around. The room resembled Rose's research lab. There were blacktop tables full of an assortment of glass containers housing a variety of biological materials, mostly small items like heart valves and tube-like sections of arteries. Much of the metal shelving was stocked with orthopedic and neurosurgical appliances, artificial knees, hips, elbows, and linked vertebrae, along with an odd collection of stainless steel rods and pins. On display in another section were pacemakers and defibrillators.

"They usually keep the transplant organs in that case over there," Steve said pointing to a freezer-sized container about six feet wide and four feet tall nestled into the far corner of the room. Steve walked over, rotated the metal handle then pulled it toward him. The latch released.

Raising the rectangular lid about head-high he declared triumphantly, "Voila!"

Marshall joined him by the edge of freezer. Peering over the rim his eye was drawn to the back right corner. There, neatly packed in a nest of dry ice, sat the cloned heart.

"Why do they pack it in ice," Marshall asked, "when they could've kept it attached to all that support equipment I saw in the lab?"

"Probably because Jeffries wants to make it look like an authentic transplant. Remember, if what I think is true, no one else in the OR knows the true nature of this organ."

"That's probably right," Marshall agreed. "What should we do now?"

Just as Steve was about to reply a voice from across the room declared, "Hey! What are you two doing over there?" Marshall pivoted. A young man, probably in his early twenties, was standing in the doorway that separated the storage room from OR six.

"Jason," Steve said to the interloper. "I got a call to assist with the operation. Who's doing the induction?"

"Dr. Heller," the young man said, his face brightening. "I didn't recognize you. Carmen Cameron is running the gases. I'm going to help with the TEE. Dr. Perez is in the building but he's helping in specials with an emergency endoscopy. I'll tell Dr. Jeffries you're here."

"You go do that, Jason."

"Who's that?" Marshall inquired.

"One of the first year thoracic surgery fellows. And a pretty good one at that. I suppose Jeffries is letting him assist."

"I'll be interested to see how Chris reacts when he learns we're here."

It didn't take him long to find out. A few seconds later, clad in full OR garb, including gown, gloves, mask, and visor, Chris Jeffries burst into the Bioprosthetics and Human Tissue storage room.

"What the hell are you two doing in here?" he demanded his tone consistent with a man used to being in charge. "And get away from that freezer!"

"We can't do that Chris," Steve replied, his tone remarkably placid in contrast to the surgeon's bombast. "We've found something in there that doesn't belong."

"What the fuck's that suppose to mean? The only thing that's in there is the heart I'm planning to transplant."

"Not if we have anything to say about it." This time it was Marshall who spoke. And for the briefest of moments he was amazed to hear the sound of his own voice. "What you have there is an illegally cloned organ that is not authorized for human implantation. And we're here to confiscate it."

"Confiscate it! You must be kidding, Friedman. And you too, Heller. This is my OR. This is *my* operation. And I'm the one who decides what goes down here."

By then a knot of surgical staff had migrated toward the doorway that led into the OR. Without taking his eyes off of Marshall and Steve, Jeffries called over his shoulder.

"Patsy," he ordered. "Ring security and tell them we have two intruders here who need to be to escorted out of the department." A member of the green-clad throng backed off and disappeared into another room.

"Now what are we suppose to do?" Marshall asked Steve.

"Get this damn thing outta here. Go check that cabinet over there." He pointed to a red and silver storage case. It looked like something a handyman might buy from Home Depot. "There should be a pair of heavy rubber gloves in the top drawer."

"What do we need those for?"

"You don't want to pick up that heart with your bare hands do you?"

"I suppose not."

Marshall started to move toward the cabinet. "Stay where you are, Friedman!" Jeffries commanded. Marshall ignored him. "Jason," the tall lank surgeon continued, "Get Brad and Tory. We're ready to go on bypass. The three of you have to make sure those two don't touch that heart. Our patient's life is at stake."

"I don't know, Dr. Jeffries," said the thoracic surgery fellow, his voice almost at whine. "That's Dr. Heller over there."

"I don't care if it's President Clinton, you little wimp! Just remember, if you want to survive this program you'll do what I say."

Meanwhile Marshall had reached the colorful metal storage case and was rummaging through the squat wide drawers. In the second from the top he found the gloves, thick and black.

"Those are the ones," his friend confirmed. "Bring them over so we can finish what we came to do."

"You'll *do* nothing of the sort," Jeffries insisted just as a pair of broad-shouldered young men dressed in scrubs and white OR shoes emerged from the crowd at the door. "They're over there, guys," he indicated pointing in the general direction of Steve and Marshall. "Would you be so kind as to escort Drs. Heller and Friedman from our department? We have work to do here."

It was evident that Jeffries meant business. Knowing that desperate times called for desperate measures Marshall reached into his scrubs and extracted an object that had been weighing down his pocket since he'd left the surgeon's lounge.

"Not so fast, 'guys'," Marshall commanded, the last word uttered mockingly. "Not one more step!" The two techs stopped dead in their tracks. They were staring in apparent disbelief down the barrel of Marshall's Browning Hi-Power.

"Are you *nuts,* Marshall?" Jeffries exclaimed. "That isn't a real gun you have there?"

"Well, it's not a toy pistol, Chris. And let me warn you, I know how to use it."

"But this is an *operating room* in a major hospital! You can't pull that kind of crap here."

"Why don't you try me?" Marshall challenged, his hand trembling a little as he warmed to the task.

"All right," Jeffries retorted defiantly. "Ignore him, boys. He's only bluffing. He's a God damned psychiatrist, for Christ sakes!"

The two burly techs looked from the gun to the freezer and then back to Jeffries. The shorter of the two must have ranked the stern glare in the surgeon's eye over the revolver's menace and decided to take a bold step forward. Marshall noticed this move and without a moment's hesitation flipped the safety on his sleek little revolver and pulled the trigger. The loud explosion was followed by a musical ping as a deadly nine-millimeter metal cartridge zipped across the room and lodged in a waist-high square of green tile about a foot from the doorjamb. The report was deafening. Everyone in the room jumped. Marshall appreciated why they'd insisted he wear ear protectors on the practice range yesterday.

Simultaneously the tech jumped back, a shocked expression on his face. Marshall, buoyed by an immense sense of power, flashed Jeffries a smug wink. He then joined Steve by the freezer case. As he turned to face the gathering with his gun hand leading, the group of people by the doorway shrank back and the two techs pinched in beside Jeffries.

Marshall instructed Steve to remove the heart from the freezer. "Let's take what we came for," he said, "and get the hell outta here."

Steve nodded, donned the thick rubber gloves, and reached into the case. Gingerly, like a mother taking her newborn out of the crib, the anesthesiologist lifted the cloned organ out of the freezer. A few seconds later he was standing next to Marshall with Rose's cloned heart in his hands.

Marshall watched Jeffries' expression as the amazing specimen appeared. He seemed to shift from wide-eyed horror to painful perturbation. Marshall wondered if once the heart were handled in this manner it was no longer a candidate for implantation—which, of course, suited him just fine.

Using the revolver as prod Marshall indicated to Jeffries and his two techs to back off. The three men, albeit reluctantly, complied. As he turned toward the exit, he was dismayed to see that two security guards now blocked their egress. One, Marshall recognized, was the stocky Black man who'd checked his ID earlier that evening at the parking lot entrance. The other, an older man with grey hair and a beer belly, didn't look familiar.

Seeing Marshall with the gun, the Black guard seemed to be appraising the situation. In one fluid motion he unsnapped the strap on his holster and removed the weapon from its leather sleeve. Pointing it directly at Marshall, he said in a commanding voice, "Okay fellas, the party's over. Put down the gun, sir."

Marshall wavered for a moment. He glanced from the guard to Steve and then over at Jeffries. The surgeon looked relieved, then pleased. Marshall hated to give him the satisfaction of triumphing, but he had no intention of seeing anyone get hurt as a consequence of all this GI Joe stuff. He looked back at Steve one more time. His friend, wearing a grim expression, just nodded. Marshall lowered the Browning.

"Now set your weapon on the floor," the guard instructed, "and kick it toward me."

Meanwhile the older guard, his face now a cherry red that contrasted starkly with the tufts of white hair peeking out from under his black-rimmed cap, slipped past him and positioned himself in front of Jeffries and his two techs. He, too, had drawn his weapon and was pointing it at the 'intruders'. The Black guard bent over and took possession of the Browning.

"Now, doctor," he continued. "Could you please return that specimen to the case."

Steve was about to comply when Marshall heard some commotion in the hallway.

"Let me through, dammit!" ordered a familiar voice from outside in the corridor. "This is *my* hospital and I demand to know what's going on here!"

Although Hunter had just survived complicated, debilitating open-heart surgery, Marshall sensed that he still retained the aura of authority and leadership that had helped propel him to where he was today. The Black guard eased forward into the room and cleared the area around the doorway. A moment later one of the nurses from the stepdown unit wheeled the CEO into the room.

"What the *hell's* going on here?" Hunter demanded.

Jeffries seemed to sense this was a cue for him to reestablish his authority. "I was just starting a transplant procedure, Bertram, when Drs. Friedman and Heller barged in and tried to confiscate the donor organ," he explained. "When I tried to have them evicted, Dr. Friedman pulled his gun on us."

Marshall felt embarrassed and exposed. He was about to defend himself. But instead of Hunter regarding him, he turned his attention to Jeffries.

"Is that so, Chris?" he asked in a tone that didn't require a response. "And you're sure that that's a donor transplant in the case over there?"

"Of course I'm sure, Bertram. What else would it be?"

"What would you say if I told you it's a cloned human tissue heart that you and Dr. Shaw—and I assume that it is Dr. Shaw that you have in there on the operating table—conspired to implant tonight illegally and without institutional authorization."

Dropping any further pretense Jeffries replied, "That's right Hunter. It's the same heart you commissioned Rose to create five years ago."

"But I also told her to shut the program down in ninety-seven when all research into human tissue cloning ceased, which apparently she hasn't. And that makes the organ contraband."

Jeffries glared back at his boss. Judging from his facial expressions he was moving quickly through a series of reactions, from defiance to surprise and finally to acquiescence. In the end he seemed to appreciate that he'd been thwarted and now there was no way he would get to do the implant.

"But Rose told me that you secretly wanted the project to continue."

"She lied to you, Chris. I wanted nothing of the sort."

After the briefest of pauses, Jeffries commented, "So she played me for a fool, too."

"That's an accurate assessment."

Marshall, who'd been following this interchange like a spectator watching a tennis match, now fixed his attention on Jeffries. The tall, proud, thoracic surgeon appeared deflated and defeated. He knew that he'd been used.

I know the feeling, Marshall reflected.

He considered sharing this with his colleague but out of compassion for the man's wounded pride, he refrained.

"Bagley," Hunter said to the burly guard who was standing near Jeffries. "Get my cardtrol to Dr. Rose's inner lab from Dr. Friedman and go down there and bring back a Plexiglas cube and a large bottle of formaldehyde. I think it's time to put this wonderfully dangerous human organ out of harm's way. As for you Steve, why don't you have your nurse bring Dr. Shaw out from under anesthesia and transport her back to the recovery room? Chris, get yourself dressed and join me up in my room on five north. We have plenty to talk about."

And with that Marshall realized that the show was over.

chapter forty-two

over

Leaning over, his elbows resting on his thighs, Marshall sat on the bench in front of an open locker in the surgeon's lounge. The bright fluorescent lights made everything appear whitewashed and sterile. He, in contrast, felt soiled and tired, like he'd just run a 10K race. Contrary to the euphoria he usually felt after completing a tough jog, now there was merely weary exhaustion.

He knew she was still in the recovery room. He knew he should take a walk over there and see how she was doing. But he assumed nurses and aides would be milling around, the nurse anesthetist that had induced her, possibly even Steve. He had to talk to her, see how she was doing, find out how much she knew, and how she was handling the disappointment. But he didn't care to compete with these others for her attention. He needed to do it away from the OR, away from inquiring ears and eyes.

Marshall wriggled out of the v-necked scrub shirt, perspiration staining its armpits black. His street shoes with their flimsy covers were followed by the baggy cotton pants. He considered leaving the mesh bonnet on while he showered but decided that a stream of hot water cascading down upon his scalp was just what he needed.

He stood slightly bent in the antiseptic shower room beneath a torrent of water. He thought about what he'd say to her. He tried to anticipate what she'd ask. She'd want to know what had happened and why. He felt compelled to share the truth with her. Would she ask him if he still loved her? And if he did, how could he have been party to this? He hoped he had the courage to be honest.

He found a towel then used the blower on his thinning brown hair. He dressed slowly, wishing he'd brought a change of underwear. Finally, nearly a half-hour after Hunter had arrived in the Human Tissue Prosthesis Room to inject some order in the expanding chaos, Marshall returned to the long corridor that bisected the Hunt's Department of Surgery.

Her room was on the seventh floor of the Tower building. He rode the elevator alone, relieved that it was after visiting hours and the on call house officers were probably evaluating patients or resting in the resident's lounge.

He checked an overhead sign. It directed him to a series of rooms of which hers was one. He strolled down the tiled floor, listening to the TVs broadcast prime time programs. A stocky nurse shouted from the other end of the hallway for help lifting a patient.

He continued past the nurse's station. Even if one of the staff had seen him and wondered who he was, he or she didn't bother to stop him.

When you act like you belong, he knew, *people assume you do.*

Marshall found Rose's room dimly lit by a pale yellow night-light recessed in an unobtrusive hollow above the headboard. Her hospital bed seemed lost in the murky shadows, its head slightly raised, its siderails up. Surrounding it was a circle of utilitarian furniture, a cadre of inanimate attendants with a resting patient supine in the middle.

He walked over to her. She looked older than he recalled, her complexion pale and wan, her hair dry and lifeless. He'd seen her without make-up before, mostly on sunlit mornings, fresh from an evening of lovemaking, refreshed by a night of restful sleep. But this was different. This was more than natural. It reflected the temper of aging. Even in the muted light he discerned penumbras of tiny wrinkles around her mouth and eyes, deepening creases like etchings in her forehead, and an arid parchness to her full pale lips. It was as if the life that she'd been promised was now oozing away.

Sensing his presence she opened her eyes. A flicker of recognition crept into her countenance. She bestowed a meek smile upon him.

"Marshall," she said, her voice little more than a hoarse whisper. "You're here. How did you know I was in the hospital?"

"Chris told me," he lied.

"He didn't go through with the operation?" It sounded more like a statement than a question.

"No."

"Why not?" She asked, her expression confused, her eyes searching.

"I stopped him."

Then, as if comprehension dawned, her face brightened for a second then fell. She looked like she had just lost her best friend—and maybe she had.

"But why?"

"Because it was wrong, Rose. Because it was illegal." At this he hesitated. He knew that wasn't enough. He had to relate the truth as he saw it. He owed her that. "And because," he added, "you didn't deserve it."

She reacted as if she'd been slapped. First she inhaled a short gasp of air, and then turned away. Just as abruptly she looked back.

"How could you say that, Marshall? It was my heart. I made it from my own eggs and genes. I carried the fetus for six long months. I went through morning sickness and stomach cramps. Finally, after I was sure I could keep the heart growing, I delivered it. After all that, how could you say I didn't deserve to have it implanted inside me?"

"It's not what you went through to get it, Rose," he explained. "It's not even that it was contraband. It's that I know about your mother, Rose. That's why you don't deserve it."

Again a look of confusion clouded Rose's face. He imagined what she was thinking. *Of course he knows about my mother. I told him all about her. He hypnotized me into revealing more. What difference does that make?*

"I went to Erie last weekend and visited your father."

"You saw my dad? Why would you do a thing like that?"

"To try and find out more about you."

"About me?" she commented. "That's so sweet of you to care enough to go all the way there. But, Marshall, what could my father possibly tell you that you couldn't find out from me?"

"He told me about your mother, Rose."

"My mother?" she repeated, her expression betraying fear and concern. "What did you want to find out about her?"

"I know about the accident. I know how she really died."

"How...?" she started to ask, but her frail voice trailed off before she could complete the sentence.

"He showed me the bookbag with the bloodstain on it. He explained how it got there. He described how the accident really happened."

He was curious as to how she would react to this information. He braced for anger, denial, or both. He expected her to lash out, attack and accuse him, or at least defend herself and her actions. But instead she became sullen and withdrawn. Her expression, which had begun to show some animation, fell again, sinking down into the depths of sadness and despair. Or was it resignation and utter defeat? He couldn't be sure.

It was a while before she spoke. Finally, in a soft voice, almost a whisper, she asked, "So I guess it's over?"

Marshall wasn't sure what she was referring to. He took his best guess and replied, "Yes, Rose, it's over. Hunter confiscated the heart. Which means you're left with the whatever God gave you." He hoped this didn't sound too harsh. He didn't know how to be more tactful than that.

"No, Marshall, I mean *us*. I guess this means that we're over."

Now this was something to which he hadn't given much thought. So preoccupied had he been with the act of confiscating the heart and thwarting the implantation that his relationship with Rose had taken a back seat in his mind.

He looked over at her and tried to conjure up the feelings that he'd had for her during their roller coaster of a relationship, to re-experience the emotional energy that had kept him enthralled and enslaved. But, to his amazement, he came up empty. Could it be that now that she was fated to live out her life sentence without a medical miracle, he was ready to abandon her? No, that wasn't it. After all, hadn't he loved her before he knew about her devastating congenital illness and then even more after he'd learned about its dreadful consequences? His reaction, he realized soberly, had more to do with whom he'd recently discovered Rose to be. She was truly the 'bad seed' Frank Shaw had talked out, the 'evil' person to whom Bertram Hunter had referred, who had murdered her mother and possibly her first husband too. Hell, she may have even killed him too with a stiletto knife in an act of rage or simply in an effort to ensure her personal survival. For hadn't it always, from the moment he'd met her, been about Rose, about what she wanted, about what she needed, and about what it took to get it?

Over the next few seconds his mental debate ran its course. He knew that she was waiting for his answer.

Regarding him intently, an inquiring expression on her face, she asked, "Well?"

He knew what his response should be. But once spoken he feared he might regret it for the rest of his life. Hesitating, he took a deep breath, then sighed.

"Yes, Rose," he replied ever-so-softly, "I suppose it's over."

chapter forty-three

of giving thanks

It was a cold gray late autumn afternoon, the kind Marshall's mother used to call raw. However, inside the two-story brick house on Caton Street in Pittsburgh's Squirrel Hill neighborhood, he felt warm and relaxed. During the first part of the afternoon he and Jared groaned then cheered as the Detroit Lions toppled the injury-riddled Dallas Cowboys. Later, toward evening, Sally served Thanksgiving dinner.

From the onion soup to the pumpkin pie Marshall found everything she made delicious and complemented her several times during the meal. She managed to deflect his kudos until finally, as she set down a cup of decaf cappuccino, she acknowledged his kind words with a pink-cheeked blush and a soft, "thank you, Marshall."

Midway through their second cup of coffee, Sally suggested they retire to the living room, announcing that her children would be happy to clean up. After their questioning looks were met with a stern one from their mother, the teenage siblings silently began their chore.

Sally's rectangular living room was divided into two unequal sections. A stone fireplace with an L-shaped sectional occupied the portion near the dining room. A second area, larger and situated closer to the front door, seemed more like a family room, featuring a large screen television, an elaborate sound system, bookshelves, and an upright piano against the front wall. A Tiffany lamp on the piano bathed part of the room in a soft amber light.

While Sally searched for a selection from her compact disc collection, Marshall relaxed, coffee cup in hand, on the sectional, absently regarding the fireplace grating.

Noticing the small pyramid of cordwood on the tile apron he called to her, "Mind if I light a fire?"

"If you can. I forgot to replace the Duraflame log."

"Not a problem as long you've got some newspaper lying around."

She indicated a magazine rack by the side of the sofa. He nodded and set off to accomplish his task. By the time Sally joined him on the sectional he had a respectable blaze going.

Still thinking about the meal, Marshall said casually, "Those Cornish hens you served were great. But how come no turkey? After all, it *is* Thanksgiving."

"It's a custom I learned from my mom. We were a small family and we rarely had company for the holiday. She hated to fuss with a big bird, so the hens were an excellent compromise."

"And a delicious one at that," he commented. "I can't tell you how much I appreciate you having me over today. It's my first Thanksgiving since the divorce and it would have been depressing spending it alone."

"It was our pleasure, Marshall," Sally replied. "In fact, Stephanie was the one who suggested we invite you."

"Well, then I'll thank her personally after she gets off K.P."

Sally smiled and turned her attention to the fire. Marshall, too, found his gaze drawn to the lambent flame, its silhouette like a yellow molten mountain range shifting and undulating near the horizon. The effect was extremely relaxing, almost hypnotic. In the background the singer sounded familiar but not the song.

"Isn't that Judy Collins?" he asked without shifting his attention from the fire.

"Uh huh," Sally replied, more a grunt than a distinct word. "It's a Pete Seeger tune, 'Oh, Had I A Golden Thread'. It's part of a collection called, *Where Have All the Flowers Gone?*"

"Her voice sounds sweet," he commented. "And that title adds a touch of irony for me."

The reference to flowers made him think of Rose. In fact, many things these days made him think of her.

Yes, I know where one particular flower has gone, he told himself.

Either Sally read his mind, or a similar association struck her. Casually she asked, "Have you heard from Rose lately?"

"I've spoken to her only once since she was discharged from the hospital." He knew Sally knew what had happened with the cloned heart. "It was a few weeks ago at her father's funeral in Erie."

"You went all the way to Erie to attend her father's funeral?"

"Believe it or not," he said turning toward her, "I grew to like the guy. When we first met over the summer I thought he was okay. Then after I visited him again in September, I became genuinely fond of him."

"That's when you found out what Rose did to her mother."

"That's right."

A pause ensued. Gradually it stretched out for a few minutes. During the silent interlude, Marshall found himself wondering what Sally was thinking. Did she appreciate that his trip to Erie was as much an excuse to see the daughter as a tribute to the deceased? Probably. Did she also know that he wasn't motivated by a passing interest, but that he desperately needed to see Rose again and come to terms with the intense feelings which still haunted him day and night? Probably not.

"Well how *is* Rose?" Sally finally asked, as if feeling obligated to make this inquiry.

"Not well," Marshall replied frankly. "After she was discharged her symptoms got worse. In October she consulted a local cardiologist who specializes in congenital heart disease in adults. She was admitted Mercy Hospital and spent three weeks there being treated for heart failure and rhythm problems."

"That's too bad," Sally commented although he heard neither compassion nor conviction in her voice. "And there's still nothing beyond oxygen and medication that can be done for her?"

"She mentioned some reconstructive procedure that they're considering, where the surgeons repair the valve then reshape the right ventricle. But it's an operation that's usually only successful in children."

"Why wasn't it tried earlier?"

"Maybe," he replied a little facetiously, "because on some level Rose was always holding out for a new heart."

"That's hard to imagine, Marshall."

There was another pause in their conversation. Marshall's thoughts wandered back to that dreary weekend in Erie. The funeral was held on a Sunday. He'd skipped the service and intercepted the mourners at the cemetery. From an unobtrusive spot on a rise above the small gathering, he saw Rose sitting on a metal folding chair a few feet from the brown varnished coffin. Even through the black net veil he could tell she was pale. She had on the same black dress she'd worn to the Rivers Club so many weeks ago. But rather than voluptuously filling out the dress, the material seemed to hang on her sagging shoulders.

Later that evening, he followed a few of the cars back to the Millcreek house. There he managed to speak to her. At first he was surprised that she allowed the conversation. Perhaps it was graciousness on her part. They managed to exchange pleasantries then he inquired about her health. She described her hospital stay. Finally she alluded to a possible operation.

She'd resigned from the Hunt. She claimed it had been motivated by a lack of professional credibility as well as her failing physical health.

Now that her ruse had been uncovered and the project terminated there was nothing more to work toward. Plus, her medical condition was her priority now. She had enough money to sustain her comfortably for a year or two without working. After that she would seek disability.

They discussed her father, about the difficult life he'd led, especially since the death of his wife, how he'd made the best of it. Marshall freely admitted that despite the old man's gruff stoicism, he wasn't such a bad guy after all. He considered pointing out the irony of his expiring on October 30, the same day his wife had passed twenty-four years earlier. It had been mischief night, then and now. But he hesitated. Rose didn't need to hear that kind of stuff, he decided. Even if she'd perpetrated one of those deaths, it wasn't his place to grind salt into her wounds.

The conversation meandered into safer territory, to Presque Isle, to Mr. Getty's Bed and Breakfast, to sunsets by the lake. When he departed the cottage-style house around six that evening it was with an aching heart and a gnawing sense of incompleteness.

A coal from the fire exploded. The image of Rose standing at her childhood door faded. Sally's fireplace came into focus.

"Good," she said softly. "You're back."

"Uh-huh," he grunted. "Sorry about that."

"You're entitled," she said, patting him gently on the hand. "You really loved her, didn't you?"

With barely a moment's hesitation he said, "Yes. Yes I did."

"I know you did."

"But I think I'm almost over her. And besides, it was all an illusion anyway."

"What do you mean by that?"

"Rose used me, Sally. You know that. And I was a willing little pawn in her elaborate chess game. Even if a small part of her cared for me, it was incidental to the primary role I played in her life."

"Which was to cast a favorable vote at the executive committee meeting."

"That," he agreed, "and to present Hunter and the members of the committee with a positive, credible psychological assessment of her."

"But how could she anticipate Hunter would even ask for that?"

"Rose was good, Sally. And she did know Hunter." Sally's solemn look of comprehension showed she agreed. "I was thinking about this whole thing the other day," he continued. "Now that Rose's story is coming to a close, there's another bit of irony."

"What's that?"

"Obviously Rose thought that by having the cloned heart implanted she could alter her own fate and temporarily change her destiny. It was almost as if she was seeking a kind of immortality."

"So?"

"And it looks like she failed in that endeavor, doesn't it?"

"That's the way it looks."

"Do you know what Bertram did with the heart?"

"I heard he turned it over to the Smithsonian. They've preserved it in formaldehyde and placed it on display in their Science and Technology pavilion."

"That's right," he confirmed, "which in a way affords her the immortality she was seeking."

Sally nodded, as if appreciating this little twist. "I suppose that was his parting gift to her," she commented.

Then, with the mention of Hunter's name, he recalled a gift of similar magnitude that Rose had given the CEO.

It's so clear to me now, Marshall thought ruefully, *how really well Rose and Hunter knew each other. Better and for much longer than was ever true for me.*

Marshall was back in his head again, driving north by northwest out of Erie along state Route 5 on the morning after the funeral. He had little trouble finding the turn-off to the Getty Bed and Breakfast. Cautiously he negotiated the rutted dirt road, already pocked by discolored patches of ice. He passed the house's small parking area, paused briefly to take one last look at the place where they had first made love, then inched over to the crest of the hill. He stopped at the gravel lot by Halli Reid Park.

Stepping out of the Mercedes he stretched his long weary limbs. The weight of the weather and the stress of the weekend were wearing him down. With a sigh, he removed his galoshes from the trunk, turned his collar to the wind, and set off across the dirty grass field.

Marshall reached the beach area near the lake. Involuntarily he shivered as a stiff cold breeze howled in off the water. Turning right, he retraced the path he and Rose had taken along the shore. Eventually he reached the intersecting creek, donned his rubbers, then gingerly crossed. Again he shivered as the surging water soaked through the bottom of his pants. At the opposite side he clambered up the inclined bank then jogged the next hundred yards or so. Finally he stopped, waited for his breath to catch up, and looked around. There they were, that familiar constellation of rocks and boulders, set beside one another about fifteen feet from the lake at low tide.

There's where it happened, he reminded himself. *There's where Rose carved our initials on that stupid slab of slate and encircled them in a crude heart. Then she buried the sentimental tribute under a pile of rocks.*

If he concentrated real hard he could almost picture her sitting there on the boulder, the rock tablet on her lap, an intense expression on her face, scratching out block letters with the key from his Manhattan apartment.

That's when she told him how much she loved him. That's when he'd replied to her in kind. It was a moment which helped define their relationship. At least in his naïve, innocent mind it had.

He knelt down behind the nearest boulder. Using his bare hands he cleared away the top layer of slate. A shallow hole, no more than an indentation in the surface of the beach, appeared. Then he dug in earnest, methodically removing one layer after another until he found what he was looking for.

There it sat, the square slab Rose had buried less then four months earlier. With sentimental reverence he lifted it up and held it to his chest. He reflected on the past few months, how intense and full his life had been, what he'd experienced and what he'd become. And despite the termination of their passionate, albeit brief relationship, he still had memories of more intimate times.

The boulder was still slick from the lake's morning mist. Carefully he sat down on it, his hands clutching that tender, loving symbol of what she said she had felt for him. The coldness seeped through his pants and overcoat. He gazed out upon the lake and watched white-capped waves dance toward him from the horizon. Where was the cigar-shaped freighter that had floated by on that morning in July?

Finally, with his heart pounding wildly in his chest, and the hint of a tear in the corner of his eye, he regarded his rocky valentine. He read the words. Rose's name was there. That was fine. But somehow the rest was wrong. His name was missing. It wasn't just gone, as if eroded or abraded by the shifting tides. No, it had been replaced. Another name was there in its place. With a certain mute incredulity he read, 'Rose Loves Hunter, 7/17/97.'

How could this amazing transformation have taken place? he wondered. Could it have been some cosmic metamorphosis? No, a much simpler truth occurred to him. In his numb fingers he was holding a different plaque. It was a similar slab of slate, all right. But it was a plaque on which Rose had indicated her love to his boss, Bertram Hunter, while *they* were sitting by Lake Erie almost three years before Marshall had met either. And just as he, Marshall, had been made to feel special and unique, so too had Hunter been subjected to the same treatment. And perhaps, Marshall wondered, so had several others before them.

His heart ached. His hands trembled. For a painful, sobering moment he stared intently at the plaque again, as if reassuring his doubting eyes that it wasn't his. Finally, after he was sure, he stood up, held the slab of slate high over his head, and smashed it into the boulder. With a violent explosion it shattered into a dozen smaller pieces, its shards flying all over the beach.

It's scant retribution for what I've suffered through, he decided.

But the gesture did seem to provide him with a modicum of satisfaction.

A dish crashed to the floor. Marshall jumped a half-a-foot off the couch.

"What was *that?*" Sally called in the general direction of the kitchen.

"Jared dropped a dessert plate," Stephanie hollered back. "It's not one of your good ones, Mom. Don't worry, we'll clean it up."

Sally gave Marshall a wry smile. Loudly she said, "All right. Use the broom and make sure you check under the cabinets for pieces."

"No problem, Mom."

When they were settled again Marshall commented, "They're really good kids, Sal. You should feel proud. You did a terrific job raising them."

"Why, thank you, Marshall," she replied. Even in the muted light he could tell she was blushing. "I guess I knew that."

"It couldn't have been easy for a single working mom. But now, when you see the way they turned out, wasn't it worth it?"

"It certainly was, Marshall."

He gazed upon her soft features. He thought about what a wonderful person she was. Then he recalled something else he wanted to share with her.

"You know, Madame Olga was right," he announced.

Sally looked confused. "Madame Olga?"

"That old gypsy who read my tarot cards at Kennywood." Sally's look melted into one of understanding. "I've been thinking about what she predicted."

"And...?" Sally prompted.

"When I asked her about whether there'd be romance in my life, she turned over a card with my particular astrological sign on it. Then she said something about how Gemini symbolizes harmony and the connection of opposites. How it also implies love and emotionality. So naturally, given where my heart was at the time, I thought of Rose." Sally nodded attentively. "Then," he continued, "she turned over a second card and predicted that although there was romance in my future, the road to finding it wouldn't be easy. She warned about danger. 'Something unknown,' was what she said. 'Danger from something unknown.'"

"I'm started to sense where this is going," Sally commented.

"I'm sure you are. But there's more. She also warned about a crisis of sorts that would arise between my personal and professional lives. That must've referred to the moral dilemma I had when I was given Don Owen's psychological profile on Rose. Turning in that forgery was wrong. I broke the law, Sally. I committed fraud to protect her."

"I know that, Marshall. So?"

"It's just so hard for me to believe I could do something like that."

"Let's just say you weren't thinking rationally at that time."

"That's a diplomatic way of putting it." He paused for a moment to collect his thoughts. "Where was I? Oh, I remember. Then, Madame Olga started dwelling on the negative. She kept tossing in words like chaos, misery, and destruction."

"Maybe she predicted what you'd go through before your confrontation with Chris Jeffries in the OR?"

"That's what I thought, too."

When he didn't continue right away Sally asked, "So what else did Madame Olga say?"

"Well, next she warned me of a period of deep sadness."

"Was that accurate?"

"I'm afraid so."

"Anything more?"

"Yes. She told me that after I moved through the sadness a brand new sense of energy would be available to me."

"And…?"

"Then—and this is the most significant—she flipped over the last card. I believe it was called Judgement. She said it indicated that I would experience 'an end to suffering, the regeneration of my spirit, and the fulfillment of several new beginnings'."

"Is that so?"

"Yes."

"And have you?"

"I believe so."

"Like what?"

"Well," he said, drawing the word out for emphasis, "I've started in earnest to write my second book. It has to do with the moral, emotional and psychological issues around cloning."

"That's sounds interesting. Anything else?"

"I made an offer on an acre lot with a quaint little three-bedroom house in Fox Chapel. The closing is two months from now."

"Excellent," she replied with what sounded like genuine enthusiasm. "So it looks like you're planning to stay around a while."

"You could say that."

She nodded approvingly. "Is that it?"

"No, Sal," he replied, "frankly it isn't."

Despite his outward cool, Marshall felt like a bubbling cauldron inside. Desperate to elaborate on his feelings, he couldn't quite find the right words to say. Just like when he'd crossed that slate creekbed in his slippery galoshes and overcoat, he felt unsteady and unsure of his footing. Instead he eased toward Sally until their shoulders were touching. Reaching out a trembling arm he reached over and took her hand in his. Her palm was soft and warm. He relished the sensation. He expected her to withdraw, which would imply that she preferred to keep their friendship uncomplicated. But she allowed it to remain there, even returning the pressure a bit. Thrilled, he leaned back and gazed into the waning fire.

Could Madame Olga have been right? he asked himself as the yellow flame danced gaily upon a charred log.

Could his most auspicious beginning be here and now? It certainly seemed right. It definitely felt right. And perhaps, when all was said and done, they had the rest of their lives to find out for certain if it *was* right.

THE END